THE THIRD SUN

DAUGHTER OF THE PHOENIX
BOOK ONE

VICTORIA J. PRICE

Editing services provided by Rebecca Jaycox
Cover illustration by Natalia Sorokina | Instagram: @jwitless_art

ISBN: 978-1-9163540-0-5

www.victoriajprice.com

For John and Brenda Gray

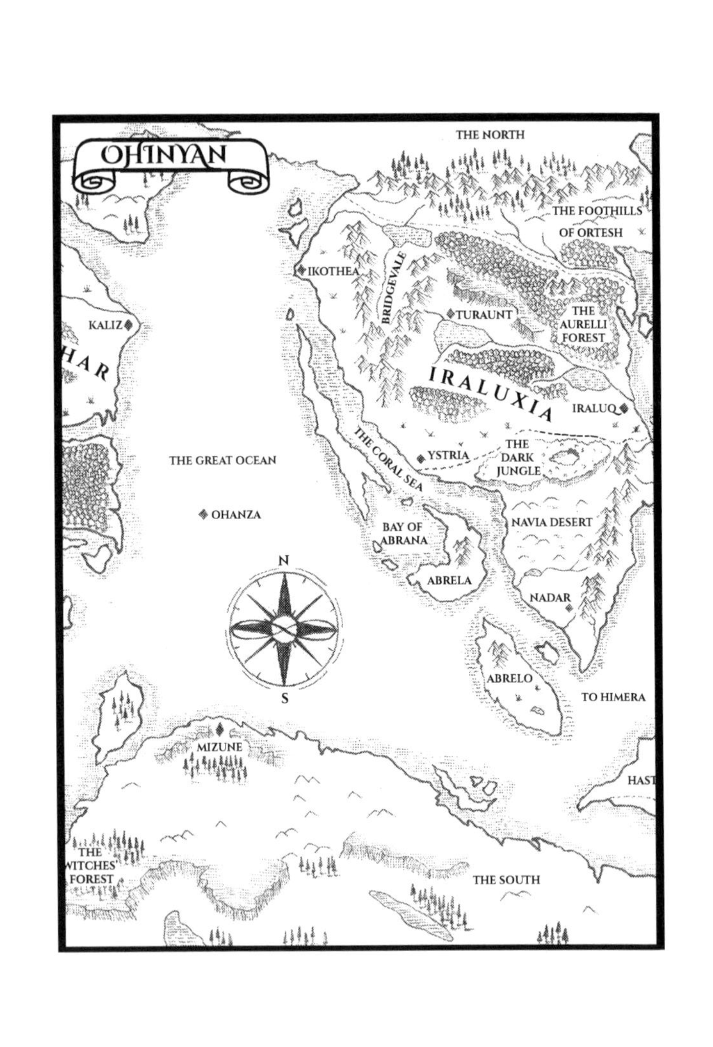
OHINYAN
THE NORTH
THE FOOTHILLS OF ORTESH
IKOTHEA
BRIDGEVALE
TURAUNT
THE AURELLI FOREST
KALIZ
IRALUXIA
IRALUQ
THE CORAL SEA
YSTRIA
THE DARK JUNGLE
THE GREAT OCEAN
OHANZA
BAY OF ABRANA
NAVIA DESERT
ABRELA
NADAR
N
S
ABRELO
TO HIMERA
MIZUNE
THE SOUTH

PROLOGUE

The Lady Noor had made her way south to join a group of witches gathered around a fire in the depths of night. She rested her weapons against a splintered tree stump and took a seat beside the fire. The scent of moss and charred wood filled her nostrils, and a soft orange glow lit up seven faces in the shadows.

"Kharsee." Noor bowed to the leader of her coven, if she could still call them her coven.

"You are all here because you have felt it," the old witch began, her violet eyes glistening like polished amethysts. She reached into the folds of her cloak and pulled out a leaf, lustrous and onyx black in the firelight.

"Darkness is creeping into Ohinyan," she announced. "A seam is slowly tearing apart—one that holds the very essence of our world together." Kharsee held the gaze of the other witches as she spoke.

Noor listened whilst the others muttered amongst themselves. Kharsee turned the leaf in her hands, ignoring the murmurs from the group until silence fell over them. Nothing but the crackling of flames broke the stillness of the dark forest beyond.

"Above the seam hangs a small village, suspended from great trees and endless, twisting vines. The broad leaves that cradle the morning dew are wilting, the vines crumbling and decaying. Like most of the people of Ohinyan, the villagers do not yet know of the tear in the ground below, or that from it escapes a darkness that has been hiding, deep and low beneath the earth like a foul breath. After lifetimes of waiting, the darkness has begun to seep into our world, rotting and ruining everything it touches," Kharsee added.

The flames turned black, and one of the younger witches shot to her feet.

"Perhaps you ignored it for a while, cast aside your worries, and blamed it on the coming of the third sun. But I think you have all heard its whispers." Kharsee ushered the young witch to sit down. Fine lines framed her eyes and mouth, but Kharsee was not frail, far from it. "The darkness tried to take hold of our world when the first sun died. We do not know why it failed. Now, the second sun is dying, and the darkness is trying to break free."

She turned to each of the faces in the firelight, her expression calm. "What do the angels know of this, Noor? You have Alexander's ear."

"Some have heard the whispers." Noor sharpened her blade on a stone, flicking her braid over her shoulder as the wind picked up.

"But what do they intend to do? What is Alexander's plan?" a young witch asked.

Noor considered her response, inspecting her blade in the firelight. Alexander was exactly where he'd agreed to be, where she'd *asked* him to be, searching for the girl on Earth.

She caught the gaze of each of the coven members around the fire, their expectant stares waiting for answers. *The* girl.

"The leader of angels is carrying out his duties on Earth," she replied, her eyes fixed back on her blade. "Alexander heeded our request. We must trust him."

"Duties?" The witch beside Kharsee leapt to his feet, hands clenched in tight fists, and his voice trembling. "What of his duty to Ohinyan? We are under attack, and yet where are the protectors of this world? Spending all of their time on *Earth*."

"Enough child." Kharsee placed a gentle hand on the young witch's shoulder. "The angels are doing the best they can, given the situation."

"But Countess, there is so much we do not know—"

"So then *assist* the angels," Noor demanded. "Do not sit idly by, just because the witches that came before us would not get involved with the matters of Ohinyan."

The group murmured, but Kharsee was silent, her lips a firm line. Wisps of silver hair brushed lightly against her cheek. She locked eyes with Noor before casting her attention back to the group.

"Come now," Kharsee said. "We are running out of time. Every witch must make their own decision: stand alone, unite with your fellow witches, or side with the darkness. In the coming months, every one of us must make a choice."

The witches stood, inclining their heads in a respectful bow before dispersing into the forest. Noor remained beside Kharsee until the coven members were nothing but shadows amongst the trees.

"Tell me all you've learned, Noor."

"I bring no good news. Attacks across the continent, mercenaries from the north venturing far away from their usual hunting grounds. Is it all connected to the darkness, to our dying sun?"

Kharsee's expression was unreadable, but Noor bit back at her questions. *So many questions.* But she could not overstep. It had taken too long to claw her way back to this point, for the privilege to sit around this fire beside Kharsee and to have any part in what was to come.

"Everything is connected in some way or another." Kharsee threw the blackened leaf into the fire, and it hissed and crackled as it burnt. "You must speak with Alexander, the moment he returns to Ohinyan."

"You really think this girl can help?" Noor asked. How could one girl unite the creatures of this world, unite its people? The continents were divided; people ceased talking with creatures long ago. Most of the people had ceased talking with each other, too.

"I do."

Noor let out a breath. "*If* Alexander returns, Kharsee." She threw a stick into the fire and followed a trail of sparks, carried upwards into the canopy. "This darkness, some say it's like a nothingness—an emptiness calling out in the night. What is it?"

"Not what, but *who*," the old witch said. "You have witnessed the changes in Ohinyan." She gestured towards the leaf, bubbling and burning still. "He is responsible. Whispering from his prison to anything and anyone who will listen. *Erebus*."

"But he must have failed before, or we would not be here now, would we?"

"There are many gaps in my knowledge, Noor, and this I cannot answer. He must have failed, yes, but at what cost? Who can say whether he will fail again? He has had many years to think of his mistakes, to spread his whispers into Ohinyan. Whilst most of our world has forgotten him, he has been waiting." She placed a gentle hand on Noor's cheek, her eyes flickering with fear. "Our sun is dying, and the darkness is coming. We need this girl, Noor. We will need all the help we can get. All of Ohinyan must unite, or what lies ahead will divide us all."

CHAPTER ONE

FIA

Endings were hard. Surely, everybody knew that. The end of your favourite book. A breakup. Saying goodbye. A death.

Fia stood at the edge of a grave, watching a groundskeeper as he laid fresh soil.

"We're keeping it level as the coffin sssettles," he'd explained when she first saw him do it a while back. He was missing a front tooth and the S sounds whistled gently as he spoke. But he spoke very little and Fia appreciated that.

The cemetery was quiet. A squirrel gave her the side-eye as it held an acorn tightly to its chest. Magpies pecked at the dirt nearby. Crumbling graves stood tall amongst dense bushes, and an angel headstone reached higher than its neighbours.

She hadn't really been seeing an angel, had she? Not a real one… angels weren't real. She *had* to be imagining it.

"*Worms.*"

"Excuse me?" Fia asked, as the groundskeeper continued his shovelling.

"Ssssorry love?" He placed his tools in his wheelbarrow and dusted off his hands, even though they weren't dirty.

"I thought you said... um, never mind." Her words came out in a rush. "Thank you," she murmured as he walked away. His Highgate Cemetery badge reflected the morning light, and he hummed to himself.

Fia arranged yellow roses in a neat pattern around the grave marker and brushed leaves off a small, laminated picture of her sister. It was still too soon for a headstone; the earth would need topping up for months.

"Hey Soph," she whispered. "I've got something for you." She placed a little carved angel in the soil, as thunder rumbled somewhere in the distance. The wind carried the smell of damp earth as a few spatters of rain hit her coat.

The most annoying thing about endings was that everyone expected you to start over. But where did you begin? What if you didn't want to begin?

She cast her gaze along the path, scanning for movement, but only wet leaves waved back at her.

"I think I saw the angel again." Fia added some of the roses to the grave beside her sister's. This one had a headstone with her parents' names engraved into it in lead-filled letters. "And I swear, I didn't dream it, but on my way here just now a fox said good evening to me. Maybe he knew it was my birthday." She huffed a laugh. "And that magpie definitely just shouted 'worms' a minute ago."

She let out a soft whistle through pursed lips. Did grief make you crazy? She'd planned on telling Henry about the angel and the voices... until *that* girl had turned up.

Something heavy fell into the groundskeeper's wheelbarrow nearby, but he was nowhere to be seen. Fia checked between the gravestones for any sight of the angel. She saw no white wings, only overgrown greenery and the grey of ageing headstones.

Could watching too much TV really damage brain cells? Or maybe it was just the trauma, and her brain was doing that protection thing she'd read about. That was it, right?

"I know you're there," she called out to the still graveyard. She didn't know, but it was worth a try. Nothing but birds chirped in response, so she said a silent goodbye to her family, wherever they were, before making her way to the exit. Just once, she wished she could hear them. Hear their voices, hear how their day was, what it was like, where they'd gone next. She didn't want to think about how lonely it was without them, not today.

As she stepped out onto the pavement, the first real drops of rain fell. Fia pulled her hood snug around her face, tucking in stray wisps of auburn hair. Thunder rumbled again as she made her way down the hill to the bus stop.

Henry.

She'd been so preoccupied with figuring out how to tell him about all the weird stuff that had been happening, she hadn't even seen what was going on right under her nose. Henry was all she'd had left. Well, other than Jo. Was it weird if your gym instructor was your only friend? Probably.

The worst part was that Henry's new girlfriend had been hanging around at the coffee shop, and Fia hadn't even put two and two together. She'd ordered an iced mocha a week or so ago and had been oddly stand-offish, but then most customers were. Fia muttered expletives under her breath as she approached the bus stop. "A bloody iced mocha!"

How long had it been going on? Was it weeks? Months? She bit back obscenities, willing herself to stay calm. *Don't you dare cry.*

The street was quiet. Parked cars lined the pavement that had buckled and cracked from tree roots breaking the surface. The bus pulled up moments later, splashing through overflowing potholes. As the smell of wet tarmac filled her nostrils, Fia pushed away the memory of her sister lying motionless in a puddle on an empty road, and instead stepped onto the bus, tapping her card as she passed the driver. If only Sophie had worn her helmet, instead of insisting Fia take it instead.

She reached into her pocket and her fingers wrapped around Henry's key. The spare key to her flat. What an idiot Henry was. What an absolute idiot *she* was. If Fia focused on Henry, she could keep the thoughts of her sister at bay. Sophie was the only family she'd had left. And Sophie was right. Henry had played her, just like she'd said he would.

Fia pulled the cord tighter on her hood, as her gaze fixed on the droplets of rain forming on the window. It wasn't really *that* surprising Henry had cheated on her. She hadn't exactly been herself lately. *Do not cry.* All the words she should have said to Henry echoed over and over on repeat. *That lying, cheating… how did you not see this coming?*

The bus reached Fia's stop and she stepped off, hesitating outside the entrance to the gym. She could just go home. She blinked up into the rain, pushing back at the panic creeping up her arms, her chest, her neck.

The red-bricked gym was set amongst shiny new office buildings, with an old wooden plaque that still sat above the entrance: a shield of purple and red feathers with "Resurgam" engraved elaborately beneath it. *I shall rise again.*

Birds chirped nearby, and Fia paused to listen. There were no words, only the trickle of rain, squeaking bus brakes, and car horns. She let out a quiet whistle, embarrassed to have expected to hear anything else. No voices or angels had followed her here, and the anxiety eased as quickly as it had come.

Training always calmed her, for a few moments at least. There was something about beating a punch bag that made the hollow feeling at the pit of her stomach a little bit easier to bear. Jabbing, hooking, kicking, elbow striking, Fia found the rhythm relaxing.

Kick after kick, left leg, right leg, knee, knee, elbow, elbow, her anger towards Henry melted away in the mangle of blows and sweat. Imagining *he* was the punch bag helped, too.

Where was Jo? It was late, but she was usually here until closing.

"That's some serious rage for a Monday night," a voice called out from the depths of the studio. Fia wiped the sweat from her forehead with the back of her arm and then gave a quick, strong punch for good measure. *Screw you, Henry.*

The gym was quiet at this hour, a couple of guys lifting weights, a woman running on a treadmill. The sparring mats were always empty, much to Fia's relief. She'd struggled with small talk since Sophie's death.

"Evening, Jo."

Jo smiled, deep laughter lines around her eyes creasing at the corners. "Pad work or sparring?"

"Spar." Fia adjusted her gloves as Jo strapped on a pair.

It could have been going on for months, this thing with Henry and his not-so-new girlfriend. He'd been distant for a while now, but Fia had been too afraid to ask, to push it, to push *him* away.

Jo flicked a long, black braid over her shoulder. "Happy Birthday," she blurted, dodging a knee kick.

Fia shook her head. *Of course* she knew. Jo always knew things. *Don't push her away, too. She's all you've got left.*

"Aldridge. You're top of my membership list. I couldn't miss it." Jo threw a right hook, too slow for Fia. "Come over to my place for a celebratory drink," she said, dodging again, this time to avoid an elbow strike. "Your eighteenth is a special occasion."

Fia concentrated on her attack, pushing aside the flutter of anxiety in her chest at the thought of having to go to a social event. She still wasn't ready for that. *Jab, jab, hook.* She willed her anger to disperse. At Henry. At the irrational spark for Jo knowing about her birthday. At the world.

"Jess will be coming. I told her to invite a few people.

Bring Henry, too," Jo finished, successfully knocking Fia off her feet with a sweep kick.

"Henry's been cheating on me," Fia said, lying still for a moment, before brushing a strand of hair away from her face, as she stared up at the ceiling. She pictured Jo's cramped flat full of people, demanding answers about her breakup. A sea of faces staring back at her, waiting for answers. *No way*. The anxiety balled in her throat.

Jo reached out her hand. "Fia I'm so–" Before she could finish, Fia jumped up and countered with a sweep kick of her own.

"It's over. I kicked him out. So I'll give that invite a pass, I think," she said with a weak smile and held her hand out to Jo. Sparring was over. She gave Jo a quick, tight hug. "Thank you, I do appreciate the offer." She really did.

Jo shook her head. "Henry… *that*… argh! If I see him around here…"

The two guys at the weights made a terrible show of pretending they hadn't been watching, but Fia didn't care. She waved goodbye to Jo as she caught her breath. What was there to say? Other than Henry was a lying, cheating…

"Ring me if you change your mind," Jo called as Fia walked away to the locker room.

The last thing she wanted was a birthday party, even though she knew Jo was only trying to help. The thought of having to talk about Sophie, her break up with Henry, of working at the coffee shop—quite possibly the dullest job she had *ever* had—of tedious University applications. That was not her idea of a celebration.

She grabbed her things from her locker, tapped out of the gym with her card, and ran the long route back to her flat. Turning down streets she knew were in completely the wrong direction and circling back through the park, her route guided by wherever streetlamps illuminated the path.

She ran until her legs could take no more, and as soon as she was back inside, she kicked off her trainers and threw herself onto the bed. Her nose crinkled as her face touched the duvet. *Henry*. The bed reeked of his aftershave, and she pushed herself up with a groan, pulling off the sheets. Her foot kicked against the little ball of hair ties he'd given her before she'd left for work.

"Eighteen of them for your eighteenth," he'd said, and then *that girl* had turned up, waiting for him in the rain. *Asshole.*

Fia's phone rang. "Hey, Jo," she said, twirling the little bird charm she always wore on a silver bracelet around her wrist. It was Sophie's, and she never took it off.

"Fia, hey. I know it's late, I just… wanted to check in on you."

Fia sighed and slumped down on the bare bed. "I'm fine, really."

"I just didn't want you to be alone on your birthday. Well, I mean, technically your birthday is over now, but you know what I mean."

"Really, Jo, there's no need to—"

"Because the thing is Fia, you're like a—you're like family to me, so this thing with Henry, I want you to know you can talk to me about it. Any time."

Fia huffed a breath. "Thank you, Jo. I mean it." She should probably say more than that, shouldn't she? Tell Jo how much her friendship meant. Explain what happened with Henry.

"Okay, well, I'll see you tomorrow, yeah?"

"Yeah, sure thing, see you tomorrow, Jo." Tomorrow she'd tell Jo the whole story, tell her all about Henry and his side bit.

Her stomach rumbled. Food. She needed food—anything to get her mind off Henry. A packet of microwaveable rice sat on the counter where she'd left it the day before, so she tore off the top and shoved it into the microwave.

She cast her eyes over her flat, searching for any of Henry's belongings she might have missed. The décor was sparse, anyway. A tattered grey sofa, a white coffee table with far too many ring stains, a striped blue rug, and her treasured collection of books. It was nothing much, but it was hers.

The microwave beeped, and she tipped her steaming rice onto a plate. It had all been Sophie's, too, not too long ago. Sophie had bought that rug at Shepherd's Bush market, rolling it out as if it were a magic carpet the day she'd brought it home. Fia pushed her rice around the plate with a fork. Home. This had been such a happy family home, once. But they were all gone now, along with any dreams of feeling like she was a part of something. That was the only real reason she'd stuck with Henry for so long—she couldn't face being alone.

A pea dropped off the side of Fia's plate, but she didn't care. The rice was awful, anyway. She reached for her phone. The lock screen glowed 02:16. There were still a few hours left until daylight. Every year for as long as she could remember, she and Sophie would lie on a blanket under the stars on Hampstead Heath to celebrate their birthdays through rain, wind, or snow. She saw no use in breaking with tradition and stuffed a blanket into her backpack as she made her way to the door, out into the rain, and towards the bus stop.

As Fia sat on the night bus, her eyes followed the shadows from the streetlamps, flickering in odd shapes over the back of the seat in front of her and over her feet, *one, two, three*. She loved the colours of London and all its rich history. After their parents had died, she would sit on the bus with Sophie, taking in the sights as it drove over Tower Bridge, past Somerset House and Big Ben and the Houses of Parliament. She would trace her fingers around the shapes on the bus window of the buildings beyond, the brickwork or the carvings.

The bus arrived at Parliament Hill Fields and Fia jumped off. A boy with similar hair to Henry's flicked his chin as she passed his seat. Had Henry ever really liked her at all? All those times at the coffee shop. *Ugh.* The more she thought about him, the tangle of emotions turned to relief. At least she didn't have to hide all the weird things that had been going on; now there was no one to hide them from. The damp, cool air hit her at once, and she flipped up the hood on her raincoat. The rain had eased to a gentle drizzle. She made her way up the path into the heath, seeking out a spot at the viewpoint.

Fia's blanket did little to keep her dry as she blinked up at the sky above Parliament Hill. The lights of the city illuminated the clouds, turning them into glowing tendrils of smoke. She knew there wasn't much chance for stars tonight. Instead, she watched her breath escape in a swirling mist into the light rain. She was alone, and she didn't belong—*anywhere.*

"Does it ever get any better, Soph?" Fia asked into the cold air. A siren wailed somewhere in the distance, as a long, white feather drifted slowly down onto her blanket.

She wiped her face. *The angel. It's here.* She was on her feet at once, searching left and right. This time she caught a glimpse of it, just a flicker of white heading back down the hill towards the bus stop and in the direction of the cemetery. "Wait!" she called out, breaking into a run.

The road leading up to the cemetery was a steep hill. A tall, brick wall lined the path to her right, and to her left were large Victorian houses. The road was dark under the dense cover of trees, and thick rain clouds blanketed the sky in a layer of grey, concealing the first rays of the sun on the horizon. But there it was again, another flicker of white up ahead in the shadows.

Rainwater ran down the hill in streams on either side of the road, and the pavement was slippery beneath her feet where leaves had fallen.

"Keep it together," she repeated under her breath, as she caught sight of gravestones beyond the wall beside her. The tip of a white wing caught the light of a streetlamp before dropping over the wall of the cemetery.

I must be crazy. With one quick check left and right, she pulled herself up, over the wall, and jumped down onto the other side.

Fia crossed the courtyard to a huge wall of arches bordering the cemetery, glancing once over her shoulder to look back at the gothic entrance building. Its tall, arched windows and stone parapets cast eerie shadows on the courtyard below.

She paused for a moment at a stone staircase at the base of the arches. Beyond the steps lay the graves. She had to know if the angel was real. Without looking back, Fia left the land of the living and walked up the staircase into the land of the dead.

"What am I doing, Soph?" she whispered, as her chest tightened. She began counting her breaths, her ritual to maintain calm. If the angel was here, she was going to find it. She had to. It *had* to be connected to the voices she'd been hearing.

At almost dawn, the cemetery had a dreamlike quality about it. Every headstone was covered in soft, damp moss, and every tree was entwined in ivy and crawlers. Water trickled softly from dripping leaves. The path wove around crumbling graves, concealing what lay ahead in the shadows. In the bushes on either side of her sat huge, decaying tombs, set back from the path, covered from top to bottom in dark ivy and twisting wood. She had to find it. If there really was an angel, she'd search until opening hours if she had to.

A moss-stained column loomed out from the wild grass with small, yellow wildflowers covering the base and concealing its engraving. Up ahead, the gloomy dawn lit up a small opening, green and lush even in the half-light. Rotting cherry trees and old oaks lined the pathways amongst ornately carved gravestones.

Fia stifled a cry as a bat flew across the expanse. She continued up the muddy pathway passing urns atop gravestones, their lids left slightly ajar to allow the spirits of the dead to escape. By now the composure she'd mustered was withering away. All the hairs on the back of her neck stood up, and her breath shortened as her nerves quietly ran away with themselves. Worst of all, she'd completely lost sight of the angel. "I know you're here somewhere," she muttered.

Branches snapped nearby, only this time it wasn't white feathers Fia saw, but dark clothing. Something wasn't right. Why would anyone be in the cemetery so early? She didn't wait to find out and launched into a run, her heart pounding in her chest.

"Stop!" a man called out. His voice was much closer than Fia would have liked. It wasn't the groundskeeper. Even she realised how irresponsible it was to come into the cemetery at this hour—any number of weirdos could be hanging around. As her feet carried her along the path, she could hear Sophie's voice in her head, chastising her like their parents would have done.

Up ahead, through the trees to her left, Fia could see the great entrance to the Egyptian Avenue, its enormous stone obelisks rising on either side. She didn't chance a look back over her shoulder as she sprinted through the corridor of tombs. Purple wildflowers and ferns blurred at the corners of her vision as she leapt up a stairway before her.

"Over there," another voice shouted.

A great cedar tree towered over the cemetery, casting shadows everywhere Fia looked. A cool breeze blew a few loose strands of hair across her face, carrying with it the scent of wet earth and leaves.

She turned right, heading towards the enormous mausoleum, the tallest and grandest in the cemetery. Something rustled in the bushes behind her, and a heavy metal gate crashed shut. Her heartbeat thundered in her ears. She ran to the nearest entrance for the raised catacombs and shook the huge iron gate until it fell back against the wall with a thud that echoed down the empty corridor beyond. *Shit. What if they heard that?* She could hide until the cemetery opened. With one last look out to the dawn, she turned and followed the feeble light of her phone into the darkness.

Fia shone the weak light at the coffin-lined walls, the smallest corner sections saved for the tiniest of coffins. A chill travelled down her spine. She pushed aside a low wooden barrier, holding her phone out to lead the way. In the distance, the first few rays of morning light began to shine through an opening above. She allowed herself a small moment of relief that she'd be out of there soon.

The clink of metal against metal from amongst the shadows echoed in her ears, and she froze, listening until the echoes became silence. The darkness wrapped around her, and she pressed on before the growing sensation of claustrophobia could take hold.

She had no idea where she was going. *Don't think about the coffins, don't think about the coffins…* She kept her eyes fixed firmly ahead of her and walked on, deeper into the chamber. A dead end.

Something moved in the shadows behind her, and she flashed the light back, fighting the rising hysteria. Her chest tightened, and her breathing grew short and sharp.

She reached a hand out to steady herself against the wall behind her, stumbled, and then all at once the world began to spin.

CHAPTER TWO

FIA

Fia was falling.

Mud, sky, mud, sky, mud, sky. Everything blurred into one continuous loop of brown and blue. *Am I dead? Is this what dying looks like?* But then she saw the angel's wings, so she had to be. Sharp pains shot through her leg, her arm, her head, so quickly it became hard to define where the pain was coming from. Her breath was knocked out of her with the constant tumbling and the mud, sky, mud, sky, a flash of white feathers, and then a *crack*.

Fia hit her head, hard. Reaching out, she felt the warm, stickiness of blood. She looked up to see the sky once more but instead saw white feathers and a pair of crystal blue eyes looking down at her anxiously. The angel's arms wrapped around her and lifted her. And then darkness.

It was warm. There was a sickly smell, mixed with damp moss and earth. It stung her nostrils, and her whole body seared with pain. Muffled sounds grew louder, faster, and then lulled. The white wings of the angel flashed somewhere nearby as she opened and closed her eyes, but the throbbing in her head was unbearable. She heard a piercing scream, *her* scream, and the voices turned to cries until she could see the blue eyes again. *Silence.* Fia fell in and out of consciousness, dreaming of the angel until the sickly smell woke her again.

This time the pain was worse. A drum was beating, or was it her heart? Fia opened her eyes to stinging smoke. The beat quickened.

"Altair, she's awake again," a deep voice said beside her, gentle and soothing. White feathers flickered at the edges of her vision.

Those eyes… the white feathers. Wings. I must be dead. The drum beat louder, drowning out the voices. An old man with a dark, weathered face leaned over her.

"Stay with her," the old man said, his voice scratched with age, as she drifted in and out of a daze.

It was hard to tell if she was dreaming or awake, as the beat grew louder, closer.

Voices sang, "Ho-yah-wa-hay-ah!" The beating was so loud Fia could feel it in her chest. Her heart was racing, but she didn't know why. All she remembered was being in the catacombs, and then she had reached out for the wall and… *fallen.* The sickly, sweet smell hit her in waves once more, filling her nostrils. But fallen through what? Her head spun.

"Ho-yah-wa-hay-ah!" followed the beating of the drum. It was so fast and so loud. She felt like she was still falling, but she was lying down, covered in blankets, and there was a flurry of movement all around.

"*Fia…*" another voice called to her, from somewhere far, far away. "*Fia…*"

She opened her mouth to speak, but fear stole the breath from her mouth. Her heart raced so fast she was certain it would burst through her chest.

"Ho-yah-wa-hay-ah!"

Her eyes began to focus. She was in a tent, with a high ceiling swathed in reams of green and gold fabric. Through the smoke, she could make out more of the old man's features: tall, tan, and leathery, with eyes as dark as an evergreen.

"Ho-yah-wa-hay-ah!" he sang again, throwing his arms above him, his great fur cloak swinging from enormous shoulders.

The echo of her name rang in her ears and left her hands trembling. On the ground before her were several men and women on their knees, rising and dropping to the old man's song, pulsing their bodies to the same beat that had been drumming in Fia's head. She couldn't move, but all the panic began to melt away, her chest was no longer tight, and her head had ceased spinning. *What just happened?* Her eyes adjusted to the light as she took in every detail of the strange little tent and the people kneeling, sweat beading on their foreheads.

"Altair," called the deep, gentle voice, "it's done."

The old man nodded and from the shadows beside him stepped… *an angel.* She wasn't crazy, after all.

He was tall, his shoulders broad and strong. He wore only some loose, hemp-like trousers, tattered at the ends and tied at the waist with a narrow piece of rope. His bare chest was neatly sculpted. He stepped lightly towards her on bare feet, his candlelit face revealing the same crystal blue eyes Fia had seen when she fell through the… whatever it was. His wavy hair was the colour of wet earth, with copper streaks here and there, almost reaching his shoulders and curling at the ends and around his ears.

She tried to speak, but her throat was dry, and no sound came out. The angel sat beside her, and she stared in silent awe at his enormous white wings as they moulded around him. She focused on her breathing, steady and slow. *Not crazy, but very possibly dead.*

Fia reached into her coat pocket and pulled out the feather that had drifted onto her blanket on Hampstead Heath. With her free hand, she gently touched one of the angel's wings. It was thick, with hundreds of large, soft feathers, and each one was slightly different. Some had a silver sheen, and some were slightly speckled, as if by sand or dust. Some had grey tips, and a few were entirely grey. But there was no doubting it—the feather was his. All this time, she'd thought she was going crazy, but here he was, her very own guardian angel. Wherever *here* was.

The angel took her hand. His pale skin was cool and smooth and his touch gentle. There was no anxiety balling in her throat, no racing thoughts in her head, or the need to count her breaths. Her cheeks flushed, and she pulled her hand away. He was more beautiful than any image of an angel she'd ever seen. His lips were pressed tightly together, his brow deeply furrowed in concern.

"Fia, can you hear me?" he said, his voice calm and soothing.

She nodded, but only the slightest, smallest of nods. All this time, the angel had been real. *Why did he never show himself? Why didn't he save Soph?* Fia felt a flash of anger. She was grateful for the coat covering up her chest—it always flushed pink despite her best efforts to will it not to.

The angel helped her to sit, his hand around hers, and passed her a small wooden bowl of chestnut brown liquid. "Drink this. Here," he said, taking a sip. "It's safe."

The liquid was sticky, and it tasted like bark. She drank all of it, relishing the soothing feeling on her throat. "Thank you," she croaked, handing back the bowl. "Where am I?" She reached for her head, and her fingers met with the rough fabric of a bandage.

The men and women were gone. When had they left? But Altair remained, his fur cloak swinging behind him, as he shuffled around in the shadows.

"What happened? I was in Highgate and now I'm here… wherever here is." Fia waved her hands, taking in the patterned fabric of the tent, the wooden bench the angel sat on, and the rugs on the floor. "And how do you know my name? Am I… did I *die*?" Sophie. She could see her sister again.

"I'm Alexander," the angel began. "This wasn't exactly—"

"Makya," cried a voice from outside the tent. "MAHKEEEYAAAAH!"

Altair moved surprisingly fast for an old man. "We're under attack, we need to move." He barked orders, already pushing his way out of the tent.

Fia was too dazed to speak. Her head didn't hurt, but it was *fuzzy*, her thoughts a jumbled mess. *If this is what death is like…* She could fight, but she felt weak, and her vision was still blurred around the edges. Alexander pulled her to her feet before she had time to decide and led her out into crisp night air.

"We have to go, *now*," he said. "This way." He guided her amongst tightly placed tents of white canvas reaching high above them. It was dark, and Fia tried to hide her unsteadiness from him.

At first it seemed as if balls of fire were being shot into the camp, spreading flames at an alarming speed. But as they ran, darting through a series of tents and wooden structures, Fia saw swirls of deep, black smoke, exploding in and *out* of the camp. Voices cried out behind them as others fled, too.

Within seconds the whole camp was ablaze, and the air weighed heavy with ash and thick, grey smoke. Fia held her mouth tight, covering her nose with her sleeve. At times, as they ran, she caught the shape of a figure sway in the dispersing smoke as it swirled, but then the figure would disappear. *What was that?* She fought back her rising panic, clenching her fists tight at her sides to stop them from shaking. "What's happening?" She coughed the words out and covered her mouth at once.

The heat and the commotion were unbearable, and the smoke burned at her lungs. Sweat pooled on her forehead and strands of hair stuck to her face as a shrill horn sounded through the flurry of flames. Screams came from behind, but they kept pushing on into the night: men, women carrying babies, young children, all running and stumbling beside them.

They ran until they were clear of the camp, across a small stream that glittered silver in the moonlight, and away into a dark forest.

"All those people!" Fia looked back, sucking long, deep breaths of clean air into her lungs. It burned, too, but in a different way from the smoke of the blaze. Her head was clear of the foggy sensation, but her legs were weak, and she knelt to steady herself. *Just breathe. Stay calm.*

"We need to keep moving, to get to higher ground," Alexander said, as his eyes scanned their group.

Fia could still hear faint cries for help from the burning camp. Alexander, ignoring her protests, took her by the waist and dragged her away with the others.

She was too weak to argue. The angel held his arm firmly around her, but she felt feathery light and was sure her feet weren't touching the ground. Her chest thundered with adrenaline, and she still wasn't sure if she'd died or if this was all a terrible dream. *What kind of guardian angel are you?*

Their group had grown larger. Altair had joined them, along with the men and women Fia recognised from the tent. Young and old clung to each other in the dark, dressed in animal skins and running barefoot through the forest. She tried to piece together what she'd seen—the primitive tents, the lack of footwear. Uncontacted civilisations still existed, didn't they? Fia was sure she'd read about them online.

The dense trees gave way to large, rocky areas where boulders jutted out of the earth at awkward angles. There were still trees here, but they were smaller and sparser as they ascended a slope with loose stones underfoot.

Finally, they stopped moving, high above the burning camp and far away from the inferno, the forest separating them. They'd reached a caved section of the hill they'd been ascending, well protected from their attackers.

"Everyone got out, but we lost a few horses," a young man said quietly to Altair.

He nodded. Fia opened her mouth to object but decided against it. *You've been hearing all kinds of things… who knows what you heard?*

The cave was vast. Areas lit up with torches and small fires by the people from the camp, each taking a small space for their families to rest for the night. A fire had been lit near the entrance, and a large group had crowded around it to keep warm. Fia looked at each of them, all bronzed, with vibrant wooden beads and threads around their necks and wrists. She rubbed her palms against her jeans, trying to figure them all out. As she counted her breaths, she looked for anything familiar—not that she knew much about cultures that refused technology.

The night had fallen still. Though Fia could smell the burning camp on her clothes, the air was crisp, and the smoke blew far into the distance. The sky was clear, and the stars, accompanied by the moon—*moons*—shone brightly through the forest. There were no streetlamps here to distort how bright they were. *Okay, so you're not dead, but this is a long way away from London.* The thought was oddly liberating. If only she could calm her nerves. She recognised nothing, and she pulled her legs close to her chest with a shiver.

An elderly woman passed Fia a rough blanket, and she wrapped it around herself gratefully. Alexander muttered a few words to Altair before making his way back to the entrance and out into the night air. He glanced over his shoulder to look back at Fia as his wings spread wide. With one smooth motion, he was airborne, and she followed his silhouette, disappearing into the dark sky until he was nothing but a shadow in the distance. *A real angel.* She ran a hand over the bandage on her head as Altair approached. Another burst of anger shot through her as she realised Alexander had abandoned her, again.

"We owe you some answers, child." Altair's voice was soft. "Come, sit beside the fire."

"You saved my life," Fia replied, tucking her legs beneath her as she sat. "Thank you." Exhaustion throbbed through her bones, begging her to lie down, but rest could wait. This was no time for sleep.

"It was Alexander who saved you, but we will come to that later." Altair threw some salts onto the fire, and it flashed in blues and greens, like burning driftwood. The flames flicked and twisted higher into the night.

"My name is Altair, and these are my people." He gestured around the fire. "Once you fell through the window to our world, you were no longer on Earth." The fire danced, and the flames swirled into an image of Fia, falling, endlessly, down a muddy slope. She gasped, but the others around the fire sat silently, waiting.

"I leaned against a wall—it might have been a grave," she replied, barely audible. *Was it only a few hours ago?* "What do you mean, this isn't Earth? Where is… where are we?" The hairs on her arms stood up, and for a moment she felt like she had as a child, locked in the empty storeroom cupboard at her old foster home, crying in the dark.

Altair looked into the flames. "Our worlds are very similar, from what the angels have told us. We do not know how or why they are linked, although there are many theories. It is not often that people fall through. There are few stories and even fewer survivors."

Fia reached again for the bandage around her head. The fire flickered with images of people falling through gaps in the air, straight into a lake, or into the middle of an ocean, or onto the peak of an icy mountain.

"You have come to us at a time of great suffering." Altair's face was grim and severe with the weight of his words. "Our world is at a crossroads, and some have chosen to take advantage of this."

The flames flickered with the forms Fia thought she had seen during the attack on the camp. *So they had been people, after all.* And she thought that being able to see an angel made her crazy. But this, this was... She breathed in deeply, exhaling through pursed lips and willed her expression to remain blank.

"We call them the Makya."

The fire flashed with images of destruction, and of the Makya—half human, half flame, solid, and yet ethereal.

How could they be fire and people all at once?

"We are known in Ohinyan as the Navarii. My people's history with the Makya goes back further than most."

The fire changed, revealing a large desert, with hundreds of tents—a camp a thousand times bigger than the one that was just devastated.

One, two, three. Each breath she counted scraped against her throat. *Other worlds, angels, fire people.* What was this place? Fia wanted to run, far away, but she knew her legs wouldn't carry her. And where would she run to, anyway?

"We were not always a travelling race, but we were made nomadic when our home was destroyed many years ago by the Makya. Many of our people went to the place of souls, and it was only with the angels' help that we survived." The fire blazed with wings of ebony, tan, ivory, and auburn, angels firing silvery arrows from the sky into the inferno below.

Fia brushed her hand where Alexander had held it and pulled her blanket closer at the thought of his blue eyes gazing into hers. They were like sunlight on water. *Get yourself together, Fia. You've known him for like five whole minutes.*

"We adapted, and we have never stopped travelling since. The nomadic lifestyle suits us best—we move with the seasons."

The flames rose above them, revealing a blaze far greater than the destruction they had fled from earlier that evening. The spitting, burning wood imitated piercing screams before fading into ash, and then black as the angels disappeared. Darkness was all that remained.

"That was the coming of the second sun, the sun you will see rising in the morning. But now, the third sun is coming, and the attacks have started once more."

The flames shot high into the sky in an explosion of light, balling at their peak into a bright circle and flashing a multitude of colours: lilac, crimson, indigo, vermillion, cyan. Finally, a new ball of orange rose from the flames, growing bigger and bigger.

"Wait, your sun is dying?" Fia asked. She played through the similarities and differences between their worlds. Surely, this was a bad thing?

"It is dying, child. Yes. But it means an end, a beginning, the cycle." The flames revealed the changing seasons, birth, marriage, and death. "It is a time of change, of new beginnings. For some, like the Makya, it is a time to take advantage of the atmospheric differences in our world, when the energy is shifting, and to use that advantage for gain and for power. Ohinyan may be in darkness for a while, but I am hopeful for the light that will follow it."

"The others don't seem as hopeful as you," Fia said, looking from Altair's face to the people around the fire, who held each other, sullen.

Altair almost smiled. "I am more than one hundred years old, child. I learned the story of our ancestors from my great-grandfather, who learned it from his great-grandfather before him. The coming of a new sun is a time of many things. Many will become bones of the earth, a part of Ohinyan, a part of forever, of the never-ending cycle. But many more will survive into the new era. It is the way of our world, of Ohinyan."

Fia watched the flames, flickering with scenes of life, of animals, of strange people in thick furs and of children laughing, of animal-like creatures on two feet walking and talking amongst them, some with pointy ears and tails. She bit back her anxiety, rubbing her sweaty palms on her knees once more. Sophie would have said something reassuring, something to keep her calm. And Jo, Jo would never believe this, even if she'd been sitting beside her. *Just breathe. They're going to take you back. Just breathe.* There had to be a way out, a way back to Earth.

Families huddled together around the fire, chatting quietly as the smallest children were tucked in for the night with palm fronds and grasses. Fia tried to return her blanket, but the old woman just smiled and pulled it tighter around Fia's shoulders.

She had so many questions. The bandage was coming loose from her head, and Fia tucked an end under itself. *How am I going to get back to London?* She felt a twinge of guilt as she pictured Jo, turning up at her flat with coffee and leaving after getting no response. She couldn't lose Jo, too. *Henry…* Would he even notice she was gone? *He used you. It doesn't matter what he thinks.*

Her eyes were bright with the fire as it shifted colours. The images faded, the flames flickered blue and green like before, and then settled back to a golden glow. She knew exactly what Sophie would say. Fia huffed a quiet laugh. *She'd probably say, what a great adventure.* It was a crazy thought, but that was Sophie.

Fia chewed her lip, silently ordering herself not to cry. She could die in this world. She touched her head again, feeling for the wound, and winced.

The group stirred, and the same young man that had spoken to Altair when they arrived in the cave rose to his feet. Whispering to the old man, he raised his bow, inclining it towards the opening.

A shadow cast over the entrance to the cave. There had been no sound from their feet touching the ground, but when Fia looked up, Alexander had returned with a young woman.

"Alexander, brother." Altair reached for the angel's arm, holding it for a moment before welcoming his travelling companion.

The woman was exceptionally tall—taller than anyone Fia had ever seen, and at least a head taller than Alexander. She was beautiful—perfect, symmetrical face kind of beautiful. Her skin was pale, even by the light of the fire as it flickered against her ebony, plaited hair. Her worn leather boots reached up past her knees, and she was decorated in silver. A large, jewelled belt sitting almost as high as Fia's head reflected the fire, whilst enormous silver cuffs ran up her arms and around her athletic biceps. On her head and dipping down towards her eyes sat a large silver circlet, with a glittering blue stone in the centre as dark as her eyes.

"Lady Noor," Altair greeted her with a bow of his head.

"Altair." She bowed back.

They sat together beside the fire, their polite introductions turning into hastened whispers. The families dispersed into different areas of the cave, settling down for the night beside their sleeping children.

Fia's tired, aching body trembled with the effort of staying awake. She had far too many questions to fall asleep, but the temperature inside the cave had dropped, and the exhaustion of the night's events had caught up with her. She wrapped the blanket tightly around herself as she waited for her chance to speak, her eyelids becoming heavier. Her questions would have to wait until morning.

CHAPTER THREE

NOOR

The Lady Noor gazed over to the spot where Fia slept. The bandage around the girl's head had become tattered and stained black with ash in some places. Dark black circles bloomed beneath her eyes; her skin pale with fresh scratches. The girl appeared too frail to have lived through such a fall.

"I've received word that the windows will become more unstable with each passing day." Alexander flexed his wings to adjust his position. "As the sun dies…" He lowered his eyes. "Unless the witches find a solution to get her back, she'll be trapped here."

"And the angels on Earth?" Noor asked.

Alexander shook his head. "They may not be able to return."

This was not welcome news. Noor didn't envy Alexander's position, but they had to focus on the task at hand. "Altair, we must take her to the nearest coven at once, if she is the one we've been looking for, we cannot wait. How much have you told her?"

"We must consider the girl's safety," Altair replied. He

shifted his weight and said nothing further. Noor knew it was likely the least talkative he'd been in some time. The old man was not fond of witches, and this was no secret to Noor. They were mutual acquaintances only through Alexander, and she trusted Altair no more than she could trust the changing direction of the wind. Apparently, the feeling was mutual.

"I've told her very little," Altair said. "Of the Makya, the sun dying. But nothing of the coming darkness or why she is truly here," he finished, looking over to Fia.

"We must hurry. Erebus will not wait for us to make a decision." Noor glanced out at the sky as it became ever lighter with the new dawn.

Altair's response did not matter. Whether he had told Fia why she was here or not, what mattered was whether she could make a difference. Whether they could *all* still make a difference.

Rays of light gradually made their way through the trees. She wondered how many more dawns she would see with what lay ahead before turning her attention back to the conversation.

It wasn't long before the sun was clearly visible in the sky, and the smouldering mass of grey from yesterday's attack could be seen in the distance. The horizon was still, with nothing but quiet birdsong breaking the rustling of the trees.

"We should scout the area. There could still be Makya foot soldiers out there. You and I can cover much more ground, twice as fast as the Navarii," Noor said to

Alexander, already on her feet. "We need to make sure the area is clear before we proceed to the coven."

Altair raised an eyebrow but said nothing. There was truth to her words, and she knew he would not argue.

Noor sheathed her weapons and readied her glider. There was no use in wasting time.

"See you on the ground," Alexander called out, as she leapt forwards into the air with precision and grace, her glider opening into the wind like the wings of an eagle.

Her arms held firm to the wooden frame, the canvas spread wide above her head. There was little that could rival this feeling. The wind against her cheeks, the morning sun enveloping her in its warmth. *We cannot let this end.* She would protect Ohinyan, no matter the cost. Even if the coven never took her back.

A thick plume of smoke soon cut through the cool wind, and Noor surveyed the damage from the previous night's attack. The camp was a blackened, crumbling mess. Alexander swooped down alongside her, his arms resting lightly at his sides. He was going slow for her sake.

"I'm going down," he called over the wind.

"Let me check for Makya." But it was too late. He was already mid-dive, making his way to the centre of the camp. She scanned the horizon for any signs of an airship and pushed down to dive after him. "Last time I checked, the leader of angels was not impervious to fire," Noor said, as her feet touched the ground. She folded her glider, resting it in its' sheath.

Alexander's face darkened but he remained silent.

The weight of her words dawned on her. "I'm sorry, Alexander, I didn't mean—"

"No, you're quite right," Alexander replied. "But I cannot lead from the shadows. My father was… unlucky. Let's hope I have better luck."

They searched the whole camp, or what was left of it. The Navarii were resourceful, and there was no doubt in Noor's mind that they would salvage most of what was left. No Makya foot soldiers remained, and the only casualties were a few horses that had already become carrion for the birds.

"This was no way for them to die." Alexander watched as the birds pecked away at the carcasses.

"The people are safe. That is all that—" The birds suddenly scattered, and at once she and Alexander drew blades.

Something hit her from behind, and she rolled forwards as heat licked at her neck. The Makya was thrown off her, taking her glider with it in a tangled mess. But it gave Noor the second she needed to push her blade through the Makya's thigh as it struggled with the canvas of the glider.

"Yield and I will spare you," Noor snarled, pushing her weight into the blade.

The Makya woman spat in her face. "Foolish witch, you'll be dead in moments."

"You're alone. Why?" Noor twisted her blade, and the Makya's hands pressed against her pooling blood.

"One of us is all it takes." The woman grimaced. She reached a bloodied hand to Noor's glider beside her in the grass, and it fell away into cinders between her fingertips. Her hands ignited, ready to attack.

"No," Alexander cried.

Noor did not hesitate as she plunged a second blade deep into the Makya's chest. She left it there until the flames ceased, and the Makya lay motionless.

"Why did you do that? You could have spared her." Alexander said, pulling the blade from the Makya's chest.

"Spared her? You saw her hands. She was about to incinerate us both." Noor snatched her blade from Alexander and wiped it on the soil. "There was no time to hesitate."

"Perhaps."

He was well known for being fair—a little too fair on occasion. *Not everyone can be saved.* She fought back a memory, one she had been trying to hide from for too long. Hands covered in blood, too much blood, and a body lying still.

"I know you think I am too soft, but Ohinyan will need a little softness after what's ahead." Alexander surveyed the camp as he spoke. They retraced their steps, checking each tent and structure again for any sign of Makya.

"I think you have played the hand you have been given with grace." Noor truly believed it. When Alexander's father had died, news spread quickly that his sister did not want to take her rightful seat as leader. She was the eldest, and it was her birthright. But she had chosen to put her children first and handed leadership to Alexander, the youngest angel to lead in the known history of Ohinyan. *A role I do not envy.*

Noor watched him as he searched the tents. He'd grown on her. She had not expected him to help when she'd approached him, all those months ago. But he had grasped what was coming and despite being so young, he seemed to understand. She stifled a laugh. She was barely older than Alexander. And yet somehow, the fate of Ohinyan was in their hands.

Silla would have liked him. They might have even been friends, in another life, perhaps. Noor had to redeem herself, and Alexander was key to that redemption. The witches might just welcome her back to the coven if Fia was the girl that could change the fate of the world.

That she wanted to redeem herself in Silla's name she would keep to herself. Noor would keep his memory alive and honour him as long as she lived and breathed.

They left the camp, returning through the forest on foot.

"What if we've made a mistake?" Alexander asked, as they walked back to the caves.

Her glider was beyond repair. She'd have to make a new one. "A mistake? You mean, if she isn't *the* girl?"

"All of it. I didn't tell her anything. I changed my mind and left Earth without her, and she still followed me here, anyway. We've deceived her," he said, pulling his fingers through his hair.

"Deceived her?" Noor laughed. "We know nothing of what will happen between this sun and the next, and your concern is that you've deceived her?"

Alexander didn't seem to notice the humour. "I should have told her everything. I should tell her everything, the moment we're back."

"We must get her to a coven—"

"She's not just some prophecy, Noor. She's a real person. We can't just play with her life because we have something to prove."

Alexander paced back and forth, a hand rubbing at his neck. What had happened between the two of them on Earth? "What do *you* wish to prove, Alexander?"

He ceased his fidgeting and stood tall. "My only wish is to honour my father."

She knew there was more but didn't press him further. As young as he was, he was the leader of angels, and she had too much respect for his position to argue. "Of course."

The trees gave way to rocks as they ascended, the forest bed turning to sparse stones beneath their feet. The scent of spices drifted from the caves above, and they returned to find Altair preparing food.

Noor delivered their report quickly. "There is much for you to salvage."

"Very well," Altair said, brushing spices from the front of his cloak. "Then it is as we have agreed. The Lady Noor and Fia are to venture to the nearest coven, hopefully, no more than a few days travel on foot. Alexander will return to his soldiers, and I shall lead the Navarii west, to find anyone who might stand beside us. Fly carefully, brother," Altair said, grabbing Alexander's hand in his for a moment.

"Look after her, Noor." Alexander glanced over at Fia, still asleep in her blanket. He stepped forwards a few paces, leapt into the air, and was away.

Noor watched Fia stir, her chest rising and falling in a steady rhythm, and she hoped they were doing the right thing. All of them.

CHAPTER FOUR

ALEXANDER

Scenarios played over in Alexander's head as he patrolled the forest floor with Malachai, his right hand. There was every chance Makya scouts were still in the area, and capturing one for questioning could prove useful. He wondered if he should've sent a soldier instead, but he'd decided against it. A hands-on approach might not have been the traditional way of doing things, but it was *his* way.

"You're sure she's the one?" Malachai asked, as they walked. There was only so much they could see from above, and there was much to discuss.

Rain had fallen, their bare feet disturbing wet earth, as they made their way through the trees. It was peaceful here outside of the cities, the noise and the commotion always pressing in on him. He breathed in the scent of earth and moss.

"The one?" Alexander hadn't been listening, and Malachai's question took him off guard. He pushed back at the urge to fold his arms across his chest.

"From the witches' prophecy?"

"Oh, the prophecy. Yes, I do. I think so." Alexander dragged his fingers through his hair, and stopped as soon as he caught himself doing it. "She's been able to understand Earth animals for some time now." Why hadn't he just told her everything when he had the chance? He knew precisely why. He'd felt something, more than he should. More than it was *right* to. He had responsibilities, a duty to Ohinyan, and he had to honour them.

"Then you should be satisfied, sire, your mission was a success."

Sire. Such an old-fashioned tradition. "I wish you wouldn't call me that," Alexander said.

Malachai pushed aside a broken tree branch with his right hand, his left holding his bow. "It's better I practice saying it, otherwise, some may think I'm undermining you."

Succinct as always, Mal. "Practice. I see."

"You've nothing to prove, you know. It's a noble thing you've done, stepping in for Mira. No one expects it of you. You're *twenty-one*... Alexander, your parents had been together seventy-five years before your sister was born. What you're doing for the angels, for Ohinyan is..." Malachai waved his free hand around as he spoke. He'd *always* talked with his hands, for as long as Alexander could remember. "Well, it's noble," Malachai finished.

"Noble. I see."

Malachai flexed a wing to nudge Alexander's shoulder.

"Are you going to repeat everything I say for the rest of the day?"

"No, of course not. I'm sorry. There is much to do, and little time to do it. The windows are becoming more and more unstable. Has there been any evidence of this during my absence?" Dead leaves crumbled under Alexander's feet as they passed more blackened, smouldering tree trunks.

Malachai reached for the gold cuff on his wrist, twisting it as he spoke. "There has been one report." He paused by a stream and knelt beside it, letting the water pass through his fingers. "Part of a wing was recovered—cleanly removed, like a very fine blade had been taken to it. We think a window closed on the angel as they passed through to Earth."

Alexander crouched beside Malachai and splashed his face with cold water. An angel was wandering around on Earth with half a wing missing, probably too afraid of what might happen if they tried to come back for help. Could they be dead already? He scooped a handful of cold water and gulped it down. *What if Fia had died, following you through?* "When did this happen?"

"Days ago. A week, perhaps."

"And there have been no further reports?"

"None." Malachai was on his feet, his eyes scanning the trees for any signs of unwelcome visitors.

Learning to trust others was proving difficult. Delegating was difficult, but it was his general's duty to manage which angels travelled to and from Earth. Alexander knew he had to trust that the situation was in hand. Still, an angel was wounded, and they were his responsibility, all of them. He let out a breath. "I fear I am falling short of my father's leadership, Malachai."

Malachai turned slowly, continuing his search of the trees. "Your alliance with the witches, sire?"

"The alliance was the right thing to do. I should not have agreed to look for Fia. We don't just take people from Earth. It goes against everything we know." Alexander rested his bow beside his blades as he spoke. "Ohinyan… it isn't safe for her here."

"It isn't safe in Ohinyan for anyone, sire. Ohinyan, Earth, it doesn't matter where she is. You said it yourself. A coven was in the cemetery before you left. If she was still on Earth, perhaps they might have intervened."

"She was only in that cemetery at night because of me. How would an Earth coven know who she was? They were already *in* the cemetery, pursuing me, as far as I know. The fact remains, there are far fewer dangers on Earth." He filled his container with cool water from the stream. *What were you thinking?*

Malachai rubbed his chin between finger and thumb. "I'm sure your father made many decisions. Some right, some wrong. The alliance with the witches, electing to go to Earth instead of sending another, that Fia is *here*—however she got here—is all leading towards the greater good. The angels know that. Ohinyan will know that, soon enough, when the third sun shines bright in the sky."

Alexander replaced his weapons. He'd tried to keep her safe on Earth, and instead she'd fallen through the window to Ohinyan. "This prophecy, something about it doesn't feel right."

"You doubt the witches?" Malachai asked.

Alexander flexed his wings to shake off the rain. "No, I don't. I believe them—I believe Noor. What I don't understand is how we didn't know about it already. How could something like this be concealed from the angels. Did my father know?"

Leaves rustled in the wind, and rain dripped through the canopy. The forest was eerily quiet.

"I don't know, sire. But you're right. It does seem strange to not know such a thing."

Fia had been through so much, and Alexander had witnessed it all, even her breakup with Henry. There was no doubting she had a gift—a spark of understanding of the Earth animals.

But then he'd seen her, the night of her birthday, alone in the park talking to the sister he'd watched die before his eyes, and something in him crumbled. He couldn't take Fia from all she had left. He couldn't do that to her. He hadn't even allowed himself to think about what he'd felt for her since leaving Earth.

And yet, she followed him, anyway. What a mess he'd made. How could one girl change the fate of an entire world?

Malachai was silent beside him as they walked. The rain had eased, and the canopy brightened as sunlight broke through the trees.

A low hum carried its way to them on the breeze.

"Did you hear that? It sounded like an engine." Alexander pushed himself off from the forest floor and up through the trees. He hovered for a moment, scanning left and right, until Malachai emerged beside him.

"There," Alexander cried out. "An airship."

Only the Makya would have access to such a vessel, loaded with weapons they could launch deadly attacks from the air, with a far greater range.

But why now? Alexander couldn't make sense of it. One thing he knew for certain. Every person and creature in the forest below the airship was in danger—Fia and Noor included.

CHAPTER FIVE

FIA

Not long after dawn, Fia found herself stumbling and feeling her way through the forest, struggling to keep up with the Lady Noor, whose long legs took strides three times the length of hers. She told herself it was the right decision to go with Noor. Altair had just saved her life, so trusting him didn't feel like a mistake.

But mostly, she'd agreed to go because it might have been her only chance of getting back to London. That little flat was her only connection to Sophie, to her parents. And what other choice did she have? Run off into a strange world, alone, with the risk of getting killed by shapeshifting fire people, or whatever they were?

She soon lost pace with Noor, replaying what had happened since she'd fallen through the… window? Yeah, that's what they'd called it. She thought of Alexander, holding her hand in his, and her cheeks flushed at the memory. Had it been him all along, back in London?

The Lady Noor laughed up ahead. She flicked her long braid over a shoulder as she looked back.

"What?" Fia asked, her cheeks burning.

"Nothing." Noor's voice was edged with amusement. "You must have many questions."

Fia whistled through tight lips. She waved her hands and gestured at the landscape around them. "Where do I begin?" she asked, as she pointed. "I'm marching through a forest in another world with a seven-foot-tall wonder woman."

Their surroundings had become strange, almost unrecognisable as a forest. Some of the trees were lush with thick, green leaves, but others were black, bare, and almost spine-like in their twisting, gnarling qualities, and they oozed a sticky black tar. The forest was damp, the air mixed with the aroma of pine needles and morning dew on grass. When the wind blew, the scent of jasmine cascaded across their path, covering the moss in tiny white petals and reminding Fia of long summer days back in Hampstead Heath with Sophie. She reached for the little bracelet on her wrist. It was still there. She counted her breaths to calm her racing heart.

"At the beginning," Noor finally replied. "The coven will tell you all you need to know. Although you fell into this world, it is not entirely by chance that you are here." Noor waited for Fia to catch up with her, climbing through entwined branches and ducking under fallen logs. "As for Alexander…"

Fia held her breath as she waited for Noor to tell her more about the angel.

"You know someone who has passed on?"

Fia felt all the air leave her lungs, and she could do

nothing but nod.

"He remained... much longer than they normally do. It is a sad coincidence that he found you in such a way." Noor pushed on through fallen branches without looking back.

"Wait!" Fia was out of breath, tripping and fumbling her way towards Noor. "Is he my guardian angel?"

"Angels are guardians in both this world and yours, but in different ways. In your world, they help free the spirits of the dead, and in ours they protect us. They protect the spirits of our world and maintain peace here in Ohinyan. In that sense, all angels are guardians, for everyone."

All angels are guardians. Fia let the words echo in her thoughts as the sun rose and dipped in the sky. She couldn't help but feel a little thud of disappointment in her chest that Alexander wasn't just *her* guardian angel. Her feet ached but she didn't complain. It had been hours since Noor had last spoken, but it was a comfortable silence.

Noor stopped, looking down. Fia followed her gaze. They'd reached a clearing exposing the land far around them; the haggard shapes of rocky hills jutted out in the distance. She could see from this great height that the centre of the forest behind them was thick and lush, and then its edges became bare and barren, like the twisting trees they'd walked through earlier. They were at the summit of a small peak, but Noor had picked out a spot well sheltered from the elements. Scattered below them throughout the woods were more ruined patches; burnt, blackened areas with barely any foliage remaining.

"Did the Makya do all of this?" Fia asked.

Noor crouched down near the crag, sifting a handful of fresh soil through her fingertips. She held her palm open and let the last of the soil blow away in the wind. "Ohinyan is at its weakest when the sun is dying, many of its inhabitants, too. That vulnerability has made many become fearful. For the Makya, it has encouraged all you see here." Sunlight shimmered off the cuffs on Noor's arms, and the stone on her circlet glittered.

Fia took in the trees reaching to the horizon, the patches of black, *of nothing,* and the pillars of smoke. Another item in the long list of reasons to get back to Earth as soon as possible. How long until the sun died—what then? How were they all so calm about it? She rubbed at her neck as she peeled her gaze away from the horizon, pushing down the rising panic. It always started in her hands, so she needed to keep busy.

Fia settled into the rhythm of helping Noor clear a place to sleep, removing loose rocks and pulling at large plants to make bedding. She twirled an enormous leaf in her hand: thick, hairy, and veined, it was larger than her head. She layered them up as Noor had shown her, until she'd made a small bed for each of them. She'd spent time camping with Sophie—it was all they could afford during the summer holidays, and they'd slept under the stars on more than one occasion. Fia bit down on her lip as she thought of her sister. She needed a distraction. *The angel.*

Alexander… He'd been the angel, all along. A real angel,

not just one she'd made up. Satisfied with the beds, Fia began collecting firewood, working her way through her thoughts. Maybe he'd set Sophie's spirit free. But why did he stay? The sun disappeared behind the tallest peak, and Fia watched carefully as Noor kindled a fire. It was more complicated than using a lighter, but Noor made it look easy as she struck two flints together.

Orange glowed in Noor's eyes as the fire sparked to life. "Perhaps tomorrow, I will tell you the story of the first angel, Gabriel."

Fia knew the story of Gabriel, at least she thought she did, but something told her that Noor's story would be very different. She followed as the witch laid traps for rabbits, tying long vines in knots to tree branches, and creating little trap platforms from sticks tied together with long blades of grass. Fia was warming to Noor. She reminded her of Jo in a roundabout way. Everything she said was straight to the point, but there was a softness beneath her words. They seemed about the same age, too, early twenties, maybe. But then who knew how old anyone was here.

"The greatest stories are often about love." Noor flashed a smile at Fia, as she turned back to check her first trap not long after she'd laid the last.

Fia felt her cheeks flush once more. *Henry, that wasn't love.* She didn't even know what it was. But the only story she was interested in hearing was the one about how to get back to London.

The first trap was empty, and Fia followed Noor to the

second. "Do you know how I can get back to Earth? The coven will tell me, won't they?"

Noor knelt down beside the second trap, collapsed but with no rabbit. Fia didn't voice her relief that it had escaped. As Noor rebuilt the trap, she paused to glance up at Fia. "I don't know how to return you to Earth, but I am hoping the coven will tell you. They are not my coven, mine is far from here." She looked to the horizon, and Fia couldn't read her expression. "But I am told they are fair witches. My experience with them so far tells me that is the truth."

"Oh, they're fair, are they?" Fia clenched her teeth together. She didn't want to say something she'd regret. Noor nodded in response, and Fia followed her to another trap.

They pushed aside bushes and branches to find a rabbit, motionless at the end of a vine. Fia's stomach twisted. She'd never seen a dead rabbit before—never seen an animal just *hanging* like that. Noor unknotted it with care and carried it by its legs back to the fire. Fia busied herself with clearing more loose rocks, not wanting to watch as Noor prepared their meal. First the voices and the angel, now a parallel world, and a witch preparing dinner. Fia counted her breaths again, hoping to fight the nausea that accompanied the panic. What if the coven didn't know how to get back to Earth?

Noor fixed the skinned rabbit over the fire to cook and took out a large container made of animal skin, passing it to Fia. It was water, and Fia gulped it down gratefully.

"So, what do angels do… what happens when we die?" She'd always wanted to know where Sophie had gone, where her parents had gone. Energy couldn't just disappear, could it?

Noor smiled and sprinkled some dried leaves on the rabbit. "In your world, who can say? Angels go to Earth to help the fallen's spirit leave its body… here, because of Gabriel, our spirits either rise and join the sky spirits or sink deep down into Ohinyan."

"They help people's *spirits* leave their body?"

"Perhaps you would prefer the word soul," Noor replied flatly.

Fia pictured Sophie lying on a wet road at night, Alexander touching down gently beside her. She fought back the familiar sting pushing at the corners of her eyes as Noor passed her a piece of cooked rabbit. Thinking of Sophie created a dull emptiness in her stomach that no amount of anything could ever fill.

She cleared her throat. "So I'm guessing the coven will tell me why it's not a coincidence that I'm here, too. Right?"

"That is correct. I would ask you not to press me on the matter."

Fia's mouth opened and closed, and she knew how ridiculous her gawking would look. Noor wasn't being rude—was it an obligation, then, that held her silence? She had an Amazonian like quality to her. Despite her long limbs, her movements were graceful, like a dancer's. She busied herself with tasks, eating a mouthful of meat every now and then as she worked. Finally, she sat, sharpening one of her weapons on a strip of leather, humming softly as she looked at it, this way and that, and inspecting it in the pale moonlight. She'd been patient today, and Fia was grateful for it. They'd walked a long way, and Noor had stopped many times to wait for her.

"Sleep, we have an early start," Noor said, wrapping up the remaining rabbit in more of the large leaves Fia had used for their bedding.

Where was this coven? As Fia lay down on her makeshift bed, anxiety pushed harder against her chest. It was always this way at night, when the world was silent, and her thoughts were loudest. But this wasn't London—this was another world. Another *world.* The pressure increased as the anxiety threatened to turn into a full-blown panic attack. *One, two, three…*

Fia's eyes flicked open to the Lady Noor shaking her from her almost-sleep. Arrows pointed at them from every direction, and small bows glowed orange in the firelight—far too many to count.

CHAPTER SIX

FIA

Fia's gaze moved from the tips of the arrows to the creatures surrounding them. There were too many to consider fighting. Maybe without weapons, they'd stand a chance, but every one of the strange, little feline people held a bow. Noor crouched beside Fia; her stance attack ready. Her right hand was raised to the hilt of a large sword she carried on her back, waiting for the strange creatures to make a move. Fia followed her lead, slowly rising, and steadied her feet, hands up, ready to fight.

Before any of them could make another move, fog filled the air around them, so thick Fia couldn't see through it. She struck out with her elbow to where a creature had been standing beside her, but it connected with nothing. Where before there had been assailants wielding bows, there were now birds, shrieking and screaming, diving and flapping around each other.

She couldn't work out what had happened. Adrenaline rushed in her ears, and everything was clouded in grey. But as quickly as it had come, the fog disappeared, and beside her on the ground laid the Lady Noor, unconscious, blood trickling down her forehead.

The birds were gone, and in their place the little feline people stood once more.

"Hey, what do you—" Before Fia could get the words out, her head was covered with cloth and her hands tied, plunging her into total darkness. "Hey, stop!" she shouted. "What do you want from us?" She kicked out, legs and elbows thrashing in all directions, but her blows met with air, until there was a *tug* on whatever they'd tied her to.

Their attackers made no sound. *Breathe, just breathe.* "Noor, can you hear me? Wake up, Noor!" *Breathe.* She twisted her hands against the binding on her wrists and kicked out fiercely, but was prodded with what was most certainly the tip of a bow.

Fia was led downwards, back towards the forest. Her hands had been fastened to a rope to guide her, and she could smell the familiar aroma from the day before: sweet pine mixed with damp soil and now cinnamon, too. Every now and again, she called out for Noor, but no reply came.

When she stumbled, a small hand would pull her up swiftly, and a tiny palm on her back directed her left or right, but otherwise there was no communication, only the sound of feet on twigs or rustling through leaves gave away their position.

She pictured their strange, yellow-green faces—human features, but feline, with sharp points to their ears, their chins, and the flatness of their small noses. Their eyes were impossibly narrow, their pupils like a cats'. They'd attacked with speed and silence, and now only the occasional sound of a twig breaking here and there told her they were still walking beside her.

In the distance rumbled the unmistakable sound of an engine, but Fia couldn't make out which direction it came from. She hadn't seen a single structure or vehicle since falling into Ohinyan, but then again, this could have been the middle of nowhere. She whistled. Where was Noor? *Please be okay*. Fia wasn't ready to lose another person, even if it was someone she'd only just met.

A woman's voice began pleading, but it wasn't the Lady Noor. At the same moment, Fia was shoved into some kind of container. She froze in panic as it began to lift off the ground.

She reached out. The container was small, only big enough for her, and the edges felt rough, like wood. The walls of the container arched up and over her head, and as she felt around the sides, she found an opening. She pushed her fastened hands through the hole into nothing. Air rushed over her hands as the container swung wildly and rose upwards, throwing her backwards.

The air chilled as the container ascended, and there were sounds: mechanical, and the smell of engine oil, a clang of metal on metal, like closing doors, and Fia heard footsteps approaching, the creak of the container door swinging open. Hands tugged at her wrists, the cover was pulled off her head, and her eyes gradually adjusted to the low, dim light inside the... thing they were in.

Fia looked around. It was a loading bay. There were wooden crates in one corner and several of the containers—like the one she'd arrived in—swung gently in another corner, attached to a system of pulleys. They were nothing but little wooden pods.

Some of the cat people cut her restraints, and as Fia rubbed her wrists, she assessed her chances of fighting and making a run for the nearest container. There was nowhere she could go. They were too fast. And then she saw Noor.

Noor was still unconscious, but blood glistened from a wound in her head and had clotted and crusted down the side of her face beneath the silver circlet. She was ashen. Strands of hair had worked free from her plait and stuck to the dried blood like veins. Their assailants had fashioned a stretcher for her from tree branches and the large, broad leaves from the forest below, but Noor was so tall it took four of them to drag her in it, the lower end with her feet scuffing awkwardly across the floor.

They were taken through dark, narrow corridors, clad from floor to ceiling in metal panels and large, rounded rivets holding the panels in place. Every door was closed, made of the same metal as the floor and the walls, with nothing unique to identify where they were or to give Fia any sense of location.

They stopped at a large room with what were unmistakably cells running down either side. Fia was ushered inside, and Noor was dragged in behind her, deposited in the corner on her makeshift stretcher.

"Wait, she needs help—" The solid metal door shut behind her as Fia fell in a bundle to the floor.

She kicked at the metal and fought back the stinging threat of tears. She was exhausted, Noor was probably dead, and she'd come all this way only to be scooped up into the sky, quite possibly to be killed. She swallowed deep breaths of air and kicked at the door again. *Don't lose it. Keep it together.*

Fia let out a soft whistle at the sound of Noor's quiet groan. It was the tiniest of sounds, but enough to snap Fia out of her panic. Noor was trying to sit up, and Fia helped to prop her up against the wall of the cell.

"I'm sorry," Noor croaked, "they must have known I'm a witch. We stood no chance."

"What? What are you talking about? They hit you on the head." Fia pulled off her hoodie and used some of the water from Noor's container to wet the cleanest part of the fabric she could find. She dabbed gently at the wound on Noor's head. "It was like I'd been drugged. Everything went really... grey. There were birds, and it was foggy, and for a few seconds I was somewhere completely different." She shook her head. As soon as it had begun, it was over, and Noor had been lying there on the floor, very still, like Sophie. She felt that sickly pain in the pit of her stomach she'd felt so many times before.

Fia wiped the crusted blood from Noor's eye, passing her the water container.

"You were not drugged, Fia. There are many things a witch can do. Illusion is just one of them."

"You did that?" Fia asked. "How?"

The dark cell changed to a lush green meadow around them. Noor's head was clean, and the wound was gone. Noor continued to talk, as they sat together in the meadow, a soft breeze rustling the flowers and the grass. "Illusion can be used for many things, defence mostly, but many use it for other reasons. Deceit, seduction, anything you can think of." The meadow faded, and they were sitting in the cold cell again.

"Wow. I would never leave the illusion if I could do that."

"Reality is usually better," Noor replied, looking around their cell. "My home is in a forest, like the most beautiful and wondrous illusion you could ever imagine, but it's real, hidden away from others for us to enjoy and feel at peace." She shifted her weight as she reached for a leather bundle tucked into her belt.

"I'd hoped to take you myself to the forest, Fia. You'd have liked it." Noor closed her eyes. "Now, we must get you out of here, and you must go to the witches. I have something I need to do before I can leave."

"Wait, me? What about you? We're both getting out of here together. Those cat-things are fast, but I think we can take them. I can fight, you know." Fia hid the tremble in her voice. She could fight, but she didn't think they stood much chance. They were completely outnumbered. But what worried her more, was how she would find the witch coven alone.

"Those little creatures are the Aurelli. They are incredibly swift and light on their feet. If we are in an airship, which I believe we are, then they must be working for the Makya, because no one else in Ohinyan would have such a vessel."

Fia got up and walked to the back wall of the cell. There was a small window, like a porthole in a ship, above her head. She held onto the edges of the window, put her feet on two of the large bolts in the wall, and pulled herself up to peer out of it. They were high in the clouds with glimpses of blue sky every now and again. She let her focus shift to her reflection in the glass, the first time she'd seen herself since falling into Ohinyan. Her green eyes were bright and alert, and her hair was so dirty it covered any tinges of red. She stepped down and looked at the floor in a daze. There was nothing but clouds outside the window.

"Noor, there's no way out of here until it lands. Unless you have a secret broomstick."

"What need would I have for a broomstick?"

"You don't—never mind."

Noor fastened a string around the small leather pouch she'd removed from her belt, turning it into a makeshift necklace. "Listen, Fia, we don't have much time. The Aurelli do not speak our language because they are more like animals than men. They rarely make any sound at all. There is no way we can convince them to help us quickly. It will take time if I can convince them at all. Whatever it is the Makya have offered them, I very much doubt we will be able to better it, unless your pockets are lined with gold coins."

"But I heard one of them saying something, she was pleading with the others, before we were pushed into the pods. I thought it was you at first, but then I couldn't make out the words, it was a bit of a jumble, to be honest—"

"You heard what they said?"

"I heard that they said something, but not the words, though."

Noor smiled, "You *are*…' She shook her head. "There are very few with this gift. You can hear what the creatures say. I have never met anyone who could. How long have you been able to hear them?"

"I didn't know. I mean, back in London, I thought I was hearing voices, but maybe they were in here," Fia said, reaching up to tap her bandage. "And I hit my head quite hard when I fell into Ohinyan."

"For now, it may only seem like just voices, but with focus, you may be able to speak with them."

"Talk to creatures, to animals? Am I… am I crazy?"

Noor chuckled. "No. I told you, you are not here entirely by chance. We have been looking for you for some time. There are stories of you amongst the witches, Fia."

"What kind of stories?"

"Of how you can help us. I'll tell you everything you need to know as soon as we meet again, but for now, I need you to look after this for me." She looped the necklace around Fia's neck and tucked the pouch into her top. "I'll tell you what to do with it when I catch up with you, but for now I just need you to look after it."

Fia patted the pouch to check it was secure and gave a dutiful nod. *You can do this you can do this you can do this.*

"Back in the loading bay, some of the pods are not just for transport. They're small vehicles for flight," Noor said.

Fia could see where this was going.

"They're easy to fly—a handle that turns will bring one to life, another will steer it. You just need to get it to the ground. I'm going to create a distraction, but you must remember that the layout of the airship will remain the same despite what you see, so that you can get out." Noor walked over to the window, faltering only slightly to look out as Fia had done before, stooping a little to examine the clouds. "Once you get to the loading bay, there will be several levers, some are for raising and lowering the transport pods, and the largest is for opening the loading bay doors. Once they're open, you need to get into one of the release pods and get out. I'll meet you down on the ground, but you'll need to hide the pod. I'll come and find you."

Fia paced the cell, counting her breaths. "We'll go together." Her hands were tight balls at her sides. *You can do this.* Could she, though? Could she fight her way through a strange world, alone? What if she never found the witches? What if they didn't know how to send her back? *You can do this.*

With a gentle laugh, Noor rested a hand on Fia's shoulder. "Fia, I have fought in many battles and been captured many times. I have survived far worse than this. I can defend myself in more ways than one. I'll see you on the ground." Noor smiled and handed the blood-stained hoodie back to Fia. "You'll need this more than me."

Fia nodded, tying the hoodie around her waist, and breathed in a few deep breaths. Within seconds, Noor had leapt up to the metal rafters above them and perched in waiting like a tiger ready to pounce.

"They're coming," she whispered, and the room changed colours. It was a forest. The smell of pine needles and damp soil filled the air. Trees dripped with fresh rainwater and there were rabbits, everywhere, little grey rabbits with round, black eyes like glass beads. Fia looked at her hands. She was a rabbit, too.

"She's awake," a woman cried out from amongst the trees. Where before there had been the doorway, now stood an arch of trees with a corridor of evergreens beyond it. Through the archway came more rabbits, scurrying about in confusion.

She didn't hesitate. Fia darted past into the corridor now lined with trees. As she ran, three rabbits glowed like the embers of a fire, and she knew they were the Makya.

She ran as fast as she could through the fake forest until the illusion faded, and she was no longer on four feet but two. Behind her were the screams and cries of a fight, and at that moment, she was more afraid for Noor than herself.

A single door remained open in the corridor, and Fia could hear voices inside. She checked no one had followed her before standing beside the door to listen. In the reflection of the metal, two figures stood opposite each other, glowing like embers as they talked.

"Once we have located Alythia, we will use the airship to destroy it," the taller one said. "Or better yet, take it for our own."

"But the angels' lands are not fixed, brother. You know that we will never be able to locate them," the second replied.

"The witch will tell us."

A loud scream reverberated through the corridor. Fia didn't wait for any reaction. She launched back into a run, as fast as her legs could move towards the loading bay.

There. The levers Noor had mentioned. Gasping for breath, she ran to the largest one, throwing her body weight onto it as she pulled it down to open the hatch to the bay. She spiralled around. She could see the flying pods now, behind where the transporter pods were hanging. They were like tiny wooden helicopters, with blades like a maple seed.

Three of the Aurelli creatures stood guard beside them, alert at once upon Fia's arrival. The first she knocked to the floor with a swiping kick, the second she grabbed, and threw it into the third. It only stunned them, but it gave her the few seconds she needed.

With just a moment's thought for how fragile the flying pods could be, Fia ran over to the closest one and dived in. The inside was much like the transporter pods, except that the front was totally exposed. There was a control handle, which lifted in and out. A large lever sat to the right of it, and above that, a crank handle. It was stiff, but the little blades above her spluttered to life as Fia pushed down gently on the lever. Adrenaline coursed through her, and she willed the pod to do something. *Anything, please.*

The three Aurelli stirred—she was running out of time. The pod scuffed and scraped along the loading bay floor as the first creature ran towards her. She pulled up on the control handle, and the pod lifted off the floor in bumps and starts towards the loading bay hatch. The Aurelli leapt towards her, but the pod spluttered up and down, and the creature missed, landing gracefully on the loading bay floor.

Voices closed in behind her, so she cranked down again on the lever to gain speed, dipping out of the loading bay. She held her breath as the little pod plunged into the sky. The pod swayed in the undercurrent of the airship but she steadied it. *Keep it together, Fia.*

Something small shot across the open part of the pod, and then another. Dread twisted in her stomach—they were arrows. She wasn't safe yet. She heard shouting from above, and accompanying the arrows were small balls of fire. The Makya.

Arrows filled the sky around her. One pierced through her arm, and a white-hot, searing pain travelled up to her shoulder as blood flowed, and an anguished cry escaped her. The little pod spun. Fia pulled back on the control handle as hard as she could but nothing happened. Her arm throbbed where the arrow hung from it, more blood flowing from the wound than she'd ever seen. Something hit the side of the pod, and it lurched left and right. It was being drawn back into the airship. Fia put her full weight on the lever to try and break free, and the pod lunged forwards, throwing her through the opening and into the sky.

She grabbed the control as tightly as she could with both hands and tried to pull herself back inside with all her strength. The pain in her arm was blinding, and blood was running over her hand and down her arm. It was impossible to hold on. Arrows and balls of flame barely missed her on either side of the pod. She couldn't do it. Her good arm was already tired. She looked down and saw the tiny tops of the trees in the forest below.

Something hit the side of the pod, big and dark, but she couldn't make it out. The seed pod had shattered, and she was falling, and she knew this was it. She'd cheated death twice, and now it had come for her.

All the air escaped her lungs as she plummeted, but no sound came with it. Above her the airship hovered against an endless sea of blue sky and the remains of the seed pod, swaying at the end of the cable.

CHAPTER SEVEN

ALEXANDER

They'd had two choices: return to Alythia for backup and risk losing track of the airship, or find out where it was going. Alexander had decided to follow it. It would have been too dangerous for them to split up. If it were a Makya ship as he suspected, then he'd be a fool to pursue it alone whilst Malachai returned to gather soldiers.

Together, they'd followed the ship for the rest of the day, flying amongst the clouds to avoid being seen. Alexander had only ever known of the Makya using airships. They were clunky, slow-moving metal contraptions with an unnatural number of wooden wings and an odour of fuel that polluted the air. How they even stayed airborne, Alexander couldn't fathom.

"It moves as though it's unfinished," Malachai said, his wings tinged amber, as the sun dipped low in the sky.

There wasn't time for this, but the Makya were too great a threat. A threat *and* a distraction, pulling them away from the bigger picture. No one seemed to have answers about their dying sun or what lay ahead, only stories and hearsay. It wasn't enough. How long would their world be without sunlight? What certainty was there that the third sun would even ignite?

If Fia was the girl, she could be the answer to everything. Guilt twisted in his stomach. She probably knew everything by now.

Alexander stopped to rest near the tip of a tree, holding onto the trunk as Malachai joined him. The sunset pushed through the clouds, and the humming of engines grew louder.

"Over there, a second airship." Alexander motioned his bow towards it.

Malachai adjusted his footing, releasing a hand to shield his eyes from the sunlight.

"We've had no reports of this. They must have launched within the last few days and from separate locations. What are they planning?" Alexander rubbed at his chin. It just didn't make sense.

"Shall I return for reinforcements, sire?" Malachai asked. They swayed with the tree they rested upon, the canopy a blanket of lush green before them. The airships' engines drowned out the sounds of birdsong and the wind, even though they were far away. Alexander considered his options. He and Malachai were stronger together, not that an attack would be an option. There was no doubting those airships were armed.

"No, we stay together." Even at this distance, the airship was the largest Alexander had ever seen. Wooden wings jutted out at different levels, several of them on each side in a haphazard arrangement. Panels of metal cladding ran up the sides, the newer pieces glistening as the sun broke free from the clouds. It appeared mostly dull and rusting, as if it had been made from scraps and parts of other machines. Likely stolen parts, all of it.

The two ships approached each other, and a seed pod sputtered out from the smaller one. Beneath the hull of the largest airship, a door opened to grant the pod access.

Another followed it and then three more.

"Passengers or supplies?" Malachai asked.

"Who can say? It could be the council but why?" Was war truly their intention? This was precisely why he'd agreed to accept leadership when his sister Mira had asked it of him. The thought of his two nieces waiting for their mother to come home or of Mira injured in a fight didn't bear thinking about. She was strong and knew how to defend herself, but she had too much to lose, so he'd gladly taken her place, despite the murmurs of opposition over his age.

But sometimes those slithers of doubt from the elder angels seeped their way into his thoughts, and Alexander found himself second guessing his actions more often than he'd like. Whenever he doubted himself, he reached down into his memories, searching for any words of wisdom his father had imparted over the years. They'd never discussed this particular scenario—why would they? Communication with the Makya had been progressing well up until his father's death, and Alexander hadn't been able to bring himself to restart the process, or to risk sending an envoy to

Nadar, not after what happened with his father.

"They're on the move. Let's go. Up to cloud cover," Alexander said, leaping from the tree.

Alexander and Malachai kept their distance, soaring upwards to thick clouds where they'd be better camouflaged. Malachai's wings were light like his own; that's why they'd been paired together for training as boys. They'd been taught to seek cover where they could blend in, like the clouds, while their friends with darker wings had been taught to stay low to the canopy. At night, it was easier. They were nothing more than a shadow against the trees in the dark, but light still remained, and they presented too easy a target.

He'd never imagined, as a child, that he would be concealing himself from the Makya. Stories of Makya attacks were from a time long before he was born, and it had taken until recent years for his father to make any progress towards an alliance with them. So when the attacks had started again after his father's death, the elder angels didn't seem surprised, but it didn't sit right with Alexander. Par, the council leader, always struck him as fair and level-headed. This didn't feel like her style.

"They're splitting up," Alexander said from their vantage point, as the larger airship began to turn away from the small one. It was much faster than the smaller ship, and Alexander chastised himself for not having been closer. "Let's follow."

They closed as much distance between themselves and the ship as they dared, close enough to see porthole windows dotted around the hull. As they approached, the loading bay opened, and another seed pod spluttered out of it. Arrows and fireballs shot at the pod.

"Bows ready," Alexander called out over the wind.

A Makya leapt out after the pod with a towing anchor, the hook slamming its way into the wood, but the Makya lost hold and plummeted through the air.

The pod swung and someone tumbled out of the front opening. *No.* Her auburn hair was unmistakable, like a red flag waving in the wind.

"Fia," Alexander cried. He didn't look back for Malachai. Instead, he lunged towards her, watching helplessly as Fia lost her grip and fell from the pod.

His stomach turned and twisted, and his breath caught in his throat. "No..." The word was carried away with the wind.

This is your doing. You brought her here. Time had somehow stretched out between them. It was as if he was flying against a wave, and Fia was falling in double time.

But just as she was about to hit the canopy, a great black bird swooped upwards from amongst the trees and caught her carefully on its back. *A Shadow.* It dove down as swiftly as it had arrived, and Alexander pursued it.

The bird landed in a clearing, its enormous black wings, twice the size of his, flapped gently as it lowered itself.

Alexander was quiet. This was the closest he'd ever been to a Shadow, though he'd tried many times as a boy to chase after them.

Twigs snapped as Malachai landed behind him, and the Shadow's head jerked to the sound. "What's it doing?"

The bird folded its wings under itself and rested like a robin in its nest, tucking low to the ground. Fia lay motionless across its back. *Please wake up. Please wake up.*

"Waiting," Alexander replied, approaching the bird with cautious steps.

The Shadow's eyes were onyx and as big as Alexander's hands, and the bird twitched its head left and right as he approached. He saw himself in the glassy rounds, dropping his bow to the ground. A gesture. One he knew would be understood.

Alexander stepped closer, scanning Fia for injuries. The bandage Altair had tied was still fastened around her head, and her arm and hands were covered in blood. Guilt washed over him once more. *This is your doing.*

He lifted her carefully from the bird's back and backed away slowly. If the Shadow was startled and took off from this position, its wings could knock him and Fia to the ground. But it remained still, its beady eyes never leaving him. Alexander felt as if he was being looked at for the first time. *What do you see?* Why intervene? This was not usual behaviour for a Shadow, far from it.

Alexander allowed himself a moment to check if Fia was okay. Her lips parted, her breaths shallow, as her chest rose and fell. He'd left her behind on Earth because he cared for her… more than he should, more than his duties permitted.

The bird let out a short squawk as it took to its feet, testing its wings for take-off. Alexander was barely clear, as the breeze from its ascent blew strands of hair across Fia's face.

And then the Shadow was gone, up through the canopy and away.

CHAPTER EIGHT

FIA

"Fia? Can you hear me?"

That voice. She knew that voice, deep and soothing.

"Fia?"

It was as if she was still falling through endless blue sky and white clouds, only it was warm. Perhaps this was what it was like when your spirit was free. Impossibly warm, with the voice of an angel surrounding you.

"Fia. Wake up."

Something shook her. The warmth was being sucked away from the comforting cocoon around her, focusing entirely on her right arm. But it wasn't just warmth, it was burning, searing heat.

"Fia, listen to me, I know it's painful, but I need you to stay awake," the angelic voice said.

She opened her heavy eyes, drowsy with pain, seeing a glimpse of feathers, white feathers, and then her eyes fell shut. *So many feathers.* The pain was sharp, coaxing her back to consciousness. Opening her eyes again, Fia was met with the crystalline blue of Alexander's, concern etched across his brow. He didn't look right. He wasn't all white and glowing.

He was dirty like he'd been in a fight.

Crimson stained his wings in places and crusted in patches across his arms and chest. She reached a hand towards him, attempting to sit up, but nausea almost overtook her. "You're bleeding."

"It's your blood." Alexander steadied her as she lay down again and closed her eyes.

"She can sleep, sire. The wound has been cauterised and will stop infection from spreading. It will heal," said a voice beside her.

She was in too much pain to sleep, but at least with her eyes closed, the throbbing subsided a little.

"Thank you, Malachai." A hand brushed strands of hair from Fia's eyes. The touch was gentle, but she kept her eyes closed to keep the nausea at bay.

"I've never known a Shadow to intervene in this way, sire. Did you see how close it flew to the ship?"

Water bubbled and boiled and then splashed as heavy items were dropped into it. The aroma of burning wood filled Fia's nostrils, along with the familiar scents of the forest.

"Two airships. What do you think they're doing?" Malachai asked. Water poured onto the ground nearby, and equipment clattered as he spoke.

"I don't know. It seems strange, even for the Makya," Alexander replied.

A hand brushed Fia's cheek, but she dared not move. *Don't open your eyes. Don't open your eyes.*

"I should not have left her."

"Sire, I will take her to the witches. She will be my priority before returning to Alythia."

The fire hissed and spat and Fia's arm throbbed. Since Sophie died, there had been an endless stream of instances of feeling like a spare part, or like she was too much for people who didn't want to be around so much *heaviness.* Even with Henry and his friends, on so many occasions, it was like she was just getting in the way of their fun. *An inconvenience, that's what you are.* She counted her breaths. She pictured Sophie's face, smiling back at her until the panic subsided.

"We will both go," Alexander said. "It will be safer."

"No!" Fia's eyes darted open and she sat up, too fast. Alexander caught her good arm as she swayed with blood rush and nausea.

"You lost quite a bit of blood earlier. You need to move slowly." Alexander searched her eyes with his. She avoided his gaze as her cheeks reddened. Her bandaged arm was throbbing, but she pushed herself up. *Don't let them know how much it hurts.*

"We can't leave Noor up there," Fia pleaded. "She saved me, created a diversion so I could escape. They know what she can do, and they'll keep her unconscious, or worse. We just—we can't leave her."

"Fia, we need to get you to the witches and back to Earth. It's too dangerous for you in Ohinyan—lives are being lost. We need to get you home before it's too late.

You don't belong here." Alexander's gaze was fixed on the fire, his expression unreadable.

Fia opened her mouth to respond but no words followed. *You don't belong here* echoed in her head, as she watched the embers of the fire turn from yellow to orange. His words stung more than they should have. *What would he know about where I belong? I don't even know where I belong.*

"This is Malachai," Alexander said. "We were patrolling nearby when the Shadow caught you falling from the airship." He shifted his weight as he spoke. "Together, we will take you to the witches, and we will find a way to return you to your own world."

"Thank you, for my arm." Fia lifted it a little to test her strength. "What's a Shadow?"

"One of the oldest creatures in Ohinyan," Alexander replied. "Great blackbirds, with wingspans twice as wide as ours." He threw a stick into the fire, embers spitting onto the soil around it.

Fia closed her eyes and felt the air rush over her as if she were falling from the little seed pod. "I should be dead."

Malachai explained how they'd heard the airship and arrived just as she fell. Fia was only half listening. *You almost died… again.* She watched Malachai, waving his hands about as he spoke. He was shorter than Alexander, but not by much. He wore the same loose, hemp-like trousers, but his were tied with a finely knotted rope of blues and greens.

He had golden skin and long, blonde hair that bounced as he moved. His soft brown eyes were edged with laughter lines, but he seemed young—they both looked barely older than she was. On his wrist, he wore a wide, gold cuff that reflected the light of the fire as he moved his hands about him. It was engraved with letters and moulded itself neatly to the shape of his arm.

"We need to know what you saw, who you saw, if you heard anything, as much information as you can tell us." Malachai unrolled a length of fabric beside him and laid wooden items and a leather container similar to Noor's on top of it. "But first, you need to eat." He handed her a cup, neatly carved and smoothed, full to the brim with water.

Fia drank it quickly and handed the cup back for more. He refilled it, and passed her a leaf wrapped around strips of cooked meat.

"I'm going to get more firewood. Eat, and then we can discuss what happened on the airship," Alexander spoke softly, the fire illuminating his wings as he stood. A wave of tiredness washed over Fia as the food hit her stomach, and she focused on the white of Alexander's wings until he disappeared into the shadows.

"Why do you call him 'sire?'" she asked between mouthfuls of food.

"We are all related to Gabriel, in one way or another, but Alexander is a direct descendant. He is our leader. It is his birthright," Malachai replied, the cuff on his wrist glittering. He followed her gaze. "From my wife," he said, touching the cuff. "It is a tradition for us. We give them to our partners as a symbol of our commitment to each other." He smiled as he wrapped his other hand around the golden cuff, gazing into the fire.

Commitment. She'd stayed with Henry because she had no one else. And then he'd cheated. But she'd used him, too, in her own way. She'd known it for a while. "That's… that's really lovely," Fia said. "How long have you been together?"

"We were recently married." Malachai beamed. "Last year. It caused quite the commotion, actually. We're young to be married, even amongst angels. My parents were in their seventies when they chose to start a family."

Fia coughed on a piece of dry meat. "Oh, that's um… How nice," she managed, patting her chest as the food eased its way down.

Malachai laughed. "Angels are a little different to humans." He flexed his wings. "We don't age as fast as you do. Our kind can live for hundreds of years if they are fortunate. I am very blessed to have found a partner. Many angels live their life alone."

"Hundreds of years is a long time to be alone," Fia replied. But time seemed different here, somehow. *A sun dying. Shouldn't that take a long time?* "How old is your world?" She tried to work out the numbers. If Altair's people had been driven out by the coming of the second sun, and the third sun was coming. *Older than Earth, surely?*

"We don't know for certain. Our evolution has been different from yours. There was life during much of the duration of the first sun, but man and creatures that can communicate had only been around a few hundred years before the first sun died. We have no record before that, which is why we refer to it as the first sun—when in reality, there have probably been many." Malachai passed more food to Fia as he spoke. She pieced together what he'd said with what Altair and Noor had told her.

"Why are you helping me? Why are any of you helping me?" She ate the last mouthful of food. None of it made sense. She rubbed her palms against her jeans and did her best to ignore the tightening of her chest, the way each breath was harder and harder to pull in.

"Angels have always been protectors," Malachai replied. "As for the others, they are friends of Alexander's, so you can be certain they are good people. Would you stand by and let a stranger die, or would you help, if you could?"

"I'd want to help," she said, as Malachai packed away his things. "And I'm not dead or dreaming?"

"No, you're very much alive."

What she'd seen so far of this world was puzzling. There had been no real signs of civilisation other than the airship, which must have meant there was a dockyard or construction yard somewhere. The angels were like nothing she'd ever seen, nothing like the robed angels of children's stories or on church windows. Here, they walked amongst mankind as if it were the most normal thing in the world.

"Now, tell me everything you saw and heard on the airship," Malachai said.

Fia recalled their capture by the Aurelli and Noor's plan for her to escape. She told him in detail about the illusion

Noor had created for her, right up until she'd been caught by the Shadow as she fell from the pod, omitting only the part where Noor told her she could hear creatures. She still wasn't certain she could, or if she'd just been imagining things.

Malachai gave a thoughtful nod. "Did you only see Aurelli on board the airship?"

"Actually, when I was running, Noor's illusion had just faded, and I heard two men talking. I only caught a glimpse of them, one referred to the other as brother." She paused to readjust her bandaged arm. "They were talking about the angels and finding that word you used earlier... Alythia? Destroying it even, and they were going to use Noor to tell them."

Malachai held his chin between finger and thumb for a moment. "Thank you for telling me."

"But we need to stop them—they can't—" Fia objected, but Malachai raised a hand to silence her, a warm smile breaking across his face.

"Rest. We'll talk more after you've rested," he said.

The first thin rays of sunlight were escaping over the horizon, turning the sky into a dim grey. The air felt still, the first few moments before dawn brought everything to life. Fia yawned and lay down, her thoughts hazy, but she was too restless to sleep, so she remained still until she no longer felt like she was falling.

Feet crunched against leaves. Her eyes flicked open to Alexander returning with firewood. His feathers were clean, and there was no trace of the blood that had dried to his arms and chest. *That chest…*

A few small birds chirped their morning melody. "So, what now?" Fia asked, patting at her bandage as she sat up.

"We find the nearest witch coven and ask them how we get you home." It was Alexander who replied, but he didn't look at her as he spoke.

"How many of these windows are there?" Fia pushed herself to her feet, testing the strength of her arms and legs.

"We don't know." Alexander tidied the camp, still avoiding her gaze. "Angels have always used the windows to travel to Earth. In all my years, I've never known of any other passing through to Earth. Only of those who fall into Ohinyan. Few survive." He threw dirt over the fire, busying himself as he spoke. "The airship took you far off the course of the coven Noor was leading you to, but there is a city, Turaunt, a few days' travel from here, where we should be able to find out where the nearest coven is."

A city. Water glistened through the bushes in the morning light, and Fia felt as if all the dirt and grime of the past few days was embedded in her skin.

"I need a minute," she said and strode off towards the water without waiting for a response. She kicked off her shoes and tested the strength in her arm by picking them up. Malachai was right; the pain had eased, although her shoulder ached a little. She took off her clothes and the little pouch that Noor had given her, looking around her once or twice as she did so, and submerged herself in the stream. It was deeper than it looked but perfectly clear and cool, and she clenched her teeth together as she sunk into the cold.

She soaked her matted hair, pulling the bandage from her head that Altair had wrapped around it a few days before. Then she scrubbed at the dried blood on her arms and hands, turning the water around her a rusty red. Satisfied, she floated on her back, looking at the sky.

At the edges of her vision, she could see both banks of the stream, lined with trees, and the small opening she had come through to enter the water. The sky was light, but soft, wispy clouds filled the space above her with a fluffy patchwork of white. *Is it spring here? Do they even have seasons like Earth?*

So much had happened, and she wished for nothing more than to talk to Sophie about it. Her name sent that familiar ball of pain twisting and throbbing in her stomach. *What is wrong with you? Just ask why you're here.*

She thought of the way Alexander's muscles disappeared below the waist of his loose trousers, of how he'd brushed the hair away from her face, of his hands on her skin, and she bit down on her lip at the memory of it. *You really hit your head, didn't you?*

"*Fia…*" a voice called to her. One that she was certain she'd heard before back in Altair's tent. The voice was far, far away, and suddenly the thought of her feet not touching solid ground filled her with dread.

Then she heard a woman's voice followed by a man's, quarrelling, but she couldn't make out what they were saying. She left the stream, her heartbeat drumming in her ears. She dressed in a hurry, carefully tucking Noor's pouch back inside her top. *That voice…* She wrung out her dripping hair, combed her fingers through it a few times, and carried her shoes and socks with her back to where she'd left Alexander and Malachai. She'd almost counted to one hundred by the time she'd made her way back to them, her breaths still catching in her throat.

"Better?" Malachai asked as Fia approached. He was alone, sitting by the remains of the fire. Everything had been cleared away, and Alexander was nowhere to be seen. *Of course he left, why would he stay? He's got bigger responsibilities than this.*

"Much," Fia replied, as she twisted her wet hair around her fingers. Malachai threw her a cloth. She leant forwards, wrapped the towel around her hair, and tossed her hair over her head to dry it. When she looked up, Alexander had returned. She felt her cheeks flush as their eyes met, and she quickly looked away.

"Time to go," he said.

"Wait, I heard people arguing, down by the stream, but I couldn't make out what they were saying. A man and a woman," Fia was rushing her words. It had been strange, and she'd left the stream in a hurry for fear of being seen.

"That's impossible," replied Malachai, "we've searched the entire area several times, and there's no one here. No one has passed by here for days."

"We better check it out. We stay together," Alexander

said.

But even as they made their way down to the water, it was clear there was no one around.

Fia said nothing. *You're not here by chance.* Noor's words echoed in her head.

"When are you going to tell me why I'm here?" she asked.

Alexander dragged a hand through his hair. "It's for the coven to tell you." He avoided her gaze as he led the way towards Turaunt.

CHAPTER NINE

FIA

They'd been walking all day. The sun was already beginning to disappear beyond the horizon, and three small moons were visible in the sky. Two small and one large, they glowed softly against a strawberry pink background. Fia lost her footing, mesmerised at the sight.

"Fia, are you okay?" Alexander reached out, but pulled his arm back as Malachai steadied her.

"Fine, I just… need to sit for a while," she replied, her voice shaky. A shiver travelled down her spine and shook her even in the pit of her stomach. "Wouldn't it be quicker to fly to Turaunt?"

"It's too dangerous." Alexander waited beside her as she pressed her hands to her knees and breathed in deeply through her nose. "We'd be too exposed and vulnerable to an attack if we carried you." He dragged a hand through his hair as he spoke.

Fia opened her mouth to speak but thought better of it. Alexander looked away. She'd told Alexander everything as they'd walked, from seeking out the coven with the Lady Noor to the moment the Shadow had caught her, tumbling from the seed pod. *As soon as Malachai leaves, I'll get some answers from Alexander.*

Alexander had listened carefully to her explanation. *Why is he so hard to read? Yesterday he's stroking my hair, and today he's… sulking?* Fia felt her cheeks redden as she tried to untangle her thoughts. He was a leader of angels, in the middle of a war, his responsibilities were greater than she could imagine. But she'd felt something, a connection. Had he felt it, too?

He'd stayed—that's what Noor had said. He'd stayed after Sophie died. Why? Fia stole a glance at his face, but it gave nothing away. He appeared deep in thought, his lips pressed into a firm line, strands of hair billowing around his face.

"There's a cave ahead, sire, it opens out into a grotto with fresh water. A good place to stop for the night," Malachai said. Fia had been so engrossed in her thoughts she hadn't even noticed he'd left.

"Very well," Alexander replied.

Does he ever wear a shirt? Fia exhaled a deep breath. *Just be normal, Fia. You've known him for what, two, three days?* She'd already lost count of how long she'd been in Ohinyan. But it hadn't just been two or three days—it had been him all along on Earth, since Sophie—she just hadn't known he was real.

By the time they reached the cave, her legs ached as if she'd been in one of her training sessions with Jo. Her head didn't throb, and her arm was sore, but it was bearable. The narrow entrance gave way to a long, winding passage of stone opening out into a large chamber. Stretched out before them in the expanse of the grotto was a cluster of trees across a bed of green moss, beside which a small brook bubbled and swirled. From high above them in the cave, a narrow shaft of light shone directly onto the trees like a golden spotlight.

Fia made her way to the edge of the mossy area by the brook, slumping beneath the nearest tree. Her fingers pressed down into soft, dry moss. She focused on the texture. Why couldn't anyone give a straight answer? *Why am I here... what aren't they telling me?* Did it have something to do with Sophie?

Malachai and Alexander prepared the area for them to sleep and built a fire. They showed no signs of exhaustion; she didn't think either of them had slept the night before. They laughed as they worked, care-free conversation passing between them.

Fia turned away, disguising Noor's pouch as she removed it from her neck and emptied its contents onto the moss at her feet. She didn't know why, but she felt like the contents were for her eyes only. She'd studied it earlier, but only briefly, when they'd stopped for water. It was a small, black flower, carved of stone, no bigger than her thumbnail with a smooth, shiny surface and cold to the touch, even though it had been close to her body all day. The detail was incredible. It should have been fragile with such fine, dainty leaves, but they were hard and strong with no signs of wear. It was like a rose or a dahlia when held one way, or a narcissus or tulip when held another. It could be almost any flower at all, Fia realised, depending on which way she held it.

"Fia," Alexander called to her as he approached, and she stuffed the little flower back into its pouch and concealed it in her sleeve before he was beside her. "How are you feeling?" he asked. He crouched low but kept his distance.

Fia flexed her arm where Malachai had sealed her wound. "Not bad, he did a good job," she said, flicking her chin in Malachai's direction.

Alexander looked to his friend and huffed a quiet laugh. "I couldn't have asked for a better right hand."

"I don't mean to sound rude, but aren't you a little young to be a leader? You can't be much older than me."

Alexander laughed again, but the sound was choked, like all the times she had to go along with an awful joke a customer had told her at the coffee shop. He rubbed at his neck and seemed to consider his words. "I'm twenty-one. I took the role for—for someone else." He smiled, but it was a tight, polite smile. "Our meal will be ready soon." He was already on his feet, striding back towards Malachai.

He took the role for someone else. What did that mean? The responsibility seemed to weigh heavily on him. The way he considered every response, in every command he gave to Malachai. The lack of answers was beginning to grow old, and Fia clenched her jaw tight instead of slamming a fist into the tree beside her.

Dinner was brief, the same meat they'd had the night

before, likely more rabbit. She watched as Alexander and Malachai busied themselves with various tasks. "Let me help with something." She was restless, and it had been nothing like camping with Sophie.

Malachai smiled. "Thank you, but I enjoy preparing food." He topped up the fire and prepared another rabbit he'd caught earlier. No doubt they'd be eating the meat for breakfast.

Alexander attended to his weapons, checking each arrow and testing the strings of his bow as he looked for signs of damage. Archery had always been on Fia's bucket list, ever since she'd been given a plastic bow and arrow as a child. She and Sophie had spent hours chasing each other around the park pretending to be fairies. That was a lifetime ago.

From the ground up, Alexander's bow reached higher than Fia's waist and was like frosted glass. It had a milky, cloudy quality to it, so it wouldn't reflect the light and give away their position. The ends of the arrows had the distinguishable white feathers of his wings. When he seemed satisfied, Alexander left the bow behind to speak with Malachai.

Fia leapt up, grabbing the weapon and pulling back on the string. Without an arrow, she looked ahead at an invisible target. It was much heavier than she expected, but she was strong and held it high.

"This bow has been made for me, considering my height, weight and, strength." Alexander was beside her. She hadn't heard him approach. "But I can show you how to use it until we can get you a bow more suited to you." His strong arms and broad shoulders had made it look easy.

Fia tried to disguise the smile she felt tugging at the corners of her mouth, as she feigned still drawing an arrow. *He's smiling back at you.*

Alexander nocked an arrow ready for her. "You'll need to use your strongest arm to draw the bow. Normally, we'd wear a guard to protect our bow arm from the string, but this should be sufficient," he said, tugging gently at the sleeve of her hoodie.

She nodded and held the curved part of the bow in her left hand, arm outstretched, as she'd seen Alexander do before.

"Now, stand straight, with your feet shoulder-width apart." He stood in front of her as he spoke, correcting her when needed. "When you draw back on the bow, you will find a point that is comfortable to hold whilst you take aim, for most it is the corner of the mouth or just below the chin."

Fia held her breath. *Don't let him see how much your arm is hurting.* She drew back on the bow, pulling her right arm up, so her hand was just level with the corner of her mouth. It was surprisingly tough to pull back with the arrow in place. She used her core to steady herself as much as she could. Alexander walked behind her, repositioning her elbow with one hand and pushing down on her shoulder with the other. Fia trembled, but not from the weight of the bow. He was so close, the scent of jasmine and cinnamon drifted from his hair, just like the forest.

"Steady," Alexander said, his voice quiet. "Over there, that tree stump."

Fia drew in a breath and held it as she took aim. Alexander stepped away from her and her concentration returned. She focused on the upturned tree stump, aiming the tip of the arrow at the centre, and released the string. The arrow shot across to the right of the tree stump and fell with a rattling thump to the floor. Fia exhaled.

"Not bad." Alexander stood in front of her again. "You were putting force on the hand that was holding the bow, rather than using all your strength to draw back, and that sent the arrow to the right of the target instead of straight."

He held the hand Fia gripped around the bow as he spoke, repositioning her so that she was just resting the bow below the soft part at the base of her thumb. His skin was warm, and Fia held her breath as she steadied herself, gazing up at him. He was still talking, explaining why it was important to hold the bow correctly, to position her feet, looking at her hand. *You have so much sadness in your eyes.* She studied his face. The traces of a frown were still slightly visible. He stopped talking, meeting her eyes. Fia's head swam. She was aching to touch him, to reach out and thread her fingers through his hair. Neither of them moved for what felt like an eternity.

"Sire?"

Alexander took a step back at Malachai's voice, taking the bow from Fia's hands.

"We've received word from the others," Malachai said.

Fia returned to her position on the soft, springy moss. She didn't want to hear what Malachai had to say, not tonight. Her head was still spinning from the moments before, her chest warm and heart throbbing. *What just happened?* She watched how intently Alexander listened to Malachai, and how Malachai responded with respect. Alexander's expressions were hard to read, but he spoke to Malachai with great kindness. Even though Malachai called him sire, they shared an easiness with each other, as if they were brothers.

A quiet whistle escaped her lips as she lay down on her mossy bed. She wanted to talk to Alexander more, to ask questions like how he'd known her name when she fell through the window, and whether he really had helped Sophie. If she wasn't here by chance, and the witches had been looking for her, he must know why. But more than any of that, she wanted to tug at the brown curls flicking around his ears, and to run her hands along his arms and his chest.

You're stuck in another world with no answers and your mind is drifting there. Great stuff, Fia. She clicked her tongue. Her questions would have to wait. She felt the warm, haziness of sleep begin to wash over her and was soon dreaming of Sophie.

***

By morning, Fia found herself alone in the cave. "Hello?"

she called out. A familiar sense of dread began to creep into her chest.

A shaft of light shone through the opening high above. Alexander and Malachai were nowhere to be seen, but she knew they wouldn't have gone far. Fia ate the berries they'd left her and washed her face in the cold, fresh water. She could hear muffled voices, lots of them. She looked towards the narrow passageway leading to the entrance of the cave, and then back over her shoulder to the edges of the grotto, across the stream. She was still alone. There was a small opening in the cave wall, and the voices were coming from within it. With another quick glance towards the entrance, she leapt over the little stream towards the opening.

It was very narrow. In places, she had to turn sideways to fit through, and the rock was cold and damp against her skin. A cool breeze touched her cheeks as she turned the next bend in the rock. The voices grew louder. She stopped at a precipice. A great expanse stretched out beyond her into the darkness. Enormous stalactites hung from the ceiling of the cave, droplets falling from them into the nothingness below.

The chill breeze became a gust of wind, and all the hairs on her arms stood up. Her foot hit a small rock, sending it tumbling and cracking onto more rocks as it finally fell, with a large splash into the water somewhere below. The sound echoed off the walls and rumbled deeply as hundreds of bats flew out from their resting place. A stalactite cracked above her and within moments, there were great white wings encompassing her and strong arms tugging her back into the passageway.

Alexander kept his wings firmly around Fia as rocks smashed onto the cliff face. They stood motionless as they heard others fall into the water far below. Fia closed her eyes. She'd almost filled the passageway when she'd come through, and now that they were here together, she was pushed up against the rocky wall, Alexander's wings cushioning her from the cold surface. Her head pressed against his chest, and she could hear his heart beating fast, matching the sound of her own in her ears.

He took her face gently in his hands, tilting her head with care, so he could look down at her, blue eyes examining her. They were curious and bright, flecked with silver and aqua. "Are you hurt?" he whispered.

She shook her head, staring at her reflection in his eyes. The air in the passageway buzzed with a familiar charge like static built up between them, waiting to be released.

"You need to stop doing that," he said softly, without taking his eyes away from hers.

"Doing what?" she breathed. Her gaze fell from his eyes to his lips, and Alexander's thumb traced her cheek.

"Almost getting yourself killed."

Fia closed her eyes as she held her breath again, swaying slightly. When she opened them, he dropped his hands from her face, and taking her hand in his, he led her back through the passageway to the grotto.

Malachai ran towards them, his bow drawn. "Sire, what

was that?" he asked, lowering his bow when nothing followed them from the passageway.

"The cave has become unstable. We need to leave," Alexander replied, holding onto Fia's hand until they were safely outside.

"How far is it to the city?" Fia asked shyly, blinking as her eyes adjusted to the sunlight.

"Less than a day's walk. We will be there by nightfall if we hurry," replied Malachai.

When they stopped later to rest, the sun sat high in the sky. Fia pulled her tattered hoodie tightly around herself. It was colder today, despite the sun. She'd been replaying over and over in her mind what had happened that morning. His wings had cradled her to him, and she could feel the strength of his arms and his shoulders, as he'd sheltered her from the falling rocks. She bit her lip, wondering what his mouth would feel like pressed against hers. Her cheeks burned at the thought. *Alexander hasn't told you why you're here, and this is all you're thinking about?* She cleared her throat. *What are you afraid of? Just ask him again.*

Alexander had gone back to how he'd been before, avoiding eye contact and only looking at her with that sullen expression, his brow furrowed into a deep line.

As they continued, the scenery changed around them. The dense forest began to drop away, and they'd been gradually ascending a gentle slope. Here and there the trees were burnt, looming structures, blackened and charred from fire. Was there anywhere the Makya hadn't been?

Eventually, the forest fell away behind them, and they emerged onto a moor, with only dull, dead grass and rock, blending into a grey sky, heavy with clouds stretching out for miles ahead.

"How much further?" Fia shouted over the wind.

"A few hours on foot," Malachai said. "Sire, I'd like to fly on ahead and check the area is secure. We should be there earlier than expected."

Alexander conceded. With a few steps, as if beginning to run, Malachai was away, beating the air downwards with his wings as he made his ascent.

Fia tried to keep her eyes on his tiny outline as it disappeared into the distance, but the wind whipped at her face, and she had to look down to shield them from the debris. She put her arms around herself. The cold seeped into her bones.

Alexander lifted his great wings out around him, and she sheltered under one of them as they walked. He moved her closer, cradling her from the wind, but not so close that they were touching. She drank in the feeling of being near him. *One ripped guy, and you've lost all common sense? Nice job, Fia. Now's your chance, just ask him why you're here.*

The sun had been dropping, making its way down beyond the horizon. The ground had levelled out some time ago, and now in the distance, they could see the landscape stretching out far below them.

"Alexander, I wanted to ask you about… well, a lot of things actually, about Soph—" Before she could finish

Sophie's name, Malachai flew up from the expanse and called out to them.

"Sire, we're too late." His voice broke. "Turaunt has been razed."

"Survivors?" Alexander asked.

"It doesn't look good," Malachai replied, gazing solemnly at the smoke in the distance.

"They destroyed an entire city?" Fia asked.

She ran as fast as her tired feet could carry her towards the horizon line stretching out ahead of them. She reached a cliff's edge and skidded to a stop. Far below them was the charred, blackened remains of a large city. Alexander landed softly beside her, and they looked on in silence as plumes of black smoke billowed from the remains of buildings high into the sky around them.

CHAPTER TEN

NOOR

The Lady Noor braced herself as cold water rushed over her head.

"Wake up, witch," said a dry, raspy voice.

Noor blinked away dirty water from her swollen eyes. Long clumps of hair that had worked their way loose from her plait clung to her wet skin. Her captors had kept her unconscious for a while to prevent her from casting any illusions. Each time the Makya would wake her abruptly and then knock her out cold again once they'd heard enough. She hadn't told them what they wanted to hear, instead giving them rambling, nonsensical pieces of information. Unfortunately for Noor, it took quite a lengthy attack to make her lose consciousness, and she suffered for it. But she had endured worse and knew she had to be patient if there was a chance of escaping.

Fighting the searing pain in her body, she glanced up at the Makya standing before her. The woman was tall, but not as tall as Noor, and even as she blazed, Noor could make out the details of her long, red coat. It was made of animal hide, one all Makya soldiers wore—resistant to fire with large, brass buckles at the cuffs of each sleeve and around the high collar that stood upright at the neck. As the Makya calmed, the intensity of her flame lessened, and her outline became more distinct. Large leather boots reached above her knees, and her coat swayed open to expose a skin-tight jumpsuit beneath as she paced. Her anger diminished, revealing ruby-red hair flowing down her back, narrow lips pressed firmly into a tight red line, and eyes the colour of embers.

"Lorn." Noor licked away the muddy water dripping from her brow onto her lips. "To what do I owe the honour?"

"The Lady Noor," Lorn replied, pacing slowly in front of Noor, who was chained from both wrists to the wall of her cell. Lorn kicked a leather boot into her stomach. "If only your people could see you now," she said, with another short, sharp blow to the ribs.

Noor's circlet fell to the floor, with the tinny reverberation of metal on metal, and it took every last inch of her resolve not to let the pain flicker across her face.

"They are not *my* people," Noor spluttered, falling forwards against her shackles. She had to concentrate, to keep her focus. "Every witch stands alone."

Lorn laughed. "Yet you still pledge allegiance to your covens. You are strange things, indeed."

"As you pledge allegiance to your Council," Noor muttered, her vision blurring. So long as Fia found her way back to the angels, she wouldn't have failed her fellow witches.

"Except I'd dare say I don't need the Council, for anything, whereas it looks as if you're in a bit of a bind right now without the help of your coven to back you. But nevertheless, I'm feeling rather generous today, as your people have been very… resourceful of late."

Noor remained silent. It was common knowledge that many witches no longer followed tradition and felt the coming of the third sun was the time to take their rightful place in Ohinyan. Erebus's whispers reached far and wide, and the Makya were not the only ones who sought to capitalise on the dying sun.

"Tell me how to find the angel's homeland. Where is Alythia?" Lorn's eyes blazed bright amber as her anger flourished. She kicked Noor again, hard in the gut, until Noor groaned and coughed up blood.

Noor was biding her time, watching Lorn's feet as she paced, backwards and forwards.

"I know nothing of the angels," Noor finally said, even though she'd been through this several times already with Lorn's brother, Jerum. She wouldn't let them wear her down, even if it meant dying alone in her little cell.

Lorn stopped in front of Noor, kneeling to look her in the eyes. "I hear Alexander rescued your little travelling companion," she whispered. "With the events taking place in Ohinyan at present, I didn't think the angels would trouble themselves with such menial tasks."

Jealousy burned in Lorn's eyes. It was unmistakeable.

Noor had seen enough jealous women in her time to recognise it. She considered her response. Lorn and Alexander had history, so she chose her words with care. "He worries for her wellbeing."

Lorn radiated to her brightest, fullest extent, her anger emblazoned across her whole being. It took all of Noor's remaining strength to conjure an illusion, one that would render Lorn blind momentarily. But she wasn't fast enough. Lorn lunged forwards, placing a searing hand on Noor's.

Okay, new plan. Noor caught the eye of a little Aurelli who had accompanied Lorn. *Now!*

She blinked, adjusting herself to her new, temporary eyes and looked back at her body in the cell, deep in a trance, or to anyone else, unconscious. Her hand had already begun to blister from Lorn's touch.

"You, with me," Lorn commanded in her direction, oblivious to the switch. Noor quietly stretched into the sensations of the little Aurelli body she had borrowed and followed Lorn down the corridor. It was a risk to leave her body unattended, but she couldn't miss the opportunity to spy on Lorn.

Two small fangs pressed against her lips, and she ran her tongue along them. Body swapping was quite forbidden amongst her coven, but sometimes exceptions had to be made. Her body would be safe enough in the cell, and once she'd walked back to it, the little Aurelli she'd borrowed would be fine, too.

They passed through the airship's long metal corridors

before stopping at a door, identical to all the others before it. With a deep breath, Lorn stood tall and walked through the doorway, reigning in the flames flickering about her.

Keep your distance.

The antechamber they entered had no distinguishable features, only the large metal rivets that held the wall panels together and reflected Lorn's auburn glow. She paced up and down for a few moments, listening, but for what? Noor heard nothing. Lorn seemed satisfied that the chamber up ahead was empty and pushed her way through the great doors.

This room was very different to the previous one. Torches lined the perimeter, casting flickering shadows on silk banners depicting the Makya emblem, the head of a phoenix in a circle of flames. In the centre of the room sat a large copper urn, filled with a fire of blues and greens. Lorn stood at the edge, gazing into the flames.

Noor remained at the doorway, assuming her position as guard, and watched.

As Lorn stared into the fire, a vision of Fia and Alexander appeared. Their bodies were entwined and writhing on the floor together. Lorn shrieked. The lovers glared back at her. Noor could see the expression on Alexander's face, his head thrown back in pleasure and delight.

"Who is she?" Lorn snarled into the flames, digging her nails into the edges of the urn, denting the metal and charring the surface where her fingers touched.

"*Only the great fire mother is worthy of the descendant of Gabriel,*" whispered the flames in reply.

Lorn leapt back, looking around the room for an intruder.

Erebus. So this is his doing, after all.

Voices approached the chamber, and Lorn stepped away from the urn, seating herself in a throne at the far end of the room. Two Makya entered.

As twins, they could easily be mistaken for each other from this distance, but as they advanced, they were easier to distinguish. Raiaan's slight limp always gave him away, and Jerum walked with perfect strides. But their short copper hair and their thin-lipped smiles were the same. Lorn smiled brightly as her brothers approached.

"That isn't your seat yet, dear sister," Jerum shouted across the room.

Lorn sat in the middle of three great thrones, her back against one arm and her legs across the other, the toes of her boot resting gently on the throne beside her. She traced her fingers around the phoenix head carved deeply into the back of the chair.

"Not yet," Lorn replied with a grin, leaping to her feet to join her brothers before the urn.

"The Council still believes you are the fire mother, Lorn. We must try to regain their favour," Jerum spoke quietly and calmly, his ember-coloured eyes the only sign of his smouldering temper.

"Their *favour*," Lorn muttered, barely audible. She gazed

into the fire again as she spoke, a wild smile stretching across her face. "We don't need them," she spat through clenched teeth. She was ablaze from head to foot, and Noor could feel the heat even from where she stood.

"What use are nine other council members who cannot make a decision quickly enough. We must continue what we have started—without them," Lorn finished.

"You know we are stronger as twelve, Lorn. It just doesn't make sense to continue without the council's backing," Raiaan interjected.

"Doesn't make sense? The council wants us to rule equally. Equally. *I* am the fire mother, my dear brothers. We are far more powerful than them. We don't need them." Lorn balled her hands into fists at her sides.

Noor braced herself, ready to run if fire filled the room. It made sense for the council to want to reconcile. Lorn and her brothers were powerful.

"Enough," Jerum snapped. "Arrogant though she is, Raiaan, she is right. Despite our current predicament, we are far more powerful than the other council members and have far more to gain. They need us. We have them right where we want them. Call for the Aurelli. We will send the Council a message. And as for you being the great fire mother, we don't know that to be true yet. There is some time until the sun dies, and we won't know for sure until then." Jerum's calm, controlled tone returned.

"But *I know*. I can feel it. I am more powerful as each day passes, as you've seen for yourself. Soon, we won't need them at all, and this world will be ours. I alone will deliver the creatures and beings of Ohinyan into a new era. Without me, *all* will perish," Lorn replied.

Noor couldn't believe what she was hearing. *Without you? Don't you mean with you? There won't be anything left to deliver.*

"We shall see. But for now, it would do no harm to have the council on our side. Let them believe we are working together. They will be our puppets to serve us in our mission," Jerum added.

"Very well." Lorn tapped her fingers on the dents in the urn she'd made moments before.

"Did you have any luck with the Lady Noor? We're running out of sky to search," Jerum asked.

"No. She wasn't very… forthcoming. I think she'd rather die before telling us anything."

"Perhaps we will have to test that theory," Jerum said, making his way towards the door. "We will prevail, dear sister. Until tomorrow, then," he called out, raising a triumphant arm to the air as he left. The tails of his coat, and Raiaan, trailed behind him.

Noor took her signal to leave. As the doors of the antechamber fell shut behind her, she heard the roar of flames and Lorn's angry cries and pictured the silk banners falling to the ground in ashes.

Time to go. She made her way back to her cell, slipping back into her body the moment she laid eyes upon it.

Noor blinked. Her own eyes. Her own blistering hands, still in shackles. The Aurelli on the other side of the bars appeared none the wiser, and beside it stood two more little guards. *Let's hope this works as well as the last plan.*

She sang to herself, soft, sweet notes, a song of longing drawing the Aurelli outside to the bars of her cell. As they watched, the ship around them changed into their beloved forest. The scents of cinnamon and jasmine, damp moss, and pine needles beneath their feet. Families with children ran and laughed and played a game through the trees. The three guards looked at the Lady Noor as she watched them, waiting patiently for a response. It had been a while since she'd tried to communicate through an illusion.

The guards nodded. Altogether, they watched the families and children running, their laughter turning to cries of terror, as they continued up and across a small brook, down over a bank, into a wall of flames. The forest darkened, blackened by the fire. The smells and the sounds were gone, and all that remained was the smouldering ruins of the forest floor.

Noor nodded and the illusion disappeared. "Thank you, I understand now."

The Makya were threatening the Aurelli, and they were powerless to refuse them. *An army created from fear.* Noor slumped against her chains, reaching for her circlet.

The two Aurelli watched her through the bars, and a silent communication passed between them, until one walked away from the cell and out of sight. Several seconds later, the door to the cell fell open, and the little Aurelli approached Noor, wide eyed and wary before dropping a skin full of water and a scrap of bread at her feet. Climbing over her shoulders, it unlocked the cuffs tethering Noor to the wall. She thudded to the floor, reaching for her circlet, and then placed it firmly back on her head before rubbing her wrists.

"Thank you," she said to the Aurelli, holding a hand gently on its shoulder. It turned to leave and locked the cell door behind it.

She ate the bread and drank the water in haste, saving a little of each for later. From amongst her layers of clothes, she took out a wrap of waxy leaf, inside of which was an oily balm. She rubbed it on her wounds and her broken, aching ribs. She would recover.

The sound of heavy boots echoed through the corridor outside. Noor carefully disguised the unlocked chains around her wrists, hanging as limply as she could from the cell wall.

"Greetings, witch."

Noor could see her reflection in the buttons of Jerum's coat, her damp, matted hair hanging in thick clumps across her face.

"Ah, one of the evil twins. Jerum, I gather, by your perfect gait," Noor spat through strands of hair. "And where is your brother today?"

"Close by, luckily for you." Jerum stooped down, close to Noor's head, close enough that she could feel the heat emanating from him, even though he wielded no flames. "But we're not here to chat about him, are we?" The embers in his eyes blazed, but he maintained his calm, quiet tone. "Tell me how to get to the angels' home and I will spare you."

"I already told you and your delightful younger sister. I do not know," Noor replied, her eyes fixed firmly on the floor.

"Lies," Jerum spat at her as he spoke, a circle of flames encompassing them both before diminishing. "Tell me how to find them, and I will make this very quick."

"I simply cannot tell you that which I do not know."

Noor didn't rise to his goading, and instead watched Jerum's leather boots, waiting patiently for the moment he would turn his back on her as he paced around the cell. She'd gathered as much information as she was going to get from being their prisoner. *Wait for it.*

"How did you get the Aurelli to help you? It is said that they communicate with no one."

"Ah, strange little creatures, aren't they?" Jerum laughed. "It seems they quite understand the notion, 'actions speak louder than words.' Our demonstrations were quite effective. Enough deflection. Tell me what I need to know."

Noor shook her head. She didn't have to wait long for her chance.

"Then you leave me no choice." Jerum turned his back to her, his arms held high above his head.

Noor sprang to her feet, pushing away the cuffs and filling the room with the image of a hundred blazing, burning Makya, arguing and fighting with each other. When she looked at her wrists again, they were blazing, too. Amongst the pushing and the commotion, she escaped unseen from the cell, outside of which she found her weapons resting against the metal wall. She smiled. A gift from the Aurelli, perhaps. Scooping them up in one movement, she ran, assessing the Makya's plans. Lorn and her brothers were part of the council, but why hadn't the other council members joined them?

There was shouting up ahead, and her illusion changed. The corridor appeared empty, as the Makya guard ran right past her towards the commotion in her cell. She paused for a few seconds before conjuring an image of herself as a Makya, slowly patrolling the ship. She knew she wouldn't be able to maintain the illusion for long with her injuries, but it was her only chance to escape unnoticed.

The entrance to the loading bay was guarded by two Makya and several Aurelli. Walking around the perimeter of the bay, pretending to check the equipment as she went, she found her opportunity.

Noor jumped, unseen into one of the pods above her, anchored in the loading bay. She needed all her strength and concentration for her next trick. She conjured a husk, a physical manifestation of whatever form she chose, in this instance a Makya guard. A risky move, because it had to remain near her in order for her to maintain it, and she was unprotected whilst she worked. Her Makya appeared below her in the space she'd occupied, scrabbling around on the loading bay floor, tripping over levers and cables, and activating the loading bay door. Now she had the attention of the Makya on guard.

"Hey, what are you doing?" one called out to her flaming husk, as it fumbled around with one of the pods. It laughed and transformed into a husk of herself, tall and elegant, before curling itself into the pod, and flying out of the loading bay door. The Makya and the Aurelli ran after it, firing arrows and balls of flames at her disappearing silhouette.

The real Lady Noor, who sat high above the loading bay, watched the scene unfold below her and was grateful for the sight of the pod, tumbling and falling away from the airship.

I can't keep this going any longer. As the commotion continued and her husk dispersed, she lay still and quiet, exhausted. Lorn's voice echoed through the corridor as the loading bay doors clicked shut.

"What do you mean, she escaped?" Lorn screamed, flames roaring from her, shadows flickering against the loading bay wall. "Which one of you is going to tell my brothers?"

Noor closed her eyes, the faintest line of a smile on her lips. She could rest for now, undiscovered, regaining her strength, and then she was going to find out what Lorn and her brothers were doing up here, above the clouds of Ohinyan.

CHAPTER ELEVEN

FIA

Fia followed Alexander and Malachai through the charred remains of the city. They passed by narrow streets lined with tall, burnt-out buildings, and the crumbling remains of a house, its wrought iron door twisted and contorted from heat. Even the trees lining the streets were bare and lifeless, like blackened skeletons amongst the ruins. There was no colour left here. Some of the buildings reminded Fia of the old Victorian houses in London, others had ornate windows and circular doors. Plumes of thick grey smoke escaped from some of the structures, and the scent of the burning city filled her nostrils.

Her foot kicked against something metal—the remains of a sign—and she picked it up to examine it. Swirling, illegible letters surrounded a black circle and flaked away as she ran her fingers across them. She dropped it to the ground, the heavy clunk echoing off the walls of the burnt-out buildings.

Malachai and Alexander were cautious, bows drawn, turning about themselves as they examined piles of rubble and the debris-ridden spaces between brick buildings. The sun had disappeared over the horizon, and the dim light remaining cast eerie shadows across the wreckage.

Fia folded her arms across her chest. *Tap tap.* She spun around. The sound resonated from within a burnt-out vehicle. It had wheels, at least, and a contorted metal chassis. *Tap tap.* She glanced over her shoulder. Alexander and Malachai were up ahead, unaware that she'd stopped to investigate. Slowly and quietly she approached, stopping when she was right beside the vehicle. She heard nothing.

It was mostly metal, now blackened from fire, with large rivets to hold the panels in place, just like the airship. Fia dropped to her knees, placing her ear against the cold metal. She looked back to see that Alexander had inclined his head towards the sound, and she held a finger to her mouth to silence him. *Tap tap.* She peered cautiously into the shadowy recess, and there, looking out from the darkness, was a small pair of eyes staring back at her.

"Hello," Fia said softly. Her eyes adjusted to the darkness, and in the light she could make out the face of a little girl, clutching a charred doll to her chest.

"Hi," the girl replied, waving her doll as she spoke. *Tap tap.* Its clothes and face were ruined, and in place of arms, it had two wooden pegs.

"She's pretty. What's her name?" Fia asked.

"Dot. She's Dot and I'm Tully," the girl replied and flicked her chin at them.

"I'm Fia. Can you come out here Tully, so we can talk with my friends?"

Tully poked her nose through a window frame and

looked Alexander and Malachai up and down before making her decision. After a multitude of creaks and clangs from the vehicle's interior, a round door fell open with a heavy *clunk* on the ground beside them. Tully crawled out, Dot tucked under her arm, and eyed Alexander and Malachai with a look of suspicion.

"Where are your parents, Tully?" Alexander asked.

Tully stared at the arrow poised at the end of Alexander's bow. "Gone. Only me and my brothers now."

Fia pushed gently at Alexander's bow, her hand steady, until he withdrew.

"Not everything is as it appears in Ohinyan," he said, searching for signs of anyone else nearby.

Fia turned her attention back to the little girl. "Where are your brothers, Tully, are there any grown-ups?"

Tully nodded. "There's some. I can take you." Clasping Fia's hand, she led them quickly through dark streets, turning left and right through narrow passageways and across wide, open courtyards. They turned another corner into an open square, flickering shadows dancing on the walls of the buildings.

"Here it is," Tully said triumphantly, dropping Fia's hand and running over to two boys sitting beside a fire. They shared some bread with her as she joined them.

Fia walked ahead of the two angels, further into the square, aware of faces staring back at her from the shadows. They were mostly children, but not all human; a child with a lizard's tail and webbed hands laughed and chased another, whose features were like the Aurelli.

An old man approached them. He used a stick to steady himself with each step, moving every joint slowly as he walked. Fia could see no creature-like features in him; he was just a regular old man with two hands and two feet. He eyed the group one by one, twisting strands of his short, grey beard in between two fingers.

"You're too late, angels. The city was razed six days ago." The old man looked at Fia's feet as he spoke, staring at her trainers.

"I'm Alexander, and this is Malachai, one of my officers. This is our friend, Fia. Are you all that's left in the city?"

The man walked slowly around Fia, dragging his stick with him. Close up, it was easier to see he wasn't short but rather bent with old age, his heavy grey coat disguising his posture. He twisted his beard again, before standing still in front of them. "Jonas," he said, patting a hand on his chest. "We're it. The rest either burnt or left." He fumbled around in his pocket for a moment, before removing a clay pipe, but didn't put it in his mouth. "There were three of your kind here, and though they helped us during the blaze, we lost them with the others." He fumbled around in his pocket again, removing a leaf, which he crumbled into the end of the pipe before resting it in the corner of his mouth.

"Three angels?" Alexander asked, stepping forwards, a frown creasing his brow.

"It seems we have a lot of information for each other. I can show you their remains tomorrow if you wish, but for tonight, I can offer you our house." Jonas turned away from them, holding his hands up towards the largest building in the centre of the square. In the flickering firelight, its exterior was blackened like the rest of the city, but the structure remained undamaged, unlike its neighbours.

They followed Jonas inside, through a dark hallway deep into the house.

"Those who are left live here now. This house has been in my family for generations, and there's plenty of space for the few who remain." Jonas glanced around. Here and there flickering lamps lit up small areas, so they could distinguish between doorways and open spaces. They reached a large, sweeping staircase, at the bottom of which was another flickering oil lamp. "We're on power from the generator. Doesn't reach upstairs I'm afraid, folks."

Jonas led them up the grand staircase into a series of interconnecting rooms, scattered with objects. It was a slow process; Jonas's movements were stiff and tired. Beyond the rubble of furniture and the newspapers strewn across the floor, he led them into a room. He lit lamps as they went before kindling the large fireplace in the centre.

"You can use this space as you please. Take anything you need, we share everything here, clothes, provisions, and there's clean water and soap. We can talk in the morning," Jonas said finally, once the fire was lit. He looked once more at Fia's dirty trainers. "There's piles of my youngest daughter's clothes around here somewhere. You can help yourself to them and anything else you might need.

Goodnight."

Fia took one of the oil lamps off the wall and wandered through the rooms, holding the lamp above her head, so she could see better. She stopped in what looked like a library. In some places, the furniture was piled so high it was impossible to see through the chairs and the desks, but there were books from ceiling to floor. Some of them lay scattered across the floor with the newspapers and the rubbish.

Alexander and Malachai's voices carried from the main room, but only the occasional word was loud enough for her to hear clearly.

"The Sacrifices of Man," Fia read aloud, bending down to pick up a torn cover with delicate, swirling letters. Inside were beautifully drawn pictures of men fighting with beasts, of the angels and the Makya. She placed it down on a table overflowing with books and junk.

Had she come here under different circumstances, she'd have loved nothing more than to spend hours reading all these books, examining every item, learning everything she could about this world. But the books would have to wait; a more pressing matter was at hand.

Fia wandered through rooms, gathering bits of clothing and soap until she found what she was looking for: a bathtub. With Malachai's help, she filled the bath with cooled kettle water. After a quick scrub, she sunk her filthy clothes into the water.

"*Fia...*" a voice called to her. It wasn't Alexander or Malachai, but it was familiar, and it sent an icy chill up her spine. She pulled a cotton dress over her head and began to rinse out her clothes.

"*Fia… why do you ignore me?*" the voice whispered.

Fia counted her breaths. *Just keep moving. A voice in your head can't hurt you.*

She leaned forwards over the bath to press the dirt from her hoodie, and then she was being sucked in, beneath the water, further and further down, as if it were a deep lake, the top edge of the bath growing smaller and smaller as she sunk. She thrashed with her arms and kicked out with her legs, her movements frenzied as she struggled to kick her way back to the surface. She reached out a hand as she swam closer to the bath's edge, but her fingers connected with glass before she made it to the surface. Bubbles streamed from her as she screamed and banged her fists against the glass.

Just as her lungs expelled the last of her air, she was back beside the bath, leaning over it, swirling her hoodie around in the dirty water, her cotton dress as dry as it was a few moments before, as if nothing had happened. Her throat was hoarse as if she'd been screaming, and her heart beat heavy in her chest. With trembling hands, she wrung out her clothes.

Fia returned to the main room with her bundle of clean, wet clothes under one arm, and her roll of found items in the other, trying to control her shaking. Neither Alexander nor Malachai were present as she hung her belongings around the fire to dry before settling into a dark velvet armchair. She pulled a checked blanket around herself; it was just like the blanket she'd taken to Highgate Cemetery. It felt like it was weeks ago that she'd followed Alexander in the middle of the night. Well, whatever she'd thought she'd been following.

One, two, three. She held her hands in her lap to try and stop them from shaking. London was so far away. What if they couldn't get her back? *One, two, three.* She twirled the little bird charm at her wrist. She'd have to think of something to tell Jo; she'd never believe the truth. *One, two, three.*

The city, what remained of it, seemed old and new all at once. Some things were familiar, like the buildings and the cobbled streets, but then there was the strange vehicle they'd found Tully in. All the furniture in the room looked old, by her standards. But then again, it *had* just survived an attack from the Makya.

She felt as if she was drowning in the bath again, pounding her fists at the glass beneath the surface. Someone, or something, had been calling to her since she'd first arrived in Ohinyan. But that had just been an illusion, hadn't it? Like Noor's illusion? Could it be another witch? Something inside her told her not to mention it to Alexander. What if he thought she was crazy?

Fia's eyes were heavy and her body ached. She sunk into her armchair beside the fire, counting her breaths once more. *One, two, three…*

***

"Fia, wake up." Alexander's hands cupped her face like before, in the cave. She froze as her eyes met his, the whisper from her dreams still soft in her ears, calling her name, over and over.

"You were dreaming," he said. Neither of them moved, and Fia couldn't help but notice the way Alexander's eyes darted from hers to her mouth. He leaned in closer, until they were so close they could share a breath. Fia looked at him, motionless, his eyes glistening like sunlight on a wave.

Alexander seemed to remember himself and stepped away, frustration laced across his brow.

"Don't go." Fia reached for his hand. "I don't want to be alone."

He hesitated for a moment before sitting beside her. "Go back to sleep. I'll stay with you." Alexander neatened the blanket and took a spot on the floor.

"Thank you."

The memory of being stuck beneath the surface of the bath water came rushing back to her, and she focused on her breathing until sleep took over.

***

The next morning, sunlight streamed through the window, and the fire was nothing more than a few embers. Alexander sat on the other side of the fire, and Fia caught his eyes shyly as she got up.

"Good morning," he said. His voice was gentle, but he barely flashed a smile. "Let's go join the others for breakfast in the square. I'll meet you down there." He left before Fia could reply.

She dressed quickly, using some of the clothes she'd found the night before: a woollen wrap and heavy leather boots paired with her own jeans and top, freshly cleaned. She'd also come across a small leather backpack, which she threw over one shoulder.

He'd almost kissed her. Had she dreamed it? She wanted to kiss him again and again. Fia let out a quiet whistle. *I never wanted Henry like this.* Alexander's mood swings were exhausting, but when there were glimpses of his kindness, of his friendship with Malachai… She shook her head, combed her fingers through her tangled hair, and ran down the stairs, through the corridor, and outside to the square. *Don't get in the way of his responsibilities.*

In the morning light, the city looked the same dreary grey as it had the night before, and the cobbled streets were lined with junk and litter. The reek of burnt hair filled her nostrils.

"Welcome to Turaunt," Jonas said with a cheery smile as he followed Fia's gaze. "I hope you slept well?"

Fia nodded, with a sideways glance at Alexander, but he avoided her eyes. Malachai passed her a bowl of stodgy porridge, steaming in the cool air.

"I'm glad my daughter's things are of use to you. She moved to Ikothea a while back." Jonas looked across the square to Tully playing with her brothers.

"Thank you." Fia smiled. Alexander's eyes met hers for a moment, but she glanced away. Had it meant nothing to him?

Jonas was quiet as he twisted his beard between his fingertips.

"Can you tell us what happened?" Alexander asked.

"It happened a week ago." As Jonas spoke, a man on the opposite side of the square reached down to a little girl, wobbling at his legs. He helped her as she took slow, clumsy steps on the cobbled streets. "The same as we had heard from our relatives elsewhere in Ohinyan. One minute everything was like normal, going about our lives, the next the Makya are fire-bombing the streets and the buildings, telling people they can either join them or die. It happened so quickly. When it was over, those that were left either ran to make a new life elsewhere, or had nowhere else to go. That's us," he finished, waving at the group in the square.

Jonas followed Fia's gaze to the man and the little girl. "That's my son-in-law, Patrick, and my granddaughter, Irina. He's like you."

Fia paled. How did he know? "What do you mean, like me?" Fia asked. Patrick was looking at them now.

"He's from your world, and I'm guessin' you're trying to get back." Jonas took his pipe out of his coat pocket and rested it in the corner of his mouth.

Fia didn't know what to say. If Patrick and Irina were in Ohinyan, that wasn't a good sign, surely?

"And the girl?" Alexander asked.

"She was born here... my eldest daughter, her mother, was born here, and she met Patrick when he fell through that hole in the sky. They built a life together, had little Irina here." Jonas held the end of his unlit pipe as he spoke.

Patrick stood up, scooping Irina under his arm, and walked over to them. "Jonas," he said, pronouncing the last part of Jonas's name with an "iss" sound.

"Fia here is hoping to get back to Earth," Jonas said, after making introductions.

Patrick didn't reply. He put Irina down, holding her coat hood as she wobbled against his leg, chewing a rattle.

"Would you, if you could?" Fia asked.

Jonas raised an eyebrow, as he chewed on his pipe.

"Go back? No. I can't. This is her home. I can't take her away from it," Patrick replied, as Irina gurgled at his feet.

Fia nodded. "But you know a way?"

"Well, no... only heard of rumours. Elena, my wife, for years we researched ways to get back to Earth." He looked down at Irina, smoothing her hair back as he spoke. "But then Ohinyan became my home. Its strange creatures and its strange ways, they kind of, take hold of you I guess." He looked around them, taking in the charred remains of the city. "Anyway, we only ever found tales, like our folklores and legends on Earth. Some were stories passed on from witches, some from the Nords, and others from elsewhere in Ohinyan. They told us we couldn't pass through a window, even if we could reach one." Patrick pulled a hair from

Irina's mouth and tucked it behind her ear.

And what if they could? For all she'd learned, she didn't know how Alexander planned on getting her back to Earth, or why she was even in Ohinyan in the first place. Why hadn't he explained it? Did he not know? Did only Noor's coven know the answer? It didn't make any sense. She wrapped her arms around herself at the memory of her fists drumming against the glass beneath the bath water.

Jonas finally lit his pipe and held it, one arm tucked under the other, without taking a drag. "You and Patrick can reminisce later, but for now, we have other things to discuss," he said, and finally took a puff. "Alexander, we've had travellers passing through this way since the attack, and they've told stories of a darkness, of whispers in the night."

Fia felt a wave of nausea wash over her and cleared her throat to disguise her uneasiness.

"A consequence of our dying sun," Alexander replied.

"A *consequence*," Jonas mimicked. He blew a perfect O with the smoke from his pipe, encircling the sun, hidden behind a film of white clouds. "You never said what brought you to Turaunt in the first place."

"We're looking for a coven. Fia needs to speak with the witches. Do you know of any near here?" Alexander asked.

"Witches." Jonas placed the pipe in the corner of his mouth and shook his head. "None around here. Besides, we may well have to leave here before long."

"Where will you go?" Fia asked.

Jonas emptied his pipe with a firm tap, crushing the

smouldering leaves under his foot. "I will show you, seeing as you might be in need of a map. These angels aren't as knowledgeable about the land as you might think." He winked and put his pipe back in his pocket before wandering off into the house. When he returned, he was holding a few large pieces of parchment, and a wooden bow with a matching quiver, laden with arrows.

"As you found my daughter's old hunting pack, you may as well take her bow. There'll be a good knife in the side pocket of the pack, here." He handed it to Fia. She nodded gratefully, placing the bow over her shoulder; it rested perfectly across the backpack.

Jonas placed the parchment on an upturned crate. "We are here." He drew a large X through the word *Turaunt* on the map with a piece of charcoal from the nearest smouldering fire.

Fia could see the contour lines making up the large cliff face they'd come down, with the moor high above, and the large, green expanse of the forest stretching on for a great distance. They'd been making their way west across Ohinyan.

"We'll go here, in time. This is where my youngest lives." He drew a circle around a coastal city, *Ikothea*. "Here." He folded up the map. "We won't need this. We know the way."

Fia slipped the map into her backpack.

"Now, you two better come with me." Jonas turned to Alexander and Malachai. "You've got some solemn work ahead of you." He handed them each a shovel, and they followed him away, into the city.

Fia's eyes followed Alexander's silhouette until he was out of sight.

"This place really grows on you," Patrick said beside her.

"Yeah. You could say that."

Patrick smiled. They shared stories of where they were from. Patrick had been in Ohinyan for eight years and had fallen through a window whilst caving in Mexico. Elena had found him, fighting for his life.

"Sometimes, I think about what I left behind." Patrick bounced Irina on his knee as he spoke. "But then I think of what I have here." He smiled at his daughter. "This world is full of so much diversity." He gestured towards a little child with lizard-like features, running around on two legs with its companions. "It might not seem like it given the circumstances, but there's a lot of beauty here. A lot of history. And community. Even before the Makya attacks, everyone would always come together, help each other out." He shrugged as he wiped Irina's hair from her eyes. "I could never take her away from this. If we make it through what's coming, Ohinyan will be a far better place than our world will ever be for my daughter to grow up, even without her mother in it. Home is not always where we come from, I guess is what I'm trying to say."

Home. That little flat back in London hadn't felt like home since Sophie had died, but it was all she had. There had to be a way back. But if it was as simple as just flying her back through, wouldn't Alexander have done that already?

Alexander returned, alone. "Where's Malachai?" Fia asked.

"I sent him to update my general and to see his wife. Then he will continue enlisting the help of all the angels across Ohinyan, before reporting back to me." Alexander was sullen, like he'd been the day before on the way to Turaunt.

"Isn't that what you're meant to be doing, instead of babysitting me?" Fia's words came out with more exasperation than she'd meant them to.

Alexander was silent. She wanted to reach for him, but the thought of him pulling away again held her back. She knew the answer anyway and felt colour flush her cheeks. "I don't have to go back yet. It doesn't have to be a priority. There are more important things going on right now." It was the truth, and she knew it.

"Fia, we've been through this. You don't belong here. We have to get you home."

She stared at her feet. His words stung worse than before. He'd made it clear he didn't want her here, in the way. It was obvious his actions the night before were a mistake, and she was a fool for thinking it meant something to him.

CHAPTER TWELVE

ALEXANDER

Alexander and Fia left the city in silence, and he found himself counting his breaths as he'd so often seen her do.

Tully had gifted Fia a copper button. "For protection," she'd told them, moments before they left. Jonas had given them provisions for their journey, warning it could take up to a week to get to Ikothea on foot.

You could carry her.

Alexander had insisted they make their way to Ikothea as soon as possible. It was the last place he knew Altair and the Navarii were headed, and witches often traded there. He'd said little since telling Fia she had to return to Earth. Guilt bristled through him since the moment he'd said it, but his responsibilities weighed heavily on him, and trying to explain that to her when he'd barely given her a reason to speak to him at all seemed like a pointless task. His behaviour had been unbecoming of a leader. He sighed. *Of anyone.*

As they walked, the husks of buildings and the burnt-out mess had given way to the city gates amongst a great wall, completely destroyed in places.

Once outside the city, they followed a river that twisted

and turned, cutting a snake-like path into the earth. Turaunt was one of many valleys amongst the mountain range they were walking in, mountains that Alexander knew well from the air. By foot, they were something entirely different, and he recognised little as they walked. They were to take the largest pass through the mountains, which was used as a trade route. Jonas had told them to follow the river path upstream, and it would lead them to the pass. Vast, black expanses of scorched earth and burnt buildings dotted the banks of the river, and with each destroyed farm they passed, Alexander made a promise to himself that it would not all be in vain.

"Lina and Anya will never believe this." He shook his head. "This used to be farmland," he explained, gesturing at black soil stretching out around them in every direction.

"Who are Lina and Anya?" Fia asked, tilting her head to one side.

"My nieces. They're always hungry for a story. They were excited when they thought my sister would be leader—they're too young to understand what it truly meant. To them, it meant adventures and gifts from far off places. So when my sister asked me to take the position instead, I promised the girls I'd make up for it by telling them about every new place I went." He stole glances at Fia's face as he spoke, at the way she bit down on her lip, as if she were waiting for her chance to speak. Why was he babbling on about his nieces? He wanted to tell her the truth—how she made him forget about all the deaths he'd seen on Earth and the carnage in Ohinyan. But what would she care about all that, when all she wanted was to get back to Earth? He pressed a hand against his thigh to stop from fidgeting. He'd behaved like a fool.

"You took the position for your sister?" Fia pulled at the woollen wrap where it had slid down one shoulder and then tucked a strand of hair behind her ear.

Alexander nodded. "I did. It normally falls to the eldest family member, but Mira has the girls. She never thought… she never wanted to lead."

Fia turned to look at him, opened her mouth to speak, and then bit down on her lip again. Whatever question she wanted to ask, whatever she wanted to say, she shrugged it off and said nothing. He couldn't bring himself to tell her more about his family when she had none of her own, not this soon after her sister's death.

They walked on until tufts of grass pushed through the soil in places. Alexander's thoughts drifted to how he'd let his guard down with Fia just for a moment—he'd *allowed* himself to reach out for her, to wake her from a bad dream. He'd wanted to reach for her so many times back on Earth. He dragged his fingers through his hair. This was crazy. He should be focused on his duties to Ohinyan and nothing else. But instead, he fought the urge to pull her close and kiss her, over and over, until the sun disappeared over the horizon.

"How did you know my name?" Fia asked.

The valley stretched out around them, barren mountains

lining its perimeter. There were trees clustered here and there, but other than the river, it was mostly an uneven expanse of grass and rock. Turaunt was a tiny grey dot in the colourless landscape behind them.

Alexander tore through excuses, the silence stretching out between them the longer he searched for the right words. "What do you mean?" he finally replied, walking ahead. *Coward.*

"When I fell through, you were there, and I want to understand." Fia jogged to keep up with him, her head in line with his shoulder. She brushed hair from her eyes and smoothed it back.

He straightened and continued walking.

"Did you help Sophie?" she asked flatly.

Alexander said nothing.

"Hey." Fia pulled on his arm. "Why won't you look at me?" Her cheeks reddened, but he knew the flash of pink rising up her chest and neck wasn't from shame. "These mood swings are starting to get old," she said, her voice tinged with anger.

Alexander sighed, looking at the sky towards the sun dropping behind the mountains. How could the angels protect Ohinyan when the sun died? What if the third sun didn't appear for weeks? Why did his scholars seem to know so little? He needed answers, and the witches might just have them.

"What did Noor tell you about angels?" he finally asked.

"She told me what angels do for Ohinyan. She said that

in my world, angels set our spirits free."

"So, you know most of it already." *I was too late to save your sister.* He knew what she wanted to hear.

The grass was sparse here, and the rocks were tricky to manoeuvre across. Fia lost her footing, but Alexander caught her arm and steadied her, his face inches away from hers. His wings pulsed against the air, balancing them both.

"Tell me," Fia said, looking up at him.

Alexander took her pack as he pressed on. "I was looking for you. The witches have been searching for you for some time. But the night I found you, you went out in the rain… on the back of a motorbike, and you crashed." His voice was quiet. He was careful with his words. Fia knew every painstaking detail of the night her sister died; there was no use repeating it. "Where possible, in your world, we try to help the deceased's spirit. There are too many cases where we cannot, where we don't get there in time. In your world, you would refer to them as ghosts. Unhappy spirits who cannot leave because they are tied to things from when they were alive, bound to them. Some can become bitter and tormented because they are stuck in an in-between state—somewhere between life and death. We help them to let go."

Fia wiped a sleeve of the woollen wrap against her face, though he knew she'd tried her best to disguise it.

"So… Sophie, you helped her… to let go?" she asked.

"Yes. Sophie left peacefully, Fia. She asked me to watch over you." He tried not to rush his words, it was important to Fia, but it mattered to him, too, that he explained it right. He shook his head. "I stayed for longer than I should have. I watched you grieve, the way you'd lay down in the park talking to the stars. Or how you'd cry, whenever you thought Henry wasn't watching. I could see how cruel and unfair you felt the world was," he finished. He was bracing himself, for anger, resentment, for all the things he'd imagined over the last few days when he couldn't bear that he'd deceived her, for encroaching on her life without her knowing.

Fia didn't look at him, and he felt his stomach twist. Instead, she fixed her eyes firmly on the ground. His heart was beating fast and loud. Her silence would be the end of him. "And I… I decided I couldn't ask you to come here, to a world you knew nothing about, so I made my way to the nearest window." His words were rushed. "But then you saw me, I mean, I didn't know if you could *see* me, and you followed me right to the window. I didn't catch you quickly enough, and you hit your head, I…" He stepped forwards. He couldn't read her expression. "I'm sorry. I was sent to find you." He chewed his lip as he waited. His apology sounded like an empty shell of a word and nothing more, but he hoped she knew he meant it.

"Thank you," Fia said quietly. "For Sophie… and for looking out for me, for saving me." She wiped her sleeve against her eyes again and walked on.

The sun disappeared behind the mountains, and three moons were visible in the sky to the east of the valley. "I couldn't see you, you know, not properly, just glimpses. I thought I was going crazy. Why couldn't I see you?" Fia finally asked.

Alexander's frown eased slightly. "There aren't many in your world that can. Those that know we are there—children or adults who are more aware of their surroundings than others."

"So, I'll be able to see you when I go back. Angels, I mean?" Fia asked.

Alexander dropped Fia's backpack and the tent Jonas had given them. "Yes, I suppose you will." He unpacked the tent at a spot beside the river. He thought about saying more, but decided against it. Every way he phrased it in his head sounded foolish.

"So now, will you tell me what the witches want from me? Why were you sent to find me?"

"After we're set up here?" he asked, almost pleaded. Was he selfish for wanting just a few more moments like this, before he told her the truth and ruined everything? *You should have told her… that first night she was in Ohinyan. You should have told her everything.*

Fia nodded. They set up the tent quickly. It was comprised of two layers, one of animal hide and the outer made of fish scales, sewn together by hand. Fia hammered in the stakes whilst Alexander attached a string to the end of some arrows.

The sky was clear, and the moons cast a pale white glow over everything. Alexander felt Fia's eyes on him as he tested the strength of the knots, fastening the loose end to the bottom of his bow, but she said nothing. He stood on the riverbank, shooting arrows at glittering targets, one after another in the dim light. As he pulled on the strings to draw the arrows back to the bank, each had a small silver fish on the end of it, flicking and thrashing in the moonlight.

She has every right to be angry. He glanced over his shoulder. Fia had built a fire, and she knelt beside it as she struck two rocks together. Had she learned so quickly from watching Noor? The woollen wrap fell low around her shoulders, and she'd scooped her hair above her head like she'd often worn it back on Earth. He thought of how her body had pressed against his in the cave, of the fullness of her lips, of her kindness with everyone they'd met.

"Tell me, please," Fia said the moment he sat by the fire to prepare the fish for cooking.

Alexander chose his words carefully. "They think you can help. A great darkness is making its way into Ohinyan, one that has been trapped for many, many years." He concentrated on the fish as he spoke. "Its name is Erebus, and he whispers to any who will listen. To the Makya, to the witches, to many of the creatures in Ohinyan, as he waits patiently for our sun to die."

"Erebus?" Fia paled at the name. "It sounds like he's recruiting."

"Erebus is preying on the insecurities of the vulnerable until he escapes." Alexander wiped his hands on a cloth Fia passed him.

"How do you defeat an ancient darkness—or prevent him from escaping?" Fia asked, brushing a hair from her eyes.

"We're working on that."

"But that still doesn't explain how I fit in to all of this."

Alexander caught her gaze. "I think you might know by now that the creatures... the animals you've been hearing back on Earth... it's not in your head. You're not crazy, but it is still a very unique gift. One that was just an old tale here, for many years. But for the witches, it's more than that. It is a prophecy."

"You knew about the voices?" Her eyes flashed, but he couldn't tell if it was anger. "What does the prophecy say?"

Alexander placed each fish onto a stick to hang across the fire. "That an Earth girl will unite the creatures of Ohinyan against an ancient darkness, or something to that effect."

"By talking to them?" Fia laughed, or more scoffed at him. What was so funny about such a thing?

"Don't underestimate the power of communication, Fia. It is a connection, an energy that makes us feel seen, understood. Imagine what that might be like for those that have never been able to communicate with outsiders before, like the Aurelli. A time of uncertainty lays ahead, and this world will need to come together if it is going to survive."

Fia was quiet. It was the truth—coming together might be the only thing that could protect the creatures of Ohinyan from what was ahead.

"Don't you ever get cold?" Fia finally asked as they ate,

her eyes moving from his bare chest to his bare feet. She pulled the woollen wrap around herself as she stared.

Alexander laughed. "Our skin is thick and strong. It keeps us warm when it's cold and cool when it's hot." He picked up an arrowhead from her pack, pushing it hard against his chest. When he took his hand away, the arrowhead was flat and crumpled.

Fia coughed on a piece of fish. "So, the angels in Turaunt…"

Alexander looked into the glow of the fire, throwing the remains of the fish into the flames. It hissed and spat. "They were burnt," he said quietly, as he watched the carcass shrivel. He pushed back a memory, too painful and raw to think about.

"That's so awful," Fia whispered.

"It's nothing compared to what I've seen in your world. People attacking each other for nothing more than looking different, children starving when their neighbours' tables are full and overflowing. I've seen so much death there, and there have been many times when I did not want to return. Life has a natural cycle here in Ohinyan. We are born, we live, we die, we return to Ohinyan, and so on. Like our sun." He shifted his weight onto one elbow, the flames flickering in his eyes. "But in your world, people are more like the Makya. They want to *own* everything. They do not return to the world when they die, but they linger, attached to their possessions, to their people, and get… stuck."

"We're not all that way," Fia said softly.

Alexander lifted his eyes from the fire to meet hers. Golden flecks glittered beside green in the firelight. "No," he said, after a while. "You're not. And we would never assume that. If we stopped what we were doing in your world, your spirits would never be free. That's something we would never allow to happen, as long as we exist."

Fia stared into the fire. He wanted to ask her what she was thinking, what she made of all of it. "Would you like to practice?" He'd risen to his feet, holding out her bow.

"Yes." She beamed, and Alexander handed her the weapon, trying to hide the smile he knew tugged at the corners of his mouth.

He stood beside her and drew his own bow. "To the tree," he said, steadying his feet and taking aim. He stilled his wings as he released the bow, and his arrow sunk perfectly into the target.

Alexander watched patiently as Fia fired arrow after arrow, this way and that, none of them hitting the tree. After the sixth arrow missed, he laughed. At first he thought Fia was angry, but then she laughed, too. She fell to her knees, shaking with laughter.

"I haven't heard you laugh since… well, for a while." He kneeled beside her. Strands of red hair swept across her cheeks, and she scrunched up her eyes as she laughed. Fia stopped to look at him. They were close again, and he ached to feel her body against his.

"It's a wonderful sound," he said, brushing the hair from her eyes. Her eyes met his, and then her gaze dropped, and she stopped laughing.

He brushed a thumb against her bottom lip, fighting the urge to press his mouth against hers. *You can't do this.* "I'm sorry, I shouldn't..." He held Fia's hands, helping her to her feet.

Alexander dragged his hands through his hair again. Fia began to say something but bit down on her lip instead.

"It's late," she finally replied, her eyes fixed at the floor. "I should get some rest." She walked to the tent without looking back, and Alexander felt as if the ground had fallen out from under him.

CHAPTER THIRTEEN

FIA

Don't get in the way of his responsibilities, Fia told herself the next morning. She couldn't bring herself to tell Alexander she could hear Erebus, or that she *thought* it was him. What could Alexander do, anyway? No one could protect her from her own mind but herself. And after what Alexander had said about taking the leadership role for his sister, Fia didn't want it to be another thing for him to worry about. If she was going back to Earth, it wouldn't matter, right? But the way he'd touched her… she shook away the thought. *Don't get in the way.*

It didn't take long for them to dismantle their campsite. Alexander made an envelope from a leaf beside the riverbed and dropped purple berries inside it. "For the road." He was gentler this morning, the sulkiness was gone, but he still kept his distance.

And the sulky behaviour made sense now—it was guilt that had driven it. His responsibilities seemed to weigh down on him, as if he thought every decision he made was closely observed. *She asked me to watch over you.* That's what he'd said, about Sophie. When he set her spirit free. Sophie left peacefully, and it was because of him.

They pressed close to the river as Jonas had told them to, until the dying sun was high in the sky, disguised behind a thin layer of white clouds. The landscape had remained bland since they'd left Turaunt, and the mountain range loomed over them as they approached. Trees were sparser, no birds sang, and only Fia's footsteps in the dirt made any sound.

"I'm sorry for not telling you sooner, about the prophecy, I just—"

"Felt like an asshole?" Fia smiled. "I know you didn't know how. I understand."

Alexander rubbed at his neck. "Well I, I didn't—"

Fia pushed an elbow towards his ribs and raised an eyebrow. "Honestly, it's fine. I think we both need to learn to open up a little." She grinned at him and his face cracked into a smile.

The trees gave way to rock, and the dirt road became stone steps before them, cut into the mountain. Alexander told her stories of Earth, of people and places he'd been. The stairway narrowed as they walked, and the rock was cool underneath Fia's hands as she steadied herself against the mountain walls on either side of her.

"What will happen when the sun dies?" she asked.

Alexander helped her over a fallen rock. "We don't know. Our scholars believe we will be in total darkness for some time, but for how long, they can't say."

"That's a little concerning, isn't it?"

"It is of great concern, I assure you." A frown etched his brow, and Fia knew better than to push the topic. Alexander was with her, instead of figuring out what to do when the sun died. And if she turned out to be a big disappointment... she couldn't bring herself to think about it.

As they reached the end of the stairway, the walls ended, and a fierce breeze whipped at Fia's hair. They studied the map before stepping out onto the pass.

"We could try this way. It might be quicker." Alexander pointed to a valley, marked out in inky lines on the rough parchment that broke away off the side of the pass. "Bridgevale."

"Sure." Fia was only half listening, as she shot an arrow at a root winding down from the rock above. Only angels travelled to and from Earth, Alexander had said. What if she couldn't go back?

"It isn't wise to waste arrows out here," Alexander said as he collected her fallen arrow.

Fia smirked. "Who says it's a waste if I have a glamorous assistant to collect them?"

He smiled as he handed back the arrow, holding onto it for a moment before she could snatch it away.

They made their way across the pass towards Bridgevale. They couldn't see much of what was below them—a thick fog had rolled in over the mountains, concealing Bridgevale in a film of grey. Fia could only see a few feet in front of her. Even though the sun was still high in the sky, the light didn't touch the rocky areas beneath them.

There was no sign of wildlife here; the wind was too harsh. Not a single spot of green escaped from the crag as they clambered uncomfortably down the mountain side.

It was dark and wet down in Bridgevale. Dead, grey trees were dotted around them, jutting out from inky pools of water. Through gaps in the heavy fog, as far as Fia could see, were hundreds of stone bridges of varying shapes and sizes and levels of decay. Some were set across great expanses of water, others sunken into the ground. It was as if someone had taken every bridge ever made and brought it here to rest.

She stepped carefully into the fog, her feet sloshing in the shallow water beneath her, and the stench of stale water hung in the air. Alexander hovered at her side, a few feet above the ground, his great wings beating silently as he flew. As they pressed on, the sun disappeared altogether, and the clouds and fog thickened. Fia pulled the woollen wrap around herself. It was cold and lifeless down here, far creepier than the catacombs of Highgate cemetery. Only Alexander's presence beside her kept her from running back up into the mountain.

She stepped up onto a crumbling bridge but spun around at a splash in the water behind her. "What was that?" she whispered, as Alexander drew his bow.

"I don't know," he whispered back, edging further onto the bridge. A low rumbling broke out from below them. Fia caught a glimpse of something black and drew her bow, but there was nothing in the thick fog.

Another splash and Fia ran to the edge of the bridge to look. Part of the side wall had fallen away, and she could see straight down into the water. Below in the darkness and the swirls of fog hugging close to the water's surface, she could make out the silhouette of an animal. Like a panther, she thought, but much bigger, pacing about in the shallow water, glaring up at her. As it moved, this way and that, its body shimmered in and out of existence, like it was made entirely of smoke. At least it wasn't made of fire.

"What can you see?"

"I don't know. It looks like a large wild cat or a shadow of one," Fia whispered. The rumbling they'd heard moments before emanated from the creature, now a low, threatening growl. "It doesn't seem very friendly."

Alexander followed her gaze. "It's a Senkah, a dark, twisted thing. They hunt the great Shadows that fly across Ohinyan—like the one that saved you from the airship. We need to keep moving, there will be more." He ushered her onwards across the bridge. "We need to stay on higher ground."

Fia nodded. Towards the end of the bridge, the side wall crossed with another, reaching up into the clouds. She leapt onto the edge, avoiding the loose crumbling stones, and pulled herself up onto the next bridge. They made it halfway across in the darkness before more growls resonated from behind them. Fia spun around and out of the fog stepped a group of Senkahs, heads low to the ground and baring large, white teeth. A guttural growl sounded from their throats.

"Fia, run," Alexander shouted, shooting an arrow at the first Senkah. The creature dispersed into a thick, black cloud of air, before reforming into its full, feline shape, the arrow splashing into the water beyond it. Fia didn't wait for the next arrow—she ran, clambering up across heavy stones as fast as her feet could carry her, until she heard another splash and stopped to scan the fog for Alexander.

"Alexander!" She couldn't see him or hear him, and panic caught in her throat. She climbed back down the bridge, but there was no sign of him or the Senkahs. Her bow drawn, Fia made her way back down to ground level, adjusting her eyes to the heavy fog. She stepped with caution through the inky water, calling Alexander's name in the darkness.

She heard a splash, and then she saw him, wrestling in the water with four Senkahs, striking out at them with the end of his bow. They became one black shadow as they dragged him, thrashing and kicking through the shallow water.

Fia shot an arrow into the mass of shadows. Then she shot another and another until one hit a solid form, and the creatures released him.

She shot her last arrow and ran, back to the safety of the bridge, but they were too fast—a Senkah had crept up behind her. It caught her by the leg of her jeans with its teeth, dragging her face down into the shallows of the dark water. She twisted and kicked out as hard she could, reaching for an arrow, but there were none left, and she thrust the end of her bow into its eye. It screamed with pain, releasing her, and then she was alone again in the filthy water.

"Alexander!" Soaking and shaking, she spun around looking for him. She ran back to the nearest bridge as Alexander's body slammed into the stone bricks beside her in a tangle of black smoke and teeth. The bridge began to shake and within seconds, Alexander was on his feet, his wings flexed to their fullest, the force of them scattering the Senkahs away from him. He leapt into the air, pulling Fia into his arms, just as the Senkahs lunged towards them.

"Hold on," he shouted against the wind, and Fia pressed her face against him. His wings beat as they flew fast into the heavy fog. Her heartbeat thundered in her ears, or was it Alexander's?

Wind whipped against her face and her eyes streamed. She gazed up at Alexander's face, spotting the unmistakeable glisten of blood. "You're bleeding!"

"It will heal," he replied, pushing on into the grey.

When the fog cleared, Alexander landed on solid ground. They were high above Bridgevale, beneath a dark sky of glittering stars, looking back down into the dense fog. Fia was stiff and dizzy as Alexander gently sat her against a rock.

"Are you well?" he asked, his eyes full of concern. A hand brushed her cheek.

She shivered, her wet clothes sticking to her.

"Come on," Alexander said, "we can't stop here. The Senkahs are strong climbers." He held her again, flying fast into the cold night.

CHAPTER FOURTEEN

FIA

It was dawn when they arrived in Ikothea.

"Fia, we're here," Alexander said, landing with a few soft steps at the outskirts of the city.

She put her feet on the ground, her cheeks flushing at the realisation that she'd fallen asleep in his arms. How long had she been asleep? She stretched her arms out, shaking her feet one after the other, as she looked around, smoothing down her nest of hair. There were buildings—skyscrapers even—enormous structures that rose all around them. They were made of metal and glass with the familiar large bolts and panels she'd seen on the airship and back in Turaunt.

"You flew all night?" She turned to examine him, searching for damage caused by the Senkahs—the cut on his face had healed. He was right; he did heal fast.

"I'm fine." He smiled, but it seemed strained. Morning sunlight shone brightly between gaps in the buildings, illuminating his wings as he folded them behind him. "Let's go and find some breakfast."

The air was thick. Fia's hair pressed against her neck and she scooped it up into a bun. There were people and creatures and *things* everywhere. The buildings were denser here, with wild, climbing skyscrapers right next to tiny little buildings as small as shacks. Some were modular and twisting. Some were fluid, like waves ascending into the sky. Fia's gaze darted everywhere, taking it all in. Skyscrapers disappeared into blue-green water, with walkways and bridges intersecting at different levels.

People pushed past them as they walked, rushing about their morning business. A woman with dark, leathery skin like an old chestnut stood behind a herd of creatures, urging them onwards. They were larger than cows and docile, with long, shaggy hair like a buffalo. But there weren't just people in all shapes, sizes, and colours. There were creatures, too, walking around, clothed and on two feet, talking to each other, as if it were the most normal thing in the world, just like in Turaunt.

Fia caught Alexander watching her, a wide grin across his face, and she laughed at him.

A man with scales for skin lifted a tattered bag over his shoulder. He threw his hands up in frustration at a child rushing past him, flicking his tongue out between a tightly closed mouth. A whiskered woman laughed and joked with a food vendor, swishing her long, furry tail out the back of her coat and trembling with laughter.

Snippets of conversation carried to them across the noise—some words Fia could make out, to her surprise, but others were just gibberish.

Enormous metal tricycles taller than a house cycled through the busy pathways, with two riders atop of each, and a great cargo of cartons and sacks piled high behind them. As soon as they passed through the streets, a swarm of people filled the empty space behind them.

There were street vendors everywhere—men with coats full of metal contraptions, all ticking and winding, and women pulling little wagons of food behind them, shouting at people to get out of the way. Giggling children brushed by Fia and Alexander, their arms full to bursting with colourful fruit.

Green birds flew in the sky above them, scavenging for scraps of food in the busy streets and diving down to grab a piece of fruit from the children's hands, before flying away into a flurry of other birds fighting for their find.

"It's so hot here," Fia said, tying the wrap around her waist as Alexander stopped beside a cart. She'd been wearing a khaki top she'd found back in Jonas's place. Together with the boots and the hunting pack, she blended in a little better, even if her tattered jeans stood out.

"It's the buildings." Alexander pointed to one as it turned slowly. "The internal mechanics create a lot of heat."

Fia watched in awe as the building continued to twist, its entire silhouette changing shape in front of them, from the base to the top. "What's powering them? What's powering the whole city?" Ikothea was nothing like London. It was unlike any city she had ever visited.

Alexander handed over a few coins to the old woman beside the cart with a smile.

"The skyscrapers have wind turbines between each of the floors and as they change shape, they catch a lot of wind. The glass is like your solar panels, using the energy from the sun. Each building powers several blocks around it. There has never been a power shortage. Here." He handed her a small, steaming parcel.

"Incredible." Fia took the warm parcel from Alexander's hands and unwrapped the tea-coloured paper. Inside it was a sweet bread, freshly baked, the smell mouth-watering. She ate it in large mouthfuls, the soft, buttery dough tasted of cinnamon, orange, and chocolate.

Alexander ate his own as they walked, stopping at another street vendor, identical to the last. To this one, he handed over a few more dirty, copper coins, and passed Fia a brick-red cylinder, steam escaping from the top.

"Try this."

It was like hot chocolate, but creamier and thicker. Alexander finished his quickly, and threw the red cylinder into a gutter, shattering it into hundreds of tiny pieces.

"It's clay, and the birds will take it for their nests," he said, following Fia's gaze to the red shards. She finished her drink before throwing her own little cup into the gutter. Just as Alexander had said, green birds flew down, and within seconds all the clay fragments were gone.

Everything really did have a cycle here. They pressed on through the bustling streets, and Fia soaked it all in. The glass on the buildings reflected the morning light, and the streets felt bright and brilliant, despite all the chaos. More tricycles passed, but this time instead of a cargo load, they carried passengers. Hundreds of people sat in the back as it wheeled through the crowds.

Fia and Alexander stepped up onto one of the walkways. All kinds of animals were being sold in cages: birds, rabbits, reptiles, and a number of furry things Fia couldn't name. Every now and again, she thought she heard a cry for help, but she couldn't tell which cages the cries came from. What could she do? She had no money, no way of knowing they wouldn't just be captured again. Up ahead, a crowd gathered around a man standing on the edge of the walkway. He was poised and ready to jump off, but as they approached, they could hear his voice over the noise of the city.

"The end is coming! Repent your sins! When the sun dies, we die, and all Ohinyan with it. The great cycle will end!" the man shouted, thrusting his hands into the air as he spoke, waving them wildly at the sun. The people below him mumbled and muttered to each other, and eventually the crowd began to disperse back into the flow of the city.

"What was that about?" Fia asked, as they walked past the man and the dissolving crowd.

"He's a vendor," Alexander replied.

Fia turned back to see the man darting through his disappearing crowd, selling mechanical paraphernalia, bottles of dark liquids, fruits, and cages full of birds.

"So, you think Altair is still here?" Fia stepped around a group of children rushing by with loose rope sacks full of fruit.

"Altair, and some friends." Alexander looked as if he might have said more, but he smiled instead. It was a comfortable smile, and Fia sunk into the easiness that had fallen between them.

The walkway widened into a large open space, with more of the strange buildings lining one side, and on the other, a fleet of ships. They'd reached what looked like a dockyard. The area in front of them was the busiest in the city, piled high with hundreds of crates and sacks that Fia had seen the tricycles carrying. Here the passengers dismounted the tricycles, making their way up winding wooden walkways onto the ships and handing over a paper ticket to a guardsman before stepping on board.

People scurried beneath the tricycles as they crossed the bustling expanse. Women shouted at their animals as they heaved them onto the vessels. A young boy wheezed as he tried to push a black bear twice his size onto one of the ships, but the bear sat steadfast on the ramp, crying out at the little boy.

The ships had copper coloured hulls, with the familiar panels Fia now recognised as an integral part of the structures here, and torn white sails that men scrambled across to repair whilst they were anchored.

The heat, the noise, the scent of the ocean mixed with the smell of the mechanical buildings, the street vendors and the animals—it was like nothing she'd ever seen.

"Alexander!" a voice shouted out over the crowds. It was Malachai. Two other angels stood beside him, a male and a female. Alexander led her beneath the great metal wheels of a tricycle, crossing the busy expanse to greet the others.

"Malachai," he said, grasping his friend's arm in his.

Malachai flashed a bright smile at Fia.

"Sire," said the male beside Malachai, bowing his head as Malachai had done. He didn't even cast his eyes in Fia's direction. The woman beamed at them both.

"Fia, this is Runa, Malachai's wife, and Oren, her nephew," Alexander said.

Fia nodded. "Nice to meet you."

Runa smiled. "It's nice to meet you, too, Fia." She held Fia lightly by the shoulders as she spoke. Runa was a whole head in height above Fia, with a gentleness that matched Malachai's.

The angels talked. They were grander, more magnificent, *brighter*, somehow, than their surroundings. Runa had darker skin than the others, with an ochre, reddish hue that seemed to radiate pearlescent light. Her long, dark hair fell in thick waves around her small face, too small for her bright green eyes. Her clothes were of the same hemp as the others, but she wore a wrap and a sleeveless top that laced up at the front like Fia's. Runa was barefoot, too. Her only adornment was the wide, gold cuff she wore around her wrist, a perfect match to Malachai's.

Oren was nothing like his aunt. Fia caught him once or twice glancing at her before looking away. He contributed to the conversation now and then, but only looked at Runa as he spoke, as if the rest of them weren't there. His emerald green eyes seemed to be the only feature he shared with her. He looked about the same age as her, too, early twenties, if Fia had to guess.

Malachai reported Makya sightings, updates from patrol posts, and information passed on from individual witches. "There hasn't been a big attack since Turaunt, sire. But we've heard rumours that Lorn and her brothers have left the council."

Alexander's brow furrowed deeply but he said nothing, a silent nod his only response to Malachai's report.

Runa took Fia gently by the arm. "Alexander, can I borrow Fia to get some provisions? We'll return shortly."

"Thank you, that would help a great deal," Alexander replied.

Fia glanced shyly at the others as Runa pulled her away into the crowds.

"Why do I get the feeling I don't want to hear about Lorn?" Fia asked.

Runa led the way past another of the tricycles unloading dozens of passengers. "I hope you don't mind heights." She ushered Fia into a glass room at the entrance to one of the buildings. She tucked her wings tightly behind herself and pushed a button, launching them upwards. At first they were on the outer wall, and Fia could still make out the figures of Alexander and the others below, but as the building twisted, the lift turned to face the centre of the structure, exposing great metal cogs and huge wind turbines of shiny copper metal. Runa pressed another button and the lift stopped, facing them towards a dark corridor between two sections of the winding skyscraper. The glass doors slid open, and Runa grabbed Fia's hand as she stepped out. London was beginning to feel like a distant memory.

"Lorn, along with her two brothers, is a member of the Makya council. The council comprises of twelve members, and they all believe that Lorn is the great fire mother, descendant of Terah, the first Makya. Many believe that Terah could hold the power of the sun in her hands, giving and taking life as she wished. Lorn believes that she will have that power when our sun dies."

"That's terrifying." Fia said, as they walked down a dark corridor lit in a few places with flickering lamps. Dark patterned fabric draped across the ceilings and walls. Every so often, they passed a doorway, swathed heavily in more fabric, voices coming from within. "But there's more, right?"

"The angels attempted to set up an alliance with the Makya, in anticipation of our dying sun and the atmospheric changes it would bring. Alexander and his father were involved in the talks with the council, and Lorn… favoured

Alexander. She felt that as he was the descendant of the first angel, and she was the descendant of the first Makya, that they were somehow meant for each other. She let her emotions get the better of her and began to convince the council that the alliance was a good idea."

Alexander and a Makya woman. The smoke from Turaunt still clung to Fia's clothes, and the thought of them together turned her stomach. "An alliance, that's a good thing, right?"

"Right," Runa replied. "Except that when Lorn tried to discuss matters of a more… personal nature with Alexander, he refused her. Lorn was furious, and, well, things didn't end well."

The heavy scent of incense filled the corridor, carried towards them by the turbines. "Why did he refuse her?" Because it was too dangerous, or because he wasn't attracted to Lorn? Fia's cheeks flushed with shame at the thought. Who he'd been attracted to in the past was none of her business. *Who he's attracted to now is none of your business, either.*

"Lorn is a very dark individual. Alexander knows better than anyone that we each have the capacity for darkness within us. But Lorn, over the years, has let it overcome her. Erebus may have been whispering to her for a long time, who can say."

Fia's palms turned clammy, fear crept up her legs, and she willed them to stay strong. *Telling them all that you can hear Erebus will come to no good. You're leaving soon anyway, so why trouble them with it?*

“Here.” Runa drew back on a fabric-draped doorway, identical to the last, and ushered Fia into the room.

It was a shop—only slightly brighter than the corridor outside, with a few more oil lamps dotted around. From floor to ceiling, there were shelves piled high with items: metal instruments, clothing, packs, weapons, and small animals in cages. Everything from the city outside and more was stacked high around them.

“Welcome, welcome, to Arc’s Emporium!” An old man, no taller than the counter, scurried out from amongst swathes of fabric at the end of the shop.

“Arc, it’s me, Runa.” She bent down, eye level with the old man, and hugged him gently. Smokey grey cataracts clouded his eyes so thick Fia couldn’t understand how he’d navigated his way through the dark mess.

“Runa, my dear, what a lovely surprise. And I see you have brought a friend.” He waved his little walking stick in Fia’s direction.

“This is Fia.”

“Fia,” Arc repeated. “Not from around here, are you? Nevertheless, a friend of Runa’s is a friend of mine.” His wrinkled old face cracked into a smile.

How does he know? Fia raised a hand to see if Arc followed it, but his eyes stared ahead.

“Any coven members drop by lately?’ Runa asked.

“No, my dear. Witches have been banned from the city since the incident at the gates.” He pulled a handkerchief from his pocket as he spoke and dusted a nearby surface. Fia and Runa exchanged a glance.

Runa's wings pulsed as she stepped forwards. "What incident?"

"Oh, you know these witches and their tricks. Some crafty illusion, no doubt."

Fia thought of Noor, trapped in the Makya airship. Had she used an illusion to trick them, too?

"I see. Arc, Fia has quite a journey ahead of her and will need some provisions." Runa took the old man by the arm and steered him towards the counter. "I'm going to need your finest goods and your best prices." Her clay-red wings pressed close to her back as she followed him to the back of the shop.

"Anything for my little Runa," Arc replied, disappearing behind curtains before returning minutes later with his arms full. Runa scooped the bundle onto the cracked countertop. There were warm clothes of thick, heavy leather lined with fur, several bottles with coloured liquids inside them, a heavy sleeping bag made from the same materials as the tent, a number of items Fia couldn't identify, and finally, what was unmistakably, a bar of soap.

Runa and Arc bartered for a while on the price and eventually came to an agreement, involving what Fia deduced to be a small sum of money, and a repair of a cart for Arc's deliveries.

Arc held Runa's hands tightly in his. "I'll have the items brought down to the dockyard for you." He shook his head.

"These are dark times for us all. I do hope you will take care, dear Runa."

"Of course, Arc. You take care, too."

"And you too, Fia, I hope you find your way home." Fia opened her mouth to speak, but Arc disappeared for a moment behind the counter, as if he'd forgotten something, and then returned with a bundle wrapped in cloth. "Perhaps this might help you." He locked eyes with her, leaning on his stick, and for a moment, Fia thought he could see her. "Sometimes being lost helps you find your way." He handed her the bundle.

Fia carefully unwrapped the fabric to reveal a knife in a leather sheath. She took it out and held it up to the lamplight. The blade was a dark, silver metal, engraved in lettering like the metal cuff around Runa's wrist. The hilt had five large green stones, the colour of Runa's eyes in a line down its centre and caught the light as Fia examined it. She looked down at Arc's old face, the milky cataracts in his eyes wobbling as he moved.

"It's a gift," he said.

"Thank you. I don't know what to say." It was truly a beautiful gift, and Fia wondered how long it had been since Arc had last seen it.

"Think nothing of it. Now take care, my dears!" He bobbed away on his stick as he spoke, back through the reams of fabric and incense smoke beyond the counter. Fia tucked the knife into the side of her boot; there was just enough height for it to remain completely out of sight.

"Let's go," Runa said, making her way to the door.

"And take care of that husband of yours!" Arc called out, as they made their way down the corridor.

Runa smiled. She led them back through the building, via the twisting lift and back to join the others at the dockyard. Fia played over the information Runa had given her, and found herself wondering just how long Erebus had been whispering to Lorn.

When they arrived, Alexander and Malachai were talking with Altair. Oren was nowhere to be seen. Alexander shot her a smile as their eyes met, and Fia hoped the heat of the city would disguise the flush of her cheeks.

"Fia, my child." Altair greeted her with an embrace that caught her entirely off guard as he lifted her off the ground. His heavy fur cloak swayed around them as he put her back down. "You look well, but I hear you've had some trouble?" he said, inspecting her before examining the fresh scar on her arm and the holes in her clothes. He reached into his cloak and pulled out a square of cloth, folded it in half and wiped at his brow.

"Really, it's nothing, I'll be fine," Fia replied. "What are you doing here? Is your family with you?"

Altair beamed. "I am grateful for your concern, child. Most of my people are here." He turned, gesturing to the largest ship in the dockyard. "We are waiting for more to arrive throughout the rest of the day, and then at first light tomorrow we set sail. It looks like you will be accompanying us."

"I will?" Fia frowned. Finding a coven was beginning to feel like an impossible task. These witches were elusive.

"We all will," Alexander said. "To travel south. Altair has some allies he hopes to recruit, and there is a witch coven nearby, the only one I know of since we haven't been able to find any here."

Fia twirled the little bird charm between her fingers. After the incident in the bath, the thought of stepping on a boat had her stomach in knots. "How long will it take?"

"A few days travel."

If the coven could tell her how she could help Ohinyan, maybe going back to Earth wouldn't be an option anymore, anyway. But then who would lay flowers at Sophie's grave? At her parents'?

As they talked, a small boy, no more than twelve, came from nowhere to stand beside them. He dumped a cart three times his size with a broken wheel and "Arc's Emporium" written in large, swirling letters across its canopy, and scurried away as quickly as he'd come.

"Ah," Runa said, "we'll follow you on board later. Malachai and I have a cart to fix."

Altair led Fia and Alexander up the walkway. The ship was just as full of life as the shoreline below it. There were hundreds of Altair's people clustered together in great rooms lit by oil lamps, decorated with painted skins and hand-woven tapestries. They were all busy: making or mending clothes and weapons, children were playing, and

the crew were bustling around on the upper decks, checking the sails
and the ropes and whatever else was needed.

In the dockyard below, the piles of crates and sacks had begun to clear, most of them carried onto their ship, some to others. Fia watched it all quietly.

"Four small ships are travelling with us," Alexander said beside her, following her gaze.

There were other races aboard, too, alongside the Navarii. Altair must have been recruiting, as he said he would, and some had chosen to accompany them on their travels.

It was several hours before Oren returned, after the last rays of sunlight dipped behind even the smallest of buildings in Ikothea. Fia and Alexander left the ship to join Runa and Malachai in the dockyard, their work on the broken cart complete.

A different kind of life filled the street around them now that dusk had fallen upon the city. Oil lamps were being lit, and bright blue lights shone up from the water beneath the walkways. It was a spectacular sight. Street vendors were replaced by pop up restaurants, flower sellers, fortune tellers, and tents of all colours and sizes with music emanating from within. Fia reached for the bird charm again, wishing she could share it all with Sophie.

Oren arrived by foot and spoke only to Runa. They stood where the piles of crates and sacks had been earlier, and now only a few remained since the tricycles had stopped passing by for the day. Oren gave a report of a Makya sighting not far from the city, but Fia was only half listening, fascinated by the sights and sounds of Ikothea's night life.

Then a flash of orange caught her eye, falling like the sparks from a firework. And then another fell, and another, and another. Except they weren't fireworks. They were flames.

"Fia, get to the ship, now," Alexander instructed. The dockyard was a scurry of activity. The pop-up restaurants, the flower sellers, and the tents all disappeared as quickly as they had come, panic sweeping across the dockyard as balls of flames landed around them.

"I don't have wings that will burn to cinders," Fia snapped back at him. She raised her arms, ready to fight.

The four angels stood defensively around Fia, and with another flash, a pile of cargo went up in flames behind them. From miniscule gaps in the ground, jets of water shot up into the sky, covering everything in a thin mist. More water poured from the skyscrapers, creating eerie rainbows in the flickering firelight, like the city had its own defence system. Not all the flames were extinguished, and where many had landed, stood Makya people, throwing handfuls of fire into the city around them.

The angels were in motion at once, breaking formation with their bows drawn and blades swinging. A Makya materialised in front of Fia, but she was ready and swung low into a sweep kick, knocking him off his feet.

"Runa, get Fia to the ship," Alexander commanded. With her wings tucked tightly behind her, Runa grabbed Fia's wrist and dragged her towards the walkway. Hesitating would make Runa a target, so Fia reluctantly followed her up the ramp. Fireballs flashed by them, and Fia leapt onto the deck, rolling to dodge the flames. Altair and his crew were already preparing to depart.

"Sails down, before they burn," Altair called out above the commotion. "We'll switch to engines."

They weren't fast enough. Fire caught the sails as the crew pulled them down, throwing buckets of water over them as they descended. Fia pulled out her bow, shooting frantically at the Makya landing on the ship. They were outnumbered here and quickly dispersed, back to the dockyard into balls of flames.

She scanned the commotion for any sign of Alexander. He was with Malachai, but Oren was nowhere to be seen. Soon, the ships would be too far from the dockyard for their arrows to reach, and they would only be able to watch the inferno stretching out before them.

The Makya were withdrawing. Alexander and Malachai leapt, wings outstretched, to make it to the safety of the ship. Fireballs surged towards them from every direction. The Makya must have been waiting for the angels to take flight.

No. Fia threw her bow aside, already running towards Alexander.

A ball of fire caught Malachai on his wing, and he fell, tumbling and rolling onto the deck of the ship. Runa was by his side at once, throwing a piece of canvas over the licking flames.

Alexander pulled Fia low beside the gunwale, examining her for injuries.

"I'm fine," she said, checking his wings as the fireballs ceased.

The city smouldered behind them in the spray of the water jets, as the ship sailed from the shore. In the centre of the dockyard, Oren stood, facing out at the ship, beside two Makya men before turning to walk away beside them.

"How could you, nephew?" Runa said, as the city blazed behind them.

Smoke carried to them on the breeze. Only Malachai had been injured, and Runa had already dressed the wound with clean bandages. It had all happened so fast and seeing how vulnerable the angels' wings were… Fia pushed out a breath, willing herself not to panic. If this was what the Makya were capable of, and Erebus was controlling them somehow, what would he do, if he broke free?

As the harbour stretched out between their ship and the dock, the last of Ikothea's flames were extinguished, and the flickering light of the oil lamps returned, glittering in the distance.

CHAPTER FIFTEEN

FIA

The ocean was dark and vast. It had taken less than a day for the land to disappear beyond the horizon, and all around them, stretching out in every direction, was deep, black water. The atmosphere was different out here, as if the ocean was a world unto itself. The sky had lost all traces of blue. At times it was nothing more than a sheet of dull white, but mostly, it was a thick, dense blanket of grey.

The air was different, too, not filled with the smells of the ocean that Fia was familiar with, but something heavier. A humid fog seemed to hang around the ship, making the air stale and lifeless. There had been no sign of life—no birds circled above them and no fish swam at the bow below them. It left an uneasy feeling in the pit of Fia's stomach.

Now and again, Alexander would take to the skies for a better view, but each time he came back with the same answer. Nothing. There was no sign of life. But that was what they wanted to hear. Altair had chosen this route because it was so far from land in every direction, as far from the Makya as they could be.

Fia was still getting used to the ship, and the way the crew swung from it to the smaller ones that sailed alongside, backwards and forwards throughout the day. There were several sets of sails, helping the engine to save fuel when winds were high, and with all the sails at full height, there was no need for the engines at all. She had watched in fascination while some of the Navarii repaired the sails, nimble hands fast at work.

The motion of the ship on the waves hadn't bothered her as much as she thought it would. She found the movement oddly comforting. The likeness between the construction of the vessel and the Makya airship was still a little alarming for Fia, but Alexander had told her they'd originated from the same dockyard. What differed here on the ship was that alongside the vast amounts of metal and nuts and bolts, there was wood and canvas, too.

Altair's people were as welcoming as they'd been on that first night in the cave. Several of the women had given Fia gifts of soaps and a comb for her hair. They never stopped making, mending, and creating. Art was appearing, more and more, throughout each corridor and across all the internal walls of the ship. There were detailed murals in vibrant chalks and inks, depicting their journey across Ohinyan, the attack in Ikothea, or the deep, endless ocean. Fia examined them as she made her way through metal passages that stretched on endlessly. The drawings were beautiful, and they filled the ship with life.

She'd been given a room the night before with a tiny porthole looking out into the grey. She woke once in the night, dreaming of white wings blazing as they sank into deep, inky waters, her eyes flicking open to the unfamiliar shadows of her room. Fia had walked the corridors afterwards, tracing her fingers over the murals and thinking about Oren's betrayal. If Oren had betrayed the angels, would there be more? Alexander had said, back in Turaunt, that not everything in Ohinyan was as it appears. He was right.

The easiness with Alexander had remained since they left land, and Fia was grateful for it. She didn't want to think about returning to London without him. It would be different to losing Sophie, a different kind of emptiness. She played with the silver bird charm as she fought against her feelings. If there was anything she'd learned since losing Sophie, it was that life was for living, but that didn't mean that saying goodbye to him would be easy.

"Fia." It was Malachai. "Aren't you cold?" The day had slipped away from them quickly, and the light had begun to shift from the grey of day to the deeper, darker black of night.

Fia shook her head. "How are you?" she asked, gesturing towards his bandaged wing.

Malachai flexed it a little and shrugged. "It's okay, it will heal, but burns take time. The bone must regenerate, and then the feathers should grow back. It can be a slow process.

Well, slower than normal." He moved his hands around as he spoke.

"Don't worry, he's in good hands." Runa stepped up behind them. She was iridescent, despite the grey hanging around the ship. Fia felt incredibly dull beside her, but Runa's warm smile vanquished the thought almost as soon as it had begun.

"I'm sorry, about Oren," Fia said, her eyes darting to the deck. What else was there to say? *Sorry he betrayed you. All of us.*

Runa frowned, and Fia thought for a moment that her eyes glistened more than usual. "It is nothing to apologise for. I should have observed him better. Perhaps I could have prevented it."

Malachai squeezed her arm.

"Come, we want you to meet some friends of ours." Runa took Fia's hand with one of hers and Malachai's arm with the other. Even with his damaged wing, Malachai was magnificent.

Runa led them down into the ship and through a painted corridor. This one showed the Makya burning the Navarii camp in the forest, and what Fia felt quite certain was meant to be herself, falling from a hole in the sky.

They stepped through a small doorway into a crowded room with dim lighting, with a few candles here and there and an oil lamp or two. Fia recognised a few of the faces gathered in the circle: Navarii men and women, Altair, and

Alexander. Alexander was making introductions but paused to watch her as she walked over to a seat opposite him.

"We need to learn what is Erebus's doing, and what is the Makyas'. How the two are intertwined," Alexander said to Altair.

Fia looked around the circle. Runa and Malachai sat beside her, next to some faces she didn't recognise. Two men dressed in a similar kind of armour. It looked light but solid, and its silvery hue caught the flickering light of the candles. They were tall, even sitting down, and Fia thought again of the Lady Noor, huddled in the airship cell and hoped she'd escaped.

"This is Maab and Enne," Alexander continued. The two men didn't reply but lowered their heads in acknowledgement.

"Hi," Fia said. What connection did they have to all of this? Candlelight flickered on their armour as they spoke quietly to each other.

Food was brought to them on trays of starched leather, consisting of great platters of meats and fruits everyone shared. Fia bit into an apple as she listened to the conversation.

"The last coven I know of, that of the Lady Noor, is on the southern continent. Noor told me her own coven was to be a last resort," Alexander said.

"We're going to Noor's coven?" Fia almost spat out her apple.

"You know how I feel about the witches, Alexander." Altair tore at a piece of grey meat with his teeth. His great fur cloak seemed to fold around him in layers where he sat, and Fia realised she hadn't seen him without it. "We know they have mixed allegiances."

"The same can be said of any race. We've known Oren since the day he was born, and yet he betrayed us still," Alexander replied.

Runa's eyes glistened as they had before above deck, but she said nothing.

Altair shook his head, and Fia caught a glimpse of sadness in his old eyes. "Very well. But one of the smaller ships has requested to break away from the fleet. I have given them permission. Anyone who does not want to continue south should go with them. They will head west to Ashar," he said, starting on an apple.

"I cannot speak for the others, only for the Nords. We will stay with you. We are greater in numbers," Maab added. His voice was deep and heavily accented, and he didn't look up as he spoke. He reminded Fia of a lion, but she didn't know why. His hands seemed impossibly big, and he had wild, wavy silver hair reaching down to his shoulders.

Enne had a wildness about him, too, but was restrained and demure at the same time. Fia focused her attention back on the conversation, picking at her fruit.

Maps were brought out, with lands indicated at and deliberated over.

Fia studied the parchment stretched out before them. Iraluxia, the continent they'd left behind, to its east, Himera, and to its west, Ashar. Islands dotted around them, and to the north and south stretched great masses of white.

Iraluxia was covered with markers, areas the Makya had destroyed, and it was a sizeable amount of the continent.

"The coven is here, in the south." Alexander tapped the white at the bottom of the map. "Altair has business in this area, too, unless anyone can provide any information about why the remainder of the fleet shouldn't travel in this direction."

"We have no objections," Maab said.

Altair rubbed his chin. "Good. What word from the angels, Alexander?"

"Runa returned to Alythia earlier to speak with my general. We have a network of angels I believe we can trust to keep us updated."

"Trust, indeed," Altair said. "These witches make me uncomfortable, Alexander. I recall one coven back in Iraluxia who were a nasty bunch back when I was a boy."

"I imagine that was some time ago," Enne said, a smile tugging at his lips.

Altair laughed. "Yes, yes it was."

"Noor's intention was to take Fia to a coven, and then infiltrate the Makya," Alexander added. "After what happened at the council meeting in Nadar, I couldn't let another angel take such a mission. Noor is adept with her illusions, resourceful. She's our best chance of finding out what the Makya are up to."

"And what has she discovered?" Altair asked.

Alexander shifted his weight. "We've had no word from her."

Please be okay.

"We'll also need a greater defence weapon," Alexander continued, "like the water jets in Ikothea. Unfortunately, they don't harm the Makya, but for most, they remove their ability to ignite. For the stronger ones, that's another matter."

Altair held his chin as he thought for a moment. "Ah, yes. Our friends in the south can help us with that." He rose to his feet. "Now, I am an old man, and I need my rest." He smiled at Fia as he wrapped his cloak around him, the layers of fur swinging behind him as he left.

"What of our dying sun, Alexander?" Maab asked.

"All I know for certain is that we're running out of time," he said, glancing at Fia.

Fia counted her breaths. All the talk of attacks and tactics, the severity of the situation pressed down on her. There was nothing she could do to help, and she was no closer to getting back to London.

They'd found the wrong girl, surely.

CHAPTER SIXTEEN

FIA

The next morning, Fia and Alexander found Maab and Enne together beneath a grey sky. As they approached, Maab's armour dropped away from him, and he transformed into an enormous black and white tiger, growling as he paced up and down the deck.

Navarii children ran screaming as Maab whipped his tail and leapt up onto a stack of wooden boxes. He let out a solitary, rumbling roar, before sitting down on top of the crates. Within moments, Enne had joined him, no longer a man, but a beautiful, white snow leopard.

Alexander approached. "Dear friends, I do hope you are going to behave. A storm approaches." He touched Maab gently on one of his enormous white paws, and Enne let out a low rumble in response.

Fia blinked at Maab, speechless. "They just… *shapeshifted?*"

"Yes, all Nords can." Alexander chuckled.

Fia let out a low whistle. "Into whatever form they choose?"

"Only one," Alexander said, before taking a few graceful steps into the air.

Shapeshifters. Fia leaned against the gunwale. Beside her, two women shifted into birds and dived into the water below. She watched them disappear beneath the surface, blurring in and out of focus as a tear rolled down her nose. *You'd have loved all of this, Soph.* The birds whistled and chirped as they dived, and Fia strained to listen.

"Fish, there!" one cried out. And then there was nothing more than bird sounds again.

She wiped away her tears and pressed closer to the railing, but the birds had already flown out of ear shot, up high onto one of the masts where they shifted back into women, naked and laughing as they talked.

A low purr pulled her attention back to the deck and to Maab, licking behind Enne's ear.

Fia cleared her throat as she approached.

"Hi. I, um, I hear things sometimes… animals. And I wondered if you could… help me practice?"

Maab stopped licking Enne's ear and raised his head to blink at Fia. His eyes were pale, with a touch of pastel green, the unusual shade she'd noticed the night before at the meeting. He opened his mouth to pant, great white teeth pressing against a pink tongue. He made no sound other than the huffing of his breath. It clouded in the cool air in front of Fia's face, and he flicked an ear.

"If I've interrupted you, then I apologise," she said, stepping away.

Enne's head shot up, and he made a peculiar chuffing sound at Maab, his teeth exposed. "Maab is not one for words," he began, but the rest of the sentence became nothing more than a throaty rumble.

Fia shook her head. "I… I see. This isn't going to be very straight forward, is it?"

Another sound huffed in Enne's throat, but his mouth was closed, and only the tip of his pink tongue remained exposed, in just the way her neighbour's cat used to do. He licked at his whiskers and opened his mouth again. "Practice, Fia. We'll help you. The Nords are restless. There will be plenty of conversations for you to listen in on."

Maab began licking behind Enne's ear again, and Fia knew the conversation was over. Still, that was the most she'd ever understood at once and it was something. Had the witches been right about her? But what could be achieved by talking? If Erebus could reach across all of Ohinyan with his whispers, nothing could stand against him.

Fia looked to the skies for any sign of Alexander, although she knew he wouldn't be back for a while. He'd flown on ahead of the ship, looking out for other angels, for signs of the Makya, or for any dangers that might be ahead of them. He'd mentioned a storm. Was it safe to fly?

A familiar knot of anxiety twisted in her stomach. Training, that's what calmed her most. Anything to take her mind off her thoughts of getting back to Earth… and of Alexander.

The familiar *jab, hook, jab, hook* soothed her as she practiced against one of the huge masts, taking care not to make contact with the wood.

"Perhaps you might prefer a real target?" It was Enne, human again, smiling as he approached. His accent rested heavily on the T's at the ends of words, and he unclipped his chest armour and placed it on the deck beside the mast as he spoke. "A fairer fight," he said with a quiet, playful laugh. He pulled two wooden quarterstaffs from his back and threw one to Fia.

"Sure," Fia replied, feeling the weight of the staff before readying her stance. She'd practiced enough times with Jo to know she wouldn't make a fool of herself.

Don't mess this up. She circled Enne. He was a few heads taller than she was—not as tall as Maab, but she knew at once this would be to her advantage.

Maab leapt up on all fours onto a pile of crates nearby, his oval eyes narrowing as he watched. Enne glanced over for a moment, and Fia didn't miss the opening. Her first strike caught him softly behind the knees, but Enne countered quickly with a light blow to her shoulder.

She swung around, feigning a swing at chest height to catch Enne off guard. He reached out with his own quarterstaff to counter, but Fia was too fast. She swung her legs low this time, tipping him off his feet. Maab let out a long, low rumble that sounded unmistakeably like laughter. Fia laughed, too, and before she could hold her hand out to Enne, he was bounding towards Maab, already a snow leopard. He rolled him over playfully on top of the crates, licking at the fur around his mouth and purring.

Fia watched them for a moment, play fighting across the deck, much to the distress of the Navarii. She laughed again, envious of how free they were in their animal form.

Runa sat down beside her, brilliant, even in this light.

"Fia, a bad storm is coming," Runa said quietly.

Fia looked above the sails; the sky was dark, and dense clouds hung over the ship. "I know, Alexander mentioned it earlier."

"Did he tell you how bad?" Runa took Fia's hand in hers, and Fia turned away from the wildcats. She could have been mistaken, but something like fear shone in Runa's eyes.

A bad storm is coming. A sickening feeling rose in Fia's stomach.

"You think he's flying through it now?" It was as if the decking was slipping out from under her. She ran to the edge of the deck, looking out into the darkening horizon. It wasn't even noon, and the sky was heavy with a black mass of thickening clouds.

"I thought he would be back by now," Runa added, joining Fia as she leant over the railing and gazed down at the murky ocean below them.

Maab and Enne stopped playing, and turned back into men, reaching for their armour on the deck.

"He will be back," Maab said. "And we will see the storm through. Come, let's not stand here and worry, but help to ensure everything is prepared. Perhaps you could clear all those with young children from the deck?"

Fia nodded. She and Runa did as he said. Across the deck, Altair looked at maps and called instructions. All masts were to be lowered and all unnecessary items cleared away.

She glanced across at the smaller ships, their decks a scurry of movement as their masts were brought down, too. She whispered a quiet wish to herself that the fourth ship had missed the storm entirely as it made its way west. The ship began to sway in the waves. *He's going to be fine*, Fia told herself, over and over.

The air around them gradually became thicker, and the sky turned an intense black. The wind had picked up, and great waves began to crash against the sides of the ship as it rocked.

Fia ran from port to starboard, her eyes darting across the sky for Alexander's silhouette. Nausea washed over her as the ship lurched, but she ignored it. *One, two, three.*

"Fia, you must get below deck," Altair called out over the wind.

"No, not until Alexander's back," she replied.

"I'll stay with her," Runa said.

With the masts down, most of the crew went below to join their families, and the deck seemed vast with only the few remaining occupants. The ship hadn't looked this big since Fia first saw it back in the dockyard. Maab and Enne remained above deck on two feet rather than four, helping wherever possible.

When the rain began, the waves were already breaking over the sides of the ship. It came down in heavy drops the size of fists, followed quickly by a crash of thunder that resonated throughout the ship.

"Fia, time to go below!" Runa shouted, gripping her arm. Beads of rain ran down Runa's dark hair, flattening it against her face.

But Fia clung to a railing and stood on the top step that led below deck, away from any direct contact with the breaking waves. Thunder cracked around them. "I'm staying here until he comes back," she said, her voice barely audible through the rain. Runa shook her head, tying a sodden rope around Fia's waist.

"I was worried you might say that." She secured the other end of the rope to the staircase. "The crew will do this, too." She pointed to the crew, and as they moved, Fia could see a trail of rope behind them, securing them to the ship.

More thunder rumbled, followed by a brilliant flash of lightning. The ship rocked wildly, as the waves climbed higher and higher. In the half-light, the shadows of enormous waves hanging over the ship were unmistakable.

The next crash of thunder was followed by a flash of lightning so great they were blinded for a moment, but then Fia could make out Alexander's silhouette, tumbling onto the ship in a ball of arms and feathers. At the same moment, a Navarii child ran out into the rain, his mother calling after him from a staircase to the lower decks.

"Look!" Fia shouted. She wriggled out of the rope and ran towards the boy. She reached out for him just as an enormous wave tipped the world sideways, and Fia threw her arms around him as the water and the wind and the angle of the ship carried them overboard.

The water was cold and dark. Even beneath the surface, Fia could see the churning undercurrent below the great hull of the ship as she kicked and thrashed, trying to find her way back to the surface. The boy's eyes were wide, and she held him to her as tightly as she could with one arm.

Fia held her mouth shut tight, fighting the urge to breathe out. Wings dove into the water not far from her. She could make out Runa's face and she reached out a hand. She didn't know how much longer she could hold her breath, but she held onto the boy, his fingers still clamped around her arm.

Runa's hand was almost touching her own when from the darkness, hundreds of creatures appeared, their long hair floating about them, all reaching out for Runa. Their upper half was like a woman's, but their skin had a silvery-greenish hue even in the darkness, and their eyes were black and empty. Where there should have been legs, there were long, deformed tails and tentacles, some with two tails and exposed flesh revealing rotting bone below.

As soon as the first one touched Runa, she screamed, a piercing, gurgling wail beneath the water, as the decaying creature began yanking at her arms and wings. Fia could hear them whispering to each other. She thrashed and kicked in the water to try and reach Runa while keeping her hold on the little boy. She reached towards the angel again, but then the ghastly things were around her, too, grasping at her hair and her arms, and one had its hands around her face. She could hear their words now that they'd surrounded her, pulling at her from every direction.

"I want this one," one said.

"But she's mine!" cried another.

"*Fia...*" a familiar dark voice whispered. A fresh wave of panic shivered through her, and she thrashed and thrashed with her legs to get away. *He can't hurt you. He isn't really here.* But it was too late.

Fia's grip on the little boy was loosening, as she struggled to hold her breath. She could barely see Runa through the mass of swirling hair and the silvery flesh of the creatures. There was another glimpse of white, and then she saw a beautiful white leopard. It dived beside Runa, swiping at the scaly flesh of the attackers. They screamed as its claws cut through their skin and their twisted tails.

Something hit Fia, hard, and then Alexander's mouth was around hers, breathing air into her lungs. As quickly as he'd reached her, they were soaring upwards, out of the water, high above the waves, and the last of the creatures fell away from them, screaming and shouting as they plunged into the water.

Their landing onto the ship was hard, but Alexander protected Fia and the little boy with his wings as they rolled onto the deck. Another wave crashed over them, but supported by Alexander, they held fast. Pairs of hands reached towards her and carried the little boy away as he coughed and spluttered water.

"We should not be above deck," Alexander said, as he helped her towards the stairs.

They joined the others in one of the smaller rooms on the first level. Enne, naked except for the blankets the Navarii people piled around him, sat beside Maab, who was still dressed in full armour. Maab said nothing and merely shook his head as he looked from Enne to Runa.

Runa was soaked but refused a blanket. Fia supposed she didn't need one. Malachai inspected every millimetre of his wife, checking for wounds. Alexander rested Fia beside them, and the Navarii draped her in blankets, too. The great ship swayed, and Maab put his foot out to stop a stool sliding into the wall.

"Runa, I'm so sorry," Fia whispered, the warmth tingling at her numb lips.

"It's all right Fia. It's not your fault," Runa said softly. "We could not have known they were going to be there."

"The Sorren have never been seen this far south," Enne added.

"Sorren?" Fia said, her teeth chattering together. "They were bickering over us. I could hear them."

"What were they saying?" Alexander asked, his wings flickering behind him.

"They um… they were fighting over who was keeping who," Fia continued, her cheeks flushing. *You heard Erebus again… tell them you heard him.*

The room was silent. The thunder and lightning had quietened, and the waves were no longer crashing against the ship.

Altair joined them. "We owe you our thanks, Fia, Hani is well. He's resting with his mother." He clasped Fia's hands and gave her a warm smile. "Let us be grateful that we are all safe," he said, his face solemn. Silence fell over them for a moment, as they sat listening to the sounds of the storm dying down outside.

"The Sorren are not immune to Erebus's whispers," Altair said. "We must expect stranger things to come. Times are changing, and there will not be one person, animal or creature in Ohinyan, that will not feel it. We must be ready when the sun dies, for whatever Erebus has planned for us."

"Alexander, why don't you help Fia back to her cabin? She ought to change out of those wet clothes." Runa's eyes sparkled with mischief, but Altair's words echoed in Fia's ears.

She counted her breaths as Alexander led her through the ship. He didn't touch her, but he stayed close. The corridors blurred into one, and Fia pushed her damp hair from her face.

How long would it be until Erebus could affect her like he had the Makya? The idea that she could help—could make a difference here—could she, really? *One, two, three.*

Alexander opened the door to her cabin and stood to one side to let her in. She threw the blanket on the bed. *One, two, three.* She peeled off the woollen wrap, and it fell to the floor with a wet smack. She sat on the bed, lay back, and looked up at the wooden ceiling, pressing at the corners of her eyes as she let out a breath.

The bed dipped as Alexander sat down beside her.

Strands of wet, earth-coloured hair fell across his face, and she resisted the urge to brush it away from his eyes.

"I'm sorry for bringing you in to all of this," he said. His wings arched up behind his shoulders, swooping low around him as he sat. It was fascinating how malleable they were.

She wanted to run her hand down his feathers, but instead she pushed herself up, catching the scent of the forest mixing with seawater. He was much closer than she'd realised.

"It doesn't matter how I got here." She took his hand in hers. "I'm here."

Their faces were inches apart, and Fia was certain the sound of her heartbeat was so loud he could hear it, too. He brushed a strand of wet hair from her eyes, and she leaned into his touch as his hand lingered. And then his lips were on hers, a soft, open-mouthed kiss, and for a moment, Fia forgot about Erebus and getting back to London. She twisted her hands through Alexander's hair as heat flushed in her chest.

Alexander pulled back, and she held his gaze, and then his eyes dropped to look down at her mouth. "You should get some rest," he murmured, already on his feet. "Goodnight."

The door clicked shut behind him, and Fia was alone in her tiny cabin, nothing but the sound of her heart beating in her ears.

Going back to London meant saying goodbye. It meant leaving him behind, too.

CHAPTER SEVENTEEN

NOOR

High above Ohinyan, somewhere in the skies not far from Ikothea, travelled the Makya airship. Suspended above the loading bay, in one of the tiny wooden seed pods, lay the Lady Noor, listening to the sounds of Makya and Aurelli below her.

Several nights had passed since her escape from the cell, and she was almost fully recovered, physically and mentally. The pod was small and cramped, but lying there had given her time to heal her wounds and understand what the Makya were doing. Only the padded footsteps and the clicking and scuffing of objects dragging across the loading bay floor indicated the Aurelli's presence.

Her thoughts wandered to Silla, of his stormy blues eyes, speckled with amber, staring back at hers. Eyes she would never gaze into again. That the witches might take her back was of little importance, but if it meant that she could clear her name and clear *Silla's* name… It was a glimmer of light in the coming darkness. One she held tightly to her chest as she listened to the Makya below her.

A voice she recognised only too well entered the loading bay, arguing with another. Perhaps an opportunity had arisen, finally.

"I expect you to be by my side for the duration of your shift. Is that so much to ask?" Lorn demanded.

"No, great Fire Mother, of course not," a guard replied.

Lorn ignited. "Don't placate me," she cried. The heat of her outburst flickered at the sides of Noor's pod. "My brothers will be back soon. Get out of my sight and send a replacement."

Noor couldn't miss the opportunity to follow Lorn, so she slid quietly out of the pod into the loading bay, projecting the illusion of herself as a Makya guard, just as the one Lorn had been talking to made her way behind the pods and out of sight.

"What?" Lorn spat, as Noor caught up with her in the corridor.

Noor opened her mouth to speak.

"Never mind. As you were," Lorn said, seething, as she led them through the ship.

Noor followed and let out a breath. She'd gotten away with it, for now. The familiar smells of the ship carried through the corridors as they walked: oil, ash, hints of the forest, and the sweat and stench of soldiers. Noor was sick of it and longed to be on a glider, breathing in the fresh Ohinyan air.

Lorn returned to the great chamber. The enormous flags bearing the Makya emblem seemed much newer than the ones Noor had seen previously. Aside from a few charred marks here and there, the room showed few traces of Lorn's outburst from a few days before.

Lorn stared once more into the flames of the metal urn. They flickered and twisted, turning into the writhing bodies of Fia and Alexander in a passionate embrace, just as they had days before. Lorn raised her arms, and Noor prepared to run or to dive behind the safety of the urn.

"Sister dear," Jerum called from the doorway.

Noor willed her heartbeat to calm. If he'd been even a second later…

Raiaan followed closely behind his brother, and behind him was… *an angel.*

Noor didn't recognise the angel. His emerald green eyes were striking, but his lips pressed together firmly, and his face had drained of colour. What part did an angel have here, with the Makya? It was without Alexander's knowing, surely.

"Brothers, tell me of your victory." Lorn sat leisurely in one of the enormous thrones at the back of the chamber. Her fists clenched as the angel approached.

"A half victory, sister," Raiaan muttered.

"You." Lorn was on her feet at once, circling the angel. "Dearest Oren, why don't *you* tell me what happened?"

"We were not aware of Ikothea's defences," Oren began, as Lorn rested a hand lightly on one of his crisp, white wings. He recoiled but Lorn's hand remained.

"Not aware?" she whispered. Her eyes flickered. "Awareness is what you were there *for*." She sent fire from her palm directly onto Oren's wing. The angel frantically patted at his smouldering feathers, crying out in pain.

"Lorn, please." Raiaan stepped forwards, placing himself between his sister and the angel. "We have learned much of use." He updated his sister on all that had transpired on the docks of Ikothea.

So Fia didn't find a coven. Where had all the witches gone? Noor thought of all the places Fia must have been to get to Ikothea. There were at least two covens she knew of in those areas, or at least there were.

"Why is Alexander heading south?" Lorn approached Oren again, as he clasped his burnt wing.

"I don't know… to find more witches, I think. He isn't really focused. His main concern is getting the girl back home to Earth," Oren replied, avoiding eye contact.

The girl. Not just any girl. It was imperative that Lorn did not find out just how important Fia was.

Lorn's eyes blazed, sparks of rage visible from Noor's post at the door.

"Very well." Lorn clenched her fists into tight balls behind her back. "We have been looking for Alythia, and we need you to take us there." She faced Oren again as he paled further.

"I… I can't," Oren said. "It isn't possible."

Lorn stood before him, hands at her sides with her palms facing upwards, flames towering out of them, ready to be thrown about the room.

"Please, it isn't possible for me to take you—only angels can enter Alythia."

"Liar." Lorn threw her arms in the air, jets of fire blazing from her palms, scorching the ceiling. "I will give you only one more opportunity to tell me. Where. Is. It?"

Oren shook his head, green eyes gazing at the floor. "I'm sorry, it just isn't possible."

Lorn let out a piercing screech as she projected every last inch of fire emanating from her hands towards the angel. Oren fell to the floor, writhing in pain as he burned. Noor didn't dare flinch.

"Lorn," Raiaan said, shoving her hand away. "We needed him."

"We don't need anyone," Lorn replied. "*We* will lead our people. As the sun dies, the days are getting shorter. I grow stronger, and we will control more than we ever dreamed possible. All of Ohinyan will answer to us."

"Lorn, we have discussed this. Only when Ohinyan is in *total* darkness will we be ready to strike, before the birth of the third sun, only *then* will we be at our strongest," Jerum reasoned with his sister, as the angel lay dying on the floor beside them. He made choked sounds and turned his face away from them. Noor could do nothing but look on from her post as Oren grasped at the last few moments of his life. She could not interfere, not yet.

"Total darkness will be months from now. We need to strike *now*. I am the strongest I have ever been." Lorn threw her palms to the ceiling once more, covering the walls above them in a blanket of fire. Noor ignored the deafening voice in her head urging her to run, far away.

"Perhaps we should continue this debate later, sister, when you are a little calmer?" Raiaan interjected.

Lorn ceased her inferno, opening her mouth to speak, before closing it, and storming out of the great chamber. Jerum and Raiaan exchanged a look before following in silence without so much as a glance back to where Oren lay.

Once she was certain everyone had left, Noor walked quietly towards the burnt body of the angel.

"Please, no more. I can take no more," he coughed out the words as she approached.

It was an unpleasant sight, but Noor had seen many unpleasant things. His wings had no feathers left, exposing sinewy muscle and bone that blistered in the aftermath. She did not step down to comfort him—it was a witch's nature to despise disloyalty, and there was no time for him to make amends. Why would he betray his brothers and sisters?

"I am not as I appear," she murmured. "I will torture you no further."

"No more, I beg of you," Oren spluttered. His face was not as badly burnt as the rest of him, but the effort of talking had him clutching at his chest, struggling for air.

"There is nothing I can do for you now." It was true. Noor could create a peaceful illusion for him, but she couldn't heal the severity of his wounds. It was too late. "Why did you betray your fellow angels?"

Oren's eyes flickered as he fought to keep them open. The beginning of a smile tugged at one corner of his mouth but didn't quite make it to the other side. "I wanted more." He fell onto his side, coughing up a mouthful of blood. "I was tired of taking orders. Everyone looks up to Alexander, as if he has all the answers. And for what? Because it is his birthright? I wanted to prove that he didn't, and that the Makya were the way forward with the coming of the new sun. That I could be a leader." He coughed again, wiping at the blood from his mouth.

"A true leader stands amongst his people, always. Never ahead of them. That is why people look up to Alexander." Noor passed Oren a rag to wipe at his mouth. "Jealousy can turn the best of us into monsters." She knelt beside him, taking in his mutilated form.

Burns covered most of his body, far too much to heal without assistance. It was no way to die. The dark room around them transformed into a brilliant blue sky, and Oren was no longer lying face down on the metal floor but on a soft, white cloud. His wings and hands were not burnt, and all traces of blood were gone. Noor was no longer disguised as a Makya guard but appeared before him as herself.

"You're a… you're a witch." It was a statement. "Thank you," he whispered. She knew he meant it. "I didn't know about the attack in Ikothea. I didn't think they were going to act so quickly—but now, now it's too late. I cannot take back what I have done." He looked at his hands, searching for the burns concealed by Noor's illusion.

"You kept the location of Alythia unknown to them, and that is something to be proud of." Had all of this only ever been about finding Alythia? But why? Had Erebus commanded it?

Oren forced a weak smile, and as his eyes closed, she watched his spirit drift away from him and sink, down through the clouds with the weight of what he had done. As his spirit fell away from his body, the clouds disappeared, and they were surrounded once more by the gleaming metal of the great chamber. The stench of burning flesh filled Noor's nostrils and she swallowed hard. She'd seen many deaths, but none deserved to die this way.

Noor rose, and without looking back at the dead angel, projected the illusion of herself as a Makya guard as she walked away to find the Aurelli. She had to act quickly. It was a risk to trust the Aurelli so soon, but after they had revealed their fears to her and helped her to escape, she had to try.

Is the council backing all of this?

Lorn and her brothers were behaving as if they were acting of their own accord, but even if they were, Erebus would be watching and waiting. Noor shuddered at the memory of his voice, whispering to Lorn in all her moments of weakness. How long would it be before he whispered to Noor, too?

She made her way to the loading bay and found the two Aurelli who controlled the doors. She showed them a sequence of illusions, asking them whether they would carry a message off the ship. They nodded as Noor's illusion turned the loading bay into their beloved forest. It was so convincing Noor could smell the jasmine and fresh rain in the air. One began to purr, the other brushed up against its companion, and Noor knew at once they would do whatever it took to get back there.

Once she was satisfied the Aurelli understood her message, Noor resumed her patrol of the ship, her route taking her past Lorn's chambers where she relieved the current guard of their duty.

"I'd stay out of her sight, if I was you," the guard said before he scurried away down the corridor.

The door to Lorn's chambers swung open. "You. In here, now."

The bedframe was charred across one side, a rug on the floor beside it nothing but ash beneath Noor's feet. But she held her composure, kept her eyes forward, and did not give any hint of a reaction to the mess Lorn had made around her.

Lorn paced her room, mumbling to herself. "A girl from Earth. Earth! And yet the fire mother and the descendant of Gabriel are destined for each other... Mother always told me it was so." Her hands balled into fists at her sides, plumes of smoke drifting up from them as she paced.

"Tell me," she said, looking Noor in the eye. "What could this Fia possibly offer Alexander that I cannot?"

Noor took in the shadows beneath Lorn's eyes, the paleness of her skin. "Nothing, great Fire Mother." She held her breath, bracing herself for Lorn to lose control.

"Then why not me?" Lorn spun to face a full-length mirror. "Am I not attractive? Am I not a pillar of strength?"

Lorn knew full well she was attractive. Even with smudges beneath her eyes and her lack of sleep, she was striking. She was twisted and tormented on the inside, but Noor could still admire the way her jumpsuit clung to her waist and her curves. Before Silla, there had been men and women. Amongst witches, it was not unusual. But appreciating beauty was one thing, being attracted to Lorn was entirely another.

"You are, great Fire Mother," Noor replied, her eyes locked with Lorn's in the mirror. She didn't dare look away, if any action was seen as an insult, there would be no time to escape Lorn's flames.

But Lorn spun around and stepped towards her, running her hand across the braid Noor had not concealed with her illusion. The gesture was gentle, and Lorn's eyes flicked down for a moment before catching her gaze again, so close they could share a breath between them.

A knock sounded on the door and Lorn stepped back.

"Sister," Jerum's voice called from outside.

"Enter," Lorn replied, spinning back to look at herself in the mirror. "You are dismissed," she said to Noor, without so much as a glance in her direction.

Noor nodded as Jerum entered, and she left in silence, but she remained outside beside the door, listening in on the news the brother delivered. Her heartbeat drummed in her chest. Lorn was about to kiss her; she'd seen that look in someone's eyes enough times to know it. Was Lorn so lonely that she'd lower herself to a guard? One kiss from her would be certain death—the Makya were well known for being uncontrollably… passionate.

"I've given instructions to follow Alexander and his party south to increase our chances of pursuing him to Alythia. If Alexander is so attached to this girl, perhaps we could use her to our advantage?" Jerum's voice carried through the wall.

Hands clapped together inside the bedchambers. "Excellent. Yes, a wonderful idea. Why not take the girl and lure him out?" Lorn replied.

"I thought you might be pleased, sister. Will you be joining us for dinner?"

"Yes, of course, brother, I'll be along shortly." The door swung open, and Noor stood tall, her back to the wall, and her gaze fixed firmly ahead of her.

"I said you were dismissed," Lorn hissed in her direction, as Jerum stepped out into the corridor.

Noor didn't give Lorn a chance to engage in further conversation, and with a polite nod, she made her way in the opposite direction Jerum headed. The roar of flames echoed behind her, and she quickened her steps as she walked. Lorn was losing control of her powers, and there was no doubting her brothers were starting to notice it, too.

What good would any of her observations come to if she couldn't manage to get a message off the ship? She poked her head into open doorways until she found a room occupied by two guards and a desk.

"Jerum sends for you both," she said, stepping inside. The guards exchanged a glance. "I wouldn't keep him waiting if I were you." She stood tall and took a step away from the doorway, gesturing for them to leave.

The guards left without a word, and Noor cast her eyes over the desk. A pile of parchment, a small lidded jar of ink and a quill sat discarded to one side. Noor clicked her tongue, it had been a long time since she'd needed to write anything down. She scrawled messages for Alexander, blowing on the ink to dry it. Before she left, she rolled up a few extra sheets of parchment and grabbed the quill and ink to take back to her pod.

She returned to the loading bay to show the Aurelli what she'd seen, handing them the tightly rolled parchment messages. Noor could only hope the messages would reach Alexander via the Shadows. She knelt before an Aurelli, its green, oval eyes looking up at her, as she showed it an image of the Shadows, flying beneath the airship.

When she was certain it had understood, Noor thanked the little creature and made her way to the dining rooms, hoping she would find Raiaan within.

"As you were," Raiaan said, walking in a moment behind her. All the guards had risen as soon as he entered, and the room filled with the scuffs of chair feet as they sat back down. It was respect that guided the guards' movements, rather than fear, like with Lorn. Raiaan was calm and quiet when he spoke, and never wielded fire like his brother and sister did to get what he wanted. Guards were often bringing him things: maps, bits of parchment, even beverages from the mess hall.

"Thank you, sir," one of the guards said, as they parted ways with him.

Noor couldn't be sure, but Raiaan was up to something.

CHAPTER EIGHTEEN

ALEXANDER

An entire ship had been lost during the storm. Three days had passed since the funeral, and the heavy mood on the ship had begun to lift. They'd held a service, even though no bodies were retrieved from the water. Hundreds of them, sinking to the ocean bed, or more likely nourishing the creatures that lived in the depths. At least their spirits would not become like the ghosts of Earth, and for that Alexander was grateful.

Fia had stood beside him as pyres of scrap wood and bundles of cloth were pushed out gently into the ocean and set alight with blazing arrows. "What happens to their souls? Are they stuck beneath the waves?"

"No, quite the opposite. They're free now. Their bodies were nothing more than a vessel," he'd replied.

They'd stood together in silence as the smouldering pyres disappeared into the horizon.

But now, sounds of laughter and chatter had returned, and the paintings in the corridors were more vivid than ever. Many of the Nords had come aboard from the smaller ships, transforming themselves into animals. The ship was full of life.

Malachai's wing had almost completely healed, and although the days grew colder, the dim grey that had surrounded the ship before the storm did not return. The sky remained clear and blue; the crisp air was fresh against Alexander's face as he observed the ship.

As well as the Navarii and the Nords who had joined them, there were other races, too. The Asharians, known across Ohinyan for their elaborate finery and feline features—distant cousins of the Aurelli—strode by them in full-length coats and thick, heavy boots. There was a group of women who kept their skin covered at all times, and the Navarii children whispered stories of women who had once been lizards, covering their skin to prevent it from drying up in the light of day. They weren't far off the truth. If they'd caught a glimpse beneath the robes, the children would see they weren't really women at all. Alexander had crossed paths with their kind once before. He recalled the flickering tongue of Anara, the way it made its way from amongst layers of robes, tasting the air between them. Anara had been kind to him and offered him refuge after the incident in Nadar, not too long before he'd left for Earth.

A familiar pang of guilt twisted in his stomach. *You led Fia to Ohinyan.* The sooner they could get answers from the witches, the better. But what if they had no intention of sending her back to Earth, what if they couldn't? He rubbed at his neck, the memory of kissing her playing on repeat. What if she stayed?

His gaze wandered to the Nords grouped together, whom Maab held authority over. In animal form, they were mostly well behaved, much to the relief of the crew. But they were everywhere: they were the birds, circling above the ship, they were otters swimming alongside them, and they were ferrets and mice and lizards scurrying about the deck.

A glimpse of red told him Fia had stepped up onto the deck. She smiled as she walked over, her green eyes fresh and bright. He pushed aside all thoughts of her returning to Earth.

One should not dwell on what could be, only what is. That's what his father would have said.

Fia pulled the hood up on her coat as she approached, and Alexander thought of how he'd pressed his mouth against hers, of the saltwater on her lips. Talking with her before their kiss had been effortless, but there had been little time for conversation since the night of the storm. So many responsibilities rested on him, so many fates tied together, as if nothing but a single spool of silk held them all.

Many threads connect us all. That's what he'd told Noor, not too long ago.

Each action held a consequence. But he did not regret kissing Fia. He did not regret the feeling of her hands in his hair.

"It won't be much longer before we're on dry land," he said, as she joined him.

Together, they watched the Nord animals running about the crates and the sail posts.

Fia gave a weak smile, the gold flecks in her eyes glistening. "I don't see how I can help. It doesn't look like you need my help to unite anything." She leaned over the edge and looked into the water below. A grey dolphin was diving and ducking in and out of the waves below them, clicking and squeaking with joy—another Nord. Alexander envied their freedom.

He resisted the urge to pull Fia to him, to press his lips against hers again, but her words hung in the air between them. Just a few days practicing on the ship talking to the Nords, Fia had improved her skill so much already. But more than that, *he* needed her: her kindness, her compassion, the way she made time for everyone they met.

He followed Fia's gaze. "We must get you back to Earth before the windows close, and only the witches can tell us if it's possible. Away from all of this." He said the last part with less conviction, as the joyful dolphin below them clicked and whistled.

"I'm losing count of how many times I've almost died since I got here," Fia said. Alexander opened his mouth to protest, but she continued, "Years ago, right after my parents died and Sophie wasn't quite old enough for custody, I was in a foster home. There was this girl there who lied about everything. Everyone knew better than to listen to her. One day I found her, hiding in one of the store cupboards, sweating and white as a sheet. When I asked her what was wrong, she told me she was cursed, forever being chased by Death, and that she could see it as we spoke, watching and waiting for her. I wanted to believe she was lying, but her eyes were filled with so much fear—she really believed what she was saying. A few days later, she was gone, and none of the staff could tell me where. They just said she'd left and wouldn't be coming back."

"Do you think Death got to her?" Alexander asked.

Fia turned to look at him. "You think she was telling the truth?"

Alexander shrugged. "There are many things we don't understand. It could be possible. But you…" He met her gaze. A few stray strands of hair fell across her eyes, as green as the forest they'd fled from. "You are not cursed. Death isn't coming for you. You just stumbled into the wrong place at the wrong time."

She chewed on her lip and brushed her hair behind her ear. What was she thinking? He wanted to ask her what it was like to talk to the Nords when they were in animal form, if she realised how much she could help them all, but he didn't know where to begin.

"Do you think Oren told the Makya where we're going?" Fia asked after a few moments of silence.

Alexander ran a hand through his hair, pulling at the ends. "I think he may have told them, yes. Although I fear they will not spare his life, anyway." He looked out to the horizon, towards the beating silhouettes of Runa and Malachai growing bigger as they approached the ship.

"Do you think the Makya are coming for *us*?" Fia asked.

Runa and Malachai had touched down on the deck, and Alexander knew at once something was wrong. Runa was already talking to Altair; he could see something in the skies had distressed her. Malachai was by her side, removing the bandage from his wing and examining the healed wound. Altair pulled a map from beneath layers of his great fur cloak and laid it out atop the nearest crate. Alexander flew over to listen to the angels' report.

"There's no land here for days in either direction." Altair waved his hand across the map.

"That may be so according to your map, but I know what I saw. Something wasn't right. There was no sign of life on the island—no birds, no insects, nothing. But there were the remains of an airship. It looked as if it had been there for some time. Sire," Runa said, turning to face him. "I'd like to go back and take a closer look."

Alexander weighed his options. He saw no harm in additional scouting. "If there are remains of a ship, there may be people stranded there. You should go."

***

When his friends did not return the next morning, Alexander felt a knot of worry pulling itself deeper in his stomach. He'd made another bad judgement, allowing them to go alone.

Altair was going over the maps again with some of his

crew across the deck. There was no good reason to ask him to risk the lives of everyone on board for the sake of two angels. No good reason other than they were his friends.

"We can't wait," Alexander heard Fia say as he approached. She was pacing beside Altair, frantic. "We all know they would have been back hours ago—last night even—they should be here by now." Fia paced, gazing out to the horizon.

"Can you spare a ship?" Alexander asked, placing a firm hand on Altair's shoulder.

Altair rubbed his chin between finger and thumb. "It does not sit well with me to risk the lives of others, but I do not think separating what remains of the fleet would be prudent, either. If we go, we go together."

"Thank you, old friend. Let's hope there are survivors from the airship, and that Runa and Malachai are well."

Fia let out a quiet whistle like he'd heard her do so many times before. He echoed the sentiment and pushed off into the air to fly on ahead of the ship.

It wasn't long before he saw the island, just as the last of the daylight faded and the moons made their way through the clouds above him. In the dim light that remained, the approach to the island was perilous. Cliffs of barren, jagged rocks stuck out in every direction, and the sea broke in crashing, violent waves at their base.

"It's cliff face as far as I can see," Alexander called out to Altair from above the ship. "I'll keep looking." And up ahead, he could see it, a break in the rocks, an opening.

Moments later, he emerged and returned to them swiftly, landing on silent feet on the wooden deck.

"There's a large cave with access to the surface. We could anchor here and take a search party," Alexander said to Altair.

"We will join you." Maab added, as he and Enne stood amongst them. They'd been running around the deck as wild cats just moments before. "Any Nord that can fly will assist with navigation into the cave."

"Is the cave large enough to accommodate this vessel?" Altair asked.

Alexander nodded. Where were Runa and Malachai? The island seemed odd, even from above, but Alexander couldn't quite say why. Why hadn't they returned?

Altair rubbed at his chin again. "Very well, the remaining ships will anchor and we will proceed."

Alexander flew above the ship as it approached the island. "Steady, watch the starboard," he called out. Two Nord birds chirped a warning. "Watch the mast."

Flickers of lamps illuminated the entrance to the narrow cave. Waves broke high and hard against the rocks, and the ship swayed with the heavy pull from the under current. He would not allow himself to think that something could go wrong, that the ship could be splintered against the rock like nothing more than a lump of driftwood.

Inside, the water was calm. Protected from the crashing waves and the wind, the tide lulled as they made their way slowly into the depths of the cave. It was a vast cavern; the ceiling stretched high above them, with great stalactites pointing down at the ship. Alexander flew close to the mast as Altair threw flares into the darkness. They sent electric blue shimmers of light across the surface of the water, falling with an echo against the rocky walls whilst some splashed into the water below.

Men and women stood on the decks of the ship with raised oil lamps in their hands, peering out into the darkness. Alexander's heart beat steady. He felt no death nearby, no dying spirit calling out to him.

"This way," he said, his voice raised.

The walls narrowed a little, and it was easier to take in details as the light reflected off the damp rocks. There were raised areas and ledges around the perimeter covered in strange crawlers with thick, gnarly roots. Alexander's eyes adjusted, and he could make out the great roots protruding through the ceiling above them, wrapping tightly around the stalactites like twisting ivy.

"Here." He landed ahead of the ship on a ledge high enough for them to climb out of the cave. Fia followed Maab and Enne onto the ledge. A few more of the Nords accompanied them, along with Altair and a handful of his men. The rest stayed behind on the ship, cocooned in the safety of the cave.

The ascent was difficult for those that could not fly. The rock was wet with slippery moss, and as they climbed closer to the surface, the air became thick and heavy. By the time the last of them surfaced, what little light remained was barely visible between the dense canopy of trees.

Something about this place didn't feel right. Altair wiped sweat from his brow with a square of cloth, and though his chest heaved more deeply than the others, he made no complaints about the climb. The old man hadn't succumbed to his years just yet. There was still no sign of Runa and Malachai, no suggestion that they'd come this way at all. They'd have likely flown above the canopy, and that thought at least gave Alexander some relief.

He'd never seen anywhere like this place. Not on Ohinyan or Earth. They stood below enormous trees stretching high above them, vast roots spread out and around each other, twisting and turning. Some of the roots arched like fallen tree trunks ten feet or so above the ground and weaved in and out of each other, creating new structures of their own amongst the forest floor.

Alexander watched as Fia removed her coat and stifled a cough against the thick air. The trees and the roots were hollow and flaking, the canopy above them dark and waxy, like the dead leaves on the ground. Fia picked one up to examine it; it was black and disintegrated into a sludgy paste between her fingertips. The faster they left the island, the better.

Altair took her hand, inspecting the remains of the leaf. "Something very dark has been to this place," the old man said quietly, before walking on into the desolate forest.

Alexander followed behind Altair. He wouldn't fail his friends. He couldn't.

CHAPTER NINETEEN

FIA

The group walked in silence. The humidity pushed down on Fia and all around her; it was unbearable. But it wasn't just the humidity. There were no signs of life here. The forest was silent. No birds or insects made a sound, no animals called out to them. Only the rain could be heard, as it fell in great drops on the forest floor. *Not immune to Erebus's whispers…* Altair's words echoed in her thoughts.

They stopped to rest, and Fia rolled the little bird charm between her fingers. It seemed like so long ago when she'd found it tucked down the back of her gym locker in London. She'd lost count of days that had rolled into nights. If only she could be like the Navarii, who behaved as if they'd accepted their great loss from just a few days before. But then, everything here had been about a cycle—life and death, the sun dying and being reborn. Fia wanted to believe there was some part of Sophie somewhere, back home in Hampstead Heath, cascading through the grass, or at the top of the BT tower, laughing and looking down at the tiny people below.

It didn't matter. Sophie was gone.

Altair's great cloak swung into her line of sight. "Don't let the darkness here get to you, child," he said, sitting beside her on one of the twisting tree roots, his cloak dripping from the rain.

"Do you miss the people you've lost?" Fia asked, staring up into the canopy, raindrops falling onto her face, as she tried to wash away the stickiness of the air.

Altair was silent for a while before rummaging around in the depths of his great cloak, and retrieved a piece of shiny wood, no bigger than a nut. He placed it in her hands.

"Turn it over," Altair said.

On the other side of the little nut was a delicate carving of a woman's smiling face, so intricate Fia could see the laughter lines beside her eyes and her long, fine eyelashes.

"She's beautiful," Fia murmured.

Altair took the nut gently from Fia's hands and placed it in between his own, cradling it with care. "This was my wife, Maia. She was beautiful and fearless and a wonderful friend. She died giving birth to our son." Altair's face softened, and his gaze followed a Nord walking by them. "Do I miss her? Yes, every passing moment of every day. I miss her company, her sense of humour, her wit. Most of all, I miss her clever insight—she was a very good judge of character and understood things far beyond her years."

"I'm sorry," Fia replied.

"Why? This is Ohinyan, child, my wife is now a part of this old tree root, the forest we fled from, and the turbulent seas we have sailed in. If I did not miss her, that means I would not have loved her. And if my years had not been filled with love for her, I probably would have been gone from this life, long ago. It has kept me going, given me courage when I needed it most, and given me wisdom when I had no words at all." Altair returned the nut back into the depths of his cloak and rested a hand on Fia's shoulder for the briefest of moments before moving on.

Fia heaved a deep sigh. Altair's words might have comforted her more had she not been in this lifeless place. Her heart was heavy, and the dull, aching emptiness would not go away.

"*Fia...*" That voice, barely a whisper. The colour drained from her face. She looked around and saw familiar faces from the ship, all occupied in quiet conversation or resting from their journey. None had heard the whisper.

"I've found them!" It was Alexander, shouting to them through the trees. "This way."

Fia was on her feet at once. "Are they hurt?"

"No, they're fine, but they could do with some help—they're just up ahead." Alexander turned back, and the others followed him into the darkening forest. The further they walked into the island, the more blackened the trees became. The trunks gave way to expanses of twisting, rotten roots and broken boulders.

Alexander waited as Fia caught up with him. They hadn't spoken about their kiss, but Fia still felt the easiness between them, and the relief that whatever it was they had wasn't broken. After the storm and the funeral, there just hadn't been the right moment to bring it up.

Something brushed against Fia's arm, and as she moved to push it away, she felt it in her hair, too. "Ugh," she said, wiping her hands at her sides.

As they continued, the forest around them became a grey-white blanket of cobwebs, thick and dripping with rainwater.

"Don't be alarmed. There is no life here at all," Alexander said.

The trees had a ghost like quality about them, and they looked to Fia like a child's drawing of a tree, except that where the leaves should have been, there was only a delicate, translucent web.

"Over here," Runa called out. She was covered in dirt and holding a long piece of tree root she'd made into a shovel. Malachai was nearby, carrying a large white bundle over his shoulder with one hand and holding a similar make-shift shovel in the other. He was covered in dirt, too.

"What's going on?" Fia asked.

Malachai placed the bundle and the shovel gently on the ground, and walked over to greet them, his expression unreadable. "Runa and I could not ignore what we found here. Those of you who wish to stay and help, we would be grateful. The rest of you can go back to the ships—there is no danger here."

A few Navarii shifted from one foot to the other, whispering amongst themselves before Altair silenced them.

"These trees are full of bodies from all walks of life in Ohinyan. They deserve a peaceful resting place, so we are burying them before we leave." Malachai looked at the trees as he spoke.

Fia followed his gaze. As she looked more closely, she could make out odd shapes in the cobwebs—a hand or a foot, or even the remains of an empty face. She shivered and wrapped her arms around herself. "I'll help." She walked over to pick up the shovel he'd left on the floor.

Maab called out commands to the Nords. Those whose animal form was of use transformed and began digging.

"Altair, take the Navarii back to the ship. We'll be along shortly," Alexander said.

The Navarii departed, and the angels and Nords made for the cobweb trees.

Fia recognised some features as she began: bodies of the little cat-like people of the Aurelli, some Navarii women, and worst of all, some Nord children.

"He's still breathing," Runa cried out from the depths of a tree. Fia rushed over as Malachai helped Runa tear cobwebs away from the face of a man. His eyes were flat against his bones, and his smooth nose led to a lipless mouth, almost a beak. His skin was covered in thick, dark scales that were dull and dry.

"You must leave this place," he croaked. Runa pulled at her water flask and brought it to his mouth, but he moved his head away.

"What is he saying?" Runa held him, trying to soothe

him.

"He's telling us to leave," Fia said, kneeling beside them as she interpreted his words. "What happened here?"

"The water… my hands…" the lizard man croaked. Fia tore at the cobwebs and snatched the flask from Runa, pouring it gently onto his hands. "You must leave at once," he repeated, a little louder this time. "Before he knows you are here, and he calls to you, too."

The unsteady feeling of being back on the ship washed over her and she swallowed hard. "Before he calls to us," Fia repeated, willing her hands not to shake.

"The others, they're all dead?" His eyes were glassy, and he seemed to stare at nothing.

Fia nodded. "Who did this to you?"

The lizard man's eyes began to flutter, and Fia poured more water onto his hands. His eyes flicked open—they were entirely black where before there had been a slither of an iris surrounded by yellow.

"Erebus," he breathed. His eyes fell shut and his chest stilled.

"Erebus," Fia whispered. As the word left her lips, the cobweb trees caught fire around them, one after another.

"We're under attack," Alexander cried. He pulled her away from the dead creature. "Maab, get the Nords back to the ship," he commanded. A fireball landed at the lizard man's feet, and within moments his cobweb-covered body was in flames.

"We will fight," Maab replied, a roar for Fia to interpret.

"They're staying," she said, as the stench of burning bodies filled her nostrils. Where were the Makya? No shapes shot in and out of the trees, only balls of fire.

A stream of flames like molten lava shot towards them, and Fia lunged out of the way, the opposite direction from Alexander. She rolled to her feet, her eyes darting to find him, but a blazing trail of fire tore its way between them.

"Don't fly. You're too great a target," she called out over the roar of the flames. Thick smoke billowed from the cobweb trees, and she held a hand over her nose and mouth. The Nords paced in their animal forms, balls of fire striking the ground beside them.

And then a fireball morphed mid-flight into a man, burning hands outstretched as he crash-landed into a black bear before him, and they tumbled through the smoke.

"No!" Fia ran towards them.

"Fia, wait," Alexander called out, but she couldn't see him.

The world went black. The smoke and the flames left with it, along with the cries and the commotion of everyone around her. Fia gazed at her feet. Where before there had been the muddy ground, there was nothing but black. Was this a witch's illusion? The only sounds were her breathing and her heart. It was as if she'd been shut inside a room with no light.

"Fia!" Alexander's voice cut through the silence, accompanied by a growl of one of the Nords and a piercing scream. And then silence again.

"Fia…"

Erebus. "You're trapped. You can't hurt me. This isn't real."

Something moved behind her in the darkness and she spun around, striking out with her elbow. Nothing. She reached for the dagger in her boot. And then another movement, to her left, and she spun again and thrust her the dagger into the air.

"Such fire inside of you. Begging for release."

"You can't hurt me," Fia said, slashing her dagger at nothing.

"Many do as I ask. As you will, too, in time. Speak a word of our exchange and I will not hesitate to harm your friends."

A ball of flame landed at her feet and turned into a man as it touched down. The darkness faded and the burning island, the smoke, and the commotion returned.

"The great fire mother sends for you," the Makya said, arms outstretched.

Fia threw the dagger into his knee, and he cried out in pain, reaching down to remove the blade. Fia used the opening to swing a kick at his head and then another at his ankles, knocking him off his feet.

The dagger fell to the dirt as the Makya jerked it from his knee and he fell. Another ball of fire landed beside Fia, transforming into a woman. Smoke surrounded them, and Fia lunged for the dagger and held it outstretched as the Makya woman approached.

"Seize her! We need her alive," the man yelled from the ground, clutching his bleeding leg.

White wings landed between them, and Alexander touched down with force and spread his wings wide, thrusting the woman away. A white tiger and a snow leopard pounced, tearing at the two Makya until they were nothing but ribbons of flesh and splinters of bone.

Alexander was beside her at once. Fia sheathed the dagger to disguise her trembling hands, her breathing ragged as Runa and Malachai touched down beside them, too. Alexander reached for her but hesitated, his hand resting on her shoulder in an almost-embrace.

"That was the last of them, sire," Malachai said.

Alexander nodded, but his gaze never left Fia's face. "Are you injured?"

Fia shook her head. "I'm fine." She was anything but fine. She wanted to tell him what had happened, about the incident in Turaunt and about all the times Erebus had been inside her head, but now she couldn't say any of it. *I will not hesitate to harm your friends.* Erebus's words rang in her ears.

"We have to go, now. Tell the Nords to meet us back at the ship" Alexander said.

Fia did as he asked, and Maab roared in response.

Alexander didn't wait for her reply; he lifted her into his arms just as he'd done back in Bridgevale and pushed up through the canopy away from the flames.

***

The only casualties were Makya. Six had attacked, and the Nords had made short work of them, despite the commotion.

They sailed for days after leaving the island, marking it on their maps, so they might tell others of what they had seen. The Navarii called it *Ohanza*, which Altair loosely translated as Shadowland, and in the days that passed, the walls of the ship were filled with Navarii drawings of the cobweb trees and the Makya attack.

Fia paced her cabin. It had been a trap all along, the fallen airship, the bodies. A trap for *her*. She peered out of her porthole, her breath fogging up the glass. The days grew shorter, and as they sailed further south, the cold air and the ice covered the surface of the ships. At night, in the distance, the sky was tinged with an electric green hue, lighting up the horizon.

She'd told no one about Erebus, about how she could hear him. Was it because she could understand the creatures of Ohinyan that she should hear his whispers, too? And as the days had gone by, she could understand the Nords more and more—even though they all spoke in a different way, their mouths or their beaks forming words differently, Fia understood almost all of it. It felt as normal as speaking to Altair. *What part of any of this is normal?*

Shouts cried out above deck. Fia tried to hurry herself, but it was difficult to climb into all the layers and furs Runa had bought for her, but without them the cold air would be intolerable. As she surfaced, she followed the crew's gaze. In the distance, jutting up from the horizon amongst dense fog, were enormous icebergs. A little wave of nausea ran over her. The ships didn't look strong enough to break through ice. They were going to have to sail very carefully.

Fia pulled her coat tighter around her. She'd taken to wearing the coat from Arc's Emporium to keep warm. It smelt of animal hide and burnt hair, but it was waterproof and lined with soft fur, and with the hood up, she was well protected from the burn of the icy wind.

"Eyes open for the marker, everyone!" Altair called out. "Alexander, can you and the others fly on ahead and look for the pass leading to the dock?" With a few steps, Alexander was airborne, followed closely by Runa and Malachai. Fia ran to the gunwale and watched as their silhouettes disappeared into the fog.

One of the Nord's cried out in her form as a bird, circling above them.

"She sees the marker," Fia shouted, "a blue flag up ahead, keep right. She said the ice spreads deep and wide beneath the surface of the water."

Fia stared in awe. The icebergs were vast. The fog cleared, and revealed ice stretched out on either side of the ship until it disappeared again into more fog. The marker, a few torn pieces of indigo rag, flapped wildly in the wind and marked the entrance to a great passage ahead of them through the ice.

The Nord flying above called out again as several large chunks of ice broke away from the walls and fell into the water below, landing in the water with a crack.

The water reflected the ice in every direction, and as the fog dispersed again and they sailed further into the passage, the air was bright and light around them. In places the ice was streaked with blue ribbons of mineral or deposit, creating beautiful, swirling patterns on the walls that pressed up around them.

Great archways of ice stretched over and above the ships, some crossing each other and some creating unusual shapes. Up ahead, Alexander sat patiently in a gap that had formed perfectly in the centre of an archway, beside another of the blue markers.

Fia found herself focusing on the fact that he still wore nothing but his linen trousers, as if it were a summer's day. They still hadn't talked about their kiss. She felt somehow, that the closer she let herself get to Alexander, the more Erebus might use that in whatever way he could.

As the ships passed beneath him, Alexander flew down to the deck. "The ice is very fragile in places. Runa and Malachai have gone on ahead."

They sailed onwards with care, and here and there they passed traces of ships that hadn't made it through; part of a stern or a mast or a crate wedged into the ice.

The passage began to widen, and the walls of ice seemed to stretch higher than before, until they reached a wide opening, and the ice peaked into an enormous archway up ahead, lined with blue markers.

Fia narrowed her eyes to make out the shapes of the

silhouettes over the archway. Her breath caught in her throat.

Beside each marker stood an armed guard, spears held ready to attack.

CHAPTER TWENTY

NOOR

"Brothers," Lorn hissed through gritted teeth from her seat in the great hall. Her shoulders tensed as the twins approached.

Noor stood guard close by. Her illusion had been easy to maintain with regular rest. Only Raiaan had questioned her, once, about why it was *she* who always followed Lorn. Lorn hadn't seemed to care—perhaps she mistook if for flattery on Noor's part after their encounter in her bedchambers, an incident which Lorn had not mentioned or acted on since.

"We are half a day away from Nadar, sister, and you will talk to the council as we agreed. Do whatever it takes to gain their trust and their allegiance. We are stronger united if we are to stand a chance of taking Alythia under our control." Jerum was very authoritative when he wanted to be.

Lorn opened her mouth to retaliate, but he'd already raised a hand, averting her murderous gaze. The decision had been made. Raiaan remained silent under their brother's watchful eye and Noor wondered why he always said so little.

"Do this for us. Visit the council in Nadar, and

everything we desire will be ours soon enough." Jerum smiled. "Come brother, let us leave our sister in quiet contemplation of her visit."

They departed in silence, without so much as a glance back in Lorn's direction. Noor could feel the loathing dripping off of Lorn, even from where she stood.

Everywhere they went, Erebus showed Lorn visions of Fia and Alexander embracing: in the reflection of the corridor walls before she met with her brothers, in the great urn's flames, even as she barked orders at the Aurelli. And with each new vision, they enraged Lorn to a point beyond control.

"*Your time is coming, great Fire Mother,*" the darkness whispered, the sound of his voice sending a chill down Noor's spine.

***

When the airship anchored in the skyline of Nadar, Lorn left her brothers behind without saying a word. Noor and three more guards followed her in silence as she made her way amongst the city. The sky was dark for such an early hour—the time of the second sun was almost at an end.

Nadar was a dreary place, trapping shadows and refracting the light. The looming buildings reached above the streets, their obsidian exteriors lavishly carved with reliefs of all descriptions: battles, offerings, great gates, and strange creatures.

Here and there, a cluster of raw shards of brilliant emerald adorned the buildings, jutting skywards at various levels and intervals, and reflecting the dark sky in its glass-like finish. The buildings themselves were odd shapes: some buildings were tall and narrow, and others were short with curved emerald ceilings, broken up by the angular shards protruding out of them. Noor detested it. She longed for the comforts of her forest, for the feel of a warm fire of her own making glowing against her skin.

Lorn clicked her tongue against her teeth, and Noor bit down on the smile that was breaking. Nadar was like an empty shell, or at least that's what she'd thought on her last mission here. A mission where she and Silla had disguised themselves as guards, and *Silla*… She pushed the thought of him away, deep, deep down, so she didn't lose her grip on her illusion. If she lost control for even a moment, they'd see her for who she really was, and Lorn would destroy her in an instant.

The stone streets and buildings were built amongst a series of canals, where in the place of water was a thick, black liquid. It was a magma-like tar, bubbling loudly as steam escaped from noisy pockets of air. Cracks in the surface revealed the orange glow of molten lava below. The buildings were impervious to it, just as the Makya's clothes were fireproof, too. How they transmuted with their garments intact, Noor had never quite worked out.

They passed the crumbling remains of the Nadar palace that Lorn had destroyed not long ago, in another of her outbreaks. Such displays were not uncommon amongst the Makya, but in destroying the palace, the repercussions had halted Ohinyan's chances of coming together. Lorn barely raised an eyebrow at the ruin.

The streets were empty; all Makya old enough to fight would be in training, and the youngest would be at school. Noor had spent enough time in the city on her mission with Silla to learn the Makya's routines and hear the gossip about Lorn.

There were no vendors, no food stalls, and no signs of life. They approached the council building, an oddity even amongst the rest. It was round with a flat, level roof, several stories high, with more of the elaborate emerald shards stretching skywards. Shiny black pillars circled the boundary of the lower levels, intricately carved with all manner of creatures.

Two guards stood on either side of the entranceway, metal staffs held firmly to their sides. "Your name, please," one of them said as Lorn and her unit approached. Lorn flicked her red hair away from her face. The other guard cleared his throat. If he knew of his comrade's mistake, he didn't acknowledge it.

A fool's blunder.

Lorn was silent, her smile sweet as she advanced. She was a scorpion waiting to strike. She touched her fingertips to the tip of the guard's staff, circling him slowly. "My name?" she said. "You wish to know my name?"

Noor braced herself, scanning her eyes left to right and

searching for anywhere she could take cover without causing a scene.

"Pardon me, ma'am, the council are expecting you," the other guard began nervously.

"How kind of them," Lorn replied, tightening her grip around the staff.

She laughed as she pressed on into the building, clenching her fists in tight balls at her sides. They smouldered into little puffs of smoke, and Noor readied herself for what was coming. She hung back behind the group as they entered the council chamber, putting as much distance between herself and Lorn as she could manage.

The members of the Makya council stretched out around the perimeter of the room, ascending higher with each rank. Three empty seats remained where Lorn and her brothers had once sat. The floor of the room was sunken and low, swirling with bubbling lava. Lorn walked further into the chamber, stepping onto stones that stretched out into the centre of the magma, surrounded by the council members. From the central stone, she was slightly higher than the lowest ranked council member, but not as tall as the highest. Noor wondered if Lorn still longed to sit amongst them, to be a part of something so great.

It was Lorn who spoke first. "Brothers and sisters of the council." She turned to face each of them for the briefest of moments before continuing. Her voice bristled with mischief. "The time is almost upon us for the Makya to take our rightful place at the head of Ohinyan. I grow stronger with every sunset, and with the coming of the new sun, I *will* be reborn as the fire mother, as you have raised me. None will stand in our way."

"Lorn, my dear sister." It was Par, the head of the council. She was as fierce as she was old. Noor had seen her wield her flames, disciplining twelve guards at once, and it was a terrifying sight to behold. But Par was level-headed, too, and well known throughout Ohinyan for her ability to negotiate—a concept which most Makya did not seem to grasp. News of how she had tried to protect Alexander and his father from Lorn's outburst at the palace had spread quickly. "We still do not know these things for certain, and—"

"If certainty is all you need, *dear sister*," Lorn replied, throwing her arms above her head. The swirling lava rose around them, suspended perfectly in the air under Lorn's control. She spiralled it with breath-taking accuracy around the council members, as if it were her own galaxy. It hung mere centimetres away from each council member, stunned to silence in their chairs.

"As I said, we do not know these things for certain," Par added, ignoring Lorn's display.

Lorn lost control of her demonstration, throwing lava around the council chamber in small eruptions and clumsy explosions.

"The priorities of the Makya have changed over the years. You and your brothers have been disruptive for long enough." Par glanced over her shoulder in the direction of the palace remains. "This is a time of great change in Ohinyan. You have damaged our coalition with the angels to the point where all communication has broken down entirely, and we must work to rebuild the relationships that were beginning to form. The time has come for us to unite."

Noor felt a flutter in her chest, like a butterfly trying to emerge from its chrysalis. Par's words were a beacon of hope amongst so much darkness. The old woman knew what mattered.

Lorn returned the lava, and it sloshed back into its resting place. "Unite? Do you not wish for the Makya to govern all of Ohinyan?"

Par sighed. "A great darkness is escaping from Ohinyan. One that is taking advantage of our dying sun. Some say they have even heard its whispers. It is destroying all that it touches. If it is left to fester and spread, there will be nothing left of Ohinyan for us to govern." Noor studied Par's expression for any sign that Erebus had whispered to her, too.

"Good," Lorn replied, as another eruption of lava swirled around the council members. "Let it crash and burn. We only need Alythia. From there, we can govern all of Ohinyan."

"No!" Par's voice resonated throughout the chamber, and as she spoke, she rose to her feet, embers and sparks trembling from her small frame. Her eyes grew brighter, and a small flicker of flames escaped from her fingertips. "We have tolerated your behaviour long enough. It is time for us to reconcile our differences, *young Fire Mother*, time for us to settle our wrong doings with the inhabitants of this world. We should have imprisoned you for destroying the palace, for the death of Zuriel—your punishment was too mild. We wrongly looked the other way when you launched your attacks, but now we ask this of you, so that you and your brothers might join the council once more. Reconcile with the angels, and together, remove this poison from Ohinyan."

Par sat down, her eyes returning to pools of black obsidian, and she was as fawn-like and tiny as she had been before.

"Very well," Lorn said, playing coolly with the lava, and emphasising each word with a flicker of flames. "I will meet with Alexander and reconcile with the angels as you wish. We will destroy the darkness together and ensure Ohinyan's safety." Lorn bowed for added effect.

Surely, they don't believe this? Par merely nodded in response, and Noor could feel her eyes following them as they left the chamber.

Lorn took her time returning to the airship, and as they each readied a seed pod, she hissed at Noor and the other three guards. "Repeat a word of what you have witnessed, and I will eject you from the ship in a ball of molten lava. Understood?"

Noor nodded. *What game are you playing now?* The pods spluttered to life, and the buildings of Nadar fell away from them. As the ship's loading bay opened, the thought of sending the pod back to solid ground crossed her mind, but there was still too much to be done.

"Well, don't just stand there," Lorn shouted at Noor. "Get the pod secure!"

Noor anchored the little pod to the loading bay moments after they landed.

"You, with me," Lorn demanded.

Jerum and Raiaan could be heard not far from the loading bay, disciplining some of the Aurelli.

"Sister," Jerum exclaimed, subduing the flames circling the terrified Aurelli. They fled as soon as Jerum's head was turned. "Tell us of your visit to the council, dear sister." His eyes flared to a deep red.

Noor dutifully followed as they made their way to the great chamber. Lorn gave details of a successful visit to the council, and her brothers beamed in response. "We are to continue south, with the full support of the council."

Noor coughed back a laugh. *You deceitful creature…*

"Well done, Lorn," Jerum replied. "With the council behind us, it won't be long before we have access to Alythia, and things will start to change for us, for the better." He turned to leave the antechamber and Raiaan followed.

"Enough." Lorn threw her arms into the air followed by a burst of flames. "What are you looking at?" she barked at Noor. "Follow me to my chambers."

Noor hid a smile as she followed Lorn through the cold, metal corridors of the ship. She had enjoyed watching Lorn become more distraught. It seemed a fair justice for the destruction she and her brothers had caused below them on

Ohinyan.

"Take these to the armoury." Lorn scowled, handing Noor her dirty boots. Noor barely had a chance to nod before the door slammed shut in her face. As she walked away, she heard the unmistakeable sounds of Lorn shouting and throwing things around her room, talking to herself… *to him.*

Dumping the boots with the first available guard, Noor made her way to the cell she had been held in days before to meet with the little group of Aurelli who had been carrying her messages off the ship. They had brought bread and water for her, as always, and she accepted it gratefully, for it gave her time to rest without her illusion. She had begun to learn the subtle differences in their feline expressions and to see mannerisms in their swift movements that she had not noticed before. One closed its eyes at her, pressing its lids together for a moment, and Noor knew it was a smile. They were an exquisite race and cared for each other and the welfare of Ohinyan immensely, going as far as to look after everything on the ship, even if it belonged to the Makya.

Noor relayed what she had learned to the Aurelli and threw in some examples of the tormented Lorn for good measure. She handed over three hastily scribbled notes. The Aurellis' eyes glistened as they watched with intent, and Noor hoped with every fibre of her being that they passed her messages on to the Shadows successfully.

Whispers hissed in the corridor beyond the cell, and she heard Raiaan's voice. "And tell me, what did you see?" He asked, his voice louder than before.

Noor quickly changed back into a guard, dismissing the little creatures at once. With a nod of understanding, they were away through the ship.

"Well, sir, just like before, it's like she's possessed," the guard accompanying Raiaan replied.

"And you are with her the most?"

"Myself and one other guard, but I… well, I can't think of her name."

"Very well. Thank you, that is all for today," Raiaan replied, and the sound of his footsteps faded down the corridor.

Noor smiled. As she walked back to her hiding place in the loading bay, she dared not let herself believe that all the threads of her plan were coming together.

CHAPTER TWENTY-ONE

FIA

"Mizunese," Altair said quietly. Fia hadn't noticed him walk up beside her and Alexander. "My wife's people."

The guardsmen gave the tiniest of nods as the ships sailed through the archway of ice. Stretching out on either side ahead of the ships was a large harbour and beyond it land bustling with life.

Mizune was a strange place. The sky flickered on the horizon in a display of vivid lilac and green ribbons, casting a glow on the snow and ice. Fia watched as the ships came into dock, her eyes darting over the land. The buildings hugged the semi-circle of the harbour, each on tiered rows of wooden stilts, stretching out on either side. The furthest tiered row was several levels up, encompassing hundreds of buildings reaching down to the shore.

The wooden houses were disorderly. Some had one storey and some two or three in different shapes and sizes. Many had large ice structures protruding from one part or another, a tower here or an odd side extension there.

On each of the tiered levels were interlacing bridges of ice criss-crossing between them, with people scurrying from one tier to another. In every gap, every structure, every bridge, there was movement from people, animals, carts, and stalls.

The bridges each contained a market, and all along the shore people worked in fur-lined, hooded coats and thick boots laced snugly around their legs. Fia watched them as silver coins were handed over for fabrics, pelts, and containers.

"Yahto." Altair walked down the jetty towards the Mizunese men that approached him.

"Altair," the man at the head of the group replied. They clasped each other's forearm in a firm hold, pausing to lock eyes, until Yahto broke into great, bellowing laughter and hugged Altair. "It is good to see you, Father," he said cheerfully, before leading Altair off the jetty.

Alexander motioned to Fia, and together they followed Altair and his son onto the shore. Alexander's kiss had played over and over in her head. The feeling of his lips pressed against hers, the warmth of his mouth, but they hadn't been alone again since. It was strange to be off the ship, and her legs were slow to adjust to the steadiness of land.

The Nords delighted in the freedom, dispersing into the dock in one animal form or another. All except for Maab and Enne, who walked silently beside her and Alexander.

"Won't you go with them?" Fia asked.

"Later, perhaps," Maab replied, his gaze fixed firmly on the Mizunese men surrounding Altair. Yahto's sapphire blue eyes shone brightly as he talked with his father.

Fia followed the group through bustling crowds, over bridges of ice, and past fragrant market stalls. They reached a large building, grander than those surrounding it, with large columns of twisting wood supporting a balcony of ice on the upper level.

Inside, a great corridor of wooden pillars manned by Mizunese guards led them to a set of doors reaching to the ceiling. Fia inspected the door carvings as they passed through: people, animals, the ocean, and an abundance of rivers, rain, and lakes.

Yahto led them into a chamber filled with a soft blue light from above. They joined a small group of men and women sitting on floor cushions, legs crossed neatly under them.

"Please sit, Father," Yahto began, "you and your friends shall join us and tell us what brings you back to Mizune." He took his place at the head of the circle making swift introductions, but the discussion that followed was long and intense. Fia could see that Yahto was every bit his father's son in the way his people spoke to him and approached him with questions with every moment that passed.

She listened intently as Yahto spoke.

"These are dark times. Safety should be the priority for everyone. The Navarii and your friends are welcome to stay here for as long as they wish. A home rests the soul, Father," he said, before clapping his hands abruptly. "Now. Let us break—eat, drink, and enjoy some entertainment for our guests."

Platters of fish, along with bowls of rice and stew, were laid out before them. Spices saturated the air, and before long a steady hum of chatter filled the chamber as they ate.

Fia chewed gratefully on a mouthful of meat from a bowl of steaming stew. Food had been in short supply on the ship, especially after the storm.

Yahto clapped his hands again, on his feet at once. "We begin." He was joined by some of the men and women who had sat beside them. Yahto stepped back across a small trench in the ground, reflections of the light revealing a shallow channel of water reaching around the perimeter of the chamber.

"For many years, as far back as our history tells us, the Mizunese have had a connection with water. Water is the very essence of life—man, creatures, plants, none can live without it." Yahto moved his hands in smooth, wide strokes, matching his words. As he spoke, Fia watched the group *pulling* the water from the little trench towards them, like they were two magnets tugging at each other's edges. Instead of splashing in a puddle on the floor, the water flowed seamlessly towards them, cylindrical and shiny, as if encased in glass.

She felt Alexander's gaze on her as she watched the display, mesmerised, but he glanced away when she turned to face him.

"Every living thing comes from water, and we return to it when we die," Yahto continued, joining the group in manipulating the flow of the water through the air. Fia sat, fascinated, observing Yahto and the group as they worked with the water. Their bodies moved gracefully around the swirling streams, as if it were an extension of themselves. In the same way the Makya were one with fire, the Mizunese were one with water. With one fluid movement, they diverted the flow upwards to the ceiling, the blue glow deepening as the last of the ice was frozen into place. Fia imagined they used the same method to hunt the fish they were eating, lancing their catch with a spear made of ice.

"The properties of water are used for many things. Healing, cleansing, purification. Tied to the ebb and flow of the oceans' tides, it is said that each night the moons return to strengthen our bond with water."

Yahto reached his hands towards the ice, and a large chunk of it broke away, falling at speed towards the spot where he stood below. Before it reached him, he waved his palms together in a circular motion, and the chunk of ice rotated around and around into a perfect sphere, like a little moon hovering above the chamber.

"Just as the water and the moons are tied to each other, so are the sun and the moons. The moons cannot shine without the sun, without the sun our days and nights would be in darkness, and our tides would lose their ebb and flow. The natural sequence of Ohinyan will be disrupted, until the third sun blesses us with its presence." Yahto dropped his hands, the little moon melting back into the trench, and sat back down in his place at the head of the group.

"And do you grow weaker with each sunset?" Maab asked.

It was Altair who replied. "Yes, they will grow weaker, but not yet."

"And perhaps, not at all," Yahto said. "Only time will tell."

Maab nodded.

"So then, my son, will the Mizunese help us? Will you stand with us and fight the Makya? Our chances of defeating them are far greater if we have the Mizunese warriors at our side."

Fia felt uncomfortable at the onslaught of Altair's stare. He was a gentle soul, but she sensed a quiet thunder beneath him, as if the swathes of his great cloak kept it contained.

"How can you ask this of me, Father?" Yahto shook his head, breaking away from his father's gaze. "Mizune could become the target for the next Makya attack. We cannot draw attention to ourselves." He thrust himself to his feet, pacing. "Our numbers are dwindling—you know this all too well. I have a duty to protect my people. Our last encounter with the Makya did not end well. We cannot fight. It is too risky."

"Whether you fight now or later, it matters not. Before the third sun graces us with its presence, there will be many battles ahead of us." Altair stood. He swung his cloak over his shoulder and strode across the chamber to stand beside his son.

"Yahto." His voice was low, almost a whisper, and Fia

could barely hear his words. "This is greater than all of us. We can hide from it, ignore it, pretend it isn't happening, and carry on with our lives." He gestured to the room, his voice growing louder. "We can continue teaching our children to fish and make bread, and we can carry on mending our nets at the end of a day's fishing. But we cannot stop what is coming. The sun is dying, and something deep within Ohinyan relishes that. Can you not feel it in the water, in the earth?"

Fia felt it in her bones.

Yahto's shoulders slumped, and he shook his head. "Father, we cannot assist you."

***

Fia stood looking out over Mizune from one of the busy bridges. The cold that filled every hidden corner of the harbour seemed to penetrate through her clothes no matter how tightly she pulled them around herself.

She'd overheard Altair's report to Alexander, and he'd met with Yahto several times to request the assistance of the Mizunese. He'd relayed their knowledge of the attacks, of the dying sun, the changes in Ohinyan, of Erebus, and how the effect of his whispers could be felt even at sea. But still, Yahto would not help. He refused to put his people at risk. Fia couldn't blame him. Before she'd arrived to Ohinyan, she'd have seen it as black and white. People needed help, and the Mizunese could give it. But she'd seen what the burden of responsibility meant, the way it weighed on Alexander, and even Altair, too. To be responsible for the lives of so many was not something she envied.

A group of Nords rested by the harbour, their distinctive silver armour scattered in heaps beside them. Maab was the most difficult to spot from this distance, his white fur disguising him amongst the ice. As a magnificent tiger, he had a much gentler way about him than as a man, more playful and carefree. He dived into the icy sea, black stripes disappearing out of sight, then returned minutes later with a seal, limp and lifeless in his great jaws. He scored down its belly with a razor-sharp claw, the steaming insides oozing onto the ice around it. A low rumble escaped Maab's bloodied lips, and in moments Enne was by his side, white fur against white fur, as they devoured the seal together. Fia looked on as Enne, feline and gentle, licked Maab's fur until it was no longer pink from seal blood.

A snowball hit her foot and she looked away. A group of Mizunese children were playing. They were having a snowball fight of sorts, directing the motion of the snowballs through the air, as if they were held by unseen cords. One feigned left and right before hurling it at another with squeals of delight.

"It does not do well to be still out here for long." Fia hadn't noticed Altair join her. He was incredibly light footed for someone so great in stature.

"It's fascinating to watch them," she said. "It's as if the water is part of them, as if they are connected to it by an invisible thread."

"It is as Yahto told you, child. Every living thing comes from water. So yes, in that sense, they are connected. We all are."

"So anyone could manipulate the water this way?"

"Perhaps, with time. The Mizunese are taught from the moment they can sit up that the water is a part of them, so it becomes as familiar to them as the act of speaking. It is said the great ice giants taught the Mizunese their affinity with water." He sighed. "Their power was not always this great. It grew in response to the Makya at the coming of the second sun. But at a great cost. I understand Yahto's hesitation to assist us. There were once ten times the number of Mizunese you see here."

A boy hurled a barrage of snowballs at a girl half his size, and just as the snowballs were about to hit, she sent a wall of ice shooting up like a tower in front of her. Fia let Altair's words unravel themselves in her head. *Ice giants. Of course there are ice giants.*

"What is it that troubles you, child?"

Fia rolled the little bird charm between her fingers. "What doesn't?" she asked, fidgeting with the little pouch around her neck and worrying about the Lady Noor. She hadn't known her for long, but long enough to know she was good and kind, and that she had risked her life to save another.

Below them at the dock, Alexander laughed with Maab and Enne, human once more, as they moved crates from the ships to the shore.

"I still don't really understand why I'm here—you all seem to be pretty well united without my help. But… I don't think I want to go back to Earth anymore," she said. *Not think… know.*

"Ohinyan has changed you, child," Altair said. "You are not the same young woman that I healed when you fell through the window."

Fia remained silent. It had only been a few weeks, but he was right. She did feel different.

"Since you returned to us in Ikothea, I have felt very proud to have you amongst us," Altair continued. "My home is wherever my people are." He followed Fia's gaze to Alexander. The day was drawing to a close, and the sun had already dropped behind the icy cliffs leading from the sea to the harbour. The soft grey light of dusk fell around them.

"Do you think you will ever stay in one place?" Fia asked, turning back to Altair.

"I doubt it. We move with the seasons. A forest that is cold and cruel in winter becomes lush and full of life in spring. When the ice melts and gives way to fresh water, ripe fruits, and animals for hunting, we can eat, drink, and feel blessed by it."

It sounded so simple. Life back in London was always so complicated, even when there was nothing in particular to complicate it at all. Fia exhaled through pursed lips, watching the little vapour cloud of breath drift away from her. She caught Alexander's gaze as he made his way back towards the cabin they shared with Runa and Malachai.

"What is of most importance," Altair said, placing a hand on Fia's shoulder, "is not how we move from place to place. But whom we move with, and who we let move us. It has been the people who have come in and out of my life that have shaped it, not the mountains I have climbed, or the oceans I've crossed." He shook his head, his old, evergreen eyes looking down at her. "I do not have answers for the questions I know you wish to ask, but the witches do, and we are very near to the coven Alexander has spoken of."

With a gentle hand to her back, Altair left, leaving Fia alone in the dusk. She blinked herself out of her daze. This was absurd. She should tell him. She should just tell Alexander how she felt, because if she went back to Earth without saying something, she knew she was going to regret it.

Fia paced down to the cabin, pushing the door open with much more force than she meant to. Runa and Malachai were nowhere to be seen, and neither was Alexander. The main room was empty.

So much for her grand declaration. She peeled off her coat and pushed through the door into her bedroom, flopping down onto the bed.

The door creaked open, and Alexander stood in the doorway. "Can I come in?"

Her room was cramped, and his wings filled the small space where he stood. Fia sat up and cleared her throat. "Of course." Her voice came out much smaller than she meant it to as she tried to think of everything she wanted to say.

Alexander sat down beside her, his wings moulding neatly around him as he sat. This time she didn't hesitate. She ran her fingers softly down a wing, the silkiness of his feathers passing between her fingertips.

Fia traced a thumb across his bicep, and his blue eyes flashed up to meet hers. She bit her lip as he held her gaze. She rose up on her knees, wrapping her arms around his neck, with barely an inch between them.

Her movement broke the stillness, and within a heartbeat, Alexander rolled onto his back and pulled her with him. She couldn't breathe. Her eyes rose to meet his and then lowered to where his lips parted slightly in the middle. The familiar stir of electricity clouded the air around them as he brushed her lips with his, and then his hands cupped her face, and he drew her in for a deep, open-mouthed kiss. Fia pulled back to catch her breath, and Alexander's eyes never left hers. She pulled her shirt over her head and held his gaze for a moment, his chest rising and falling with his ragged breathing.

And then Fia melted into him, all of her at once touching every part of him. His hands tangled in her hair as he kissed her fiercely this time, a quiet moan escaping from her, as his tongue found hers.

Alexander held her face in his hands, his eyes on hers, as they paused to share a breath. And then his mouth was on hers again, hungrier than before. His warmth flowed through every inch of her as she tasted him everywhere, with equal urgency. She didn't just want him; she *needed* him.

His breathing was fast as he grazed her neck with his lips, and she dug her fingers into his shoulders, breathless, as the electricity pulsated through her. Alexander rolled her gently onto the bed, the rhythm of their bodies intensifying as they fit together perfectly, like two fragments becoming whole.

***

The shadows of flickering oil lamps danced against the wall of Fia's bedroom.

Alexander pressed a kiss into her hair, his fingers entwined in hers.

"There's something I think you'd like to see." He was on his feet, passing Fia her bundle of clothes from the floor. "We need to hurry," he said with a warm smile.

Fia pulled on her clothes and smoothed her hair, and Alexander yanked her to him, playfully kissing her neck.

"Are you ready?" He took her hand in his, and they stepped out into the cold air of Mizune.

They moved quickly, across ice bridges and past traders packing away their goods for the day, down through the docks, and past houses. Lights flickered on inside the windows of homes. Soon, they were out of the town onto the bare ice stretching outwards on either side towards the cliffs, blue, capillary-like ribbons streaking across it.

"Where are we going?" Fia asked. It was getting darker,

and the moons were already visible in the sky. Alexander urged her onwards, over ice that gave way to rocks and a pathway of stone leading up into the cliffs.

"Alexander, really, where are we…" With one more step, they were high above Mizune, on the cliffs where they'd first seen the guards standing watch, the flickering oil lamps of the town far below them. In the other direction, the moons cast a milky glow on the still ocean. Ice stretched far to the east and west, powdery blue in the moonlight. The stars reached out as far as they could see, far brighter than the oil lamps of Mizune, glittering like fireflies in the endless inky sky.

"Just a few more minutes," Alexander said, pulling Fia back against him and wrapping his arms and wings around her. She breathed him in, savouring the feeling of his body pressed against hers, as her mind wandered to their warm bed back down in Mizune.

Moments passed, then a single note carried quietly to them on the breeze. And then another, and another, chiming melodically, until the sky filled with bands of colour flickering in time to the music. Hues of green, pink, purple, and blue flashed before them as the chimes became voices and then chimes again.

It was like a waterfall of light dancing before their eyes. Fia felt she could reach out and touch it. "It's so beautiful," she said, leaning deeper into Alexander's embrace, the scents of the forest drifting from his hair and wrapping around her.

The whole sky in every direction brimmed with colour.

Like a gentle smoke screen, the stars and the moons glistened beyond the ribbons. "What is it?"

"They are sky spirits, and they are very, very old."

"*They?* Older than the angels?"

"Much older. They protect the skies above Ohinyan, and they can harness the power of air, much like the Mizunese can with water. But most importantly for me, they protect my home."

Alexander pointed to their left, and Fia looked out at the streams of rose, lilac, azure, and ruby. As the ribbons rippled, gently, Fia could see… She wasn't exactly sure what she could see.

They looked like upturned mountains, with loose rocks and boulders floating nearby, and atop of the upturned mountains were forests, lakes, and hills. As the ribbons of light flickered, Fia could see more clearly.

"Is that... is that a city?" Even amongst the colours of the sky spirits, it was golden, as if the sun was at the very centre of the city, and its rays burst from every opening.

"Alythia. My home. It moves through the skies above Ohinyan under the protection of the sky spirits, never remaining in one place. The sky spirits guide us home," he said.

"You can understand them?"

Alexander turned Fia around to face him, and she felt the chill of the night air fill the empty space between them. She tugged gently at his hair, at the strands that curled under at the ends, as she examined the contour of his lips, the way they rested in a firm line when he wasn't speaking.

"Understanding is a complicated thing," he murmured, holding her hand in his. "We hear their song, and it guides us home."

"And the Makya?"

Alexander shook his head.

"So they'll never find it. They can't?"

"Not unless another angel leads them to it."

Oren. Alythia flickered in and out of sight. "Why do they want to reach it so badly?"

"For what it represents. A city in the sky above all of Ohinyan… a place of great power from which the wrong person could govern all of its inhabitants. But if Erebus is behind their search, then that's something different altogether…"

"And do the angels govern them? The people of Ohinyan?" She traced a thumb over his lip as she bit down on her own, and she felt the familiar sensation of longing pulsating through her.

Alexander shook his head. "No, we listen." He pressed a soft, teasing kiss to her lips.

"I can hear them, too, the sky spirits. A little, anyway. It's so strange. Sometimes, I just hear words, sounds. With some of the races we've met, even more. But it's not like learning a language it's… it's something more, it's like you said, understanding is… complicated. Am I the only one like this?"

"Loquere," Alexander said. "Very loosely translated, it

means 'one who speaks.' I have only ever heard of one other here in Ohinyan, but they died long before I was born. It is a very special gift, Fia." He dragged his fingers through his hair. "I never meant to lead you here. It wasn't right. It's not fair to ask this of you—"

"But what can I even do? You all seem to have it figured out without my help. I've just been in the way the entire time I've been here."

Alexander shook his head. "You haven't been in the way."

Fia rubbed her forehead and let out a soft whistle between tight lips. "I need to know more, Alexander, about so many things. And I need to know if Noor will be safe. Please, it's time for me to go to the coven. And then I can make my own decision. You don't get to choose for me, even if you're trying to protect me."

The breeze picked up, and Alexander brushed a few strands of hair from her face and tucked them behind her ear. "Of course, I never meant to take anything from you," he said.

"I need to do this… alone. Tomorrow then?"

"If it's what you want. The moment the sun is up." He glanced up one last time towards Alythia. "We should go." He held out his hand, and together they made their way back down the stone path to Mizune.

CHAPTER TWENTY-TWO

ALEXANDER

In the early hours before Fia left to seek out the witches, Alexander received news from a sentry regarding the activities of the Lady Noor. It was time for a visit home.

Malachai and Runa joined Alexander in their ascent to Alythia. Perched high on a series of rock formations that cut their way gracefully through the skies above Ohinyan, Alythia was a cluster of islands floating on a sea of clouds. Long vines hung from some of the rocks whilst others held waterfalls cascading off their edges, pouring clean, crisp water into the sky below. In a certain light, the waterfalls created rainbows, revealing glimpses of forest amongst the rays of sunlight. Some of the smaller clusters of rock sat at different heights, others were linked together by old, crumbling bridges uniting a mountain range as it rested in the air.

It had only been a few hours, and already he felt the absence of Fia's warm body against his. He longed to show her Alythia, to have her flying beside him above the clouds, but she'd chosen to go to the witches alone and he had to respect her decision.

Being intimate together hadn't been as it had with other women, not simply because it was his first time with a human. It was unlike being with any angel. But he knew it was more than that, more than her humanness or the novelty of a woman without wings. It was the hum of the air around them when he pulled her close. It was the spark in her eyes and the sound of her hungered breathing matching his. It was the way they'd both laughed at Fia running her hands over his wings and her quiet whistle when she'd rested her head on his chest.

"Are you ready to find out Oren's fate?" Malachai asked Runa. They passed over a waterfall, and Alexander forced his attention back to their journey.

"We've already lost him, no matter what happens," Runa replied, and they flew on in silence.

Alythia was lush with forest and running water. As they approached the centre, nature overtook the structures, as if there had been a battle over time and nature had won. The lush green ivy and crawlers wrapped tightly around the magnificent buildings. Each edifice shone with a golden lustre in the light of dawn, brilliant and majestic, as they stretched upwards into the clouds. *Home.*

Alexander was the first to touch down on the largest and grandest of all the structures in the heart of Alythia, a cluster of towers supported by great columns of marble, Ehnalia. Several guards stood waiting for them as they landed on a glistening platform, stretching out across Alythia.

"Sire," the first addressed Alexander. "Jarl is waiting for

you in the Hall."

"Runa, Malachai," Alexander said to his friends. "Debrief, and then go home—we leave in a few hours."

"But sire," Malachai began in protest.

"You have worked long enough, Malachai. Runa, take him home for some rest." It was true. They'd barely rested, either of them, and dark shadows smudged under their eyes from days of patrolling with little sleep.

Alexander left them on the platform before they could utter another word. Ehnalia's exterior was majestic, but its interior was something else. Tall, twisting columns stretched upwards to the ceiling high above, and golden light shone through countless openings in the façade to reveal an endless sea of clouds. Clouds that had been his refuge many times before his father had died but never in the days since. *A leader faces his duties, head on.* His father's words echoed in Alexander's head.

"It is good to see you, sire." Jarl greeted Alexander with a soldier's salute.

"Jarl, old friend. It is good to see you, too."

The angel's golden eyes shone brightly from behind his helmet. He was the general of the Alythian army, and one of the oldest angels known to be on Ohinyan. Alexander held him in the highest regard and had learned much from the general over the years: how to fight, how to earn the respect of the soldiers, and how to command an army. He'd spent many days with Jarl's son, Halvar, practicing with a sword under the general's watchful eye.

"The Shadows have delivered news from the Lady Noor, sire." Jarl removed a gauntlet and picked up three pieces of crumpled parchment, pale and tattered against his umber fingers. He handed them to Alexander.

"Makya air fleet approaches the South. Searching for Alythia." This came as no surprise. If Oren had been feeding them information, he'd known where their ships were destined before they left Ikothea.

"Oren dead." Sadness washed over him as he thought of the charred remains he and Malachai had buried in Turaunt. Oren had betrayed them, but to die at the hands of the Makya did not bear thinking about. It would have been long, painful, and lonely for him at the end.

"Fia is the target." Alexander's breath caught in his throat, and he stifled the panicked sound that escaped him into a cough, aware of the general's eyes on him. *Fia is the target.* He'd left her to go to the witches, alone. How could he have been so stupid? The attack back on the island, it wasn't random. It had been about Fia, all along. He took a breath to calm the nausea, to quieten the beat of his heart in his ears. *This is your doing. All of it.*

He crumbled the parchments, throwing a fist down onto the table. The angels standing guard shifted uncomfortably from one foot to another.

"Inform Oren's family," Alexander said quietly. "Runa has just returned today. Tell her she may stay with her family if she wishes. I will speak with her directly later."

Jarl called a guard over to relay the message.

Fia is the target. But why? Was Lorn trying to spite him… for rejecting her? Alexander shook away the thought. There were other matters to attend to.

"We don't have enough soldiers to face such an advance," Alexander said gravely.

"No, sire. I have already had to recall most of our legion from Earth."

Alexander exhaled. This was not good. It had been many, many years since such a thing had happened, before his father's reign. "How many remain?"

"A few hundred only. Many who have returned have been directed to patrol stations across Ohinyan, but most have been ordered to go south, to wait."

"Very well." Alexander nodded. "We will need to draw the Makya down—we must not fight them in the air. We're trying to secure the help of the water wielders in the south. If we are to be successful, we must lure the Makya to us, away from Mizune." Oren had just been one angel. But Alexander knew all too well where there was one, more might follow.

"Why are they after this Fia, sire? Whoever she is, they will go to wherever she can be found."

"I don't know, for certain," Alexander replied. Lorn was capable of many things, but he couldn't be sure if she was alone in her intentions.

"The Makya have become increasingly aggressive over the last few months," Jarl continued.

"Yes, and something about the attacks… doesn't seem

right," Alexander replied. Par, the Makya council leader, was a fair woman. Her intention had been reconciliation not too long ago. Could she really be supporting this? It was more Lorn's style, but why would she act without the council? "Jarl, I trust your judgement," he finally said. "Thank you for recalling our brothers and sisters from Earth. I have a few more things to do here, and then I must return to the Mizunese to try and secure their help." He was preoccupied with worry for Fia, and he hoped it didn't show.

"I will ready the soldiers for the attack in the south, sire."

"Let's hope it doesn't come to that." But he knew, without doubt, that it would.

They clasped arms, and Alexander left, turning through the long corridors of Ehnalia. A cool breeze passed through the archways, and he longed to hear the sounds of his mother and father's voices echoing through the hallways.

In all his years of passing through the windows to Earth, helping lost souls and watching those left behind, he'd never felt a connection with any of them, until now. He stopped at the balcony outside what were once his father's chambers, where they had spent countless nights standing side by side, watching the sky spirits. Their nightly performance never ceased to be spectacular, enveloping Alythia in a display of lilac and turquoise and delicate chimes, revealing milky star constellations and far beneath them, the glittering lights of Ohinyan.

His thoughts drifted to the night his mother had died. His father had said nothing all day, until their nightly ritual on the balcony. "Your mother is... She was a wild one, the kind you would follow to the edges of Ohinyan and back. She was, and always will be, my heart, my home." They had stood for a moment in silence, engulfed in the display of the sky spirits. "I hope one day that you know love like that."

Alexander glanced up towards the garden at the uppermost peak of Ehnalia where his parents were buried, bathed in the light of the sun all through the day and beneath the glittering of the stars and the sky spirits each night.

I hope one day that you know love like that. His father's words followed him as he made his way to the library to search for Gnossaan, his father's sage and Alythia's most honoured scholar. He hastened his steps as he thought of Fia, knowing every moment away from her could mean she was walking closer into a trap.

"Gnossaan," he called out, not wanting to waste any more time. The angel appeared from behind a row of bookcases. His grey wings, speckled with black, matched his scruffy beard.

"Come to learn more of the fate of Ohinyan, Alexander?" Gnossaan was not one for small talk.

"Tell me all you and the other scholars have learned in my absence about our dying sun."

"We have evidence so far of its effects on our world. I cannot say for certain when the windows between Ohinyan and Earth will close, but it would not be wise for our brothers and sisters to continue to journey to Earth without knowing the risk they place on their lives. Should a window close as they are passing through…" The old man fell silent for a moment, and Alexander recalled Malachai's report of an angel missing part of a wing. "There is more. Reports have made way to us of dark happenings, strange things all over Ohinyan. I am concerned that it is—"

"Erebus," Alexander finished.

Gnossaan paced up and down, his wings flickering behind him. "How can this be?" he asked, tugging at his beard. "There is so little information about him in the archives. I must go at once to continue my search…"

"Wait, Gnossaan. I have one more thing to ask of you. I am travelling with someone who needs to return to Earth. She is from Earth, that is, and fell through a window."

The old angel shifted from one foot to the other, flexing his wings, as he considered Alexander's words.

"Gnossaan, I cannot stress the urgency of this matter. The windows are already unstable, and time is of the essence. How can I return her to Earth?" Alexander ran his fingers through his hair, ignoring the knots tugging at his stomach and realising that what he wanted most was for Gnossaan to tell him it wasn't possible for Fia to return.

"Well sire, I have never known of any other than the angels passing freely between worlds," Gnossaan said, his wings flickering.

"I see." Alexander balled his fists at his sides, as he fought back the rise of anger in his chest. Red hovered in his vision, and he willed himself not to lose his temper. He'd failed her.

Trapped her here. *You could have prevented this.*

Gnossaan mumbled before clearing his throat. "The windows are unstable, sire. It would not be prudent for you to travel back to Earth again until the third sun is here." His gaze remained fixed to the floor.

"From what I've learned so far, we don't even know if that's going to happen at all," Alexander said, as calmly as he could manage.

Gnossaan's eyes finally met his, wide and glassy. "It will happen. It is already in motion. The days grow shorter, colder. The creatures of this world are behaving more and more unusually. The very air is tinged with the sun's death. Can you not feel it, sire?"

Alexander *had* seen and felt it, even in the last few days. Gnossaan was right—it wasn't *if* the sun would die, but *when*. How long would they have to live in darkness?

"As you learn more, I wish to be updated. I'll leave instructions with Jarl of where to reach me," Alexander said.

"Of course, sire. I want you to know that—"

"Brother!"

Alexander turned to greet his sister. When he looked back, the old angel was gone.

"Mira," Alexander said, embracing his sister briefly. "I haven't much time, but it would be good to walk together. Tell me, are my nieces well?" he asked, his anger fading.

"Lina and Anya are well. They've missed you dearly, as have I." Her words were rushed. "Runa tells me you've met someone," she said, her eyes glistening with excitement.

Alexander told his sister about Fia, as they returned to the main hall. He spoke of his concerns about returning her safely to Earth and of his duty to the angels. "She must go home, until it's safer here, and maybe then, I don't know…"

He rubbed his jaw as he replayed Gnossaan's words over and over. Something about what he'd said didn't add up, but Alexander pushed the concern to the back of his mind. Gnossaan was loyal, wasn't he? He'd served his father for years. "Gnossaan knows of no way to return Fia to Earth."

Mira turned to face him. "You've been searching for a way to get her back, but have you asked her what she wants to do?" She didn't wait for a response. "I thought not." She placed a hand on her brother's cheek. "Alexander, if you have found someone, do not let them go. Wait here."

Alexander tried to protest, but Mira had already left him, flying down the corridor to her chambers. He looked out over the lush expanse of Alythia as he waited, to the horizon where the land dropped off to nothing but sky beyond. Within moments, Mira returned with a small, carved cuff.

"This was mother's," Mira said, placing it in Alexander's hands.

"Mira, I can't."

"Mother and father would want you to have it, please. It doesn't need to mean a union—it can mean whatever you want it to, but I think it is important she has it, whether you decide to help her to return to Earth or… here." Mira folded his hands around the little cuff. "Now," she said, kissing him on the cheek. "I know you must go. It seems to me you've found something worth holding onto. Something you've never found here." She smiled and flew back towards her chambers.

Alexander tucked the cuff away in his quiver and made his way to meet Runa and Malachai for their journey back to Mizune. As he reached the platform, dozens of angels were returning in groups of three or four, recalled from Earth following Jarl's orders. As he greeted them, he searched their eyes and their faces, as if there might be some tell-tale sign of another Makya informant.

Oren was not the first to betray the angels in their history, and he would not be the last. But there was still their duty to Earth, a duty that had to be upheld no matter the cost. Alexander shook hands with each angel that landed, as he had seen his father do so many times before.

"We cannot abandon the people of Earth," Alexander said to Jarl as the general joined him. He still wore his helmet, and his armour was polished to a shine. Alexander didn't think he'd ever seen a spot of dirt on it.

"What would you have me do, sire?"

"I cannot expect any angel to leave Ohinyan without knowing the full extent of the situation. Alert everyone and request that a few come forward who will be willing to remain on Earth for an extended period. Anyone with a family, send them home," Alexander commanded. He didn't like it, but at least they would be given the choice. He hoped a few would decide to remain on Earth for the sake of the humans, and for the angel's safety, but he could not guarantee it.

They were joined by more soldiers who shared their reports of what they had seen across Ohinyan. The more Alexander learned, the less he believed in the Makya council's intervention, or whether they were even involved at all.

Runa and Malachai joined them to add their own reports. Runa described all of the destroyed sites she had visited before joining Alexander and the others in Ikothea.

"We need to be absolutely certain this is the council's doing," Alexander announced. "I had thought more of Par than this. We must be certain, or it could cost many lives."

"No angels have been sent to Nadar since your father's death, as per your request. I agree with your decision to send no more," Jarl replied.

Alexander nodded. "But we do need to determine whether there is any civil unrest. The sheer volume of destruction points to a unified front, but the manner with which the attacks have been carried out… the locations… it does not seem like Par's doing to me."

Jarl nodded. "You're right, sire, their attack pattern indicates little or no strategy. It has been random, but what of the council? How do you wish me to proceed?"

"We'll have to let them come to us. I can't risk sending any more angels," Alexander replied, and conversation broke out amongst the soldiers once more.

"Runa," Alexander began whilst the others talked amongst themselves. "There are no words that hold enough meaning.

You should stay here with your family, if you wish."

"Thank you," Runa replied softly. "But I would not wish to be anywhere other than at Malachai's side if the Makya come to Mizune."

"Let's hope it doesn't come to that. It's time for us to go."

As they returned to Mizune, the sun disappearing beyond the horizon, Alexander thought of the little cuff his sister had given him, and of the life he could have had with Fia had things been different. But none of it mattered. By now, the witches would have told her of a way to get back to Earth, and he would not be able to follow her.

CHAPTER TWENTY-THREE

FIA

Fia followed Ilawu, the Mizunese guardsman, who had been assigned to lead her to the witches' coven, away from Mizune and deep into the forest. The ice had melted in patches, revealing bare earth and tufts of yellow grass. They'd travelled since dawn on sledges pulled by huskies as large as stags. On all fours, they towered above Fia's head, and their excited howls echoed through the silent forest. Now and then, she could make out words of exhilaration from the dogs, and after a while, she found herself listening eagerly to their excited snippets of conversation.

The cool, crisp air began to dissipate as they went deeper, and the temperature had risen slightly. Ilawu stopped after what felt like hours, stepping aside to let Fia pass.

"This is my limit," he said, turning to Fia. "None from Mizune will enter this forest."

A wave of panic washed over her. "I understand. Yahto made that clear. Thank you for taking me this far." She'd argued with Alexander to let her go without him. Pleaded, even. Now it felt like a hot-headed mistake. She straightened her backpack and adjusted her bow neatly across it. *You can do this.*

Fia gave a faint smile before Ilawu turned back, taking both sledges and huskies with him. For just a moment, she was reminded of crisp winters back in London. *Just how much of our worlds are alike?* She thought of the histories of Earth, of its myths and legends. How much of that had originated from Ohinyan? There was so much to learn here, as life unfolded differently in this world.

She played with the little bird charm on her wrist as her thoughts drifted to Alexander and of returning to Earth without him. She rested against a tree to calm her breathing. It wasn't the walking: it was the thought of losing him. *You admitted it to Altair already. You don't want to go back.* But she had no way of protecting herself from Erebus. What if his whispers corrupted her like they had so many others?

"What would you do, Soph?" she whispered to nothing but trees.

Fia walked on through the eerie quiet of the forest and dripping leaves, until she recognised the vibrant forest of Noor's first illusion back on the airship. The witch's home.

Pillow-like grass swept across the forest bed, and in every gap stood swathes of giant, bell-shaped flowers with azure and fuchsia blooms. Moss-covered tree trunks stretched upwards beyond sight, and from them hung wisps of glittering leaves.

Hues of lilac and crimson, cyan and vermillion surrounded her; the trees and the plants were awash with vibrancy. She reached for the little black flower she carried around her neck as if it were a beacon to guide her and held it tightly in her palm.

Fia had expected to see many witches here, but instead she saw only one approaching through the trees. She looked much older than Noor, but not as old as Altair. But here, Fia knew that could mean anything. The witch was as tall as Noor and wore a similar silver circlet, resting neatly on her ashen hair.

"You hold the dahlia of the Lady Noor. Come, child," the old woman said. Her eyes reflected the colours of the forest as she approached, before settling into a beautiful violet.

Fia hesitantly stepped forward, and the black obsidian unfolded into a real flower in the palm of her hand. The witch reached out and picked it up with care, closing her eyes as she did so. She drew in a deep breath and returned it to Fia's hand, closing her fingers around it. When she let go, it was a stone again. Fia blinked at her palm, wondering if she'd imagined it.

"Welcome, Fia," said the witch. "I am Kharsee, friend of the Lady Noor. We have been waiting for you."

"Is Noor—is she alive?" *Please be alive, please be alive.*

Kharsee smiled. "Yes, alive and very well, I am pleased to report. She gave you this dahlia with good reason. We do not let just any stranger into our forest."

Fia resisted the urge to pump her first in the air, but didn't stop the grin she felt spreading across her face.

Noor is alive.

"Now, I am sure you have many questions, which I will try my best to answer, but first you must tell me everything—from your arrival in to Ohinyan, to now." She guided Fia to a seating area covered in moss, set down amongst the flowers and trees of the forest. In the centre, a small fire crackled into life as they approached.

Fia began with the cemetery in London. It felt like a lifetime ago. She described how she and Noor had been attacked when they'd set out for the nearby coven. She spoke of the creatures she could understand, and the absurdity of it all, omitting the part where she could hear Erebus. She didn't doubt how loosely he might interpret the meaning of *friend*, but she was certain it would extend to any of her new acquaintances.

She finished her explanation and slumped down into the moss, finally grasping the distance she'd travelled, and how far she'd come since arriving in Ohinyan.

"Very well," Kharsee finally said. She'd been silent, listening to Fia carefully. "Now, what do you wish to ask me?"

Fia let out a low whistle and rolled the little bird charm between her fingers. "Noor, will she be safe? What about Ohinyan and Erebus? What will happen to the sun, and how can I help with any of this?" Her words tumbled on top of each other.

Kharsee smiled, wrapping her cape tightly around herself. "I will answer as many questions as time permits. But first, I owe you an apology, on behalf of the witches. We should not have asked Alexander to retrieve you. It was... *short sighted* of us. A distant relative of yours, Talina, was a member of the coven Noor first tried to take you to."

A *relative*... She was related to the witches of Ohinyan? Fia knew so little of her family history—there was no one left to ask. She waited for Kharsee to continue.

"Talina fell in love with an angel when she was young. He showed her a window to Earth, taught her how to walk through, and together they would heal the dying and save the lives of those that were almost lost. But when her coven found out what she was doing..."

Fia watched the fire, afraid of what was coming.

"You must understand, Fia," Kharsee said. "Long ago, that same coven worshipped Erebus and did not accept the angels' dominion over our world. Erebus despises angels, so for Talina to be *involved* with one of them... Her coven tricked them, trapped Talina and her lover and burned the angel alive. Talina was banished to Earth, forbidden to return, or she would receive the same fate."

Burned the angel alive. Fia looked away from the fire. The thought of burning wings made her stomach turn.

"So you see, Fia, you are a child of Ohinyan. We knew where to find you because we have watched Talina and her blood line since she left this world. This knowledge has not been shared with the angels."

A child of Ohinyan.

"Was Talina like me? Could she… talk to creatures?" Fia asked.

"She was a loquere, yes. Like Talina, you have a gift. And like Talina, you can wander freely between worlds."

Something knotted inside of Fia. She stared blankly at Kharsee, shock coursing through her. "What?"

Kharsee was quiet, as if she were waiting for her words to sink in.

"So Alexander just has to fly me back through? That's it?" Fia asked impatiently and felt the knot grow tighter. Alexander had escorted her around what felt like half of Ohinyan for this. *This.* So much time wasted, when there was so much else for him to attend to. She pushed the thought away.

"Yes, child. For you alone, that is all it would take."

"Can all witches travel to Earth?" Fia wondered if Noor had been to Earth, and what she might have thought of it.

"No," Kharsee said. "There are very few remaining who can. It is a closely guarded secret, one that has been hidden from the angels, even amongst other witches. But as with many of the other myths and histories of Earth, all Earth witches once came from Ohinyan, so we know Talina was not the first to cross over."

Secrets from the angels, there was so much to Ohinyan she didn't understand. "Cross over?" Fia asked.

"Our worlds seem to be slightly out of alignment with each other, the material plane of your world sits higher than ours, which is why all the windows here seem to be in the sky." Kharsee reached for a stick from the fire and began to draw in the ashes around it. "There are many worlds, and ours are just two of them. But there are two planes of existence or two realms. That of spirit and that of matter. All worlds, like Ohinyan and Earth, are connected by both physical matter and the spiritual realm that encompasses them." As she spoke, she drew interlinking circles encompassed by a larger one, her violet eyes reflecting the firelight. "We are made up of both matter and spirit. And when we die, our body—that which is matter, remains with Ohinyan—or in your case, with Earth. Our spirit becomes part of the spiritual realm." The witch drew a figure of eight for Ohinyan and around it a circle with a cross in it for the Earth.

Fia leaned onto her knees for a closer look. "We have these symbols, too. This one represents infinity. And this one represents the Earth, with its equator and meridian."

"And that is where they differ. The ends of each line represent the four elements: fire, air, water, earth. The circle around it represents the fifth element, aether. Aether is what fills the universe… it is the travelling of light and gravity, or of worlds. Some say that the spiritual realm resides in the aether," Kharsee continued.

"And the sun affects the elements, so the dying sun will affect the aether, too?" Fia asked, pushing herself to her feet.

Kharsee nodded.

Fia chewed her lip and paced, piecing everything together.

"The windows between Earth and Ohinyan, what will happen to them?"

"They are becoming unstable, more unstable with each passing day. They may even shut completely."

A quiet whistle escaped from Fia. "But not permanently?"

"We do not yet know." Kharsee shook her head and threw the stick into the flames.

Fia followed the trail of embers as they flickered up into the air. "So angels won't be able to travel to and from Earth?" She thought of Sophie, alone and waiting, with no angel to come for her, and countless others like her.

"That is what we think, but we cannot be certain. Do you know the history of the angels?"

"I know a little," Fia replied, settling back down into the moss. She'd lost all sense of time. The light was strange beneath the canopy, and the colourful foliage cast long shadows in the firelight.

Kharsee smiled. "Ah, but do you know how they came to be?" Her violet eyes sparkled. "Light is born from darkness, and so the two are interwoven. At the very beginning of time, a phoenix appeared in the aether." Kharsee threw something onto the fire, just as Altair had done on Fia's first night in Ohinyan.

She thought of her kickboxing club motto as the flames turned into a phoenix, wandering alone in the aether. *I shall rise again.*

"It spent many days in darkness, searching for others. The darkness had a name, *Ahriman*, and he would whisper to the phoenix, taunting it in the empty void of the aether."

The flames blackened, and a swirling cloud of darkness whispered incomprehensible jeers and taunts. "In the loneliness of the darkness, the phoenix bore two children: a winged son, who could command the air at his will, and a daughter encased in flames. They were to be a beacon of light in the darkness. Together, they were a symbol of limitless light and hope."

"They were siblings? An angel and a Makya?"

"Yes, child, they were, once. But as light is born from darkness, so to darkness it can return. And that is what happened with the Makya. The boy, Gabriel, was too swift in flight to be caught by Ahriman's heckles. He used the winds to carry himself to safety, but the girl, Terah, she could not escape. Without her brother, Ahriman's darkness consumed her and in the embrace of darkness, she became the fire mother."

A Makya woman appeared in the fire, surrounded by a cloak of darkness. Her hair was the same colour as Fia's, but her eyes glowed crimson.

"Over time, Ahriman nurtured Terah's gifts, and she looked to him as a father. The phoenix thought she had lost her daughter forever, unable to see that love had grown in the darkness. Together, Gabriel and the phoenix fought Ahriman whilst the fire mother watched and wept. Torn between darkness and light, she became too tormented to help." The fire swirled with darkness and light and flashes of orange and gold.

Fia's cheeks warmed as the fire intensified, and the light obliterated the darkness.

"Eventually, light won, and Ahriman was defeated. But just as the phoenix bore children, Ahriman bore a son. Erebus. The fire mother was devastated by the loss of Ahriman and begged her mother not to destroy Erebus. The phoenix realised that the darkness was now part of her daughter and feared for her life if Erebus was destroyed, too, so she trapped Erebus inside the dust from a dead star, forming Ohinyan around that dust and imprisoning him in darkness. Our sun restrains him, enveloping his prison in light."

The fire turned black once more, swirling into a sphere as a planet formed around it. *Ohinyan.*

"And when the sun dies?" Fia asked, her heartbeat pounding in her chest. *Fire, air, water, earth.* She pressed her fingers into the moss, as if she might feel the energy Ohinyan contained.

"Erebus is planning his escape. His whispers have already been heard across Ohinyan. As the sun grows weaker, Erebus grows stronger."

"And the Mizunese grow weaker, too." Fia thought of Yahto's demonstration just a few days before. "What about the angels, the other creatures in Ohinyan?"

Kharsee shook her head. "This I do not know. There are many gaps in my knowledge, but I have told you all that I can. When the sun dies, a time of darkness will fall over Ohinyan, and from it, we can only hope will come a time of light."

Fia counted her breaths. What if Erebus didn't need the sun to die in order to escape, what if he only needed it to be weak? Her head spun. "How do you know all of this? Why don't the angels have this information?" It seemed strange that the protectors of Ohinyan knew so little.

"How does the grass know how to grow? I know these things through time and through living, as living things do. Witches do not share their knowledge so readily with others." Kharsee smiled. "As for the Lady Noor, she makes her way here via the Makya airship. They plan to bring war, and they plan to use you, Fia."

"Me?" Fia felt the familiar tightening in her chest, a lump in her throat that made it hard to swallow.

Kharsee nodded. "Lorn, the Makya leading the army, has a history with Alexander."

Fia cleared her throat. "Yes, one of the angels told me. Lorn had proposed a union to Alexander and he rejected her." Her chest fluttered at the words *he rejected her,* and she instantly felt guilty for it.

"Something like that. She told Alexander they could rule over all of Ohinyan, the great fire mother and the descendant of Gabriel. She felt their power could be overruled by none." Kharsee held her hands out to the fire, and in the flames Fia saw a Makya woman with long red hair, brighter than her own.

"But Lorn wanted power, destruction, and darkness. Alexander represents everything that is light in Ohinyan, and he wanted nothing to do with her. Lorn never quite got over the rejection so it seems. She wishes to capture you in order to force Alexander and the angels into revealing the location of Alythia," Kharsee finished, and the image of Lorn faded.

"But they'll never reach it." It was a wish, more than anything.

"In these changing times, who knows what can happen?"

Fia shuddered at the thought. An army of Makya were on its way because of her. She thought of the children throwing snowballs back in Mizune, of the way Altair's face lit up when he spoke with his son, and she clenched her fists into balls at her sides.

"Lorn will be coming here soon, and we must *all* prepare to fight," Kharsee added.

"We tried to tell the Mizunese, but they won't help us." Fia poked a stick into the fire. It was a great risk, even she could understand that.

"Yes, I imagine you will need more than words to convince them. They have many reasons not to help. Painful memories and fear, fear that holds them back." Kharsee paused. "But for a loquere such as yourself, I think you might find other ways to convince them. Do not think it strange, child. It is a gift."

"Like what? And why now, why never before in my life could I speak to animals? I just thought I was going crazy, back on Earth, hearing all those voices."

Kharsee shrugged. "There are many things that could have awoken this gift within you. But it has been with you since birth. Perhaps passing through the aether has heightened your gift. But it was always there, and now it always will be."

"Even if I return to Earth?" Fia couldn't bring herself to imagine it, wandering around London and talking to pigeons and squirrels, alone.

"Even if you return to Earth." Kharsee nodded. "Embrace it. It sounds like you have already learned to listen well in the time you have been in Ohinyan. Nurture your skill, don't neglect it. You will need it in the days ahead."

Fia wanted to ask more, but Kharsee rose to her feet, stepping out of the mossy seating area and away from the fire. "Do not be alarmed," she said softly.

Through the thick canopy and colourful foliage came a great black bird, its wings outstretched as it flew fast and low to the ground. It came to a standstill a few feet away from Kharsee, dropping a piece of parchment from its beak. Kharsee knelt before it in a bow as she collected the parchment. "Thank you," she murmured as the bird flew away.

"You can talk to the Shadows?" Fia asked, on her feet now, too.

"Not quite," Kharsee began, "illusions are not a very effective means of communication. Your friends will be expecting you soon." She smiled.

"Countess, the others are waiting for you." A man appeared through the trees. He spoke quietly, but Fia didn't miss the urgency in his voice.

"Very well," Kharsee replied. "Come here, child, it is time for you to return to your friends."

"How? And what will happen to Noor and the airship? Are you coming to Mizune? Will you fight with us? Will I serve whatever purpose it is that you needed me for?" Her questions tumbled over themselves, as they had before.

The old witch opened Fia's palm, placing in it a small violet stone, shaped like a tiny rose bud. "Keep this, alongside Noor's. It might be of use in the times ahead."

Fia gazed down at the little stone. She didn't know what to say.

"Noor will be fine, and you and I will see each other again soon. There is a valley not far from here. You'll find your way back to your friends from there." The witch raised a slender hand to point.

"But I—"

"You may ask more questions when we next meet." Kharsee smiled and disappeared into the shadows of the forest.

CHAPTER TWENTY-FOUR

NOOR

If the Lady Noor had not already known of the airship's position by posing as a Makya guard, she would have known from the excited buzz filling the corridors that they were nearing the south, towards Mizune, her home, Fia, and the others.

The ship was vast. When she'd arrived, she thought there were less than a hundred passengers on board, but now she knew there were several times that. What was worse, they had been joined by the Makya's latest recruits and three smaller ships, and from what she had heard of Lorn's discussions with her brothers, the passengers numbered a small army.

Noor had discovered as much of the layout of the ship as she could, and in doing so she had learned about many of its inhabitants. The most abhorrent of which were a large group of mercenaries originating from the foothills of Ortesh, below the bleak mountain range bordering the Nord's country. They looked similar to the Nords when in human form, but they were rougher around the edges. Their big, brutish arms and necks, calloused hands, and scarred faces singled them out at mealtimes. Amongst them was the odd Asharian, and some others Noor did not recognise. Collectively, they seemed to think they would bring some extraordinary talent to the battlefield, speaking loudly of their past successes to whomever would listen.

She considered taking a blade to each of them as she walked past a doorway where they dined, snippets of their drunken tales escaping into the corridor, but thought better of it and let her hands fall loosely at her sides.

"I will crush the angels in my bare hands, one by one," the largest man said. He sat at the head of a table, a group of six or so accompanying him. His head was shaved, and a black tattoo ran down the side of his neck in a language Noor couldn't read. When he banged his fist on the table, it sent wine splashing from their mugs. His tattooed arms were bare, and above tattered brown trousers, he wore a grey, rotten vest. Their weapons were crude, mostly battle axes, daggers, and maces, and Noor detested the way they spoke—forever goading each other and ready for war.

"We'll take down the bloody lot of 'em," one replied, caressing his axe and polishing its blade until he could see himself in its reflection. "It'll be our greatest glory."

Noor shook her head in disgust and continued down the corridor. The Makya had brought some of the Senkahs on board with them, too, and despite how dark they had become, it pained Noor to see them in cages along the hold of the ship. They were wild things, after all.

A large group of them paced in their cells, piercing eyes

gazing back at her—at the Lady Noor, not the face of the Makya guard she hid behind.

She'd encountered them on several occasions in her lifetime, none of which had been pleasant, but to Noor these particular Senkahs seemed a shadow of their former selves, tormented and taunted. Could Erebus have reached these poor creatures, too?

Beyond the hold and into the loading bay was the largest of all the creatures Lorn and her brothers had procured for their attack in the south. Its roars could be heard throughout the airship, night and day. Layers of great chains were wrapped around it to prevent it from banging its heavy hooves against the floor.

When they had first captured it, the creature dented panels and buckled the floor of the loading bay, preventing the hatch from closing properly. It took several Makya guards to hold it in place at all times, even with chains. Their flames only enraged it further, and nothing seemed to penetrate its dense, leathery skin.

Noor entered the loading bay, filling it with images of forest, only to be seen by the creature. It slumped, submissive, onto the loading bay floor. A wave of nausea pressed at Noor's temples as the effort of creating so many illusions began to take its toll.

"I thought it would never rest," one guard muttered, still struggling with the chains, as the creature lay quiet. Najins were rare. Their great size meant that they had few predators—except for those that wished to keep them captive to demolish buildings and to haul rock from quarries. Noor examined its horned face and great, black eyes as she walked past. Like two black spheres of onyx, even from a distance, she could see her reflection in them—her true reflection. For like the Senkahs, this beast was far more intelligent than the Makya. It was too large an illusion to maintain for long, and as soon as she was out of the loading bay, the wild roars of the beast filled the ship once more, and Noor breathed deeply through her nose to steady herself.

"Hold it down," a guard cried out behind her.

Noor was familiar with much of the airship, its layout, its inhabitants, its hiding places, but she'd never accessed the control room, and this she sorely needed. She made her way to the great hall to take her place as guard, resisting the urge to run to her hiding place above the loading bay. Instead, she focused on her breathing. It was becoming too difficult to maintain her disguise, but she could not risk revealing herself yet. *Not much longer now.*

Inside the hall, Lorn and Jerum were locked in a heated debate.

"We are two, three days away at most," Jerum said. "Can you be certain the girl will still be with them in the south?"

Lorn nodded. "I'm told Alexander is in Mizune, and I know he will not leave her side."

Noor watched Lorn as she spoke, tightening her fingers around the edge of her throne until her knuckles were white.

"They won't know what hit them," Lorn continued.

"It would be naive of us to think they do not know we are coming, sister," Jerum replied. Raiaan remained silent. Noor had rarely heard him speak in the last few days. A trickle of sweat rolled down from her hairline to the base of her neck. *Two, three days away at most. You're so close.*

"They may know of our coming, but they won't know of our numbers, or that we have the Senkahs and the Najin at our command," Lorn replied, small sparks cascading from her hands down the side of her throne.

At your command? Noor stifled a laugh. Watching Lorn attempt to control the beasts would be entertaining.

"And what of the mercenaries?" Raiaan asked.

A low, guttural sound emanated from the back of Lorn's throat.

"They will be our frontline," Jerum added. "We will use the valley. You there, do you have the maps my sister requested?" He sat on the largest throne, the buckles of his coat reflecting the firelight from the dented urn.

Noor nodded and laid large parchment maps out on the table before them. She stepped back just in time to conceal the shaking of her exhausted arms—it took all her concentration to stand and listen whilst maintaining her disguise. Weak as Noor was, Lorn and her brothers did not seem to notice.

"The valley?" Lorn asked. "Why not Mizune, and take them whilst they sleep?"

"Because the Mizunese defences are tenfold that of what we witnessed in Ikothea—we would be too great a target.

Better to draw them out, away from the town, and to a location big enough for us to land the ships," Jerum said. "We will come in low, flanked by the three smaller ships," he continued, pointing to various positions on the map. "The mercenaries and the Aurelli can take the pods down first before we touch down."

"And how do you intend on getting the Aurelli to fight?" Raiaan asked. He was leaning over the table, inspecting the maps.

"They will fight, or I will destroy what remains of their forest. It's that simple," Lorn replied.

"But—" Raiaan began to protest, but Jerum interrupted him with further plans. Lorn and Jerum bickered, and various revisions were made before they came upon a final agreement.

"We must inform the council of our progress," Raiaan added before they departed for the night.

Noor caught the look in his eyes and the tilt of his head as Lorn replied too quickly.

"I'll do it," she said.

"Really, sister, you do too much. It will be of no hindrance to me."

"No, no, I insist, dear brother." Lorn smiled, leaving the hall before he could object.

"Goodnight, brother," Jerum said. "Soon, we will have our victory, and the council will celebrate our success."

Raiaan was left alone to look over the maps.

"You," he murmured to Noor.

Noor looked to the door, calculating how far she could run before his flames would reach her.

"To whom are you loyal?" Raiaan asked her.

"Sir?" Noor replied, examining the expression on Raiaan's face. Where was this going? She had to be absolutely right about his character. If she had him wrong, it was all over.

"I said, to whom are you loyal?"

Noor swallowed hard. "To the council, sir."

Raiaan's expression changed, his shoulders relaxing. "Good, then I can trust you?"

Noor nodded.

"I need you to send a message to the council, to Par. Update them on our plans and find out if this matches up with their instructions for Lorn. Tell no one I asked you to do this. If you get caught, you are alone, understand?"

Noor nodded again. She'd been right about him, and trembled ever so slightly, relief and exhaustion weighing down on her.

"Do not be afraid, the council will come." Raiaan placed a hand on her shoulder, and for the first time, Noor could see how different he was to his twin. His eyes were the shade of autumn leaves, and the lines around them moved as he spoke, softening his expressions.

Without another word, he left the hall, leaving Noor alone. She slumped to the floor, dropping her façade. Not much longer now. She allowed herself a moment's rest before she was back on her feet and out the door as a Makya guard once more.

She used her Aurelli friends to send a message to the Makya council and doubted that Lorn had sent out any messages of her own via the other guards. When Noor could finally rest for the day, she dropped, exhausted and unshielded by her illusions into one of the rooms used only by the Aurelli, too tired to climb up to her usual spot.

Before she'd even taken off her boots, the distant roars of the Najin echoed throughout the airship. The scurrying footsteps of the Aurelli rallied around the doorway, a quiet warning. Noor came to her senses, slipping into the guise of one of the little feline creatures just as Lorn entered the room.

"Hush your gibberish," she demanded, sending handfuls of flames up the walls either side of her and outwards across the ceiling. The Aurelli ceased their scurrying, frozen in fear. Noor eyed Lorn carefully, whilst trying to mimic the movements of the Aurelli.

"Stupid, pathetic little creatures." Lorn looked down to where Noor sat slumped against a wall. "Pretend all you like, but I know you understand me well enough." Lorn sent sparks cascading around the room. "In a few days, we will land and when we do, you will fight whatever attacks us, or I will destroy what remains of your precious forest leaf by leaf. Understood?"

Lorn's retort was met with blank stares from the Aurelli. Her eyes blazed as she set fire to the nearest one. It shrieked and rolled to the ground, desperate to extinguish the flames engulfing its arms and legs. Noor rushed forwards with the others to help their friend.

"So we understand each other." Lorn laughed and made her way out of the room.

When Noor was sure it was safe, she slipped down the corridor disguised as the guard, following Lorn to her chambers.

"Why do you whisper to me from the shadows. Show yourself!" Lorn cried, followed by the familiar roar of the flames she projected from her fingertips.

Erebus. Noor shuddered as she thought of all the witches who could easily be coerced to follow a darker path.

The door to Lorn's chambers creaked open. "Oh, it's you again," Lorn said, her gaze rolling from Noor's face to somewhere lower. Her expression hardened. "You are to remain here until morning, unless another guard dismisses you."

Before Noor could utter a reply, the door was slammed shut in her face. *An entire night of this.* She considered her options. She'd have to steal whatever moments she could to drop her façade. Fortunately, the corridor was long and empty, and footsteps could be hard far before anyone would be able to see her. Noor stood tall, letting her illusion fade away whilst she remained alone, and settled in for a night of guard duty.

***

Footsteps echoed down the corridor, and for a sleepy moment Noor considered an illusion to make it seem as if she wasn't there. But that wouldn't do. She slipped back into her illusion of the guard.

"You are relieved," the Makya said as he approached.

"What time is it?" Noor asked. "I shouldn't leave my shift early," she added.

The guard smiled. "It's morning. Your shift is over."

Noor hesitated, listening for any sounds of Lorn moving around in her chambers. There were none. Good, perhaps she was still sleeping.

"Very well," Noor replied. She made her way back towards the loading bay, eager for the safety of her seedpod. Exhaustion coursed through her. *Not much longer now.*

Her route took her past the dining hall, where she hoped to pass by unnoticed.

"You there," one of the mercenaries called to her.

Noor clicked her tongue in disgust.

"Why don't you come and sit on my lap for a little bit?" the brute said.

Noor calculated the efficiency of throwing a dagger into his heart, and how many of them might fight her if she did. "I'm on duty," she replied through clenched teeth.

"I said, why don't you come and sit on my lap." He banged a fist to the table.

"Guard! Back to work." It was Raiaan. Noor was disappointed. She would have enjoyed a fight, even though she knew she would not have been able to risk it. Instead, she walked away, and Raiaan caught up with her a few moments later.

"Have you done as I instructed?" he asked, glancing left and right.

Noor gave the smallest incline of her head. "I will find you as soon as I hear from them." Her words were strained, but she'd hoped he would mistake it for intimidation.

Raiaan nodded and departed as quickly as he had arrived. Another guard walked past in the opposite direction, holding long sheets of metal. Aside from Lorn and her brothers, the other Makya on board seemed to have lost all sense of rank. None of them knew what they should be doing, or where they should be, except to wait for Lorn and her brothers to command them. It was why it had been so easy for her to follow Lorn around.

"Where are you going with those?" Noor asked with as much authority as she could muster.

"T-to the control room, er, ma'am," the Makya replied, confusion spreading across his face.

"I'll take those from here. You're needed in the loading bay with the Najin."

The guard hesitated.

"Now," Noor demanded, snatching the metal from the guard's arms, and then she walked off in the direction of the control room.

This had been the opportunity she was waiting for. A single guard stood watch at the control room door. She held her head high and walked straight towards him, waiting for the guard to open it without saying a word. If she looked like she knew what she was doing, no one would question her. It worked.

Inside the control room, a handful of engineers operated the airship. Beyond the bridge, Noor could see out the windows to the sky beyond—white cotton clouds broke every now and then to reveal a pink and lilac sky. She surveyed as much of the room as she could, its layout, its instruments, and where the engineers were positioned.

"Place them over there," one of them said to her without looking up. Noor rested the metal on a workbench. "Well, don't just stand there, guard, that will be all."

Noor nodded and left almost as quickly as she had come. But it was enough. She had exactly what she needed.

On her way back to the loading bay, a group of Aurelli adeptly slipped her a message on fine paper with a dark, black seal. It was from the Makya council. She tucked it into her clothing before making her way to the great hall to find Raiaan.

He was speaking with his brother when she arrived, so she relieved another guard and took his place, waiting for the brothers to finish. It was time for her to find out where Raiaan's allegiances sat. Once he was alone, she waited patiently for him to address her.

"You have news?" he murmured.

She nodded, handing him the sealed letter.

"You haven't read it?" Raiaan asked.

Noor shook her head. She didn't need to.

Raiaan read the letter, his eyes flickering across the page. "She *lied*." He crumpled up the paper, and with a gentle rush of heat, it smouldered into ashes. "She lied," he said again, and Noor saw his eyes darken for the first time.

She resisted the urge to step back. If he thought she was Makya, it would not be a problem for him to have outbursts like his sister often did, but Noor would not be safe from such a display of anger.

Raiaan, however, clearly had more control than Lorn. "Do not speak of this to anyone, do you understand?"

Noor nodded. "Yes, sir."

"We will wait for further news from the council before we act. Thank you," he said, without looking at Noor, and left the hall.

Noor breathed a little sigh of relief. She gave herself only a moment's respite from her illusion before making her way to the loading bay. It was time to call upon the coven.

CHAPTER TWENTY-FIVE

FIA

Fia was lost. She knew she'd travelled south with Ilawu, but the landscape had changed so much she'd lost her bearings.

The sun was high, obscured by great trees with glowing, tendril-like vines. She tried climbing the one closest to her to breach the canopy, but the vines were slippery, and she couldn't get a strong enough grip.

She picked through everything Kharsee had told her. *A child of Ohinyan.* Was that why she could hear Erebus?

Anxiety twisted in her stomach but Fia ignored it. "Not far," she said to the empty forest. "Easy for you to say." She looked up once more to try and catch a glimpse of the sun through the dense canopy. It was strange how the forest still felt so light and bright despite the sun's absence. Little orbs of light drifted in the air like miniature stars, glittering and glistening with a warm yellow glow. But then they weren't just drifting like dust motes anymore; they were flying around her in a delicate swirl, whispering in excitement.

"This way," the little fireflies said. "This way!"

Fia didn't need to be told a third time. The glittering swarm circled around her once more before darting off and away through the forest, and she followed them just as swiftly as they had departed. She ran, stumbling after them, but the little specs of light wouldn't slow down. Fia ducked under branches and jumped over tree trunks, struggling to keep up with them.

Gasping for breath, she wasn't sure how much longer she could pursue them. And then, they stopped, just inches from her face. The forest dropped away before them, and the familiar cool air of Mizune hit Fia's lungs—only it wasn't Mizune in the valley below them.

The fireflies had brought Fia to a precipice. Behind her, the forest beckoned with a lush array of flora and warmth. Below, *far* below, was a glacial valley home to creatures the likes of which Fia had only read about in fairy tales. The largest travelled in herds, moving slowly and steadily like weary elephants. Their top half was like a giraffe's; long, elongated necks stretched skywards from a muscular body propped up by thick legs, and their dark fur was ragged and matted. They wandered along in large groups dotted around the valley, moving slowly as they munched their way through the foliage.

"Herbivores," Fia said to the fireflies, with a little air of relief.

"This way," they chirped, and Fia wondered if that was all they could say.

She thought of the phoenix, flying alone through the aether, and wondered what had become of it. She surveyed the rest of the valley. A glacial river ran down the mountain range to her right, but as the river travelled deeper, the snow gave way to gleaming blue pools of water and dark foliage amongst the alpine landscape. There were ruins, too. Huge stone structures stood with their insides exposed, clean and shiny like hollowed out bones, dotting throughout the valley in odd shapes and formations.

"*Fia...*"

She froze, drawing in cool breaths of air to calm herself. Not here, not now.

"*Fia...*" the voice whispered again. She counted her breaths and thought of Alexander.

"This way," the fireflies called as they swirled around her, and reminded her she wasn't alone. And then they were gone, darting over the edge of the precipice. She stepped forward and examined the descent. The little glowing orbs were smart. She could see a route down the rock edge, and warily began her descent, her hands grasping at rocks.

"This doesn't look as if it's going to end well," Fia whispered to the little speckles of light, wondering if they could understand her.

They cooed and called sounds of encouragement as she kept going, one foot steadily after another. By the time she'd reached halfway, her hands were cut and bleeding. She balanced herself against the edge as she ripped her spare shirt into strips, wrapping it around her palms. The cotton stained pink almost immediately, but it would have to do.

Kharsee had told her so much, but she felt like she knew so little. She was still no closer to understanding what she could do to help, but the witch had said she'd answer more questions when they next met. When would that be?

Fia could see more of the valley now, the path became less steep a little further below, and it looked like she might be able to walk rather than climb. The valley was full of life. High above, huge, dark, moth-like birds rested on the breeze and floated motionless on pockets of air. *The Shadows.* Her glittering companions urged her on so Fia continued.

Soon, she found she could walk upright amongst the rocks with care, making her way to level ground. The little fireflies swarmed around her, chirping in praise before drifting ahead, guiding her through the alpine landscape. Her feet crunched in crisp snow, and her breath hung in the cool air. She fastened her coat and pulled up her hood, glancing up at the rock face as hundreds of angels passed by her in the skies above. The absence of Alexander's presence had been an ache in her side all day, and she scanned the angels for any sign of him.

She couldn't risk calling out for help. If Oren had betrayed his kind, who knew how many others had, too?

The valley was difficult to navigate. The herds of giant giraffes, although slow, moved in large groups and timing the run between their feet was tricky. The smallest, a baby, no larger than a double decker bus, moved slowly between the legs of its elders.

A path through the creatures led to an icy blue lake and was her best chance to keep going without being trodden on. She dropped down to the edge of the water. The lake was vast, and a biting breeze swept across her face. The little orbs of light chirped frantically, flurrying around her.

"This way, this way," they cried.

"I need to rest a moment," Fia said, slumping at the water's edge and unwrapping her bandaged hands. She gazed into the blue, cleaning away the crusted blood and drinking the crisp water. It was so clear she could see herself, the sky, and the little fireflies reflected as if she gazed into a mirror. It was mesmerising. Her reflection rippled, and Fia saw herself back in her flat in London. She watched, captivated, as Alexander joined her in the watery scene, wearing nothing but a pair of faded jeans and chopping tomatoes for their dinner. Fia ran a hand through the water, shaking her head. She was more exhausted than she realised. But the scene remained. She watched herself rinsing a spatula in her kitchen sink, and Alexander reaching in for an embrace as he dropped a colander on the countertop.

The fireflies fluttered around her head. "This way, this way. Hurry!"

The water began to ripple fiercely, distorting the image of her and Alexander. Fia looked up as the little glittering swarm frenzied around her.

"Hurry, hurry, hurry!" they cried, but it was too late. Surging towards her and towering over the water loomed a giant serpent, covered in scales and rotting flesh.

Fia leapt up, her little bow drawn, an arrow nocked and ready. As the thing hurtled closer, she doubted her arrows would have any effect against it. She ran back as far as she could, hoping the creature would be water bound, but she was backed up against a rock edge and still within its reach.

The fireflies hovered above her head. "Hurry, hurry, hurry!"

"Wait!" Fia cried out.

The thing stopped far away from her in the water, but it was so vast that its neck leered upwards and outwards, its dripping head metres away from hers. It sent a surge of ice-cold water towards the shore that came crashing down over Fia as it stopped abruptly at her call. From this distance, she could see its scaly skin was torn and broken all over, barnacles and shelled creatures feeding off its wounds. She retched at the thought of the water she'd drunk just moments before.

Its eyes were like a lizard's, and it had a long muzzle of a mouth full of large, sharp teeth.

"It speaks," the thing said, eyeing Fia. Bits of fish and bone spattered from its mouth in a gust of wet, warm breath.

"I do. My name is Fia." She tried her best to conceal her tremble as she spoke. She stepped to her right, searching for a way up the wet rocks, whilst holding an arrow outstretched on the tip of her bow. If she slipped…

"Mmmhmmmm, Fia." It spoke as if it was tasting her name and checking the size and the shape of it. "I have not seen your kind here in some time. And certainly not one I could converse with. No matter, I've no doubt you'll make a better meal than you do conversation."

"But wait," Fia cried and took another step to her right. The fireflies circled above her, squealing incomprehensible cries of panic. "You… you haven't told me your name, or how you came to be here?"

The thing threw its head skywards and laughed, a booming, scraping sound that sent water and creatures soaring from its skin. It blinked, two eyelids touching over the glassy whites of its eyes and meeting at the inky grey pupils in the centre.

"I have not spoken my name in many moons, nor would I wish for you to know it. I know what you are doing, and I do not care for it." It reared up at the last word, throwing more cold water towards Fia, like a thousand icy shards.

She didn't hesitate; she aimed arrow after arrow at its eyes, hoping one would hit. The creature wailed as one pierced the corner of its eye where all the others had bounced off.

"You will suffer for this," it cried. "I shall savour every limb…" It lunged towards Fia, and she leapt across the wet rocks, continuing her attack. The thing laughed again as it snapped its great jaw towards her, missing her by inches.

"Enough, Behrog!" a deep voice called from above Fia. The fireflies were nowhere to be seen. Maybe they'd fled in fear—she didn't blame them—or worse, had been washed away by the water. Air rushed around her, and she wished for an angel to touch down beside her. Whatever it was that had spoken, she was grateful for its timing, but didn't dare take her gaze away from the monster trying to make a meal of her.

"Arion," the creature in the water shouted. "This is no concern of yours!"

A great winged horse, as large as the creature's head, and as shaggy and rugged-looking as the giraffe-like animals in the valley beyond, landed on the glacial shore between Fia and the monster.

"Leave here, Behrog, or I shall have the waters boil and cook you where you sit."

"But it *wounded* me, Arion..."

"*After* you attacked. It tried to reason with you, did it not? Now go. Leave this place." The horse rose, beating its wings with such a force that the serpent was shoved away from the shore. It was enough of a warning and with a grumble, the creature sunk into the icy depths of the lake.

"Thank you," Fia said through chattering teeth, pulling barnacles and bits of debris from her hair.

"Think nothing of it," Arion replied. "It is not safe here. Behrog could have a change of heart and return. I will take you somewhere safe." He knelt, head low to the ground, and waited for Fia to climb astride his great back.

Fia hesitated. She was soaking wet in an icy valley and had almost been eaten. She'd no way of getting back to Mizune. What did she have to lose? With as much care as she could muster, and with a fistful of mane to balance her, she climbed up onto the back of the winged horse. Within moments they were airborne, up and away from the lake and over the rocks Fia had so desperately tried to traverse.

A little way above, but safely out of Behrog's reach, Arion settled down on a rocky ledge leading to a small opening in the rocks, just wide enough for shelter. From here, Fia could see the whole valley, and to her left, the witches' forest. Within moments, the fireflies returned and lit fires at safe distances along the rocky ledge to ward off the cold air. Fia stripped off her outer layers and hung them to dry before sitting near the largest fire to get warm. Arion sat on his hind legs, head held high, wings folded neatly behind him.

"I'm Fia," she said, once the warmth returned to her muscles. "Thank you for your help back there."

"You have thanked me already," Arion said, in smooth, deep tones. "And I know who you are. It is good to finally meet you. I am Arion." He bowed his head a little as he spoke, dark strands of mane falling across his face.

"You know me?" Fia asked.

"The Sprites have told me who you are." He flicked his head in the direction of the fireflies. "Fia, a fallen from Earth, friend of the angels, the witches, travelling companion of the Navarii, and a loquere, so it seems. You have made quite the mark on Ohinyan, wouldn't you agree?"

"I… when you put it that way, yes," Fia replied, hoping Arion would not understand the heat in her cheeks. "Behrog, what was it?"

"Behrog was once, as many things in Ohinyan were, something entirely different. Much like the Sorren, who I believe you have had the pleasure of meeting. He once delighted in the simple life he had. He has the run of the glacial waters for much further than the eye can see from here. The water in this valley and beyond is connected by a series of icy tunnels beneath the surface, and he dominates the water. There was a time when Behrog would roam the waters and would come to the aid of anything in danger in the cold depths. But the darkness began to whisper to him, lonely as they both were, and he eventually became the thing you saw just now."

"That vision that I saw in the water. Behrog did it?"

Arion nodded. "Yes. He has learned a few tricks over the years from the darkness."

"Erebus?"

Arion hung his head low, his ears falling forwards. "Yes. He has been busy over the years. Patient, luring the creatures of Ohinyan to his side. Biding his time. Waiting."

The chill returned to Fia's arms and she wrapped them tightly around herself, shifting closer to the fire. "Waiting for the sun to die?"

"Waiting for the sun to die, for the right moment, yes," Arion continued quietly. "At first I could only feel him." He moved a great hoof outward in the dirt before him. "But then, I could hear him. He whispers to me. Calls me by name. Tells me we are alike, he and I, because we are alone."

Fia rubbed her palms against her knees. Erebus had been whispering to her, but she couldn't bring herself to think about what it meant, not after his threat. "Are you alone?" she asked.

Arion raised his head a little, his ears flicking upwards. "Alone in that I am the last of my kind. I was once connected to all the creatures of Ohinyan. By land and sea, I spoke with all those who were willing to share information and to keep abreast of all that is happening. I never *felt* alone." Arion's eyes were bright in the firelight.

Connected to all the creatures of Ohinyan. Fia rose to her feet in a fluster, the realisation of how long she'd been gone settling in. "I need to get back. Alexander… they'll be wondering where I am," she said, gathering her belongings.

"You'll not make it back before dark. This valley is not safe even during the day, as you have discovered. Why would you risk the journey in darkness?"

"I need to get back. I have information that could help—the Makya, they're coming, and I need to warn the others what they're up to." As she spoke, she tested the dryness of her coat and heavy trousers, patting them over before pulling them on.

"I can see you are very headstrong, Fia," Arion said, as Fia put out the fires with fistfuls of dirt. She didn't reply. She had been, before Sophie died, but she hadn't felt that way for a while. But being in Ohinyan, there was a sense of purpose—everyone and everything had its place. Even Arion, the way he'd dealt with Behrog, the creature had recoiled in fear.

Fia gathered the last of her things. "I appreciate what you did for me today, Arion. I won't forget it. Will you come with me to Mizune, will you help us?" Her words came out in a rush. "If you don't want to help, I'll understand. It was a pleasure to meet you, truly."

He rose gracefully in one swift movement, stretching his wings to their fullest before folding them back. "I will take you. I would like to be of some assistance." He knelt once more, head low, and waited for Fia. This time, she didn't hesitate. Fia let the winged horse carry her back to Mizune.

Herds of the giraffe-like creatures ambled below them, and the chill air stung against her cheeks as Arion picked up speed. The sun was setting, and the days were already growing shorter. What would become of this world when the sun died? "What do you know of the dying sun, Arion?" she shouted against the wind.

"I will tell you all I know when we reach your friends," he replied. He said no more, and they flew on in silence as Fia peered down at Ohinyan, far below.

"Can you believe this, Soph," she whispered to the wind, as the glacial valley disappeared from view, and the dense canopy of the witches' forest swept across the ground, almost black in the twilight. The fireflies had been travelling with them, but now they spun around her head like they'd done several times that day, before diving into the canopy below. As they descended, they cried, "hurry, hurry," one last time. She smiled, protecting her watery eyes against the wind as Arion carried her back to Mizune.

CHAPTER TWENTY-SIX

ALEXANDER

"What do you mean, you didn't go with her?" Alexander dragged his fingers through his hair as he pressed Ilawu for a response. The snow fell thick and heavy, the wind was biting, and panic filled him as he thought of Fia out there alone.

The huskies growled, and this time it was Maab who spoke. "Something big approaches."

"Alexander," Fia called out through the blizzard. She sat comfortably astride a great winged horse, as if she'd done it every day of her life. *Arion.* His old friend touched down gently in the snow, and Alexander willed himself not to run to Fia.

"Fia, where have you been? Are you all right?" He examined her quickly before pulling her into an embrace. She buried her face into his chest. *She's fine. She's here.*

"Arion." Alexander peeled himself away from Fia to place a gentle hand on the horse's mane. "Thank you for bringing Fia back safely."

Arion whinnied in response, his head bobbing up and down.

"He says it's good to see his old friend." Fia smiled.

She could *talk* to Arion. Of course she could. Her cheeks were flushed, but she stood tall beside Arion. Alexander took Fia's bow and quiver, noting the lack of arrows. He raised an eyebrow. "Did you meet with Noor's coven?"

"I did." She pulled her arms across her chest. She was freezing.

"Please, let's go inside," Alexander said. He took Fia's hand in his, leading them through thick snow to the building where they'd watched the Mizunese perform their water skills. It was the only building big enough to house Arion comfortably, and what they had to discuss would need to be heard by everyone.

Faces peered out from lamp-lit windows as the winged horse accompanied them through the streets of Mizune. Some stood at their doors in awe, drawing blankets tightly around their shoulders in the heavy snow. Alexander held his chin high, his hand around Fia's, as Arion walked beside them.

Blue light flooded the chamber of the meeting house, even though it was almost dark outside.

"Alexander," Altair began, with a deep intake of breath. "I see that you found—" He clasped a hand to his chest as Arion stepped into the light. "A winged horse…" He approached Arion slowly. His eyes were like a child's as he gazed up at the great wings and the thick, shaggy mane. "I thought they had gone, long ago." Astonishment glittered across his face.

A snort erupted from Arion's nostrils, and another soft whinny escaped from his lips.

"He says all but him. His name is Arion," Fia said.

Arion bowed his head, as Yahto hesitantly stepped down into the chamber to join his father.

"This is Yahto, leader of the Mizunese people, and his father, Altair, leader of the Navarii," Fia continued.

"It is an honour." Altair bowed his head in return, and Alexander did not doubt his words.

"It is indeed," added Yahto. "Please, won't all of you join us? There is much to discuss."

Alexander felt his chest swell with pride as Fia interpreted for Arion without hesitation. Was her finding him the witches' doing?

Arion sat, heavy hind legs folded with his front legs outstretched, towering over them. Maab and Enne had joined them. They were like two sides of the same coin; wherever one went, the other would follow, and their movements complemented each other's.

"Fia, how did you find the winged horse? How can you speak with him? He is the centre of many Mizunese myths, a symbol of our people. I have no doubt many trembled at the sight of you walking together through the streets of Mizune. It is, as my father says, a great honour to have you join us here tonight, Arion." Yahto looked from Fia to Arion as he spoke, waiting patiently for Fia's explanation.

Arion folded his wings tight to his sides, as a Mizunese woman passed Fia a blanket. Alexander had not seen his old friend for many years, not since his mother was alive. But Arion had showed no signs of age.

"I can speak with animals, creatures, um, all kinds of things really," Fia said, with a quick glance at Alexander. He squeezed her hand in encouragement. "After meeting with a witch, Kharsee, I followed some fireflies to a valley, where I got into a bit of trouble, and then Arion appeared."

Alexander examined her bandaged hands as she spoke, and another ball of guilt twisted in his stomach. The bandages were pink with blood and filthy.

Fia described her visit to the forest of the witches, how she could return home, and how the worlds were connected. Yahto made a little pile of snow for her and she drew a symbol the witch had shown her, a figure of eight for Ohinyan surrounded by a circle with two intersecting lines for Earth.

"Kharsee said that all worlds are connected by the spiritual realm, and that it is being affected by the dying sun. This is why the windows will grow increasingly unstable."

Alexander nodded. Why had his sage not provided such detailed information? Surely it was not only the witches who knew such things. "The situation with the windows is much worse than we previously thought. I have recalled many of the angels from Earth."

"Kharsee said the effects would only remain for a while, but that a time of darkness was coming to Ohinyan. Erebus—it's all him, everything we've seen and heard. Arion can hear him," Fia explained.

The Mizunese and the Navarii began to whisper to each other in short, frightened bursts of chatter, but Fia sat calmly, as if she was taking it all in.

"You can hear the darkness?" Altair asked, looking up into Arion's dark eyes.

Arion tapped a hoof on the ground.

"Erebus has been calling to many… creatures of Ohinyan," Fia said. She struggled for words, and her cheeks blushed at the word "creatures."

"This is why there have been so many changes. He has been working, slowly, patiently waiting for the sun to die, for his moment to return," she finished, looking up to catch Alexander's eye. He felt his jaw tighten as realisation hit him. Something he should have already thought of, something he should have *noticed* before, but he didn't interrupt her as she spoke. *Can she hear him?*

"This is grave news, indeed. But unfortunately, we have a more pressing matter at hand," Yahto replied.

"Yes, the Makya." Fia wiped away the drawings in the little pile of snow at her feet. "Kharsee told me that Noor is safe and sent messages to say that Lorn intends to capture me and force Alexander to tell her the location of Alythia."

"That's right," Alexander said, squeezing her hand gently. "Noor has been delivering messages via the Shadows. The Makya air fleet is indeed searching for Alythia, and Lorn *is* after Fia." He pulled his fingers through his hair with his free hand as he spoke. What a mess he'd made of all of this. Some leader he'd turned out to be.

"I see. How do the Makya have such intel?" Yahto asked.

"My wife's nephew, Oren, betrayed us. Lorn did not spare him," Malachai said quietly, his eyes fixed on the dirt at his feet.

"Oren's death will not be in vain, Malachai. We cannot risk too many angels returning to Earth. They could become cut off from their families here in Ohinyan, and right now we need all the help we can get. Especially with this news of Erebus…" Alexander shook his head. Their numbers on Earth were few. He could not recall another time when such a thing had been done. But he would not trap his people there unwillingly.

"One thing at a time, old friend," Altair said, his voice gentle. "We have more pressing matters at hand, and it is good that you have recalled your brothers and sisters back from Earth. Let us hope it will increase our numbers enough when we face the Makya."

Arion tapped another hoof on the ground, whinnying quietly. "Arion says that he will assist us in any way that he can. He is even prepared to fight, if it comes to it," Fia said.

"It will come to that, in the next few days, according to our sources," Alexander replied.

"Very well," Yahto added. "The time for standing idly by has come to an end. You know my opinion of the witches and their prophecies and my concerns for my people. But if the great winged horse will help you, we must be humble and assist you, too. For the good of Ohinyan."

The witch coven. They must have known Arion's alliance would assist them, but how could they have known Fia would find him?

"Yahto," Altair began.

"Father, I should have heeded your request. The sky spirits have sent us the winged horse as an example, and we will follow him. I hope you will forgive me for being naive." Yahto clasped his father's arm in his hand.

Altair nodded, a broad smile stretching across his weathered face, as his son continued, "Let us sleep on what we have learned here this evening. Tomorrow, we will talk of war."

Arion sat patiently, waiting as the room emptied.

"Arion is welcome to join us and the rest of the Nords on the outskirts of town should he wish for some company. We prefer to spend most of the night in our animal forms, so we can guarantee a little conversation should he wish for it." Maab had approached them, closely followed by Enne.

"He says he'd be grateful for the company," Fia replied. "And that there will be more joining us in the morning. Wait, more what?" She tilted her head towards Arion. "Tremors in the ground, footsteps coming this way. They will be here by morning," she interpreted. "Should we be ready to defend ourselves?"

Arion shook his head. Alexander breathed a quiet sigh of relief. They couldn't afford to damage the morale of the Mizunese soldiers so soon after Yahto had agreed to help. He watched as Maab and Enne shifted, their armour dropping away, bounding alongside Arion in a mass of white and black. With the addition of the Mizunese soldiers, their chances of winning this fight were significantly improved. But at what cost? Lives would be lost, and it was his responsibility to bear.

Alexander and Fia returned to the wooden house they'd been sharing with Runa and Malachai for the last few nights, the scent of spices and sweet cooked fruit overwhelming them as they stepped in out of the cold night.

As they sat down to eat, Runa interrogated Fia on the details of her day. "I should have gone with you," Runa said, shaking her head and dishing out steaming spoonfuls of stewed fish.

"I'm so sorry," Alexander began. "I had no idea you could return to Earth… no one has ever… I can carry you back, at first light…" He poked at his fish with a wooden fork. Foolish. That's what he was. Utterly foolish for dragging her into this, deceiving her and dragging her halfway round Ohinyan. Nothing but a fool.

"We could not have known it was possible, sire. Not to mention how dangerous it is," Malachai said, pouring water into four wooden cups. "There are several windows near here."

"Don't be absurd, Mal." Runa elbowed Malachai gently. "Fia needs to go home, not to be dumped in the middle of nowhere."

"Runa's right," Alexander said, his eyes meeting Fia's.

Home. This could be her home, couldn't it, if she wanted it to be? "Fia?" Alexander held her gaze.

"Sorry, what was that?" She shook her head, and something in her expression reminded him of how she'd paused earlier when she spoke of Erebus.

"We'd have to wait a few more days to take you back, but I'll take you back as soon I think it's safe for us to leave Mizune. That is, of course, if you're okay with the risk?" Alexander asked.

"The risk?"

"Going home, the windows could be unstable." He searched her eyes, wet and glistening in the candlelight.

"Yes, of course," Fia finally said, pushing a bit of fish around her bowl. "And what about Erebus?" She asked casually, too casually, taking her bowl to the sink.

Alexander put down his fork. "We'll need to find a way to stop him."

"Well," Runa said, sipping the water Malachai had poured, "perhaps for tonight we should not think of such things."

***

Whilst Fia was getting ready for bed, Alexander sat by the window, inspecting the cuff his sister had given him. The pattern swirled and flourished from one end to the other, delicately carved into the metal.

She'll go home. You'll say goodbye.

And when this is all over, you can go back to her. It isn't safe for her here.

He put the little cuff away and lay back on the bed, flexing his wings and running his hands through his hair. He'd watched in awe as Fia interpreted Arion's words for everyone in the great chamber, so effortlessly and with conviction. Ohinyan had changed her, and he loved her all the more for it.

Alexander had known he'd loved her since she saved the little Navarii boy from drowning. When he thought *she* had almost drowned. His breath caught in his throat. He gazed out the window. Three moons glowed, and the sky spirits had begun their nightly ritual. What if all the windows collapsed, and he could never see her again? But if she could hear Erebus… His breath grew faster at the thought, and he closed his eyes to calm himself.

He'd never felt this way about anyone. The thought of losing her. He couldn't bear it.

"What is it?" Fia asked, taking his hand in her own.

He hadn't heard her come out of the bathroom. He inspected the damaged skin where her bandages had once been.

"It doesn't hurt." She pulled his hands up to meet with hers, flexing her fingers through his. "What are you thinking about?" Green eyes, the colour of the Aurelli forest, looked back at him, searching, concerned.

"Can you hear him?" he asked, his voice soft.

Fia stiffened and paled.

"It's okay. I understand why you didn't tell me—but you realise..."

She nodded, biting her lip as it trembled slightly. "I'm sorry for not telling you before."

"You're a target, Fia. Not just for the Makya, but for Erebus."

"I know. I've seen what he can do. That thing that Arion saved me from, the Sorren, the Senkahs." She wiped at her eyes. "I have no way to stop him."

Alexander pulled her closer. "I keep telling myself it isn't safe for you here. But…"

"I know," she whispered, and he brushed away a hot tear as it rolled down her cheek.

Soaked in the white glow of the moonlight, Alexander wrapped his wings around her, kissing her softly. The air changed, *intensified*, just as it always did when he was close to her.

Just a few more moments.

CHAPTER TWENTY-SEVEN

FIA

"I have felt the tremors all night. Our visitor is almost upon us," Arion said to Fia, as she followed him sleepily to the outskirts of Mizune. Alexander squeezed her hand as the huskies howled into the morning air. Maab and Enne followed close behind them, their paws silent in the snow.

Fia couldn't shake the feeling that there was going to be a consequence to admitting that she could hear Erebus. Would Erebus wait until Alexander was at his most vulnerable, during the battle, maybe? Would he target Altair, or Maab and Enne?

"State your purpose, Jǫtunn," Arion called out to a silhouette in the fog. At the outskirts of Mizune where the Nords slept lay a cluster of woodland, and beyond it stretched snow covered tundra for many miles until the witches' forest. The slow and steady tremors became deeper as they approached and then stopped.

A voice replied from the dense fog, loud and echoing, "Winged horse. I am Gymir of the Jǫtnar." His voice was crystalline, like thousands of pieces of glass shattering at once. Two more tremors shook the ground, and Gymir appeared through the fog.

Fia steadied herself, tilting her head back to take in his full height.

"An ice giant, in all my days," Maab muttered, his white fur camouflaging him against the snow.

"He says his name is Gymir," Fia said, taking a step closer.

Gymir was as tall as the strange buildings of Ikothea, with two long arms and legs protruding from a torso encased in armour. Where there should have been skin, there was nothing but ice, reflecting all the colours of the glacial drift Fia had seen throughout the south. His face was like the ragged edge of a mountain, and his eyes, from this distance, were nothing more than crevices. When he spoke, chunks of ice broke away and fell from his mouth, shattering on his chest. In his right hand, he held a weapon, a staff reaching right up to his shoulders.

"My name is Fia. What brings you here, Gymir?" She stepped closer, so he would see her better, willing her voice not to shake in front of the others.

"Fia. Many things are changing in Ohinyan. Many things," Gymir said solemnly, coughing chunks of ice and clearing his throat. He rolled each word around in his mouth before he spoke it. Crunching, rumbling, and murmuring were underscored with the tinkling of ice. "When the ground beneath us tremors with the whispers of unfathomable darkness, we listen. As the days grow darker when they should not, we watch. And when the winged horse speaks with man, then perhaps it is time for us to speak, too."

"I think he wants to help," Fia said. "Arion, can you take me higher up?"

Arion nodded.

"Gymir, perhaps the winged horse and I might come and speak with you?" Fia gave a sideways glance to Alexander and he nodded in response.

Gymir coughed and wheezed ice like a tired old man. "Very well," he finally said.

Once more, Fia climbed onto Arion's back, holding onto his mane to balance herself as he flew up through the fog towards Gymir. As they approached, Gymir held out a hand like a slab of ice over a lake, streaked with white and blue. Arion set down gently, encouraging Fia to speak.

"Gymir," she shouted as loudly as she could through the wind. "These things you've mentioned, there's more—the Makya, the fire people, they are taking advantage of Ohinyan's situation, and they want to fight and cause destruction." She held her arm up to shield herself from the wind.

Gymir coughed once more and a chunk of ice fell from his face towards his upturned palm where she stood beside Arion, but Gymir swatted it away with his free hand before it hit them.

"We are familiar with the Makya. We are not so distant with the creatures of Ohinyan as you would think," the ice giant replied, wheezing through his words, as he shook his great head. "No fight has ever come to any good."

Fia examined his features as he spoke. Deep within the crevices in his face, framed by finer, wispier pieces of ice, sat deep, dark eyes like brilliant blue sapphires.

"The Jǫtnar will assist, but we must do so from afar, or I fear we may do more harm than good." He was silent for a moment. "The wind, have you any use for it?"

"What's he talking about, Arion? What about the wind?" Fia asked.

"The Jǫtnar could command the winds, it was once said," Arion replied.

Fire, air, water, earth. "Yes," Fia shouted once more to the giant. "An airship is coming, maybe several, flying beasts made of metal."

"And these flying beasts are foe, I gather?" Gymir asked. Heavy snow began to fall, and it was hard to see his face anymore.

"Yes," Fia called out through the blizzard.

"Fia, time to go," Arion bellowed into the wind, and he leapt into the air.

"Very well," the giant's deep voice echoed, "when the flying beasts come, we will assist you."

"Thank you, Gymir," Fia called as Arion made one last circle of the giant's head before returning to the others.

"Time to discuss strategy," Arion said, as his hooves rested in the snow.

***

"The Makya know of Mizune's defences, so they will not land here," Alexander explained in the great chamber, as they looked over maps of brittle parchment. "There is a valley to the south, close to the witches' forest. It is the only place suitable for them to land."

Altair nodded. "We do not wish to draw the attack to Mizune. It is too risky. They will be exposed in the valley. And what of the council?" he asked. Even when seated, his great cloak hung about him in endless layers.

"We've had no word from them, and I cannot risk sending another envoy." Alexander ran a hand through his hair. "My general will have more information for us soon, but I think our suspicions will be correct. I do not think this is the council's doing."

Fia thought of Lorn and of Terah, the fire mother. Were they one and the same?

"That does not mean we will hold back," Yahto added. "We cannot trust the information from your witch friend to be accurate or complete. What does the information from your guards tell us of the Makya?" *Your witch friend.* The loathing tone was not lost on Fia.

Yahto paced up and down the chamber, and Fia's eyes flickered between the men as they spoke. She would not miss this opportunity to learn how she could contribute—how she could repay them all for saving her life.

"The Makya are not natural fighters," Alexander said. "They rely heavily on their ability to create fire and are easily caught off guard." He spoke with confidence, despite being so much younger than the rest of the men in the room. Fia admired the way he never let his age fluster him. "None are as adept as Lorn and her brothers or as the other members of the council. The rest will be clumsy, easily exposed."

Fia cast her gaze across his wings, willing away the creeping panic at the thought of those feathers catching fire in battle. He'd worn nothing more than his loose hemp trousers, much to her distraction, the entire time she'd known him. Did angels wear armour?

"Do they carry weapons?" Yahto asked.

"The less adept ones carry a fire staff, which causes extensive damage but are slow to target, and as for their ship, it is armed, so they may cause destruction from the skies without deploying their guards. But I cannot speak for any allies they may have with them," Alexander replied.

"They have the Aurelli from the forest where I… arrived," Fia said. "They're light but nimble, and really fast. They carried bows, but I'd put money on it that their teeth and claws could do some serious damage, too."

Yahto pressed Alexander with more questions about the Aurelli when Fia could answer no more. Instead, she listened intently. If she was to be of use, she needed to hear everything that was said, and would not leave the discussion, even though Runa had tried to coerce her with offerings of archery practice. She'd practiced so much on the ship and since their arrival in Mizune. She sat in silence, only speaking when interpreting for Arion, considering carefully every new piece of information the group had to offer.

"Arion," Alexander continued. "Will you stay by Fia's side throughout the attack?"

Arion nodded, tapping a heavy hoof on the ground. He had said little, but Fia had no doubt he'd seen his fair share of battles.

"My people will create a shield of ice," Yahto said. "How many angels have you called for?"

"There are several hundred in the skies above Mizune and the surrounding area as we speak. The airships arrive tomorrow," Alexander added. "Can the Mizunese create a shield big enough if we can come in low to the ground?"

"We cannot guarantee it, but we can try," Yahto replied.

"It is as solid a plan as any." Altair stood, holding his chin between finger and thumb. "We had hoped against hope that it would not come to this. Let us still have faith that it will not. To each of you, I cannot give you any better words of advice than to tell your loved ones what they mean to you, and to kiss them goodnight before you climb into bed this evening. Tomorrow may be our last day on Ohinyan." He pulled the layers of his cloak around himself and folded his arms across his chest.

"Yes, Father, and tonight, we will celebrate life," Yahto said.

The fire fizzled out as one of the Mizunese channelled water across it, and the chamber became tinged with the pale blue light from above as the room emptied.

"Walk with me?" Alexander asked, taking Fia's hand.

"I know," Fia said. "It isn't safe for me here. And I have to go home. But I keep thinking about what home means to me, Alexander, and it isn't that empty flat back in London. It isn't that life."

They crossed the bridges of Mizune, past market stalls packing up for the day and fisherman as they wound up their nets for the night, ready for the next day's catch. The wind carried the salty scent of the ocean across the harbour towards them, and seals barked somewhere in the dusk.

"And what life is there for you here?" Alexander said, shaking his head. "For anyone here in Ohinyan? We don't know what's coming, and it isn't safe for anyone. If we make it through tomorrow, then what?" They walked for a while, making their way up the path leading high above Mizune.

Fia looked out at the icy passage they'd navigated their way through on their arrival to Mizune, at the flickering silhouette of one of the blue markers, nearly black in the little light that remained. Blue veins streaked the ice from their tip right into the inky water below them, glowing in the twilight.

"We don't know what the next day will bring, or the day after that when Erebus could return and destroy everything, and then in moments the sun could vanish forever," Alexander added as they reached the cliff top overlooking

Mizune. "If you can hear him, that means he can get inside your head, manipulate you..."

A sinking feeling in her stomach told her it was the truth. She had no defence against Erebus. No way of keeping him *out.*

The glittering lights of oil lamps being turned on twinkled below them, and the fog had finally begun to disperse. Maab and Enne were nearby, playing together as wild cats, almost invisible against the backdrop of snow.

"I've almost made my decision," Fia said. "Sometimes, the right thing isn't always the easiest, do you understand?" she asked, turning to look at Alexander, his wings tucked behind him. The last of the light had slipped away over the horizon, and the night was settling in. She put a hand to his face and gazed into his eyes. Silver flecks glistened in the darkness.

"I can't lose you," he finally said.

"You won't." Fia bit down on her lip. She couldn't lose anyone else; it would be the end of her.

Alexander reached out to her. "If anything were to happen to you…" He glanced up at the sky, to where the sky spirits had begun their nightly dance. Fia stood beside him, and he took her hand in his as the colours unfolded before them.

"I've never…" he began, and with his free hand, he traced a thumb across her cheek. "I've never felt this way about anyone."

Fia felt the familiar stir of electricity surrounding them.

"I can't lose you, Fia." He kissed her, and she never wanted it to end.

"You'll be safe on Earth, no matter what happens here," he said, as he pulled back.

Fia breathed in a deep, cold breath of air and laid her head on his shoulder. "I'm not ready to give this up. Not now. Not ever." She lifted her head up to look at him.

"Alexander," Maab called out from behind them. He fixed the last piece of his armour to his chest as he approached.

"Maab, what is it?"

They walked ahead together, and Enne joined Fia as she watched the sky spirits.

"My people say that these are the spirits of those that have passed," Enne said softly, following Fia's gaze.

"The sky spirits?"

Enne nodded. Fia couldn't bring herself to look amongst the stars for Sophie, not tonight. "Why did you leave your people, your home?"

"Home and where you come from are two very different things, Fia." A gentle smile spread across his face. "There are many things going on in the north, and it is no longer the wonderful place that people speak of so fondly in tales and legends." The sky spirits chimed as they turned from ribbons of cyan to magenta.

"I think memories of a place can often be much more beautiful than reality," Fia replied.

"Yes, I think that's right." Enne looked away to the footprints in the snow. Fia followed his gaze to Maab and Alexander. "So tomorrow, we fight, and the next day you will return to Earth, as if none of this ever happened."

"I notice you don't refer to it as my home, like the others do," Fia said, with a small laugh. She pulled her hood up over her head, hoping the cold wind would hide her reddening cheeks.

"Home is wherever this is, Fia." Enne broke his gaze away from Maab to point at her chest. "In the end, it was love that liberated me from that tormented place. Being with him is the only freedom I need in life. Anywhere he goes is my home." Enne's face lit up as he watched Maab walking ahead with Alexander.

Fia smiled. Enne was full of light and life. His words were gentle, but she'd seen his fierceness when he'd saved her from the Sorren. "Tomorrow, we fight, the next day, Earth," she repeated with a sigh, letting the words sink in. "But it certainly couldn't be as if it had never happened. How could I forget this," she said, waving her hands at the sky spirits, "or forget all of you?"

"Forget him, you mean?" Enne gestured to Alexander. "He will come back for you, you know, when it's safe. He's right to tell you it isn't safe here, and besides, what's love without a little heartache?" He laughed. It was an infectious sound lighting up his whole face.

"You think he's right?" Fia asked.

"I do. It is the logical thing to do. You'll be safe on Earth. Erebus's whispers cannot reach you there," he said, winking.

"But how did—"

"And if you are safe, then you can build a life together when this is all over," he finished.

"You make it seem so simple."

"Ah, life is not so difficult really, Fia. It's all happening inside of us. All this love, this fear, this worry. It's not in Ohinyan, or in Earth. It's in here." He pointed to her chest once more. Enne laughed again, scooping up some snow and then throwing it at her playfully.

"I never thanked you properly," Fia said, dodging a snowball. "You saved my life Enne, back on the ship, from the Sorren. Thank you."

Enne smiled and nodded, as they were joined by Maab and Alexander.

"Come now, or we will be late for the celebrations," Maab said, reaching out to take Enne's hand.

Fia leaned into Alexander as he wrapped an arm around her. "It seems odd to have a party with what's coming,"

"It is the perfect time," Enne replied. "We should always celebrate life as if we are about to take our last breath." His armour dropped away from him, and he was a snow leopard once more, leaping and bounding through the snow beside Maab as a magnificent white tiger.

CHAPTER TWENTY-EIGHT

FIA

Fia hesitated at the perimeter of a clearing in the heart of Mizune, a gathering place, for ceremonies and celebrations Yahto had told her. The party was bright and lively: Navarii, Mizunese, and Nords laughed and danced together around an enormous fire in the centre.

Barrels wrapped in strips of blue fabric and fastened bundles of fishing nets made seating areas around smaller fires, all bustling with people, drinking, eating, and talking.

There was a time when the thought of a party, even just a few quiet drinks with friends, had filled her with dread, but things were different now. Everything had changed since coming to Ohinyan, and the thought of leaving it all behind knocked the air from her lungs.

The night sky was clear, the shimmer of stars still visible in the firelight. Even the sky spirits had joined them. Fia could make out their colourful ribbons on the horizon. Couples whirled past in an energetic dance, one pair after another spun by her.

She recognised Maab and Enne, their silver hair catching the light as they danced. Maab held Enne's hands in his as they moved, a broad smile across his face. The only time he ever smiled was when he looked at his partner. The music stopped, and Maab pulled Enne towards him, his hands on Enne's face as they kissed, quickly and hungrily.

Fia knew she shouldn't watch, but the way they touched each other, the way they gazed at each other like there was no one else around, she couldn't look away.

Enne pulled back, a bright smile lighting up his face as breath clouded the small space between them. His lips moved, but Fia was too far away to hear. Enne reached for Maab's hand and led him away from the crowd.

Home and where you come from are two very different things. Enne's words had stayed with her as they'd prepared for the party. It still seemed strange that anyone would want to have a party with what awaited them the next morning, but Runa had told her that was *precisely* why, so they spent less time sitting up worrying about it and more time simply being together. Fia understood, but she preferred the more poetic way Enne had put it.

"Fia, I've been looking everywhere for you." Alexander wrapped his arms around her the moment he was beside her.

"I'm not used to parties," she said, leaning into him and breathing in the scents of the forest clinging to his skin—pine, cinnamon, jasmine.

"Stay here tomorrow, stay here away from the fight, where I know you'll be safe." Alexander's breath was warm in her hair, and he pressed a kiss against her head.

Fia spun around to face him, the cold air filling the space between them instantly. How was he still not wearing a shirt? "I'm not going to sit here and make all of Mizune a target, Alexander. We need to draw them out. I can fight—I want to fight." She reached a hand up to his face, her fingers rubbing against the stubble lining his chin. "I want to be where you are."

He took her hand in his and sighed. "You've no idea what Lorn can do." He swallowed. "I can't let her do that to you."

"Tell me." Fia rested her head against his chest. "What happened between the two of you?" Music still played, drums and wind instruments carried a lively tune, but Alexander's expression was stern.

He cleared his throat. "It wasn't long before I left for Earth to find you, a few months at most. My father had been making progress with Par, the Makya council leader, for a new alliance between the angels and the Makya." He took her hand and moved them closer to a smaller fire that was unoccupied. "I might not feel the cold, but you do."

Alexander sat on a barrel beside Fia, his hands resting on his thighs. "My father agreed to attend a meeting in Nadar, the Makya's home country, at the southernmost tip of Iraluxia. But Lorn requested my presence, and my father said it would be rude to refuse, so I accompanied him." His hands rubbed at the fabric of his trousers as he gazed into the fire.

A sickening feeling worked its way up Fia's arms, balling at her throat.

"When we arrived, Lorn requested my presence immediately. She was wild—rattling off ancient history about why we should be together—why we were *meant* for each other. She even kissed me." He laughed, but it was a choked, forced sound. "You have to understand Fia, angels are protectors. In all of the history I have ever been taught, the Makya have destroyed, taken, or controlled. When she kissed me, I saw no love in her eyes, only all of the things she *wanted*, and it certainly wasn't me." Alexander stood, flexed his wings, and sat back down again. Was he counting his breaths?

"When I refused her, Lorn lost her temper, throwing flames. She destroyed the banners in our meeting room within minutes. Moments later, my father and Par joined us, and Lorn—she was out of control, she—" He closed his eyes. "My father stood between us, to reason with her, but she'd already shot a stream of flames in my direction, and my father took most of the force of it. I couldn't do anything. I didn't *do* anything. I pulled down a banner to extinguish the flames on my wing, and when I looked up Par was trying to help my father." He reached a hand to his wing, as if he were recalling the wound.

"And then Lorn attacked Par, too, and Par fought back—she's old but she's fierce, and she sent Lorn running. My father…" Alexander swallowed.

Tears pressed at Fia's eyes, and she wiped one away as it rolled down her cheek.

"Par got us both out. The room was gone—it was ash. My wing was badly burnt, but my father, he was—he wasn't breathing." Alexander shook his head, and his eyes flicked open, lined with tears. "Par did everything she could, she called for healers, but they're not equipped to deal with those kinds of injuries in Nadar. They've no need for it."

Fia reached for him and took his hands in hers.

Alexander straightened himself and cleared his throat again. "These attacks, I truly don't believe them to be Par's doing. She did everything she could to save my father, but I couldn't risk sending any more angels to Nadar, not after what happened. And Lorn—I don't even know if they punished her, if she regrets what she did. Probably neither of those things. But I know exactly what she's capable of Fia, and the thought of the same thing happening to you…" He pulled her into his lap and pressed his face into her hair. "I can't lose you."

Fia stifled a sob. "You won't. I'm so sorry about your father—I had no idea. Why didn't you tell me?"

His wings wrapped around her, and she looked up into his eyes. They were glassy in the firelight, and the thought of him grieving alone broke her heart.

"You lost Sophie and it was… it was like the world had been pulled out from under you. Your love for her, Fia, it's in everything you do. I didn't want to take away from any of that by burdening you with my own loss."

The tears flowed freely now, and Fia didn't wipe them away. They fell down her cheeks until the space between her and Alexander's chest was damp. "Burdening me?" She choked a laugh. "Grief is so lonely. I'd have given anything to know somebody understood how it felt, to know what I was going through, what I've been going through." She fought back at the anger rising in her chest. It had been this way since Sophie died—anger at people who still had their sister, their parents, anger at people who glazed over when she told them her sister was gone. It was a completely irrational anger and she knew it, but it was grief, and there was nothing she could do but accept it and hope it would pass.

"I understand," Alexander said quietly. "I know." He brushed the hair out of her eyes and wiped at her tears. "I wasn't ready before, to talk about it. But I want to share everything with you."

Fia's cheeks flushed with shame. She understood. She knew what it was like to not be ready, to hold onto every shred of emotion threatening to shatter her completely if she allowed herself to feel.

They sat together, listening to the music and the sounds of the party. Laughter erupted nearby, and all Fia could think of was Alexander's father, burning alive.

"I'm going to get you something to eat," Alexander finally said, pressing another kiss into her hair. "I'll be right back."

Fia watched the flames as she waited, the party still lively around her. There was no way she could eat anything now.

"*Fia...*" a voice whispered. *Erebus.* Nobody else had heard. The dancing and laughter continued, and no one else paused at the sound of his voice.

"*Why do you ignore me? I understand, you know, what it is to have no one left. To be truly alone.*"

"You are nothing but a shadow. You can't hurt me, Erebus," Fia breathed, her voice barely more than a whisper, too. Where was Alexander? She knew she should get up and find him, but something held her to the spot.

The fire flickered for a moment, the flames turned black, and she felt her hands moving towards them, watched as they plunged into the fire without her control. She tried to speak, but no sound came out, and the black flames burned at her skin, as they wrapped around her hands and up her arms.

"*Not now, no. But you and I will meet soon enough. You disobeyed me, Fia. Next time, I will not hesitate. Return to Earth, or I will destroy everything you love.*" The fire hissed and turned orange once more. Fia was back on her seat, her hands in her lap, as they had been moments before, no signs of burns on her skin. The music and the laughter drowned into nothing, and Fia's heart was like a drumbeat in her ears. Tears streamed down her cheeks and she tried to count her breaths, but it was no use, fear caught in her throat.

"Fia, you're pale. Is everything okay?" Alexander was beside her, a bowl of steaming stew in one hand, the other cupped gently on her cheek. "I'm sorry, I didn't mean to upset you."

Fia cleared her throat. *I want to share everything with you, too.* But not this. She couldn't bring herself to tell him about Erebus tonight.

CHAPTER TWENTY-NINE

FIA

"Let us hope the sky spirits bring us fresh snow," Altair said, preparing the huskies for departure.

Fia looked up, the last of the fog had lifted, and Mizune had awoken to a clear, blue sky stretching as far as the eye could see. This was not the weather they'd wished for. "Are there enough sleds for everyone?" She'd skipped breakfast to help in any way she could. She couldn't eat. Not on a morning like this. Not after Erebus' threat.

Altair shook his head. "I'm afraid not. Many left under moonlight to make the journey south on foot."

Fia said nothing. It was a long way to walk in this climate, and worse, to the possibility of imminent death. She pushed back at the thoughts telling her she had led the Makya here. That this was her doing. They crept up her spine and whispered in her ears.

The group travelled a few hours south of Mizune, close to the witches' forest. The location had been chosen based on several factors: the forest that lined off one side of the snowy tundra, a glacial lake sitting to the east, and the beginning of the rock formation that went down into the valley beyond the witches' forest lining the west. Behind them to the north, although sparser, the land was not suitable for a ship and was more difficult to navigate on foot, so this was the only place the Makya would be able to land. Fia sucked in the cold air as steadily as she could and then concentrated on the clouds of breath as she exhaled.

She watched the soldiers as she approached, chatting quietly in groups or smoking crumbling leaf from pipes. Mizunese and Navarii alike, they huddled around fires telling each other stories. For a moment, she felt the urge to run, like she was back in Highgate cemetery with the sound of footsteps pursuing her. Instead, she sucked in more of the cool air as she surveyed the soldiers.

The Mizunese wore quilted vests with inky blue sleeves beneath them and thick, heavy gloves—a uniform of sorts. The Navarii had no sense of similarity to their attire; some sat beside shields carved with symbols, whereas others wore crude metal helmets and sharpened the blades of their long swords.

Panic rooted Fia to the spot; she could see hundreds, but certainly not thousands, of soldiers. How could they win this? Alexander landed beside her, following her gaze along the line of men and women. He was covered in armour, but she'd recognise his lips, the contours of his chest, his strong arms, no matter what he wore. A golden helmet covered the top half of his face, with a matching chest plate, gauntlets, greaves, and boots that glistened as the light caught them, polished to their best. He wasn't entirely covered, but few exposed spots remained—his wings amongst them. Across his back were two long swords and his bow and quiver full of arrows.

Fia allowed herself to feel a shred of relief. "I thought there might be more of us than this."

"We don't need numbers. We have strategy on our side," he replied, calm and composed. His eyes sparkled from within his helmet. Their numbers were doubled by the angels in the sky above them who were skilled archers, armoured, ready, and waiting to launch an airborne attack. "It's not too late for Arion to take you back to Mizune," he said.

"I want to fight. You know I do. And we've discussed this. If I'm here, they'll be looking for me, and that means Mizune will be safe."

Alexander nodded and held her face gently in his hands. "Be careful, don't leave Arion's side." He brushed a thumb gently over her lips.

Fia nodded, she was too nervous to speak. *Please be okay.*

Alexander kissed her swiftly and flew in line with the other archers to prepare, their glittering armoured bodies hovering above her.

An angel flew in beside Alexander, his helmet tucked under his arm as he greeted his leader. Golden eyes met hers for a moment as the angel turned to look at her. Fia was too far away to hear their exchange, but she knew from Alexander's description that it was Jarl, his general.

Jarl gave a bellowing instruction to the soldiers to put out their fires and their pipes and called them to formation. He stood in line beside Alexander as the hum of engines carried to them on the breeze, and Fia recognised the sound at once. A large airship flanked by three smaller ones advanced from the east, just visible over the horizon of the lake. The soldiers cried out, rallying each other as the enemy approached. Fia leapt up onto Arion's back, her fingers burying into fistfuls of mane. She was making him a target, too.

A fierce wind picked up across the tundra, forcing snow off the trees in drifts.

"Gymir," Fia said under her breath.

The airships advanced over the horizon. Each of the flying beasts had a multitude of metal and wooden wings protruding from the underside in a disordered manner, surrounding what looked unmistakably like large metal canons. *Shit.*

The soldiers moved in sequence; a line of Mizunese footmen dotted amongst the rest of the allies. They created a shield of ice large enough to encompass the entire army and launched it upwards into the sky. Like a glass dome, it protected the angels above them, too.

Fia sat astride Arion's back, bow drawn, waiting for the mark. She'd been practicing with Runa and she was ready. If she was to be a target, she could at least put up a fight.

Maab and Enne flanked Arion's sides, joined by the other Nords that could attack more fiercely in animal form. Those that remained stood as men, wielding swords and spears.

The angels and the Navarii archers raised their bows ready for attack. The air was so tense Fia was sure the ice shield was creaking from the weight of it.

"Hold!" Alexander cried out from somewhere down the battle line. Their makeshift army was several rows of soldiers deep, split off into organised rectangles of men and women, each with their own group of Mizunese to protect their unit.

The ice giant's wind became fiercer as the airships flew closer; a violent gust of air dug into the trees around the lake, snapping them in two. The scent of pine and fresh snow drifted across the expanse.

"Hold," Alexander commanded again over the wind and the drumming of the airships' engines. The ships attempted to fly in low, but the Jǫtnars' wind blew the Makya off course, sending them rocking and swaying in the air dangerously close to each other.

The Makya regained formation, launching an airborne attack during their descent. Fireballs zoomed like meteorites through the sky towards Fia and the others. Still, Alexander cried, "Hold your positions, wait for my order!"

Fia fought back a tremor as she held back the draw on her bow. Fireballs struck the ice shield one after another as the Mizunese worked together, transforming shards of ice into droplets of water. The Jǫtnar increased their attack, and the airships were blown across the lake to the bare tundra, but now they were low enough that men were jumping down to the ground from ropes.

Gymir and his companions cried out as they sent one

final commanding wind, spiralling like a cyclone towards one of the smaller airships and engulfing it in seconds. The cyclone dispersed, and pieces of the airship fell as it eddied into the snow below. The ship crashed hard into the tundra in an explosion of metal and wood, breaking up into small pieces and dragging chunks of earth and snow with it as the wreckage came to a halt in a contorted mass beside the lake. *Go Gymir!* Fia's stomach was doing somersaults.

As the airship crashed, a fireball struck the ice shield above the angels and it shattered, sending shards of ice as sharp as glass across the soldiers. Fia sat tall. She would not show weakness amongst so much courage. Instead, she held her bow steady as the Mizunese replenished the shield.

"Keep an eye on those men," Alexander cried as the three remaining airships lurched in the wind back towards them. Little pods fell from the ships, one after another, bobbing in the wind towards the front line. The three remaining ships touched down, and an outpouring of black dots covered the snow: Aurelli and Senkahs.

The wind dropped, and the ice shield was down. The enemy was in range.

"Fire," Alexander called, and a curtain of arrows whistled high through the air towards the creatures. Several of the wild things dropped to the ground, but the rest raced on through the snow.

The Nords didn't wait for a second command. Those in animal form broke formation and ran across the snow, eyes only for the Senkahs. The Nordic foot soldiers remained, filling the gap their animal counterparts had left. Their matching metal armour was strong and light, and they brandished a multitude of weapons. Steel battle axes and swords, carved wooden spears, and mace-like staffs swung about them as they sang battle cries and launched into the approaching Aurelli, who bounded towards them on all fours. Fia released her arrow, striking a Senkah in the flank, just as it leapt towards a Nordic wolf, buying enough time for him to clasp his jaws around the beast.

The Makya launched themselves into the front line. One by one, they came from the ships as fireballs, before turning back into people. Arion dodged fireball after fireball, and Fia pressed her body low to his mane, squeezing her legs against his flanks to hold on.

A Navarii soldier cried out in pain, rolled out in the snow by a Nord footman, as the snow hissed around him from the flames. But the Makya were slow, as Alexander had said they would be. Once they'd landed amongst the soldiers, it took too long for them to get their wits about them and as they hesitated, it gave enough time for an opposing attack—another barrage of arrows from the angels.

The Mizunese countered as much of the fire with water and ice as they could, graceful with their movements, even in the height of battle, wielding the ice like a blade. The Navarii attacked the Aurelli with swords, who fought back with spears and shields and swift, frenzied movements. Fia and Arion flew low over the frenzy, keeping watch over their friends as Fia fired steady arrows that hit their targets. She aimed to harm, not to kill. She didn't know if she could bring herself to do that, not yet.

"The mercenaries are trying to break off the east flank!" Yahto called out beside Altair as he tackled a Senkah. It writhed and disappeared in a ball of black smoke. One of Fia's arrows dropped to the snow in its place as Arion touched down beside Yahto, and she leapt onto the ground.

"Something isn't right," Altair replied. "There should be more of them. It is as Alexander suspected. This cannot be the council's doing." He brushed snow from his arms. He must have fallen, but he showed no signs of injury. An Aurelli ran at him, and with one smooth blow of his battle staff, Altair sent it sliding through the snow, unconscious. "There are as many creatures as Makya and those mercenaries, Par would never lower herself to work with such a breed."

Yahto snorted in agreement as he dodged a fireball, trapping a Makya soldier in a block of ice up to her waist. Fia took great pleasure in landing a kick in the centre of the Makya's chest.

Alexander joined them, flying in low to scoop up a group of Aurelli and hurl them into an approaching Senkah. "We need to deal with the mercenaries," he called out, rallying soldiers from the eastern side of the frontline to advance their attack on the men. *Mercenaries?* Fia swung around, surveying the men running from the direction of the airship, and she knew at once who they were. She grabbed a fist full of mane and leapt up onto Arion's back.

The mercenaries fought wildly: they bit at skin, and they pulled hair, and they swung maces made of nails and double headed axes that sliced through whoever approached them.

Arion took to the air once more and Fia could see Maab and Enne ahead. They were fast and light-footed despite their size, and they worked together to tear through the mercenaries in a mass of blood and flesh, their white fur already stained pink. Maab was amongst the men, a deep, rumbling growl emanating from him and revealing a bloodied mouth of sharp teeth. Enne flanked his side, launching himself at the enemy with razor sharp claws. He crushed arms and legs between his teeth, as if they were nothing more than powdered snow.

Adrenaline thundered in her chest as Fia fired an arrow at one of the mercenaries. It struck him moments later. He ripped it from his leg, looking up at her as a great black bear slammed into him and shook him from side to side like a rag doll. *Good.*

Arion swooped low again, close enough to the ground for his wings to knock several Aurelli off their feet. Altair and Alexander joined them. Alexander held a long blade in each hand and cut his way through the first of two mercenaries that approached. Fia held her breath, but his attack was fluid and strong, with no hint of hesitation.

A third mercenary spat on the floor in front of Alexander. "I'm going to enjoy cutting those wings off your back."

Arion pulled up as Fia drew an arrow, ready to fire.

The mercenaries were wild, but they moved carelessly with attack after attack in slow, clumsy motions. Alexander was graceful, circling each of the men, blades crossed, considering each move until he saw an opening. His blades silently sliced through flesh and bone. The mercenaries didn't stand a chance. Fia let out a whistle, her lips numb against the cold.

Arion flew higher, far from the reach of the Makya fireballs. Below them, Jarl fought with a Senkah as Fia fired arrows strategically and carefully down to the ground. Arrows from above whizzed past her, extinguishing balls of fire into screaming, writhing bodies of wounded Makya below. "Thank you," she called out to an angel as he flew on to the next target, bow drawn. She sucked in a cold lungful of air, searching for her friends below.

"We're driving them back," Arion shouted through the wind.

"The ships are taking off," Fia cried out in reply. "We have to stop them before they escape."

Arion grunted his reply, flying high over the battlefield towards the two smaller airships. As they approached, a horned beast, equal in size to Behrog, erupted from the hold of the last ship still sitting in the snow. Enraged and frenzied, it tore through any soldiers in its path: Makya, Mizunese, Navarii, Senkahs, it seemed to make no difference to the creature. Its legs and torso were wrapped in chains, and on its back, thrashing the tethers wildly, sat two Makya: a man and a woman dressed in leathers.

"Lorn and her brother, Jerum," Arion called out.

Stay focused.

"The last ship is taking off," Fia replied, "We have to hurry."

Arion pressed onwards towards the ship, as Fia continued her onslaught of arrows. An idea struck her. "Arion, get us in underneath. We need those ropes."

Hanging beneath the ship as it ascended were the ropes the mercenaries had dropped down from, swaying wildly in the wind.

Swiftly, Arion descended beneath the largest ship and Fia reached out, grabbing the three ropes closest to her. "Take us up to one of the smaller ships," she cried.

Arion beat his wings, rising up to the underside of the closest ship. Much smaller in size, it still had rotary blades above and many smaller wings jutting out at various angles underneath.

"We need to attach these to the wings, quickly," Fia said. "Once more!" she shouted through the wind, as Arion flew up and over the ship, releasing the ropes so they fastened the two ships together.

The snow had finally come, but it was light and blustery. The larger airship groaned beside them. "What was that?" she shouted.

Arion ascended high above the smaller ships just as an explosion shook the largest one, setting fire to the front set of rotary blades. The ship swung wildly around one hundred and eighty degrees, pulling one of the smaller airships by its tethers and billowing smoke from the open hold.

"The ropes are holding—it's working," Fia cried, and her chest fluttered with adrenaline and satisfaction. A tall, dark figure appeared in the doorway of the hold, swinging violently on one of the ropes. "Noor! Arion, we have to help her."

Arion dived low beneath the ships; the larger one had set the smaller ship on fire, and they were now grinding and falling together in a mass of metal and flames. Arion swooped low under the loading bay. Fia reached out for Noor, pulling her onto Arion's back just as the rear blades shattered and both ships fell, spiralling and tumbling in a mass of smoke and flames into the glacial lake.

"Did you have anything to do with that explosion?" Fia called out to Noor.

Noor laughed. "Very nice touch with the ropes. I'm impressed Fia."

They swooped down to dodge a Makya firing at them from a seed pod. Through the snow and the smoke below, Fia spotted Lorn, revelling in sheer delight as fire flooded from her fingertips with as much speed and strength as the Mizunese controlled water.

"Lorn," Noor cried over the wind as Arion flew lower.

Lorn stood alone in the snow, surrounded by charred bodies, frantically shooting flames at her assailants, as the two airships crashed into the tundra. Two bears charged at her from the masses, flanked by men brandishing spears.

"Do your worst," Lorn called out, laughing and shooting

streams of fire towards them. Three Mizunese soldiers accompanied the Nords and sent shards of ice to meet her flames, hissing into steam as they collided. A group of angels joined Fia, firing arrows as Lorn attacked.

"You'll never defeat the great fire mother!" Lorn spun around, flames shooting outwards from her palms.

Arion took them away from the commotion, and Fia lost sight of Lorn.

"Wait, I need to go lower," Noor shouted through the wind.

Fia opened her mouth to respond just as a fireball flew past them. One of the little seed pods chased them again.

"It's Lorn," Noor said. "She's coming for you. We have to move," she yelled through the snow and the smoke.

Fia gritted her teeth. She was ready.

Fireballs shot past their heads through the blizzard. "Arion, we need to set down. It isn't safe for you up here," Fia said. Arion descended, but a few metres from the ground fire clipped his wing, and he spiralled downwards, throwing Noor and Fia into the snow.

Lorn dived after them, right out of the seed pod. "Do you know who I am?" she screeched.

Fia fought for the breath that had been knocked out when she landed. She fumbled for her bow, her spare hand searching for an arrow, as she clambered to her feet.

Lorn's feet touched the snow a few metres from Fia. Fire shot from her palms, up her hands to her arms, her neck, her head, until her whole body was engulfed in flames. "I am the fire mother." Lorn's voice was a twisted mess of laughter and crackling flames. She pushed her hands outwards, but no fire came. "Do you really think a little arrow will stop me?" A piercing sound escaped her.

Fia fumbled with the arrow, and with one short burst of Lorn's flames, the bow was searing hot, and Fia dropped it in the snow, falling to her knees. She plunged her palm into the icy powder.

"You're coming with me," Lorn seethed, grabbing Fia by the arm and shoving her into the seed pod before taking to the skies once more.

Fia cried out in pain as Lorn's hand wrapped around her, searing heat shooting through her whole arm and up her neck, but she kicked and thrashed at Lorn regardless.

"Move and I burn the whole pod," Lorn spat.

"You'll kill us both," Fia said through gritted teeth. She steadied herself against the wall of the pod with one hand—the other was already beginning to blister. The scent of burning hair filled her nostrils, and someone called her name through the snow as arrows came down at the pod. Lorn screamed as one caught her in the arm. The pod swung wildly as she fought to fly. At the same time, she furiously fired jets of flames randomly into the snow.

"Fia!" Alexander called out to her. She couldn't see him. But if she couldn't see him, neither could Lorn, and that was a good thing. The thought of his wings meeting with Lorn's fire was enough to send her into a blind rage, but she kept her cool as she felt in her boot for the dagger Arc had given her. *Breathe.*

"You can have him, you know," Fia said, drawing Lorn's attention away from her attack. "It was never going to go anywhere, anyway."

"What?" Lorn called out, still distracted by her flames and the seed pod.

"I said you can have him," Fia shouted. "To yourself." And she lunged forwards, pressing her dagger into Lorn's shoulder blade, her burnt hand biting with pain.

Lorn laughed. And then again, and again, louder and more hysterically, the intensity of her flames increasing outwards and into the sky as she laughed, like endless orange ribbons escaping her fingertips. She reached for the dagger, throwing it into the air.

Fia took her chance; she grabbed hold of the pod's controls and it lunged sideways, tipping her out of the side into the blizzard. A fireball followed her as wings encased her and arms wrapped around her waist. "No," she screamed, "Alexander!"

They fell hard into the snow, rolling and tumbling, the smell of burning hair and flesh filling her nostrils. "Alexander," she called out again.

"Are you okay?" he said, crystal blue eyes looking up at her from the snow.

"I'm fine," she sobbed, "you're hurt." She held a blistered hand over his wing, charred and smouldering, and he took it in his.

"It looks worse than it is." He held his free hand to an

open wound on his wing.

"Well. Isn't this just precious," Lorn called out from behind them.

Fia stood with her back to Alexander as he wearily pushed himself up from the snow. She'd get in a few punches at least.

But as Lorn launched her inferno, a flash of black and white dived past, tackling her to the ground. It was a Nord. They let out a deep roar as they attacked, a blurry mass of fur and flames until Lorn pulled herself free. She cried out in pain as arrows rained down on her, and she withdrew to the safety of the seed pod, shouting obscenities as she took off, sparks and embers trailing her as the pod spluttered into the air. Fia grabbed Alexander's bow and chased after her, firing arrow after arrow, despite her blistered hand and her bloodied arm. But it was too windy. Snow fell in thick curtains. Lorn had already retreated to the remaining airship. Fia loosened her grip on the bow, her blisters already breaking, and fell to her knees with exhaustion.

The airship disappeared over the mountain range, and the skies cleared almost instantly.

Kharsee knelt on the snow beside Noor, surrounded by dozens of witches attending to Alexander and the other wounded.

"You frightened her off," Fia said, her gaze following the trail of a mercenary, fleeing towards the lake. "The snow, it was you?" She looked back to Kharsee, her violet eyes flickering in acknowledgement.

"Just in time, too," Noor added, pulling herself to her feet.

"Arion?" Fia called out, panic trembling in her voice.

"He is fine," Kharsee replied. "We are seeing to his wounds."

"Enne, Enne!" Maab cried out as he ran towards them. Half clothed and barefoot, he almost threw himself at the mass of black and white fur in the snow. The Nord had saved Fia's life. Maab pushed away at the witches surrounding him.

Victorious soldiers cried out around them. Cheers and whistles escaped from amongst the Navarii and the Mizunese, even the Nords were celebrating. The Makya were retreating. Senkahs and Aurelli fled in every direction.

But Fia's world fell silent as she saw Enne's charred body in Maab's arms. "Do something," she whispered to Kharsee, "please."

Maab stroked Enne's singed fur as he hugged him close. "You hold on. Keep your strength up. Don't change back. You need your strength."

But Enne ignored Maab's plea and changed back into a man, holding a charred hand to Maab's cheek.

Kharsee took off her cloak and placed it over Enne's scorched body. "It's too late," she said quietly.

"No," Fia replied, tears streaming down her cheeks.

Maab rocked Enne softly back and forth as the victorious cheers reached a crescendo around them. "Keep your strength up," he said, stifling a sob.

"Nothing warms my heart more than knowing my last breath was for you," Enne said, gazing up at Maab. His eyes became still, and his hand fell from Maab's face.

Maab took Enne's hand and kissed it, over and over as he cried. He closed Enne's eyes. Enne's spirit rose from his body in the shape of a beautiful white snow leopard, leaping and dancing in the wind.

Through the cheers and the laughter of the soldiers celebrating victory, Fia watched Enne's spirit above them until it joined the sky spirits in a flash of blue and was gone.

CHAPTER THIRTY

NOOR

The Lady Noor and Fia sat quietly beside Enne's body with Maab and a group of Nords. Alexander joined them, folding his wings behind him as he sat. Noor inspected him from where she was seated. The witches had healed his wounds, but bald, featherless patches of wing revealed the extent of Lorn's damage.

"The feathers will regrow," he said softly, as Fia examined him, too.

Noor shifted her attention to Fia's bandaged hands, to the bulkiness at her shoulder where more bandages sat, after Lorn's hands had pressed down on her. She felt a surge of pride—Fia had fought well.

"You could have been killed," Fia said to Alexander, as he gently took her bandaged hands in his.

"We all could," Alexander replied. None of them spoke.

Enne's body had been covered except for his face. Eyes closed, he could have been sleeping peacefully. Their paths had never crossed, but Noor knew from his mate's stifled movements that he was loved. It was enough to tell what kind of man he'd been.

The crowds around them had departed as soon as they'd realised what had happened, beginning the arduous job of clearing bodies from the battlefield. Their victory had not been without casualties.

Alexander placed a hand on Maab's shoulder.

"It's my fault he's dead," Fia finally said. "I'm so sorry, Maab. It's my fault." She clasped a hand over her mouth and her shoulders shook.

"We all knew what we were getting ourselves into today. He died an honourable death, saving his friend," Maab said quietly.

Kharsee walked by, a silent summons. Noor rose to her feet to join her coven leader.

"You are needed for what lays ahead, Lady Noor," Kharsee said, as their feet crunched in the snow.

Noor chewed over possibilities. Was this an olive branch or another test? "Anything to keep the coven united."

Kharsee smiled. "You know I never wanted you to leave, but some things are beyond even my control. What happened with Silla…" Her gaze fell to the snow. "You made a choice, Noor. The more I think of it, I like to think I would have done the same for the man I loved."

Noor sucked air through her teeth at the sound of his name. *Silla.* They walked through the rows of pyres being constructed, past solemn soldiers preparing their friends for a final goodbye. So much death.

"The coven has been impressed with your initiative to work with the angels, to find the girl. We want you back,

Noor. To be our envoy."

Noor felt a glimmer of something she hadn't allowed herself to feel in a long, long time. They'd circled back around to Fia and the others. "Arion. I take it you had something to do with their meeting?"

Kharsce smiled. "I merely pointed her in the right direction. Arion is just the beginning."

Noor turned to her, a frown creasing across her brow. "She's leaving. Erebus is calling to her, she can't stay here, if she was our only chance… She's leaving."

"The prophecy never said anything about her having to fulfil it from Ohinyan, if I recall." Kharsee's eyes glittered. Noor looked back at Fia, chatting with Maab. Just one girl with so much to achieve and so much already achieved since her arrival.

Alexander walked up beside Kharsee, closely followed by Yahto and Altair.

"Par awaits us," Altair said, caution laced across his face. Earning his trust would take time. But Noor was patient. She followed them to meet the Makya.

Altair made introductions, Par the Makya council leader, and *of course*, Raiaan stood beside her.

"I fear we have failed Ohinyan," Par said. She was small in frame, but Noor recalled her fierceness from the council chambers. "We raised Lorn to believe she is the fire mother. Her corruption is our doing. She has deluded some of our soldiers into following her and brought shame on us once again."

"She has even deceived our brother," Raiaan added.

"I saw you come from the airship with the others," Yahto spat, eyeing Raiaan suspiciously. Altair held back his son.

"I can vouch for this one," Noor said, stepping forward, and flashed an image of herself as a Makya guard for all to see.

Raiaan smiled. "Very clever. I ought to thank you, for your astuteness. And as Par has said, the council wishes to have no association with Lorn and Jerum. There are much bigger things at stake here that affect us all. We are as invested in Ohinyan as each of you. It is our home, too."

"We will all need Lorn alive. When the third sun comes, we will need her. That is why some have chosen to follow her. Lorn was taught the wrong values… had I been there, things might have been different." Par shook her head, tapping a black, glossy cane as dark as her eyes in the snow.

"I do not think Lorn's current state of mind is entirely the council's doing," Noor added. "The darkness has been calling to her."

"It has been calling to all of us, but it is whether or not we choose to listen that matters," Par replied, her old eyes glistening with knowing.

Noor caught Alexander shift with discomfort.

"The council have given their word," Kharsee announced. "We will work together in the months ahead. It has been agreed amongst the key covens that the Lady Noor shall be envoy for the witches."

Par held both hands on her cane and nodded. "We have

given our word, and we stand by it. Jerum has escaped with his sister, and we will not rest until we find them."

"Very well," Alexander said. "We have much to discuss."

Noor did not join Alexander and the elders as they departed. She was too weary from her days aboard the ship to follow. She'd heard enough for now. Raiaan remained beside her, perhaps he felt the same.

"So just how long were you spying on us?" he asked, no hint of anger in his voice. He held his hands behind his back and motioned for Noor to join him as he walked.

"Long enough," Noor replied. But she knew there was no ruffling his feathers. She'd seen his kindness on board the airship. He was never cruel to the Aurelli, and his soldiers had respected him.

"So Erebus has been taunting my sister. That explains… rather a lot." He surveyed the pyres as they walked, his expression blank.

"Tell me something." Noor stopped to face him. "Do you believe she is the fire mother?"

His brow furrowed, but his eyes were bright, hopeful. She saw her reflection in the flecks of copper, gold, and carnelian. "I have been raised, as she has, to believe so, yes. Whether she will decide to take ownership of her responsibilities to Ohinyan is another matter entirely."

Noor nodded in understanding. They walked on together in silence, and Noor felt a new beginning taking shape. Hope fluttered in her chest.

In Silla's name, then.

CHAPTER THIRTY-ONE

ALEXANDER

Snow had fallen heavily in the last few hours. What had earlier been a muddied expanse of lifeless bodies was now covered in pristine white, with the exception of the funeral pyres slowly being built in the snow.

Alexander watched Maab prepare offerings and blessings to accompany Enne's body. It could have been Fia lying there.

In the distance, a handful of witches lead groups of Aurelli back towards Mizune. Fia, at Noor's instruction, had spoken with the odd little creatures, assuring them they would be returned to their forest by the Navarii ships. They'd responded with skittish, frantic movements, but with the help of the other witches soon calmed after watching illusions of what it was like to be at sea, and how quickly they could be home.

More witches coerced the Najin down into the valley below their forest, after much cooing and calling. It was a shy thing when not shackled. The surviving Senkahs had fled, in every direction into the shadows of Ohinyan. The darkness had taken hold, and there would be no way to bring them back from its depths now.

Fia had made up her own mind about returning to Earth. At least it was her choice. He could give her that. With her safe on Earth, he could focus on his duties. On being a leader. Perhaps even a leader his father would be proud of. But above all, perhaps Ohinyan might even see its way out to the other side of the darkness that lay ahead. He clung to the hope that she might want to return, that she could see Ohinyan as her home.

She walked towards him now, her auburn hair loose below her shoulders, and her eyes wet with tears. *Loquere.* She'd brought Arion to them. Alexander's chest swelled with pride at the memory of her interpreting for them all just a few days before. How wide eyed they'd all been as she spoke for the great winged horse. He took her bandaged hand gently in his.

"Come, the others are waiting." He led her to the witches' forest, and though they barely spoke, he committed to memory every detail of how she pushed back her hair, every brush of her thumb against his.

Amongst glittering emerald trees, Alexander announced an alliance with the Makya council, one they all hoped would remain strong in the coming months.

"Aid and provisions have been promised," he said. "Par informs us that Lorn and Jerum have only a handful of Makya who remain loyal to them. Together, we will defeat them."

Large, bell-shaped flowers in bright purples and blues surrounded them, filling the air with a sweet, vanilla scent.

"Our priority will be the declining temperatures," Kharsee said. "It's going to get cold, and fast, so we will need to work closely with the Makya to maintain a sustainable living temperature across all inhabited areas of Ohinyan."

Alexander watched the old witch as she spoke. She'd welcomed Noor back, at least that was something.

Kharsee caught Alexander's gaze. "Our only alternative is relocation."

"Relocation?" Fia bristled beside him. "As in, to Earth?"

Kharsee nodded.

"That is an illogical solution," Altair interjected, rubbing his chin. "Most people don't even know of Earth's existence. How can we expect them to evacuate?"

How would they even get them all through? Alexander had already tasked his fastest scouts with searching for windows that might allow for a departure from Ohinyan. They couldn't possibly fly everyone through, and he wouldn't ask it of the angels, either. It wasn't simply an evacuation, it meant only the angels would ever be able to return. *And Fia.* Would she want to come back?

"The alternative is that we leave them here to die," the Lady Noor chimed in, sharpening a blade quietly as she listened. "That is, of course, if the windows between worlds do not close entirely."

"But how can you take Par's word, after all that's happened?" Fia said, her voice laced with frustration.

"We must take responsibility for shaping our own future. This alliance will ensure that," Altair replied.

"And what of Erebus?" Yahto asked. "How do we prepare for him?"

Alexander felt Fia tense beside him, and he rubbed his thumb over the back of her hand.

"Our knowledge of Erebus is still limited. Arion has told us more than we have known for many years. We will need to learn all that we can about him if we are to ensure he does not take a hold on Ohinyan when the sun dies," Kharsee replied.

Alexander sunk into the rhythm of instruction. The Navarii would return the Aurelli to their home, before continuing in their ships across Ohinyan to raise awareness of the dying sun, and to learn whatever they could about Erebus. Maab, at Alexander's request, agreed to lead one of the ships. Arion and the witches were to work together. The angels he had split off into various tasks: scouting for windows, for Lorn and her brother, and searching for any information that might help.

"It's time to help the others with the funeral preparations," he said finally, his hand reaching for Fia's waist.

"Did you know when you sent me into the valley? Did I serve my purpose, fulfil your prophecy?" Fia asked Kharsee before they turned to leave. Her jaw tightened and she chewed at her lip.

The old witch rested a hand on Fia's. "Prophecies are not set in stone, Fia. Often, they are a seed, a catalyst in a chain of events. We need Arion for what lies ahead. He is connected to all the creatures in Ohinyan, he is the key to uniting them all. Only a loquere could have reached out to him."

"You needed someone who could bring him to you," Alexander said. These witches and their secrets. Working with them was going to require patience.

Kharsee held Fia's hands in hers for a moment before leaving them in silence.

Fia looked up at Alexander, and he drew her into an embrace, breathing her in. Runa had lent her some jasmine soap, and the scent mixed with the smoke from the Makya's fires.

In that moment, he knew he would always be distracted if she stayed. He would always be looking for her, checking she was safe. He would always put her first. She'd said it herself at the party in Mizune—she wouldn't let herself be priority over an entire world full of people and creatures. Over his world. He fought away the sting of tears, as he brushed one of her own away from her cheek.

She'll go home. You'll say goodbye. And when this is all over, you can go back to her. But she must go home.

CHAPTER THIRTY-TWO

FIA

Building the funeral pyres calmed Fia's mind. It was easier to pass the time with her hands rather than with her thoughts.

"I wanted to thank you," said the Lady Noor, passing a handful of branches to Fia.

"Shouldn't I be thanking you? You saved my life. What happened to you up there?"

Noor smiled. "Let's say we're even." She laid down a branch, interlocking it with others around it. "Up there?" Noor looked up, sapphire blue eyes searching the skies. She sighed. "A lot happened. It felt like a lot longer than it was. But from what I understand, a lot happened down here, too." She glanced over at Alexander, stacking wood on a nearby pyre.

Fia gave a weak smile. "Yeah, a lot. But I'll be back on Earth soon, and it'll be like none of this ever happened."

A few snowflakes fell, and Noor held out a hand to catch them. They transformed into dandelion seed heads, white and feathery in her palm. "We are, all of us, like these little seeds, Fia. Once we collide, we either lose a little bit of ourselves, or take a little of another with us. But we are never the same again." She blew gently at her palm, two seeds stuck together as they drifted towards the snow. "I think you have given part of yourself to Ohinyan, and in return it has given part of itself to you. That cannot be erased. I, for one, am very grateful our paths collided, and I shall not forget you."

Fia's lip trembled, and she bit down on it hard. This was the first of many goodbyes she wasn't ready for. "I'm coming back when this is all over," she began, removing the little pouch from around her neck and with it the little black stone she'd been carrying. "This is yours," she said, holding out the little black dahlia.

"Keep it." Noor smiled. "For when you come back. These stones are very special amongst my people. It will always identify you as an ally of mine, and you never know when you might need a friend. Here." Noor fastened a few strips of red leather to Fia's wrist in elaborate loops and knots. "Witch knots are very powerful. Untie this in your greatest moment of need, and you will be able to bind winds and release them much like the giants did today," Noor finished, with a smile that reached her deep blue eyes.

She left without saying another word, and Fia found herself alone again, imagining Enne and Sophie together somewhere—wherever it was people go when they die. She watched Maab speaking quietly with Altair, inspecting a little pebble. Maab held Altair's arm gently before they parted ways. He looked up at Fia, waving her over.

"It is a gift," he said, turning the pebble over and over in his hands. It was like the one Altair had shown Fia of his wife, only this one was double sided. On one side was Enne's likeness as a man, and on the other, a delicately carved likeness of him as a snow leopard.

"It's beautiful," Fia replied.

Maab was silent, rubbing his thumb over every line of the carving, turning it through his fingers, as if he were committing every detail to memory.

"Maab, I… Enne and I… last night, up on the lookout…"

"Yes, the two of you spoke whilst I discussed strategy with Alexander," Maab said, his eyes fixed on the likeness of Enne smiling back up at him.

"Yes, that's right." Fia forced a smile. "Enne said some really wonderful things."

Maab nodded.

"He loved you," she whispered. "So much. He told me love had freed him. That you were his home. You know that won't ever change, right?" Her words came out in a rush. She tried to recall all the things people had said to her at Sophie's funeral. There was nothing worth repeating.

"Thank you, Fia. Those are kind words," Maab said, but his eyes did not meet hers. Low, heavy drums were beating slowly; it was time to light the pyres. Maab nodded, and together they made their way to Enne's pyre.

Altair spoke to the people gathered around. "The memory of those we have lost can never be taken from us.

They live in our minds and in our hearts, as long as we choose to keep them there. Their spirits join Ohinyan." He knelt, scooping up a fistful of snow. "They are part of the water you wield, and they are the particles of dust floating in the sunlight as it shines through your window each morning. They are with us, always."

He scattered the snow in the breeze, and as the drums sounded once more, the fires sparked into life. The crowd broke off into groups, each holding their own little service.

Fia wiped away her tears. She thought of Sophie's funeral, how strange it had been watching the coffin lowered into the ground.

Alexander took Fia's bandaged hand as they stood beside Enne's pyre. Maab clasped his hands in front of him and cleared his throat. "We Nords have a saying: no tree grows to the sky. Or as you would say, nothing lasts forever. I told Enne this once, and he told me, '*ah* but this is the beauty of Ohinyan.' He said that when it was his time to die, I would see him dancing in every gust of wind, swimming in every stretch of open water, and running in delight in every drift of snow. He believed, as I know many of you do, that his spirit would go on living in Ohinyan forever."

Murmurs of agreement came from the Nords gathered around the pyre.

Maab was quiet for a moment as the pyre was lit. "You told a friend that love had freed you, but it was your love that freed me. You will forever have a place inside my heart. It will always be your home. We honour you now, Enne, forever dancing, swimming, and running in delight." He fell silent, holding his head high as the flames engulfed Enne's body.

Alexander wrapped an arm around Fia, and together they watched as Enne's body became part of Ohinyan. Fia twirled the bird charm in her fingers as she let the tears flow freely down her face. She fought back the knot tugging at the bottom of her stomach and snagging the air from her lungs when she tried to breathe calmly. Enne was gone. She was leaving. This might be the last time she saw many of these faces again. She could lose all of them. She could lose Alexander for good.

It was time to go. Erebus had made her decision for her. If she stayed, Alexander and all their friends were at risk. She wouldn't do that to them. Couldn't. If Alexander truly knew of Erebus' threat to her, she'd only be in the way. There was too much at stake in Ohinyan, and she couldn't put her own feelings before an entire world.

She was quiet on the sled ride back to Mizune, listening to the dogs chatting in cheerful outbursts. They were enormous, happy things, undisturbed by the day's events. Fia and the others hadn't heard from Gymir since he and the Jǫtnar had helped them during the attack, but every now and then, she thought she could hear the crystalline sound of his coughing and spluttering into the wind.

The huskies raced onwards, and at the edges of her vision, the snow hung from the trees in glistening shapes and the blue sky blanketed the horizon beside a bright, white expanse of snow. The smell of the ocean filled her nostrils as they arrived at the outskirts of Mizune. She was going to miss this place, despite the biting cold.

"Fia?" Altair's great cloak swung from side to side as he approached. "Fia?"

She looked up as the huskies came to a stop and climbed wearily from the sled. "Altair." She tried to smile but couldn't.

"You have endured much since your arrival in Ohinyan, child," he said, examining her arm in a sling and her bandaged hands.

Fia sighed. "All those people. Enne… It's just the beginning, isn't it? When the sun dies, everyone could—you could all be gone."

Altair smiled gently, wrapping an arm around her shoulder. "Life and death are like breathing in and breathing out. As with so many things in Ohinyan, one cannot exist without the other, and they cannot be separated. Just as night and day cannot be separated. Day will find a way to return to Ohinyan eventually. This I know for certain."

"But how can you know?"

"It is the way of Ohinyan. Like meeting and parting. At some point, we have to say goodbye. Some goodbyes are just more final than others."

"Do you think this is final?" Fia watched the huskies bounding off through the snow before turning her attention back to Altair.

"Who can say," Altair replied, rubbing his chin. "But the encounter was worthwhile, was it not?" A smile spread across his face from ear to ear, and for a moment, Fia forgot she was going back to London and leaving all of this behind.

More goodbyes followed. For most, it was short and sweet. Noor had hugged her—a wordless hug that almost took the wind right out of her. Maab clasped her good arm, shaking it firmly with his. "It has been an honour, Fia. Until we next meet," he said in his thick accent.

Malachai said a few quiet words. Runa embraced her in a fierce hug, tears flowing freely down her cheeks. She laughed as she wiped them away. "We'll see you soon, okay?"

Fia nodded. All the air had escaped from her lungs, and she had to use the tiny bit she had left just to keep breathing. There wasn't enough for speaking, too.

Arion knelt in the snow for Fia to climb up onto his back one last time, and she carefully dug her hands into his matted mane. The sun was setting, and the sky spirits were dancing and spiralling in ribbons of colour above them.

The snow had stopped falling, and a light breeze carried with it the scents of salt and seaweed. Oil lamps flickered in Mizune, casting long, black shadows. Fia breathed it all in deeply and closed her eyes. "Okay, let's go."

Alexander flew silently beside them as they made their way to the window. The journey would be faster if Arion carried her, he'd explained, but he stayed close, never leaving Arion's side. The fireflies had come, perhaps to say their own goodbyes, but they were quiet as they danced around

Fia and Arion, their shimmering glow finally disappearing before they reached the coast.

Fia studied as much of the changing landscape as her streaming eyes would let her, committing it to memory. She shielded her face against the wind. Below them was the deep, dark expanse of ocean, and to their left the sun dipped down into the horizon, melting into the water. She listened to the rhythmic beating of Arion's wings, and felt the strength of his legs as they galloped through the air, closing her eyes when the wind became too much.

What had taken days of travel in the Navarii ships passed by them in a single night. They crossed over rocky terrains, forests of lush, tall trees, and cities with structures even stranger than in Ikothea, and all the while, Fia felt the darkness of the night sky close in around them as the light faded away. She couldn't see the sky spirits this far north; she might never see them again.

She thought of Sophie, and whether she'd joined those spirits. Her chest ached at the thought of her sister, but it didn't knock the air from her lungs as it had done in the days before. She'd thought her grief would grow smaller over time until there was nothing left, but instead she had grown around it.

Fia's legs were numb by the time Arion slowed his pace, circling wide as he descended. He followed Alexander, who had dived low into the forest. He touched his heavy hooves to the ground gracefully and knelt once more as Fia awkwardly climbed down from his back, stiff and aching from the journey.

"Thank you, Arion. For everything," Fia said, burying her head into his neck.

"I have enjoyed having a human to talk to. I'd forgotten what it was like. For that, I thank you, Fia."

"Will you miss it?" Fia asked.

"I will. But the witches and I have much to learn from each other, and I wish to help with what lies ahead. Whilst I cannot talk with them as I can with you, they have a rather unusual way of communicating with me, which will have to suffice." He laughed. He was quiet for a moment, dragging a hoof across the grass. "I turned away from the people of Ohinyan many years ago. Thank you for reminding me that they still have the capacity for good in them, just as the creatures do."

With a slight nod in Alexander's direction, Arion was airborne, beating his enormous wings and pounding the air with his muscular legs.

"Goodbye!" Fia tried to call out, but her voice cracked and came out small and quiet. She breathed in the smell of pine needles and jasmine one last time, trying to control the unravelling ball of anxiety in her chest. She counted her breaths.

"It's time to go," Alexander said. He pulled her close, his forehead resting against hers, and they stood for a moment, sharing a breath before he scooped her up into his arms. He carried her with care, flying slow above the canopy into the velvety blue of the night sky. "Are you ready?"

"Is this it?" Fia asked, looking up at the stars.

"Look ahead."

It was hard to make out in the dark of night, and it had no discernible shape, no edges that Fia could clearly see. But straight ahead of her in the night sky, as if it were carved into the air, was the window. And through it, Highgate cemetery's dark catacombs. She held her breath. Neither of them spoke as Alexander carried her through, and Fia couldn't bring herself to look back. One moment they were under the starry sky of Ohinyan, and the next they were in the damp and musty catacombs of Highgate cemetery.

Silently, he carried her above the shadowy streets of London. It was late; the roads were quiet, and all the lights in the homes were off. The lights of the city sparkled in the distance, and somewhere a car alarm was going off. Everything seemed so out of place to Fia.

The parked cars looked peculiar, and the perfect rows of houses so awkward. That sinking, gnawing in her stomach pulled itself further and further down, and tears threatened to spill over her cheeks.

They arrived at her flat, and Alexander dropped in gently through the top window. In the moonlight, her bedroom was cold and empty, and the alarm clock by the bed cast a red glow across the floor. Fia dropped her backpack and her bow and let her feet carry her to bed. The numbness was creeping in, and the waves were crashing over her once more. Alexander sat down beside her and took her hand in his. She bit her lip. This couldn't be it. But it was the only way to protect him. To protect all of them.

"My father gave this to my mother. I want you to have it, so that you know I'll come back for you, once this is all over—so that you know I mean it when I tell you I want us to be together." His words were rushed, and he held out a golden cuff like the ones Fia had seen Malachai and Runa wearing. It was beautifully carved, with fine, delicate lines that flicked and flourished in intricate patterns.

"What if something happens to you?" she asked, her glistening eyes searching his.

"It won't, I promise. I'm coming back for you as soon as it's safe."

Fia took the cuff and placed it on her wrist. It fit snugly and reflected the moonlight, as it shone through the window. She kissed him, her hands tugging through his hair and her tears mingling with their kiss.

She fought back a sob, and traced a hand along the stubble of his jaw and placed another at his chest, breathing him in deeply. "Stay with me a while?" She felt as if the room was crumbling around them, as if all the air had been sucked out of the world.

Alexander pulled her close one last time, stroking her hair until she fell asleep.

Her dreams came quickly. At first, she thought she would live forever. She was infinite. Eternal. She was flying, soaring, stretching her wings wide. Beside her flew

Alexander, soaring and diving with her. His elation was contagious—she tried to laugh, but the wonder of it took her breath away.

She delighted in it, turning gracefully in the gentle wind. They flew together until day became night. Alexander was ahead of her all the while. She turned in the wind once more, but then he was gone. She searched for hours, flying through the night, until the first light of dawn began to creep across the sky. She searched amongst trees and caves, under waterfalls and across oceans, but he was nowhere to be found.

When Fia awoke, she was alone. The quiet morning sunlight filled her empty bedroom. Golden rays lit up the particles of dust floating in the air after weeks of being undisturbed. Alexander was gone, and on the empty pillow beside her was nothing but a long, white feather.

IF YOU ENJOYED THE THIRD SUN...

Please consider leaving a review on **Amazon** or **Goodreads**.

Reviews give authors much needed exposure and let other readers know what they can look forward to, too!

FIND OUT WHAT HAPPENS NEXT IN FIA AND ALEXANDER'S STORY...

The Eternal Dusk:
Daughter of the Phoenix Book Two
Available on Amazon

Find out more about the world of Ohinyan and read the prequel:

The Angel's Calling:
Daughter of the Phoenix Prequel
Available at www.victoriajprice.com

ACKNOWLEDGEMENTS

The Third Sun took many years to get it to where it is now and I'm incredibly grateful to everyone who has listened to me talk endlessly about it. To all those who have read a chapter or a complete draft, I would not be writing this without you. Special thanks go to:

Chrishel Smith for your support, feedback and enthusiasm for Fia and Alexander—and for all the kind things you've said, it means a lot.

Amy Eversley—thank you for the many, many emails and thoughts during the last few months. I'm looking forward to swapping many more manuscripts!

Brie Tart for all the time you've given me, and the late-night chats about anything and everything.

Kayla Maurais for your insightful observations and for your encouragement.

August Head—thank you for your feedback over the last year, it's been a huge catalyst to get me to where I am now.

The SPF and 20Books communities, two incredible resources that any aspiring author should check out.

My editor Rebecca Jaycox for being as awesome as everyone says you are.

And finally (always save the best for last) thank you to my husband Ali—my first and biggest fan. Your belief in this story, the characters, and the world I've built has been the driving force that's kept me writing for all these years, and I couldn't have done it without you. Thank you for believing in me and for your love, support, friendship… and for your amazing editing skills.

About the Author

Victoria lives in leafy Surrey, in the South East of England. She loves fairy tales, myths and legends, and grew up creating stories both in words and pictures. When she's not writing you'll find her exploring with her husband and their two dogs, searching for beautiful hidden places and secret picnic spots.

Go to www.victoriajprice.com for free downloads, including a collection of short stories about the parallel world of Ohinyan.

Follow on social media:

Instagram @victoriajprice

Twitter @victoria_jprice

Facebook @authorvictoriajprice